RED
ICE

visit
www.susiecornfield.com

RED
ICE

Susie
Cornfield

To Terence & Tricia,

Happy reading.

GARRET
BOOKS

2015

Red Ice
Published by Garret Books in 2015
ISBN 978-0-9552279-6-7

Garret Books Ltd Reg. No.: 5647052
Registered address: Suite 210, Maddison House, 226 High Street, Croydon CR9 1DF,
Surrey, England, UK
www.susiecornfield.com

A CIP catalogue record for this book is available from the British Library

Illustrations by Jamel Akib
www.jamelakib.com

Designed and typeset by Caroline and Roger Hillier, The Old Chapel Graphic Design
www.theoldchapelivinghoe.com

Copy editor: Ros Lavine
ewordwizard@gmail.com

Printed by TJ International, Trecerus Industrial Estate, Padstow PL28 8RW, Cornwall, UK
www.tjinternational.ltd.uk

To family, friends, colleagues, and experts in many fields
who have given kind support to me and the bookbabies
– thank you.

And to
Mother Nature –
all good wishes for the future.

An injustice anywhere is a threat to justice everywhere.
Martin Luther King

Also by the author

Fiction
Black Light; a satirical thriller, first in the series The Chronicles
of Dekaydence (Garret Books, 2008, ISBN 978-0-9552279-2-9),
produced originally as *The Sticky Rock Café*
Green Fire; a satirical thriller, second in the series The Chronicles
of Dekaydence (Garret Books, 2009, ISBN 978-0-9552279-3-6)

Non-fiction
Farewell, My Lovely; a collection of tributes to much-loved
departed pets. Original paperback (Garret Books, 2006,
ISBN 978-0-9552279-1-2); hardback, revised and extended edition
(Garret Books, 2009, ISBN 978-0-9552279-4-3)

Poetry
Catch 36; a collection of poems by Susie Cornfield inspired by
love and loss, friendship and nature, children's nightmares and
grown-up steam-venting about life today (Garret Books, 2010,
ISBN 978-0-9552279-5-0)

History
The Queen's Prize; the story of the National Rifle Association of
Great Britain (Pelham Books, 1986, ISBN 0 7207 1751 5)

Susie Cornfield trained as a journalist on a local newspaper before
joining the staff of *The Sunday Times* where she was the paper's
radio critic. She went on to become a columnist for the *Sunday
Telegraph Magazine*, a writer for BBC TV and a presenter/producer
for United Artists TV.

What they said about *Green Fire*:

Reminds me of Mervyn Peake
– John Carey, Emeritus Merton Professor of English Literature, University of Oxford

A courageous and imaginative fable
– David Selbourne, writer and thinker about our times

A brilliant book. Even better than Black Light.
– Andrew Weatherston, Teen Titles

I couldn't put it down. Rich characters, humour, pace, originality ... This deserves to make waves.
– Sally Chattaway, actress

CONTENTS

Dramatis personae 12

Glossary 14

The story so far ... 15

SECTION 1

1 Holy disorders 19

2 Massacre of the innocents 24

3 CO_2 or not CO_2? 28

4 The new disorder 32

BREAKING NEWS 35

5 What am I going to do about Maria? 40

6 A new Dekaydence dawn 42

7 Overture and beginners 46

8 Out of the frying pan 52

9 North's about-face 56

POLITICAL WHISPERS 60

9.5 A Tartan dream 63

SECTION 2

10 God and PMT 67

11 Boa constrictor 72

12 The return of Innit? 76

13 What are we going to do about Maria? 79

BREAKING NEWS 81

14 The sand pit 87

15 When did you last see your fathers? 91

16 If you can't stand the heat ... 94

17 Found and lost 96

POLITICAL WHISPERS 101

17.5 Six of one, 1.5 dozen of the others 106

SECTION 3

18 Holy vanishing act 109

BREAKING NEWS 112

19 'Oid to freedom 114

20 The staffie of life 115

21 Walking back to unhappiness 119

22 The dog it was that died 123

23 The other truth 126

24 Train of thoughts 129

BREAKING NEWS 133

25 Tea and sympathy 136

POLITICAL WHISPERS 138

25.5 A child is born 142

SECTION 4

26 Heaven's above 147

27 Mama mia! 149

28 The killing fields 153

BREAKING NEWS 157

MORE BREAKING NEWS 164

29 The grapes of wrath 165

30 Sunday crunch 168

31 Good, Innit? 171

32 A talent to diffuse 175

33 A stranger in the gallery 178

34 Where is Cromarty? 182
POLITICAL WHISPERS 186
34.5 Nigel's news 189

SECTION 5

35 A claw in heaven 193
36 First aid 196
37 Face in the lead 199
38 Vigil 202
39 Royal questions 204
40 Angelica's secret 209
41 Face on fire 215
BREAKING NEWS 217
42 Lost and found 221
43 Re-wrendering 223
BREAKING NEWS 224
44 Musical thoughts 228
POLITICAL WHISPERS 230
44.5 Homeward bound? 233

SECTION 6

45 New angel delights 237
46 Chips with everything 239
47 The Tower of Eden 243
48 Losing a friend 249
49 Judging times 252
50 Golden oldies 255
51 A right turn 258
BREAKING NEWS 262
52 Relative values 267
POLITICAL WHISPERS 271
52.5 Seeds of change 275

SECTION 7

53 The invaders 279
54 North to the fore 282
55 Golden moments 286
56 The taming of the shrewd 290
57 What is Maria doing about Maria? 293
58 Love bugs 295
BREAKING NEWS 297
59 The Phoen'oid goes independent 299
60 Ashes to ashes 305
61 Heartbreaking news 310
POLITICAL WHISPERS 313
61.5 Special delivery 317

SECTION 8

62 A heavenly uproar 321
63 Dust to dust 324
64 The future 328
65 The chocolate killer 330
66 The chase 334
67 I once met a girl called Maria 338
BREAKING NEWS 343
68 Goo hoo-ha 347
69 Miscarriage of injustice 352
70 Cooking up lies 354
71 A Royal funeral 356
72 The lost brain 359
POLITICAL WHISPERS 363
72.5 Holy recycling 369

SECTION 9

73 Heaven on red alert 373

74 Brotherly love 376

75 MacBangers and burgers 380

76 A mother writes ... 382

77 Sound bites 386

78 Out-Dek'd? 390

79 Indigo to the rescue 393

80 Make-up time 398

BREAKING NEWS 401

81 Queens together? 406

POLITICAL WHISPERS 408

81.5 Home from home 413

SECTION 10

82 Heavens above 417

BREAKING NEWS 423

83 Tears and rage 429

84 Busy buzzy 432

85 Future imperfect 434

86 Country cousins 436

87 Diabaloic mutterings 439

88 A musical request 442

89 Travels with my doorkey 445

BREAKING NEWS 452

90 Murder most foul 453

91 One dark night 456

POLITICAL WHISPERS 460

91.5 Jam'd up thinking 466

SECTION 11

92 Beware the haggoid 471

93 Rough justice 474

94 What's innit for Innit? 480

BREAKING NEWS 487

95 Rome alone 490

96 The woman in blue 493

97 Crowning glories 497

98 The Phoenix is fading 504

99 A bedside farewell 507

100 Grout, bee-ware! 511

101 A Roman morning 515

102 Papal summit 517

POLITICAL WHISPERS 523

102.5 Justice and jam 526

SECTION 12

103 God rides out 529

104 Seeing is believing 534

105 The Queen's promise 537

106 Fangs ain't wot they used to be 543

107 Unholy father 545

108 Strawberry jam goes indy 551

109 What's up, North? 553

110 Baby blew it 557

POLITICAL WHISPERS 560

110.5 Hive of industry 562

SECTION 13

111 God's stand-in 565

112 HOH and the MCC 567

113 Coronation celebrations 570

114 Di'Abalo's speech 574

115 Spring 578

116 Summer 580

117 Autumn 584

118 Winter 587

119 The jackpot prize 590

120 Fear and fury 593

121 Brain fever 595

122 Arrival of the ALFs 599

123 'Oider and 'oider 604

124 Mixed box 611

125 A relative problem 613

126 Mother of reinvention 617

127 Beware chaos 621

128 The Phoen'oid's gift 623

129 O, Father, who art not in heaven 626

130 Flying tonight 635

131 Adieu 638

POLITICAL WHISPERS 640

132 The Phoenix rises 645

So, what does THE FUTURE hold...?

1 God and Mother Nature 653

2 MacNoodle and MacMinor 656

3 Petty and Hunky, the Face and Schneek 659

4 Grout and Indigo 662

5 Claud Canapé 668

6 The Catguts 670

7 The Martin family 673

8 Ruby Q 678

9 HOH Randall Candelskin 682

10 The Noteians 686

11 MacCavity 688

12 McCarbon 689

13 Hilli 690

14 Comprendo 691

15 Bodkin 692

16 Lars Sparks 693

17 Innit 694

18 Will and Piccolo 696

BREAKING NEWS 702

19 Piccolo and Will 704

20 The Suit and Phlegm 708

21 Bhupi and Spaghetti Sureshi 712

22 Boston 713

23 Spiky Hair 714

24 Goo and MacSoya 715

25 The man in the pink shorts 716

26 Ruby Q 719

27 Lorenzo di'Abalo 726

28 Ruby Q 729

29 Lorenzo di'Abalo 731

POLITICAL WHISPERS 736

30 HQ 739

31 Mother Nature 743

32 Angelica Nera 745

33 Heaven 753

34 Will and Piccolo 754

35 Ruby Q 756

36 Grout 758

37 Grout 760

37.5 (RECURRING) Ruby Q 763

DRAMATIS PERSONAE

Angelica Nera *Ruby Q's mother*

Bhupi *temporary head of Heaven*

Bianco *a young man in a black bird's body*

Bodkin *Dekaydence laboratory assistant*

Cage Martin *the Martins's eldest son*

Cataract *senior partner at accountants Cataract, Cyclops and Mote*

Lady Catgut *wife of Sir Harrison Catgut*

Claud Canapé *internationally renowned designer*

The Crown Prince *the King's son and heir and father of the Princess Indigo*

The three Clives *good men and true, now Heaven-based*

Comprendo *leader of gang of three young men*

The Dipstick Five *a pop group*

Driver *Noteian schoolfriend of Handcuffs, Will, the Phoenix*

Edwina Gardening-Fork (pronounced Spade) *Editor*, Shed Monthly

Elsa D. Cooper *Ruby Q's grandmother*

Er *a gladiator*

The Face (Verona) *leader, the GeeZers, Petty Masters's sister*

GeeZers *peaceful activists for action on climate change*

God *Heaven's Top Man*

Goo *trainee chef, son of MacGluten*

Grout *Head of Innovation, Dekaydence*

Handcuffs *Noteian schoolfriend of Driver, Will, the Phoenix*

(Sir) Harrison Catgut *composer, knighted for his services to loud music*

Hilli *the Face's minder*

Hunky Doré *US pop star, husband of Petty Masters*

Indigo *the King's granddaughter, Will's cousin*

Innit *a young Dekaydence worker of many unsavoury talents*

Jack Martin *the Martins' third son who died in the London tsunami*

Jake *Waat and Jack Martin's baby son*

Jarvis *journalist/manager on Dekaydence's* Daily Unigraph
Jezza *Innit's girlfriend, who died in the London tsunami*
Jojo *a Phoen'oid, modelled on the Phoenix's younger brother Josef*
Kane Martin *aka Stanley Halls, the Martins' second son*
Killivy *Dekaydence gardener*
The King *constitutional monarch of Great Britain*
Lars Sparks *internationally renowned photographer*
Lily Nera *Ruby Q Cooper's aunt*
Lord Lorenzo di'Abalo *head of the Company of Dekaydence*
MacCavity *Head of Dekaydence Security*
MacGluten *Head Chef at Dekaydence*
MacMinor *Red Tartan guard*
MacNoodle *Red Tartan guard*
MacSoya *Dekaydence trainee chef*
Maria *the President's daughter, sister of the Phoenix*
McCarbon *deputy head of Dekaydence Security*
Meryl Martin *the Martins' elder daughter*
Mother Nature *carer of the natural world*
Mr and Mrs Martin *parents of Taylor, Jack, Kane, Cage and Meryl*
Nigel *a violinist, miniaturised by Dekaydence*
North, South, East and West *regional leaders of the GeeZers*
Nayr *Indigo's personal guard, son of Sid*
Petty Masters *avant-garde fashion designer, married to Hunky Doré*
Phlegm *Lord di'Abalo's butler*
The Phoenix *a freelance activist for worldwide justice*
Piccolo Smith *a musician and composer*
The President *elected head of the Federation, formerly the Union*
The Professor *Head of Dekaydence Research & Development*
Rallan Cooper *a drummer, Ruby Q Cooper's father*
Randall Candelskin *Signor di'Abalo's right-hand man*
Real GeeZers *eco-activists, prepared to use violence*
Ruby Q Cooper a *journalist on the* Daily Unigraph
Schneek *rollerblading assistant to Petty Masters*

Sid *Will's personal guard, Nayr's dad*
Sinus *the King's butler*
Solomon *City bishop*
Spaghetti Sureshi *Heaven's peacemaker*
Spiky Hair *Editor, Dekaydence's* Daily Unigraph
The Suit *a tabloid journalist, friend of Spiky Hair*
Taylor Martin *the youngest in the Martin family*
Tommo *Will's brother, damaged in the Dekaydence White Room*
Mr and Mrs Treasure *Elsa Cooper's gardener and housekeeper*
Verona see The Face
Waat *half-sister to Innit*
Wassit *a gladiatior, Innit's cousin*
Wiggins *a King's Counsel, brother to Cataract*
Will *the King's great-nephew, a Prince of Scotland*
Young Miss Burgess *right- and left-hand woman at* Shed Monthly

GLOSSARY

adservarum, or ad'um
  multi-communications device, worn on the wrist or hidden under a
  lapel, used as a phone, etc.

Eye-Spy, pl. Eye-Spys
  multi-lensed Dekaydence cameras that film anything untoward and
  much that isn't

TTT (thought-talk-transference)
  the silent way of communicating in Heaven

The Chronicles of Dekaydence begins in book one, *Black Light*, continues in book two, *Green Fire*, and concludes with book three, *Red Ice*. This is the story so far ...

Teenage heroes Will, Ruby Q and Piccolo, together with eco-warriors the peaceful GeeZers and Real GeeZers (committed to action, often violent), have been battling to save the planet from global meltdown and adult apathy – to no avail. They are now young adults, and eminent scientists are disputing the idea that man is the cause of climate change. Secretly, as it has to be, Will, the King's great-nephew, once an active 'green', is now among the sceptics' number.

As is Will's former Noteian schoolfriend the Phoenix, rumoured to be the son of the President of the Federation. Working undercover, via the journalist Ruby Q, the Phoenix continues to inspire people worldwide to combat evil-doers – through revelations of child abuse and murder, 'honour' killings, the skinning of live animals, and much much more.

But when Lord di'Abalo's mysterious global media company Dekaydence takes the Phoenix captive, his friends and followers learn that there are plans to sell the secrets of the Phoenix's mind – an action that will be watched by a global audience—before he is destroyed.

As young adults, Will, Ruby Q and Piccolo face problems, old and new.

Much to his disgust, Will finds himself branded a pin-up to revive the fortunes of a fast-fading Royal Family, while dreaming – oh, how he dreams – of a lost love.

Piccolo – the abused runaway who saw his father murdered before his eyes – is now a successful musician with an unknown but exciting project on the horizon. He lives a country idyll but, secretly, struggles with depression.

Ruby Q writes for Dekaydence's most prestigious newspaper but yearns to find out more about the company's head, Lord di'Abalo of Croy Polloi. Alas, she will discover more than she wanted to know.

Perhaps the future lies in Justice, a new group set up by North, a former GeeZer, with the aim to make the world a better, fairer place for all, for example, by bringing to court for war crimes the President of the Federation himself. It's a long and dangerous shot as the President is known to be a survivor of immense resilience, with breathtakingly enormous reserves of disposable cash.

Meanwhile, mysterious sudden deaths are happening in high and faraway places while great changes are soon to take place in the lives of many, including Indigo, the King's granddaughter, Innit, a Dekaydence thug, and Grout, the shy lab technician now the steady genius and Head of Innovation at Dekaydence. Then there's the sudden arrival of a new global currency that may spread sweetness and light before …

SECTION 1

Politics is the art of looking for trouble, finding it everywhere, diagnosing it incorrectly and applying the wrong remedies.

Groucho Marx (1890–1977)

1 HOLY DISORDERS

'I'm just popping out for a bit,' says God airily.

Mother Nature glances up from a pile of papers.

'No need to tell me where you're going,' she says. 'Those old trousers speak for You.'

'There's a crisis on Earth,' says God.

'So what's new?' asks Mother Nature.

'I had such faith in this model of mankind but now...'

'Why do I sense the hand of Di'Abalo?' Mother Nature sighs.

'Spot on, as ever,' God says sadly. 'Human beings are in desperate need.'

'Aren't we all?' Mother Nature says sharply.

'In many ways, yes,' God says reflectively. 'What's your problem?'

'The TV licensing people,' says Mother Nature crossly. 'They're suing You for zillions in unpaid licences. They say every home on Earth has a TV and thus conclude that each and every church worldwide must have one, too.'

'Even when there's no one in them.' God shakes his head.

'You're exaggerating, as ever,' says Mother Nature impatiently.

'Not by much,' says God.

'I get the feeling your makeover isn't working out,' says Mother Nature.

God brushes the cracker crumbs and feathers off his trousers.

'Do you want to come with Me?' He says. 'You've missed the last few trips.'

'Why do you bother with Planet Earth?' says Mother Nature. 'You always come back from it stressed out.'

'We've been through this before,' says God.

'Yes,' says Mother Nature. 'But this is the last time.'

'Jolly good, because I'm not giving up on them.'

'Suit Yourself,' says Mother Nature, stacking up a pile of papers. 'Because I am.'

'You can't!' God looks appalled.

'Yes, I can. They're a bad lot. I don't know how You've kept faith with them when they have so little faith in You. You keep expecting them to see the Light. They won't. They're blind to it. Why? Because, they're the most self-centred, greedy and despicable life form You've ever created. You got the formula wrong. You made a mistake, certainly in getting me involved. Why not admit it and walk away?'

God is aghast.

'But they're Our children,' he says. 'They're experiencing droughts and floods, and an increasingly toxic environment. They're fretting about man-made climate change. While they see "real" food, water and fresh air running out, along with jobs and a future. The only constant in their lives is war.'

'Whose fault is that? Theirs! And the execrable politicians they insist on electing over and over again.'

'Not entirely fair. The fault lies with the President of the Union, or Federation, as he has chosen to call the lands under his bullying domination.'

'I've told You over centuries, they take Your name in vain. And the President is no different from the rest of them,' Mother Nature sighs. 'They set up churches in Your name to escape paying taxes and continue their abominable abuse. And they drag Your name through the mud and blood of countless wars and unnecessary deaths. They are cruel, dishonest, avaricious hypocrites.'

God is staring at His centuries-old sandals. They're showing signs of wear. No one makes them any more. And He's long forgotten the necessary skills.

'Look at the way they treat me, their mother,' Mother Nature continues, her indignation rising. 'Every minute of every day they abuse, pollute, ravage, burn and rob me. They develop chemicals to kill me. Only now are they discovering ancient crops don't need fertilisers and can survive floods without chemicals. And that answers to human health are often in the natural world. But what do they do? Nothing. No, it's too late. I've had enough. *They* are the problem on Planet Earth and I want nothing more to do with them.'

'But what about the innocents?' God protests. 'What about Will, Piccolo and Ruby Q Cooper? And Indigo,

Tommo, North, Grout and poor wee Nigel, the talented violinist miniaturised by Dekaydence? What about the Phoenix? And all the other young people fighting for good causes? All of them need Our help.'

'It's too late,' Mother Nature interrupts. 'You're too indecisive. You can never decide whether You are the angry God of the Old Testament out for revenge or the loving God of the New who's into forgiveness. You've no idea whose side You are on. Though one thing is crystal clear, it is not mine.'

God stares at Mother Nature in shock and disbelief.

'What are you saying?'

'I'm saying Our union is at an end,' says Mother Nature. 'So take this in remembrance of me!'

She pushes several mountains of papers across her desk towards Him.

'But...' begins God, watching aghast as piles of paper avalanche to the floor.

'Look, as it was in the beginning it was fun, and interesting,' says Mother Nature. 'But I can no longer stomach humans and their arrogant, ignorant ways. Neither can I tolerate working under Your hands-off, non-interfering, liberal policy. From now on I fight only for the planet, for wildlife and nature. If it comes to it, I'll fight You. To the bitter end.'

'Oh, My God!' says God, staring into the eyes of His long-term partner.

'No point talking to Yourself,' scoffs Mother Nature.

'You never listen.'

'What am I going to do?' He cries out.

Mother Nature slips her spectacles into her pocket and stands up.

God swallows hard; she's wearing the blue dress he created for their first date, albeit while He was struggling to recover from a broken rib.

'You know all the answers,' she says, 'as well as all the questions. You don't need me. You can work it out for Yourself.'

And with that she walks off.

God stares dumbstruck at her departing figure.

'And get someone to fix this!' she shouts out, forcing the rotting, unpearly gate to shut behind her. 'Otherwise You'll be having trouble with the neighbours from Hell. Again.'

God is staring at the cloud matting beneath his feet. Is it a raindrop or a tear from His eye that runs down his cheek? It's impossible to say for sure.

Locking His worries and a handful of private thoughts inside an innocent-looking fluffy white cloud, God sighs. He's about to switch Heaven to remote when He remembers. There is something He must attend to before He leaves.

2 MASSACRE OF THE INNOCENTS

The Phoenix knows you can't alter the ways of the world overnight. But he is impatient for change. From time to time he works for the Real GeeZers, young eco-warriors committed to activating climate-change policies, if necessary using violent action. He believes they are fundamentally mistaken, that climate change is bigger than and beyond man, but he takes on an assignment if he can ally it with his own fight for people and animal welfare and against governmental and corporate corruption, greed and cruelty.

Much has been achieved by youngsters following the Phoenix's daring, headline-grabbing actions. And he sees his army of active followers is fast growing. But now he is injured and there is still so much to do. No matter, he tells himself, his health will soon improve.

'Your flight leaves tomorrow at 6.40am,' North, the new leader of the Real GeeZers, tells the Phoenix. 'The Minister for Tourism has heard of your official assignment and requests a meeting at your hotel on your arrival just after midnight.'

The last thing the Phoenix wants is some government official breathing down his neck, late at night, after a long-haul flight. Could the official know the real objective of his trip? Is it a trap? Whatever, he has to take the risk. He cannot, will not turn back. Neither will others who are involved. It'd be dangerous to stop now. But timing on this job is tight.

Information arrives by courier. He's advised to pack a suit and tie. The Phoenix smiles grimly. That can only mean the job's status has changed from 'high profile' to 'red alert'.

He boards the packed plane as T-J Jenkins, a photo-journalist on a visit to photograph new buildings rising in the capital of a newly booming economy in Africa. It's a plausible enough front for covering another thriving local business – the murder of innocents.

The plane lands and a swell of passengers disperse into rivers of extended families and tributaries of couples, children and siblings. No one takes much notice of him. It's been a long flight. It's after 11pm. He's a white man alone and exhausted, with a camera and a guidebook. A tourist, they conclude casually, knuckled under by the unfamiliar steamy wet heat.

A taxi takes him to a nearby hotel where a room has been booked. He's drying off after a welcome hot shower and entering the bedroom to get clean clothes when he sees a large envelope has been shoved under the door.

Inside is a handful of statements, some signed in childish writing or a simple sign. Mostly, there are photos. Of young children, dead, dismembered, beheaded. Of young children, with deep scars across their heads, with an ear cut off, a limb missing. And babies dug up from shallow dust bowls or lying dead in pools of dried blood, covered in flies.

The Phoenix has seen much in his young life, more than most, but nothing has prepared him for this. It dawns on him that he's old enough to have a child the age of one of these savaged creatures. Anger ignites within him.

He stares at the photographs of three men. He already knows who they are – a witch doctor, a high-ranking policeman and a wealthy businessman who scour and savage villages and farms on the outskirts of the capital. The first two take money from the third, who pays to take the blood and life of a child because he, like others in his country, believes the sacrifice of a child will bring him luck and riches.

Meanwhile, the authorities ignore the Church's claim that there are more child victims in any one parish than official statistics show for the entire country.

The Phoenix has little more than two days for his official and unofficial work, with a deadline to get information under the wire a.s.a.p. to the journalist Ruby Q Cooper, who is writing a piece for *The Daily Unigraph*.

A phone by the bed rings. He picks up the receiver and notices a drawer in the bedside cabinet is part open.

'The Minister for Tourism has arrived, Mr Jenkins,' says the receptionist enthusiastically. 'He apologises, but he won't be able to stay long. Also, he begs you not to bother with formal dress.'

'Thank you. I'll be down in five minutes,' says the Phoenix, staring fixedly into the drawer at the Baldwin revolver.

3 CO_2 OR NOT CO_2?

Beneath the traffic's roar – the noise of the crowd, the sound of a butterfly's fluttering wings – there are voices. Two young men, hundreds of miles apart – both eco-activists, one a prince of Scotland, the other a dour but steady Northerner – are talking under the government-imposed wire and below the level of the Eye-Spys' tracking devices.

'What's up?' says North. 'D'you want my job back?'

'Och, no,' says Will, with a mirthless laugh. 'Thanks, anyway.'

'So why this conversation?' says North.

'I never told you why I resigned.'

'No, you didn't, but so what? says North. 'The work of the Real GeeZers continues without you.'

'I should've told you this before, it could've changed everything for you, the Rear GeeZers and—'

'I'm not good at change,' North interrupts.

Will takes a deep breath.

'Look, I need to tell you this: I don't believe in what the GeeZers, Real or otherwise, are doing.'

'What d'you mean?' says North.

'I don't believe mankind is the root cause of climate change.'

'Then check out the data,' says North coolly.

'I have and I don't believe it,' says Will.

He pauses, waiting for a response that doesn't come.

'I've done research. The data comes from computer-generated climate models,' Will continues. 'The software is practically programmed to foresee disaster, and scientists come to believe the models echo reality exactly. They don't. They examine atmospheric motion and water levels but not the chemistry and biology of trees, soil and sky.'

'I don't understand,' says North.

'The reality is that human activity is causing levels of carbon dioxide to rise rapidly,' says Will. 'And that might be a good thing. Or not. The earth is going through a relatively cool period. Warming is not global but local, making cold places warmer rather than making hot places hotter.'

'You're saying the opposite of what most scientists believe – that carbon is good for us?' says North aghast.

'Possibly, but I don't know for sure,' says Will. 'The rise of carbon dioxide might be insignificant. But there are those who believe that no chemical compound in the atmosphere has a worse reputation than CO_2. That it is, in fact, a natural and essential atmospheric gas.'

'Really?' North says dubiously. 'Send me the links.'

'OK, but there's something else,' says Will.

'The earth's flat?' says North.

Will gives a dark laugh.

'It may or may not be greenhouse gases or CO_2 emissions

that'll cause the planet to die. Worse perhaps, climate changes are natural recurring process that happen over long periods of time. But now, man is exacerbating changes over infinitely shorter periods of time, sometimes within a few years.'

'Sounds like a double Armageddon,' says North reflectively.

'Who knows for sure?' says Will. 'But isn't that the basis of science? That there is a finite answer, until the next finite answer comes along. That's to say, there is no certain certainty.'

There's a pause.

'I admit I've put my faith in the mountain of scientific evidence rather than read and research it all myself,' North says thoughtfully.

'You're not alone,' sighs Will. 'Some of that mountain comprises digestible science fantasy. And there are high priests of climate change who berate man and cows for farting too much. Equally, they're more than content that the Federation President has set up a secular body with an unchallengeable right to create "green" money-making taxes.

'Don't get me wrong, I believe in climate change. Sunspots, volcanoes, tornadoes, tsunamis, earthquakes. But you can't stop naturally recurring processes. Unless you're God. Or Mother Nature. It's happening elsewhere in the solar system – on Mars, Jupiter, Saturn – and there's not much evidence there of humans driving around in gas-guzzling Dekaydence Mostro Marinas ... You've gone very quiet.'

'If you're right,' says North, 'it means what I do, what I tell others to do in the name of the Real GeeZers, and others prepared to die to save this planet...it's all for nothing.'

'Who knows for sure?' says Will.

'OK, I'd better do some research and get back to you, as soon as,' says North, 'but there are projects already under way. I won't pull them. It'd be too dangerous.'

'I understand,' says Will.

And who better than Will to understand the dangers of operating undercover, at night and mostly alone? He, a prince of the realm, who has lived a public lie as an undercover eco-activist. Who is now an increasingly popular pawn in the game plan of his great-uncle, the King, to promote the monarchy and ensure its survival.

There is much undercover work to do, Will considers, and two important issues to resolve:

1 Why has Dekaydence taken teenagers from the streets and turned them into smiley, empty-headed slaves? They did it to Will's older brother, Tommo, once a big, brave chap and now a simple-minded child. Will there ever be a cure for him and the other damaged youngsters?

2 For causing innumerable deaths and wounding thousands of soldiers and civilians in endless wars throughout the world, the President of the Federation *must* be tried and, if found guilty, jailed for war crimes.

4 THE NEW DISORDER

The early morning light is as sharp and bright as a fresh lemon. Grout, Dekaydence's young Head of Innovation, has to squint to take in fully the splendour of the new, ancientised Dekaydence Amphitheatre – based on the Colosseum in Rome – with a great tower at each compass point, containing shopping malls, cinemas, offices and apartments that will launch tonight as the Federation's largest action-packed entertainment centre.

Flashing his VIP pass, Grout walks the site, the size of six football pitches. He visually scales the 500-metre towers and the six stacked rows of arches, constructed of concrete, Roman red brick and the new Dekaydence fabrication, plithanium, that he, Grout, has created.

The amphitheatre heaves with activity: musicians and acrobats rehearsing; vendors setting up stalls of Dekaydence food, clothes, and souvenirs; animals and animal'oids (part being, part metal) herded this way and that. Underground, Grout travels countless passageways, lifts, staircases and ramps. He views the numerous chambers, large and small, containing warriors, animals, armourers, rangers, cooks, child runners, doctors, physiotherapists, first-aiders, vets, cleaners, morticians and refuse collectors. He climbs through a trapdoor that leads into the arena, comes face to face with a snow leop'oid, which attempts to bite him through the metal wire. He quickly retreats.

It's hard to believe that six months ago on this site stood the royal palace, home to the Royal Family for generations, until they were evicted by Lord di'Abalo, Head of the Company of Dekaydence. He had the Royal Family rehomed in a set of decaying summerhouses in the neighbouring park and dismissed the staff. Then he had the audacity to request His Majesty officially open the new amphitheatre. His Majesty accepted the invitation, graciously, to help safeguard the future of his son and heir.

At the main entrance a smiley young woman in the daffodil-yellow suit of a Dekaydence Guide checks Grout's pass.

'Can I go through the gate over there?' he enquires, casually.

'No.' She beams brightly. 'Each visitor archway equates with a different social standing. Your DNA match shows you must use the Great Archway over there, that's for the exclusive use of politicians, bankers and VIPs, such as yourself.

'That other archway is for the masses. That's to say the penniless young and the sadly, badly educated. Nearer, but still at a distance, is the gate for the sturdy, put-upon middle class, who sit up in the gods and are robustly exposed to the elements.

'I must also inform you, sir, that should you enter a prohibited area you face on-the-spot enslavement – unless, of course, you have sufficient and immediate cash to buy your way out.'

Grout breathes a sigh of relief. The project Di'Abalo asked him to create is working. Later tonight, after the launch, he'll return to work on a new project, an antidote to a new deadly virus that's broken out in the Far East. How much better, he thinks, to be working to save lives than footling about with an entry system and software for yet another suspect Dekaydence project.

He catches sight of a tour guide with a sheaf of writers, among them the Dekaydence journalist Ruby Q Cooper. He's about to acknowledge her when he sees Di'Abalo approaching from the opposite direction.

He walks off briskly, away from them both. He must be careful. Dekaydence has trained and nurtured him, and now relishes and exploits his techno-scientific mind. He cannot, must not, ever let Di'Abalo learn that he works secretly for Ruby Q Cooper; for Prince Will; for Will's young cousin, the king's granddaughter, the Princess Indigo; and for the human and animal rights activist the Phoenix. All four of whom work undercover with groups campaigning hard for a better, fairer and just world.

BREAKING NEWS

Ruby Q Cooper and T-J Jenkins report from Africa for *The Daily Unigraph*

It's early evening and the queue at the car repair shop is dwindling as mended and tended cars and trucks are driven away by satisfied customers. Though hidden away in the back streets on the edge of this African town, the shop is nevertheless renowned for the quality of its vehicle maintenance and bodywork repairs.

The light is beginning to fade and the few customers remaining are enjoying the company of the large man at the counter whose kindly nature cheers and soothes even the most impatient customer.

A man in the workshop, his big feet sticking out from underneath an ancient long-bed pick-up truck, slides out and whistles softly to the man at the counter. Knowing that this is their cue to depart, the few customers remaining reluctantly shuffle out.

The two men shut up shop, holler to those left in the workshop and drive off into the darkness in the truck.

In the workshop the three women, who have spent the day working on vehicles, carburettors and blown radiators, quickly clear and sweep the floor area. They

LIVE FROM AN ILLEGAL INTERNET SERVICE PROVIDER

drink tea and talk in nervous subdued tones as they prepare for the evening shift, which tonight will be different and dangerous. They fall silent as they uncover three slightly concave sheets of stainless steel, each a dozen hexagonal shapes of scrap metal in a mix of colours, and three more, like reversed pancakes, flat but for a raised border at the edge rolling up about twenty to thirty centimetres.

They hear the old truck pull up outside. Cautiously, a woman opens the door. The two men have returned with a third, and each is dragging a deadweight body along the ground. They place one limp body face down on one of the flat pieces of metal. They do the same with the other two bodies. The three men then heave a concave sheet on to the back of each.

The women set to work. One of the bodies groans. One woman lifts up her mask.

'Are they going to wake up?' she demands crossly of the men.

'Not until we reach our destination,' the large man reassures her. 'And if they do, we're ready for them.' He pats a pouch on his hip, which she interprets as indicating he has the drugs necessary for the job.

The women are fast workers, their tools relatively quiet. The work is soon done and the three men's bodies transported via a pick-up to the truck. A tarpaulin is thrown over them and the truck moves off. The women check and inspect the workshop and lock up. They hurry home in silence, each deep in her own thoughts. One woman starts to weep, another shushes her as one might try to calm a crying baby. The third says nothing but squeezes the sobbing woman's hand and quietly urges her onwards.

The next morning the city is awoken by shrieks from the main square where stands in the middle of a rose garden a magnificent statue of the President and the remains of a very old truck.

Three tortoises – of a size never before seen – are chained by their legs to the legs of the President's statue, which has one foot planted firmly on a globe. Of course, people realise at once the creatures aren't tortoises, they're men inside colourful metal shells encasing them from the base of the neck to their ankles, the side welding allowing no more than a shallow breath of movement.

'It's witchcraft,' some mutter, fearful of being heard.

'Then it's of his own making. This is the witch doctor!' says one old woman loudly, giving the leg of the nearest 'tortoise' a resounding kick. 'And that one...' She lands a boot in the face of another 'tortoise'. 'This is his friend, the policeman.'

'And this one's a builder,' says a young man, equally

loudly. 'That new shopping mall is his. He got enough greed to starve the world of food. Killing babies ain't nuffin' to him. Dirty murderin' bassard. He paid a man to take my sister's child. A year old it was. May he rot in hell. Or better still, inside his stinkin' shell.'

The crowd turns its gaze to the mass of photographs stuck on sticks in the flowerbeds. There are pictures of young children and babies, abused and maimed. Or left to bleed to death in the roadside dust. A woman sobs as she looks at a picture of her six-year-old grandson found decapitated in a field near her home. She refused an offer of money; she was denied justice for her grandson. Her story is not unique. Neither are her tears.

Among the pictures are banners making demands.

'Stop those who pay to kill our children.' 'Sacrifice the guilty not the innocents.' 'While we are trapped by grief, may these shelled men live trapped until they die.' Another banner asks simply, 'Why?'

A teenage girl kneels to pick up an unusual feather of red and gold lying in the dust.

'It's the Phoenix!' she whispers, as she holds tight to the baby on her hip. 'He's come to help us!'

The word spreads like wildfire. The excitement in the crowd is almost palpable. They know the Phoenix acts worldwide for people in need and distress. So he must've

LIVE FROM AN ILLEGAL INTERNET SERVICE PROVIDER

come to stop this butchery. To protect their remaining children. But where is he? How did he do this? He must have had help, but from whom? Will he and his helpers be discovered and punished? Will any of this stop child sacrifices in their land?

In the night the car repair shop catches fire and is burnt to the ground. In the morning the police search the wreckage but find nothing. Or anyone or anything of interest at the homes of the three men and three women who worked there. Borders and airports are alerted but to no avail.

By lunchtime the photos and T-J's undercover interviews are exploding worldwide via newspapers, websites, adservarums and TV, alongside the horrific reasons why three men are imprisoned in metal shells.

The Phoenix lives

5 WHAT AM I GOING TO DO ABOUT MARIA?

Sooner or later someone will crack open the shells of the tortoised men. The Phoenix hopes that all three men are tried in court and imprisoned indefinitely. And that this must act as a deterrent to those who consider following in the men's bloody steps.

The Phoenix wants Ruby Q's story to so outrage people worldwide that they'll demand the practice of child sacrifice be stopped. That people worldwide will demand that regular work with a living wage is paid to those who might otherwise be tempted to stray. And that there will be education sufficient to stop the practice.

Global support and action is essential because this is not about oil or rare minerals and, thus, few politicians will lift an eyelid to get involved. The Phoenix knows and understands this more than most. His father is one of those politicians. His father is President of the Federation.

The Phoenix cares about the men and women who produced the 'tortoise suits'. He knows that they are walking free in another country, with funds to start new lives. He also understands that within that freedom they will never be able to escape their memories, or their sorrow at the fate that has befallen their children.

He cares about the Minister for Tourism, who secretly

organised the firing of the garage as well as the car workers' escape, and prays the man escapes suspicion.

The Phoenix, who'd been uneasy at meeting the Minister, immediately recognised the schoolboy in the young man.

'All for one and one for all,' the Minister had whispered to him, with a grin. 'My dear fellow Noteian.'

The Phoenix feels a sudden, sharp pang of guilt as he thinks of his sister, Maria. How long has it been since he's seen her?

He reflects on her troubled life. When she'd learnt their father had been responsible for the bomb attack on their home that had killed their mother and younger brother, Josef, she'd gone to stay with friends. When a tidal wave of electoral sympathy had elevated their father from Prime Minister of the UK to President of the Federation, she'd disappeared without trace.

The Phoenix can't recall when he last saw her. Let alone spoke to her.

When he lands back home he contacts his Noteian schoolfriends, the two doctors, to ask them to find her. Just that. No more. He'll pay. He'll do the rest. His friends are well connected and discreet, and they've known Maria since she was a baby. Teased her through childhood into young womanhood. One of the Noteians, he recalls with a rare fleeting smile, had taken rather a shine to her.

6 A NEW DEKAYDENCE DAWN

A sunset sky of purple and gold embraces the arena where a 500,000-strong audience is clapping and cheering, singing and shouting, ravenous for the action to begin.

Awaiting his cue to enter the Dekaydence Royal Box, the King assembles a brave face under the Day Crown that sits on top of the Bowler Hat that hangs from a pole, held by a bewigged footman. The pole is made of constantly fracturing plastic. Somehow, the centuries-old gold, from which it was originally made, has found its way into the Dekaydence vaults.

The King will wave, smile and nod graciously but not arrogantly. He will perform thus till the day he dies – in order to secure the monarchy. Will knows the King will do all this and more to ensure the succession. If necessary, he suspects the King would kill. Indeed, some say that is how Will's father met his 'accidental' end. After all, the trait is not unknown in the family genes.

As the sky fades from blush pink into burnished gold and on into a deep ink blue, a plithanium forest of trees and shrubs bursts forth from the sand. Giant fountains of plaited rainbow-coloured water shoot up into the air, and firebirds of green, gold, white and tangerine fly back and forth across the stadium, creating fantastic pictures and patterns.

As the firebirds spell out the word 'Dekaydence' – in giant capital letters with the company crest at all four compass points – the cheering and applause grows louder.

'Ladies and gentlemen, boys and girls.' A commanding voice fills the arena, hushing the crowd. 'Please welcome to the new Dekaydence Amphitheatre His Royal Highness, His Majesty King Edmund, the Crown Prince with his son, the Crown Princeling, and his daughter, the Princess Indigo!'

'Here we go,' the King says jovially, leading the family into the Royal Box.

The applause is polite. The Crown Prince, with his spiky blond hair and shades, yodels and punches the air. Given he's dressed in tight white leather, it's about the only movement he can manage. Several thousand young men, similarly attired and imbibed with Dekaydence alcohol, punch the air and yodel back. The King smiles at the Crown Prince's enthusiastic reception but inwardly despairs at the lack of dignity needed to attain it.

Will steps forward. The roar from the crowd is overwhelming. He grimaces. He hates these official engagements, and so imagines himself on the loch at home, sailing with his older brother Tommo. Only a few years back. When life had been easy. And problems and responsibilities had hitched themselves only to adults.

When Tommo had been Tommo. A big glorious character with a great kind heart. Before Tommo had joined the GeeZers. Before Dekaydence had messed with Tommo's mind. Before Dekaydence had taken the GeeZers' message to fight global warming and turned it into an enormous money-making opportunity. Before—

A sharp prod in the ribs startles Will back to the present.

'Give 'em a smile rather than that damn scowl you're always wearing,' the King says, snowflake soft and thunder dark, as he waves, smiles and nods in all directions.

'Leave him alone, Grandpa,' the Princess Indigo says under her breath.

Will tries a grin but can't make it appear on both sides of his face.

'I suppose that'll have to do,' the King sniffs, as he continues smiling and waving. 'But don't forget, my boy, they'll want to see you married soon.'

'No need,' Will retorts. 'You have a son and heir, who has given you a grandson and a granddaughter. And I'd say the Princess Indigo is an extremely clever and capable young woman.'

'Insurance, dear boy. If I'm honest, I would've liked more boys,' says the King. 'One can't have too many insurance policies.'

'Don't think you're getting any produce out of this "policy",' says the Princess Indigo indignantly. 'The genes show they'll be either mad, bad or dangerous to know. Or all three in one.'

The King laughs.

'You are far too determined a creature to allow your offspring to be anything other than as pretty and perfect as you, sweetie pie!'

Indigo tosses her dark curls.

Will says nothing. His thoughts are focused on finding someone in the crowd. He knows that someone is out there somewhere but...

He's seen the boy he rescued from the streets once or twice, and only at a distance. If ever Will catches his eye, Piccolo always scowls before fleeing fast. Will wonders about the reason but is fearful of the answer. Piccolo is now a young man, a successful composer and musician. Will has learnt that Piccolo is close to Grout, the young boffin within Dekaydence, where they both work. And that every weekend they stay with friends in Sussex. Will tortures himself, wondering, How close is close?

7 OVERTURE AND BEGINNERS

'Great story about the tortoise men, Ruby Q,' says the Suit, a widely travelled, late-middle-aged journalist who works on a Dekaydence tabloid that specialises in ferreting in dustbins, gutters and ad'ums, as adversarums are now generally known, to find spicy news that'll drive up newspaper sales and outdo rivals.

The Suit is a friend of Spiky Hair, editor of *The Daily Unigraph*, a respected broadsheet newspaper and Ruby Q's boss. All three are sitting in the VIP box, waiting for the event to start.

'I've never heard of your co-journalist, T-J Jenkins,' the Suit continues, slurring his words between drinks.

The Suit looks quizzically at Ruby Q, waiting for a response.

'T-J works undercover,' Ruby Q replies.

'Stop snooping about for your rag,' Spiky Hair says, firmly, to the Suit. 'Find your own T-J.'

'As if I were a common thief!' the Suit protests.

It's obvious the Suit has been drinking. Ruby Q knows from Spiky Hair that this is most unusual and that something must be up.

The Suit snorts. Something on his ad'um has caught his eye.

'So Lord di'Abalo springs his friend Candelskin from jail and within weeks appoints him officially His Overall Holiness. Now His Overall Holiness Candyfloss is to appoint that sleazy old cur Solomon to be his right-hand man and Financial Bishop to the City of London.'

'Oh, my,' says Spiky Hair, distracted, like Ruby Q, by the arrival of the temperamental fashion designer Petty Masters and her personal assistant, the rollerblading Schneek.

Petty is wearing something akin to a large tent. It's summer blue and covered with bright golden orbs of sunshine and fluffy white clouds that float slowly across the fabric, while her earrings are silver twittering swallows that every so often take off and soar through the sky before returning to the PMT ear.

Petty is stuffing her mouth with cream crackers (as usual) and broad beans (unusual). Rumour is she's pregnant; but her staff remains mum. Schneek helps her divest herself of a backpack, avoiding her high-flying hairdo and the dense feathery wings on her back.

'Look at that.' The Suit slurps and hiccups his words. 'Such is the state of the nation that even an angel is discarding her wings.'

'He's in a bad way,'' Spiky Hair whispers to Ruby Q. 'I wonder why?'

The lights dim, the music plays, the audience hushes. The first set begins.

The stage set is a Parisian nightclub packed with designer-attired customers, handsome young waiters and pretty waitresses, and a language of looks, touch and danger.

The band, the Studs 'n' Sluts, known better as the SS, are slick and slinky, like their songs, written by Piccolo Smith and Sir Harrison Catgut. The Sluts, Apple and Citrus, wear off-the-shoulder, figure-hugging tangerine leather dresses and slashed black fishnet tights. The Studs, Biff and Slosh, shirtless and emphatically muscled, are in braces and skin-tight black trousers. Their dancing is precise, precocious and perilous.

Ruby Q makes notes in her pad, such as 'SSpecial, SScintillating SStuff!'

The next set is a dingy London street. The music, last year's popular, sentimental hits from Bread 'n' Water (songwriter, Piccolo Smith) remind Ruby Q of Jack Martin, who died the previous year in the London tsunami, leaving a widow and an unborn child, and Ruby Q with a broken friendship as well as a broken heart.

Luckily, she's distracted by Hunky Doré, the American superstar singer married to Petty Masters, who leaps on to the stage for the next set.

Dressed in a leopardskin loincloth, HD is Tarzan, surrounded by numerous scantily clad Janes, who emerge from a wild jungle. The audience is transfixed by the sight of the young white American rapper with his Dekaydence implant add-ons of two pairs of arms, three hairy black and one hairless white. As well as the pair he was born with.

Alas, towards the end, HD's wild performance has an

abrupt end as one of his black hairy arms comes loose and flies off into the crowd. It's hurriedly retrieved by Black Tartan guards from a drunken lout stuffing the arm into a baguette full of ketchup. HD is rushed to hospital, accompanied by Petty Masters, and her assistant, Schneek, and the interval is called early.

Ruby Q takes a phone call. It's the care home. Elsa, her grandmother, is causing trouble and the home wants her out immediately. Rallan is in no fit state to help. Although Ruby Q knows now that Elsa isn't her biological grandmother and Rallan isn't her biological father, she has grown up with them. They are her family. She will do whatever is needed to help them.

Spiky Hair is sympathetic and practical. She contacts the Dekaydence chauffeur to take Ruby Q to the care home and then take her home.

'She ought to stay here,' mutters the Suit.

Spiky Hair ignores him.

'Good luck, Ruby Q,' she says. 'Let me know how you get on.'

Ruby Q is touched by Spiky Hair's kindness. So she misses the finale, the most awaited event of the day. She misses the VIP reception, and the opportunity to talk to Lord di'Abalo, Head of Dekaydence, who she has learnt is her real father.

She also misses a chance encounter with the woman she has been searching for years — her mother, Angelica Nera.

But there is something she doesn't miss.

As she goes to leave the Suit takes a firm hold of her arm with one hand and of Spiky Hair's with the other. His face is pale, his eyes wide and scared.

'We haven't got long,' he says, looking from one to the other. 'There's a new, deadly virus out there.'

'There always is,' says Spiky Hair, removing her arm from his grip. 'It never does much damage, does it?'

'This time it's for real,' says the Suit agitatedly. 'We're all going to die. I have it on the greatest authority.'

'Who is this great authority?'

The Suit looks about nervously.

'Phlegm,' he whispers.

'Lord di'Abalo's butler?' Spiky Hair sounds surprised. She'd heard the old man had died.

'You know we meet for a drink every so often,' says the Suit.

'Yes, but you don't drink...and he is...'

'Yes, yes, usually, I drink cordial,' the Suit says tetchily. 'Elderflower, if they've got it. It's Phlegm's favourite, too. After Scotch, of course.'

'OK,' says Spiky Hair slowly. 'But I think it's safe for Ruby Q to visit her grandmother tonight. Any news of Armageddon, Ruby Q, I'll contact you a.s.a.p.'

Sitting in the back of the Dekaydence limousine, Ruby Q can't decide what to worry about first. Her family, that isn't. Her mother, who appears to be lost for good. Or a deadly virus that'll get her before she gets answers to the questions rattling around in her life about who she is and what she can do to make the world a better place.

'I'm looking in the mirror,' she says to herself. 'I'm there, but only in part.'

Get a grip, Ruby Q.

Where have you been?

Where I've been for a while. In your head, keeping an eye on you. Somebody has to.

8 OUT OF THE FRYING PAN

The young composer Piccolo Smith sits huddled at the back of the VIP box. His face is hidden by a wide-brimmed old hat. He's among strangers, and out of the view of TV cameras. He catches sight of Will below him in the Royal Box and pulls down the brim of the hat still further.

A bureaucratic or planned mix-up? Whatever, Piccolo is separated by a dozen rows from his friends, his mentor and his mentor's wife, Sir Harrison and Lady Catgut, Grout, his friend from Dekaydence, and Nigel, former first violinist of the Imperial Orchestra of the Union, miniaturised by Dekaydence and saved from death by Grout. Luckily, as Piccolo sees it, he is further away from Will...

Dressed in cricketing whites and a blue and white striped jacket, Catgut, knighted for his services to loud music, is as over-excited as a child to hear his music (co-composed with Piccolo) played in the arena and to such a huge crowd. He accompanies the songs, cheering, clapping and whooping such that the man behind remonstrates with him, telling him that he's not at Lord's now. Catgut's behaviour doesn't change, except for the worse, when he hears the Bread 'n' Water songs composed by Piccolo.

In an interval Piccolo catches up with Lady Catgut, Grout and Nigel in a slow-moving queue to the lavatories.

He advises her to leave before the second half because he has heard it might upset her. Lady Catgut, touched by Piccolo's concern, has, nevertheless, flicked through the brochure and seen the herd of handsome hunks.

'I may be old, Piccolo, dear,' says Lady Catgut. 'But I'm not *that* rusty.'

'Keep an eye on her, man. Rumour has it the fight scenes will be wild,' Piccolo tells Grout discreetly, before quickly returning to his seat.

'I shall keep two eyes on her,' Nigel declares fiercely. His devotion to the kindly lady who has cared for him over many months knows no bounds.

Come the next interval, as VIPs head towards the official reception, Piccolo turns in the opposite direction. He must avoid Will at all costs and, as his ticket allows him through many barriers and Red Tartan Guards...

He takes a turn here and a staircase there, arriving in a subterranean world throbbing with activity, heat and clamour. Here, the Dekaydence Tartan guards, Red and Black, show one another nothing but antipathy. Here, prison guards and animal minders prepare their beasts for the fights. On standby are blacksmiths and armourers, physios, doctors and hi-tech morticians, ready for hi-tech repairs and departures.

Piccolo is inspired by the operatic grandeur of it all. Melodies, plots, songs and stories start fizzing away in his head. Then he feels a rough hand taking hold of him by the scruff of his neck.

He is spun round to face the big man he knows to be MacGluten, Head of Dekaydence catering.

'Game's up, laddie. Unless you got some cash.'

'I've nothing but—'

MacGluten strikes a blow to Piccolo's head.

Piccolo's brain reverberates in shock.

'The rule here is "Food and paupers don't answer back." Understand?' says MacGluten.

Piccolo is too stunned to say the words 'VIP pass'. He tries to reach for his pocket when he's grabbed again by the scruff of the neck and lifted off the ground by a big, brawny Black Tartan guard.

'Puddings or savouries?' the guard calls to MacGluten.

'Casseroles. It's bony but it'll have to do.' MacGluten sounds harassed. Probably because he is. He's overseeing food for the VIP reception, a private banquet for Lord di'Abalo's personal guests, and a secret vanload of puddings for the His Majesty.

Piccolo, meanwhile, realises slowly that Dekaydence cameras appear to be inside every oven and saucepan MacGluten is using. He struggles to open his mouth but he's hit again.

'Carry on like that, young man, and you'll get a long drawn-out and painful ending,' the guard says. 'Bear that in mind if you've got a mum, a sister or a lady friend out there. They could get mighty upset. And we don't want that, do we?'

Like a slow, cold mist creeping across an abandoned

graveyard, Piccolo understands suddenly what it means to be related to the word 'food'. The contents of his stomach turns to liquid that wants to evacuate fast from his body.

He's been through enough beatings in his early life. Enough breaks, bruises and bashings about the head to make his brain spin off-key... And now this.

Suddenly, the exploits in the kitchen bring it all back to him. As before, he feels he's losing the will to live. He imagines in death that his murdered father will come to greet him. That maybe he'll meet up with Bianco, the handsome young man who promised to rescue him from the streets and who then disappeared. Whatever happens to him, Piccolo prays fervently that God will keep His side of the bargain. That He will keep Will safe from harm forever if he, Piccolo, has no contact with Will ever again. Forever and ever. Amen.

9 NORTH'S ABOUT-FACE

'So what's this emergency meeting about?' the Face demands of North. 'Had *another* change of mind? Want to quit your violent mob and return to the peaceful GeeZers with me? Or you got other ideas, dearie?'

The twenty-odd young men and women – assembled in a room at the old George Inn near Southwark Cathedral – shift in their seats. It's not the chairs making them feel uncomfortable, it's the tension in the air generated, as usual, by the Face.

North scans the faces in the room. He knows them all. GeeZers, of both persuasions, committed to saving the planet from environmental meltdown. The GeeZers, the original non-violent activists, and the Real GeeZers, prepared to take violent action to effect speedy changes.

There are missing faces. Lost campaigners, friends and family. Lost, disillusioned or wary of exposure to hostile authorities.

'I thank you for taking the risk to come here tonight and meet in a public place. I want this "open" way of doing business to continue,' says North. 'However, we know our exits and safe houses – should the same situation occur as before when the Black Tartans made their unannounced, armed entrance on our meeting, and a young GeeZer, a friend of us all, was murdered.'

He pauses to give time for GeeZers to reflect on the night friends and colleagues were injured or taken into custody where, it is said, some remain.

'I hope the information I sent you is enlightening and will help prepare you for what I'm about to say,' North continues.

There is muttering and mumbling, and a static apprehension in the air.

'I'm not here to argue or persuade anyone to my way of thinking,' says North. 'But I implore you to research and read the links I've sent you and make up your own minds. Read the thoughts and beliefs of sceptics and the believers.

'As you know, I was committed to the idea that man is responsible for climate change. It's what I learnt in school. It's what I saw on TV. Recently, I've read sufficient to persuade me otherwise. That climate change is a natural, recurring process. That man plays a part in it all. And what man *is* doing is making money out of a global climate change bandwagon and extracting money from well-intentioned but misinformed people.'

Amidst the boos and hisses, jeers and cheers, there is a smattering of slow hand-clapping and warm applause.

'Get angry. Disagree all you like,' says North, raising his voice above the fracas. 'But read the research you'd never normally look at. Explore the opposite of what you believe.

'And think on this. There are other important issues in the world today that need addressing. We can blame successive governments and bankers, at home and abroad, for our collapsing social and economic structures. But better we ask "How has this come about?" and "What can we do to improve things? Why wasn't sub-prime lending made illegal? Why weren't those fiddling the Libor banking rate tried and sent to prison? Is there a law that would prevent such events happening again?"

'We need to discuss these issues openly with other campaign groups. We won't agree on everything but there is strength in numbers. We have youth and energy on our side. And, possibly, a tad more IT expertise...'

Laughter makes a small but welcome ripple through the audience.

'Like the Phoenix and Ruby Q Cooper, we can shock people into an awareness of what's happening in our world. And, hopefully, shock them into action, into demanding and insisting on change. Who doesn't want an honourable, honest, caring and open society that deals harshly but fairly with liars, robbers and cheats that fester in banks, governments and almost anywhere?'

There is enthusiastic applause.

'But what exactly is our aim?' shouts a voice.

'And how long before we win?' shouts another.

'We're talking about a revolution,' says North. 'Hopefully, a bloodless one. Ideally, national governments must be abolished. Governance must be on a local scale.

We all agree we want politics to be devoid of politicians. Politics is too important to be abused by a bunch of self-centred, naïve, overgrown mainly male schoolchildren.

'It's unlikely we'll get reform in our lifetime but, God in Heaven, we have to ensure that it's emerging before our children leave school.'

There is muttering and undercurrents. North holds up his arms.

'I am sorry but I must catch a train. I'll meet you here same time next week.'

As he leaves the room words are hurled at him hard, like rocks. Turncoat. Hypocrite. Fool. Wimp. Some words, he hears, are thrown by the Face. But there are a few cheers, some applause and the odd supportive pat on the back.

The revolution has started, thinks North. It's simply in the wrong place, on the inside, among the revolutionaries. But as he runs along the street towards the station, a thought comes into his head. Maybe a revolution among revolutionaries is the best place to begin? Yes, it may be the very best place.

1

'As we feared, sir, it's just been announced there will be another tribunal,' the civil servant informs the President of the Federation.

'Oh, God, not another one.' The President groans. 'That makes four over the past four years. I can barely squeeze in my six months' annual holiday. What do they want out of me, blood?'

'Mmm, could be.' The civil servant nods, thoughtfully. 'More likely, they want the truth about the war on the eastern borders of the Federation.'

'Are you accusing me of lying, Cyril?'

'I'm a civil servant, Mr President. I wouldn't presume to employ such language or actions. But the press and public are after you, sir. They are furious at the million-plus deaths of soldiers, civilians, youngsters and babies still in the womb. The more so now it's been shown that statements made to justify the war have proved to be false.'

'Typing errors, Cyril. The people here aren't properly trained.'

'For sure, but that's now true of every workplace and place of education, sir.'

'Is it?'

'Yes, sir. It was one of your earliest policies, if you recall.'

'Are you sure?'

'Yes, sir.'

'Remind me, what was I thinking?'

'You needed to abolish education and training at every level to ensure the government had the funds for Lord di'Abalo to build the Colosseum. If you recall, sir, you also created the term e-con – Entertainment for Controlling (the Masses). And you received a substantial seven-figure creator fee from the Federation. There were posters everywhere. Alas, only the bright, privately educated and old 'uns such as ourselves could read and understand them.'

The President bangs his fist on the table, rather than admit to the civil servant that he was state educated.

'Bloomin' waste of money, then,' the President sneers.

'Pretty much, sir, yes. But as you may recall, the public is now paying off the debts through the many taxes, etcetera, that you introduced...'

'Hurrah, for the middle class and the mugs!' says the President. 'We couldn't do without them, could we, Cyril?'

'No, Mr President. But research shows they could do without us.'

'Oh, my lord, we can't be having that,' says the President. 'There's your pension as well as mine to protect. Get someone on the case, would you, old boy? Someone legally minded. Wiggins might know of someone. Pity we can't use Wiggy himself. He's just one halo short of being a saint. And that would make things rather difficult for us, wouldn't it, Cyril?'

Cyril nods.

'But, just in case there's trouble,' the President continues, 'let's get Di'Abalo's young thug on board. The one he's been training up. What's his name?'

'Bodkin, sir. Personally, I wouldn't allow him within whiffin' distance of a sewer.'

'Excellent, Cyril. It would appear Bodkin is our man.'

9.5 A TARTAN DREAM

'How'd the exam go, MacMinor?' MacNoodle enquires of his fellow Red Tartan guard.

'I think I did all right,' MacMinor says, after a moment's thought. 'Mebbe not gold but p'haps silver or bronze? I hope I don't disappoint the wee lassie who was my Open University tutor. She was excellent, most generous with her time. Even though she hailed from Aberdeen.'

'So, are we celebrating?'

'Och no, it's far too early. But I got lucky.'

'Not an Aberdeen pay rise? Known otherwise as a brutal, unannounced-in-advance deduction from your Dekaydence pay packet.'

'No, man.' MacMinor chuckles. 'You know I want to go to Florence to look at the art I'm studying.'

'Every Red and Black Tartan guard knows that, MacMinor. Dream on, man.'

'No need, Mr MacNoodle. His Overall Highness, Mr Candelskin, wants me to accompany him to Rome. I'm to carry a letter that he will present personally to the Holy Father.'

'Holy haggoids! Have you landed on your sporran or what?'

'I'm sure you could come wi' me. Maybe not to see the Pope himself but...'

'Och, no,' says MacNoodle. 'That's kind of ye, but Cromarty cannae do travel. You know he gets sick going up the stairs on the Tartan Bus. As for what comes out of his *derrière* on the way down—'

'Quite, quite,' MacMinor interrupts quickly, as he recalls the incidents. 'But you could come wi'out him.'

'Thanks, man, but he's ma baby. Ma boy. And what would wee Rossie do wi'out his brother? Anyway, where I go, they go. Or not at all.'

SECTION 2

Let us be the ones to say we are not satisfied that your place of birth determines your right for life. Let us be outraged, let us be loud, let us be bold.
Brad Pitt (1963–)

10 GOD AND PMT

'How's my makeover coming along, Miss Masters?' enquires God, as optimistically as His infinite enthusiasm allows, given His newly separated status.

'The beard must go,' says Petty Masters in her loose elastic cum south London accent. The globally famous fashion designer — dubbed PMT by the media for her temperamental mood swings — is currently staring at a monitor while chomping on raw broad beans and cream crackers. 'How long's it been around?'

'The beard?' the King of Kings muses. 'For ever, I s'pose.'

'Thought so,' mutters Petty, glancing Heavenward before recalling she needn't bother. She's already sitting in Heaven, working for the top man.

'I use it in the way others use worry beads,' says God, curling strands of long grey whiskers between His fingers. 'I couldn't possibly remove it.'

'The deal is I modernise your image and then you get me 'ome, pronto!' Petty says sharply, shovelling beans into her mouth.

'But—' begins God, mesmerised by the number of beans Petty consumes in one mouthful.

'You can*not* go back on Your Word!' she interrupts

fiercely, swivelling round to face the Almighty. 'It's in your contract. I've seen it.'

'I beg your pardon?' says the Almighty, aghast.

'That tall, good-looking bloke on reception showed it to me. The one with the big wings I had to refurb.'

'Gabriel? Well, I'll be…' A rumble of thunder sounds close by.

'He told me that you wanted a new look and that I was the one to create it,' says Petty. 'Very flattering, but I've got a big show coming up for a VIP client who, unlike you, will pay me megabucks without killing me off.'

'I have not killed you off.' God sounds wounded. 'I said you'd be in beta string theory nine for a short while. And take it from me, Lord di'Abalo is used to waiting.'

'How d'you know who my client is?'

Even though she speaks through a sea of mushy beans, He hears suspicion in her voice.

'I am God,' says God, with one of His mysterious smiles.

'So you know Lord di'Abalo is not someone to cross.'

'Yes. And neither am I, Miss Masters,' says God. Another rumble of thunder draws closer still. 'Now, let's get on. I'll never hear the end of it if you're late for your appointment with Mother Nature. At least—'

'Hold on, hold on, how did you…?' Petty Masters demands, as she checks the voluminous tent in which she arrived heavily but unrevealingly pregnant.

'As I said, I *am* God,' God repeats, with another of His mysterious smiles.

'Is there anything you don't know?'

Is there just a tinge of sadness in the Almighty's steady impenetrable gaze?

Petty Masters feels His look reach into her very being. She retreats to view the monitor.

The clamour of voices and the cacophony of hymns in His head are making God exceedingly weary. It's all prayers and pleas, moaning and cursing. And if He hears 'All things bright and beautiful' one more time... It's been like this all day. All year. All...

When *was* the last time someone told Me a joke? he thinks but can't answer.

He groans inwardly. It's an incoming message from that wretched man Randall Candelskin – Lord di'Abalo's right-hand man and now His Overall Holiness (whatever in *his* name that means). He's talking to Him, God, as though they're equals! Who does this lower case think he is? And who gave out His number? It could be only one person. The Pope.

True, the poor man is very busy. Like the rest of us, God shakes His head sadly. Perhaps if they took a short break. Just the two of them. Or with all the others. Hang on, it must be about *that* time, mustn't it? Goodness, it's come round so quickly. He'll check the diary. Suddenly, He feels infinitely better. And not quite so alone.

'God! The equipment here is *so* outdated!' Petty Masters cries out. 'Look at this before the firkin' thing crashes. Your old white nightie thing goes. As does the beard. Dark red tartan spex are an option. A regular hedge-trimming on the beard etcetera; white trews and a blue-and-white striped seersucker jacket...'

Petty turns to God. He's still wearing those grubby old corduroy gardening trousers. She's about to remonstrate when He disappears. In His place stands a clown, its grin revealing teeth made of tiny skulls. She stares at it in horror. The clown laughs as its long spindly arms and twitchety fingers reach out to ensnare her.

She hears herself scream. The earth is moving beneath her. All Heavenly memories are erased and...

Petty is back in her bed. Alongside her husband the American rock star Hunky Doré, who is stretching out three or four of his six arms to embrace her.

'HD! I need another cream cracker and broad bean sandwich! And—' She groans. 'HD! The baby's coming!'

'OMYGOD, THE BABY'S COMING!' cries Hunky Doré, extricating himself from the embrace, grabbing his jacket from the bedpost and struggling to get all his six arms into the six sleeves. 'OMYGOD! OMYGOD! OMYGOD!'

He leaps out of bed and immediately falls back on to it.

'Did the earth just move for you, honeypot?' says Hunky Doré, laughing.

He staggers across the floor, trying to pull on his trousers, and falls over. From the floor he uses his ad'um to tell the chauffeur to have the car at the door, pronto.

Petty knows that HD's unsteadiness isn't caused by alcohol because he doesn't drink. So, is it a sign that his body is rejecting the recent four-arm implants?

No. Hunky Doré is closer to the truth than he realises. The earth has indeed moved. Thrice within three minutes.

God has felt it, too. He wishes He could ask Mother Nature what's going on. World weather is in turmoil and there are these odd, earthly hiccups. Is this part of her anger against Him? Or is it a 'time of life' phase? God sighs. Now He'll never know.

He hurries to put Heaven on remote. For all the good it'll do. For in Heaven, as on earth, hiccups and climate changes aside, strange forces are at work.

God sighs, sensing His time has come.

11 BOA CONSTRICTOR

A girl with a scarlet feather boa round her neck is stirred from sleep by the sound of an engine approaching. Puzzled to find herself curled up on a doorstep, she looks up and sees a young man run past, his face white with terror. There's a flash of light as a beam from a RasaLasa gun immobilises him. The girl freezes. She lies still and quiet, watching, waiting. A Dekaydence Tartan Bus draws up in the street. The young man is bundled aboard. The bus moves off.

It's some time before she feels confident to move on, before she makes her way carefully along the road, from shadow to shadow.

A man opens the front door of the familiar house. She puts her foot in the door and sees in his eyes a flicker of recognition that's hurriedly suppressed.

'What do you want?' he says imperiously, ramming the door against her foot as he scans the street from left to right.

She stares at him blankly, her fingers toying nervously with the feather boa. She's lost it again. The thought, the connection, the very reason she's there has disappeared in the crumbling maze that used to be her mind.

'I thought...'

She frowns, murmurs and turns to go but he grabs her by the arm.

'Oh, no, you don't!' he says, dragging her into the house.

He slams the front door shut and locks it. The abrupt rough action disturbs memories she wishes could remain buried.

She stands in the hallway, swaying and unsteady, staring at him. Suddenly, the wall behind him appears to capsize into the floor. She goes with it, vomiting as she falls.

As he goes to hit her, he realises there's sick splattered all over his long, flowing purple vestment.

'You filthy, drugged whore!' he shrieks, kicking out at her.

Hurriedly, he divests himself of the garment and stuffs it into an empty charity bag filed in a letter rack on the hall table.

As he pads into the front room in his vest, pants and socks, she watches him from beneath her eyelashes, a dead smile on her lips. He still has the scar on his stomach from the scalding tea she threw at him when... A tiny light flickers in her mind: purple vestment is for death, isn't it? Has he been officiating at a funeral? Her mother's? Her brother's? No, that was before, wasn't it? But when?

She hears his voice ebb and flow as he talks on the phone in the next room.

'Despatch? This is Solomon. Account number...? Good

God, man! Do you not know who I am by now? Yes, all right! 777! I beg your pardon? I don't care if you are on a tea break. This is top priority! And it will be done now or I'll have your guts for... Yes, good, at last we understand one another.'

He slams down the phone and realises that he's shivering. He goes into the hall to get a coat from the rack, only to find the carpet is bare but for the feather boa. The front door is wide open. She has escaped, with the key he left in the lock.

Cursing, he grabs a coat and runs out into the street. He looks up and down the road. It's deserted apart from an old drunk in an old green mac on a bike, cycling slowly and unsteadily. She's gone. Disappeared. He curses under his breath and looks heavenward, thereby missing the twitching of a curtain in a house opposite.

He picks up the feather boa. Donating it to the cleaner or a charity shop might raise a few eyebrows. Better to burn it. It's only when he returns his coat to the rack that he realises the old green mac isn't there. His face and fists tighten. Damn the girl! It was probably her on the bike. Why hadn't he...? He hears a vehicle pull up and brisk footsteps approaching.

'She went that way!' he informs the young uniformed man on the doorstep, and points along the road. 'She's on my bike. Get rid of her, the bike and the old green mac she's wearing!'

The young man – known to be skilled in many nefarious

trades and known also as Innit – touches his cap, strides back to the van, presses for search-and-assist help from the Eye-Spys, and drives off.

Solomon stares at the vehicle proclaiming itself a Dekaydence Diner in flashing lights as vibrant as the feather boa he's holding.

He catches sight of twitching curtains at the window opposite, remembers he's semi-naked and jumps back into the hallway, slamming the front door shut.

'Nosy blighters!' he mutters, aware his heart rate is thunderously high.

12 THE RETURN OF INNIT?

Some minutes on, some streets away, Innit climbs back into his van. Bodkin is pouring his friend a mug of hot, sweet cocoa from a flask.

'Ta, Bods. Just what I need,' says Innit, taking a long swig.

'What did you do with the ol' drunk?' says Bodkin.

'Turned him upside down and shook out his wallet and small change,' says Innit.

'You did well, In,' Bodkin says admiringly, relieved that his friend appears to be returning to normal.

'You sad case, Bods,' says Innit gravely. 'What I did was help the old gent into his house. Made him a cuppa with the last tea bag in the place. Poor ol' codger. I gave him fifty quid.'

'Fifty quid! What about the girl? The bike and the mac and everything?' says Bodkin, wide-eyed and anxious. 'Solomon will go volcanic. And we'll get into trouble, we will, for not finding her.'

'Look, the girl's vanished,' says Innit. 'It's well dark. There are technical problems with the Eye-Spys and that covers our backs. Well, mine anyways 'cos, officially, Bods, you ain't supposed to be in 'ere. And I dunno, but whoever that girl was I have a feeling she deserves a break, well away from that dirty old man in his saggy, baggy knickers and a red feather boa.'

'Two good deeds in one night, In, and fifty blinkin' quid gone,' says Bodkin. 'That'll do you for a couple of lifetimes.'

'Yeah.' Innit laughs. 'But I got one more good deed to do tonight, Bods. MacMinor, one of the Red Tartans, has got an Open University essay to write. That means MacNoodle needs back-up at the arena launch. So, me and Colin are going to help him out.'

'In, why don't you give Colin to Grout? Given how busy you're getting? Grout is besotted with that tin lizard.'

'Grout's got the choice of any ol' 'oid in your lab,' says Innit sharply. 'He ca*nnot* have my Colin! Don't you understand? Colin was Jezza's baby. And now she's dead... I ca*nnot* let him go, Bods.'

Innit's voice and temper rise to an emotional high Bodkin hasn't seen in a while.

In the back of the van, behind a metal grille, Colin grrrargles, a sound like metal marbles crashing into one another at high speed.

Bodkin shifts his body away from the liz'oid and closer to the door.

'And while we're on the subject,' snaps Innit, 'Colin is not a tin lizard. He is a liz'oid and he's me mate. I ain't giving away me mate. To you or no one. Don't you forget that, Bods.'

'Sorry, In. Sorry,' says Bodkin dejectedly, realising that

Innit isn't yet his old self. That he is still grieving the loss in the tsunami of his girlfriend, Jezza. Bodkin looks up. Colin is staring at him and salivating horribly.

Bodkin grabs hold of the door handle in case an emergency exit becomes an emergency necessity.

Innit slurps an over-dunked biscuit from his mug of tea. He's flicking through the photos he took with the hidden camera in his cap. Solomon hadn't recognised him. No surprise there, thinks Innit, Solomon recognises only those he deems worthy, monetarily, of acquaintance.

Bodkin looks over Innit's shoulder at Solomon in (almost) all his glory, a scarlet feather boa thrown casually over one shoulder.

'Firkin' 'ell, In! Those pix are dynamite. They could come in well useful,' says Bodkin, smacking his lips.

'Yeah, I reckon so, Bods. I reckon they could be extremely well useful.'

At last Bodkin sees the hint of a calculating glint in Innit's eyes. His heart soars. Good deeds and the love of a crazed tin liz'oid aside, Bodkin thinks Innit is on his way to becoming once more his old normal evil self.

13 WHAT ARE WE GOING TO DO ABOUT MARIA?

Inside the house opposite Solomon's, behind the twitching curtains, stand two young friends. Doctors. Old Noteian schoolfriends of different religious faiths. Proud of their heritage, their friendship and brotherly love for one another.

'How weird is that, we're watching him and we see her?' says one. 'It was her, wasn't it? I mean, not many girls today wear a feather boa, do they? Funny, I remember her playroom was full of them when she was a little girl.'

The second young man moves away from the window.

'Yes, it was her.'

'And you got her tagged from this distance? We'll know where she goes?'

The young man puts a comforting hand on his friend's shoulder.

'I hope so, my brother.'

'When will you tell him?' says the first young man.

'After we've brought her in and when she's on the road to recovery.'

'What? That could be a year down the line, at least. Or never.'

The second man nods.

'Listen, the world is changing simply because of what

he does. As the Phoenix he connects with ordinary people, young and old, worldwide. His actions inspire their actions. He must keep his cover. If this were to get out...everything else aside, you know what he'd do.'

'But he asked us to find her. He's our friend. She is all he has left.'

'No. He has his work. That is his passion.'

'But not to tell him...it's tantamount to lying. We must tell him. He has to know the state she's in. In case—'

'If we tell him, he'll go insane. If he hasn't already. The less he knows the better.'

'What if we fail? What if we don't find her? Or she refuses our help?'

Dark eyes look steadily into dark eyes.

'She dies sooner rather than later. And we are all lost. Because if he learns the truth he'll run amok, turn over the world in search of her abusers and killers. People might stop believing in him. His radical campaigning might fade and fail. And then the most likely scenario is that he'd kill himself, because he'll believe he's failed his sister as well as his mother and brother and the world. Then the Phoenix will rise no more.'

'May God protect him.'

'If He, or She, happens to be around, amen to that. Keep your faith in your God, my brother, for now I have no faith in mine or any other. But let us both keep faith in the Phoenix. Let's protect him from himself. Let's enable him do his work as long as he is able.'

BREAKING NEWS

HOME | NEWS | MUSIC | VIDEOS | DIARY | BLOG

RUBY Q COOPER reports from the East Federation for *The Daily Unigraph*.

Anastasia and her husband, Ivan, are excited. They're awaiting the birth of their first child. Boy or girl, they don't mind. As long as it's healthy. They plan to have three more children. A small family by the country's current standards. But times are hard. Anastasia has five siblings, Ivan six. There are numerous nieces and nephews so the baby won't want for admirers, playmates and babysitters. Anastasia's waters break during a hospital appointment. She's rushed to the delivery room. It's a painful birth; she is given drugs. Anastasia glimpses the baby boy before he is whisked away. She slips in and out of consciousness.

'I need you to sign this document immediately,' says a harassed doctor outside the delivery room, waving a piece of paper in Ivan's face.

'What is it? What's the matter?' Ivan's eyes widen.

'Your wife needs emergency surgery.'

'Oh, God!' Ivan cries out, his hand trembling as he signs the document. And then he remembers.

'The child? What about the child?'

'A son. Someone will come for you,' the doctor shouts

LIVE FROM AN ILLEGAL INTERNET SERVICE PROVIDER

over his shoulder as he hurries through the squeaky swing doors to the delivery room.

'Of course,' says Ivan, dazed. 'A son. I have a son.'

'Come with me,' says a nurse, arriving a moment later.

The boy is asleep in an incubator, attached to tubes. He is small and thin.

'Can I hold him?' he asks the nurse nervously.

'No,' she says, firmly. 'Maybe tomorrow.'

He says nothing. He goes outside. A friend sits in a battered old taxi that brought them all into town. They were expecting to return home that night, with the newborn. Now Ivan will have to pay for a second journey. He prays for more overtime. He goes back to sit at his wife's bedside, and holds her hand. It is late when the doctor finds him with his head resting on the bed. He is sent to sit in the waiting room where, again, he falls asleep, only to be awoken by a nurse.

'Come with me, please,' she says urgently.

Through the window he watches them detach his son from the tubes. He leans his head against the glass and, through tears, stares at the little body lying lifeless in the incubator. The nurse beckons him in, handing him his son now wrapped in a frayed blanket. A thought flies into his head – that the old blanket will have a longer life than his son's. He cradles the baby with such gentleness, such

LIVE FROM AN ILLEGAL INTERNET SERVICE PROVIDER

love, kissing away the tears that fall on his son's blue, chilling head.

'My wife, can she see him?' he asks the nurse.

'I am sorry,' a senior nurse interjects. 'But—'

'Is she dead, too?' Ivan asks, alarmed.

'No, no,' says the senior nurse. 'She is sleeping but our policy... Seeing the baby will upset her. And the last thing we want is for her to be upset, isn't it?'

He can't answer, because he can't think straight, let alone speak.

Gently, as though the fragile body is alive, he hands his son to the nurse. Try as he might, he cannot stop crying. He returns to the bedside of his sleeping wife.

'Is it true what they've told me? That our boy...?' she says when she awakes.

He nods, his grip on her hand gets tighter. He watches her. She is as still as her dead son, except for the tears falling freely from under her shuttered lids.

He kisses her hand, and strokes her forehead.

In the morning, the friend returns to take them home. The couple are silent and withdrawn and remain so for the entire journey. Only when they step out of the taxi does the friend speak.

'Mourn your son and never forget him but remember,

you are both young and, in time, a child will bring new life and joy into your home and heart.'

It's a year since the couple's son died and there is no sign of new life. They start to fret, to argue, as they have never done before. They return to the hospital. Their doctor has left and a woman doctor introduces herself before examining Anastasia.

'Did you ask for this operation?' the doctor asks, looking up from the notes at one, then the other.

Anastasia shakes her head.

'My wife was sedated,' says Ivan. 'The doctor told me the operation was essential to repair her. I had to sign a document quickly because it was so urgent.'

'What have they done to me?' Anastasia pleads. 'Why can't I conceive?'

The doctor looks at Anastasia with compassion.

'I am truly sorry for what I have to tell you. But it's better to tell you the truth, not fabricate a lie. The operation means you no longer have the ability to conceive.'

Anastasia covers her mouth with her hands to mute her scream.

'In our country,' says the doctor, 'the procedure to sterilize women without their knowledge is now an epidemic. We are talking economics. We are talking statistics that look good when we negotiate with foreign powers with better statistics.'

Anastasia looks utterly bemused.

'So, if I hadn't signed, if I'd asked questions, if...' says Ivan.

'Don't go down that path,' says the doctor, 'it will destroy you both. Whatever questions you asked, they would not have told you the truth. Neither would they have informed you of the quotas of such operations the government demands doctors achieve.'

'I cannot take this is in,' says Anastasia. 'All I can think of is I have failed my son and my husband.'

She bursts into tears. Ivan takes her hand and reassures her that he will not leave her. He would not do such thing. He loves her and that is that. He recalls several men in the village who have gone off with new women when their wives have had one, two or three children. And suddenly, he is torn with an understanding and an anger that he has never felt before.

'Listen,' says the doctor, 'this is not a perfect solution but I suggest you leave this godforsaken country. Live your lives together elsewhere and one day, maybe, you can open your eyes and your hearts to a child who has no home, no family. Give love and you will live and love again.'

Anastasia turns to look at her husband through a veil of tears. She sees confusion in his tired, wounded eyes. Could giving love to an abandoned child bring them both love? She takes his hand and prays for courage to face a new and different future.

That night, the doctor leaves the land of her forebears, with a similar prayer for courage. She will tell the world about the suffering of her countrywomen who, like women elsewhere in the world, are forced unknowingly into a secret sterilization programme to reduce population figures.

The doctor can no longer tolerate this practice. She leaves her homeland where whistle-blowers, men and women, are imprisoned, or worse. She will become a whistle-blower for her countrywomen in another land and tell everyone she meets about the wrongs being done in her country. And, as a symbol of her campaign, she will carry with her for ever the red and gold feather of the Phoenix.

The Phoenix lives

14 THE SAND PIT

'Come to see your cousins in action, Deskboy In?' a gladiator shouts to Innit who is leaning over a balcony above a pathway into the arena where scores of armed men and women are assembling for the final event.

'Get back to your pink skipping rope, Er!' Innit shouts back, a big grin on his face. Colin the liz'oid grins, too. Or so it seems to Bodkin, who's come with them to the finale and is sweating profusely in the monsoon heat and because of the close proximity of the haggoid.

'Oi, Er,' Innit shouts. 'Say hello to Wassit. Tell the hydrogenated deaf noodle that I love 'im, too.'

Er prods his brother, Wassit, in his armoured chest and points to Innit. Wassit grins at Innit and both he and Er send back a double thumbs-up sign.

'See you later, Deskboy In!' Er shouts, as he and Wassit move towards the gate to the arena.

The gladiators, about five hundred of them, are strong, mighty muscled men. They're standing, waiting in an underground corridor leading into the vast arena. They're restless. They want to get on with the fight. So does the goodly scattering of muscled women. All are in classical costume, dressed as in ancient times, carrying ancient weapons and wearing protective headgear bearing an emblem that assigns them names – Kronos, Loki, Medusa, Thor, Medea, Satan, Boudicca *et al*.

A man mountain in tartan appears before them at the arena entrance. It is MacCavity, Head of Dekaydence Security, with Lucretia, his human-hungry pet spider'oid, its body the size of a cat, which clatters along close by, climbing up and down the walls.

'Dekaydence is transmitting the battle live to theatres and cinemas round the globe,' MacCavity tells the gladiators. 'So hard fighting is expected. Dramatic grunts and operatic groans are vital. And, of course, don't get carried away, but blood is essential.'

There is dark laughter.

'You'll have signed your papers?' MacCavity asks.

The gladiators nod contentedly, recalling the words 'lucrative long-term contracts'. Alas, they never did read the small print.

Meanwhile, above their heads, numerous dead and dying animal'oids are being cleared from the arena. Silently, scientifically. For reassembly. Blood, metal, bone is separated. For more fights, in a different 'oid format. It takes but minutes.

The audience doesn't see this. They are distracted by a cloudy overlay of popular Dekaydence cartoon and film characters that intrigue all ages, while music (composed by Piccolo and Catgut) floats into their ears.

Catgut is furious. He was told the music was for a meeting of the Women's Institute, not this bloody mayhem with added chiffon. He glances over his shoulder to where Piccolo is sitting but he's not there. Catgut fails to calm a sense of panic. He has never recovered from the loss of his son, his only child. He doesn't want to lose Piccolo, with whom he shares so much. He's about to stand up to search the crowd when Lady Catgut rests her head lightly on his shoulder.

'Etti,' he murmurs tenderly. He always knew Piccolo would leave one day. To do his own thing. Live the life of a man, far away from the two old codgers that he feels he and his beloved wife, Henrietta, have become. How will she cope? How will he cope? He imagines a horribly lonely, futile future.

The music stops, the chiffon evaporates and the crowd, alerted by a fanfare of trumpets, looks down on the gladiators entering the arena and applauds the mighty spectacle. They are in pairs, each bearing a club or an axe, a sword or a shield or other weapon.

Lady Catgut looks around and grabs Catgut's arm.

'Careful, Etti, that's my composing arm, dearest,' says Catgut chirpily.

'Catgut, he's gone!'

'I know, dear,' he says sadly. 'But I'm sure he'll be back to visit. We are home to Piccolo, you know that.'

'Piccolo?' Lady Catgut frowns. 'No, he's sitting at the back, remember?'

Catgut is about to interject but Lady Catgut isn't in a listening mood.

'No, Catty, it's Nigel! He's disappeared. Grout found this under Nigel's seat. Something's happened to him.'

Lady Catgut holds up Nigel's violin case, containing his beloved violin with his bow, spare strings and resin.

'He wouldn't leave this behind, Catty. Would he, Grout?' She turns to Grout for confirmation but...

'Oh, my goodness, where is Grout? Where's my little Nigellus? And now you say Piccolo's gone, too! What's happening, Catty? All our boys are missing! I have a bad feeling about this place, Catty. What do we do? What do we do?'

15 WHEN DID YOU LAST SEE YOUR FATHERS?

'Where have you been?'

The amphitheatre. I left early. The second half is still going on.

Oh! So...was it fun?

It was bloody, actually. I'm glad you missed it.

Aren't you supposed to hang out with me? Being as you're my inner voice.

Come on, you're an adult. You don't need me nagging you any more.

Don't be too sure.

Sounds ominous. What's up?

I'm finding it difficult to get my head round the fact I have two fathers.

Ah, yes. Sorry.

My non-grandma, Elsa, is having a nervous breakdown, while her son, Rallan, my beloved non-dad, is on the verge of one after being kept underground for months by my 'alleged' father, the head of Dekaydence who is also my boss, Lord Lorenzo di'Abalo.

Any sightings of your mother?

Put it this way, she isn't exactly leaping out of the bushes to contact me. I haven't seen her since I was six and I'm beginning to forget what she looks like. What's more, in some ways I'm beginning not to care.

Sorry to hear that. But you have now got an aunt.

Yes, how could I forget the woman who set a catastrophe among the pigeons? Who was Lord di'Abalo's fiancée before he ran off with her sister, my mother? Yes, Auntie Lily has gone reclusive on me. She's sent me a few apologetic emails ducking out of any meeting I try to arrange.

Oh, dear. Any other plans?

Work.

Anything else?

Care for my dad and Elsa. Get to see Auntie Lily. Find out more about Di'Abalo. A bit of investigative stuff.

Sounds interesting? What's it about? No need to be coy. You're telling yourself, remember.

So you know there's talk of a deadly virus.

Not another one? How many is that in the last decade?

They say this one could wipe out most human life.

Ah, a benevolent virus. Excellent.

Be serious.

I am. So what does this virus do? How many has it killed? And who are 'they'?

One: I don't know. Two: I don't know. Three: I don't know.

If I were you – which to an extent I am – I'd want to know who 'they' are. And what 'they' are up to before I started to worry.

Yes, but first I need to talk to someone.

I can guess who that'll be.

You should be able to if you're in my head.

Then I'd say it's Grout.

Well done, Sherlock. The problem will be getting hold of him, he's always so busy.

16 IF YOU CAN'T STAND THE HEAT ...

'Get this!' 'Fetch that!' 'Clean this until it bleeds! Yes, I know it's a carrot!' 'Don't answer back, you stick of wimp-weed.'

It is bedlam in the kitchens. The heat. The noise. The high density of people. And the short tempers.

'Do it, or you'll get another one of these!'

Piccolo is struck again. He falls to the floor, knowing he must get up quickly before the blow becomes a kick, the kick becomes a broken rib and he's sent to waste disposal.

'Stir the soup, milksop!' someone shouts, thrusting a ladle the size of a sword into his hands. He stands at the oven, drenched in sweat. It's like a jungle, he decides. The ferocious heat together with wild men and women out for one another's blood. Each breath is an effort, and his aching arms scream for him to cease. Immediately.

Death must be easier than this, he thinks. And his mind drifts off to his father – a poorly paid postman, a nifty guitarist who did the odd underpaid gig. Murdered, in front of his eyes by his mother's boyfriend. Piccolo's eyes are watering. It could be the onions but...

He hears music. Debussy. *En bateau*. At once he's in a different place. The little wooden piccolo in his jacket pocket hears it, too. Piccolo feels as if it's nestling closer into his chest. Reminding him. He's a musician. He's not a cook. Not a bottle-washer. Not a slave. Reminding him that, above all things, he is a creator. He can create a picture of sounds with a handful of notes. He cannot move mountains or cook an omelette but he can inspire minds and make hearts beat faster.

His eyes are streaming. He looks around. All are busy, many are shouting and rowing. He steps away from the ovens. He walks quickly and quietly through the heat and the arguments. He's a minor irritant not worth bothering about. He's on a mission and, perhaps unconsciously, people move out of his way. He arrives at a door. He has no idea where it might lead. He opens it and closes it behind him.

He's in a dark corridor. A tumultuous noise engulfs him. He can't distinguish what it is. What is causing it? Is it to be this way or that...? He feels a waft of warm air and heads towards it.

The noise increases. It's like sitting in an orchestra pit filled with drummers and percussionists. It is the rhythm, the heartbeat of music.

'You can create music,' the little wooden piccolo tells him. 'You can weave this noise into order and beauty. That is what you were born to do, Piccolo Smith.'

'I know,' he whispers to it. 'Thank you for reminding me.'

17 FOUND AND LOST

'Oh, my God!' Will leans forward, clutching the side of the box. Piccolo is standing in the centre of the arena. He's conducting, using a huge ladle. Why? And what is he conducting? There's no music. Only the sounds of metal crashing on metal, and the grunts, groans and growls, screams and screeches of the competitors and the crowd.

Piccolo's eyes are glazed over. He's staring at nothing, oblivious to everything around him. The gladiators ignore him. He's not part of the script. And they're too busy performing for the worldwide audience, and a cash bonus. Aside from fighting for survival.

The crowd, in part, is confused. What is the boy doing? Is it a set-up for something? A spoof? If so, where are the signs to tell them how to react? They titter, uneasily. They fret, nervously. But they are a minority. The rest continue to roar at a good, dramatic hit with a sword. Or a fall. Or a spectacular comeback. Or a death. Yes, the crowd marches on and tractors over everything. It knows it has a need, and a duty, to carry on reacting.

Will is on his feet in the Royal Box.

'Be seated!' the King orders, shooting him a look of thunder.

Will glowers.

Di'Abalo shrugs.

'The Tartans will save him, Will,' Indigo pleads quietly, a restraining hand on Will's arm. 'They'll know he's not part of the act.'

'And if they don't?' says Will.

He doesn't wait for an answer.

Outside the Royal Box, Tartan guards, Black and Red, are ready to bar Will's way...and then they recognise him. They see fire and danger in his eyes. They also see Sid, his personal bodyguard, emerging from the shadows to walk by his side.

The two young men find their way to the arena entrance. They see the fighting gladiators. The blood-splattered sand. They hear the roaring crowd. They come across an injured gladiator lying in a corridor on the ground, tended by Dekaydence first-aiders, his body blocking their progress into the arena.

They try to edge their way round the throng. Will stumbles. Someone has grabbed hold of his ankle. He looks down. It's the injured gladiator who screams out that he can no longer see. Suddenly the tight grip is no more. Will kneels, wanting to say something, but it's too late, the man is dead.

Will wants to dash into the arena but Sid takes hold of his arm.

Piccolo has disappeared.

There's a roar from the crowd that's sprinkled with

wild applause and cheers.

Sid scans the arena. Will searches the groups of fighting gladiators and then, in the distance, sees Grout and Nigel. They are briskly walking Piccolo away from the fighting and heading for the far exit.

Will follows them keenly with his eyes. Thank God, Piccolo is safe, he tells himself, clenching and unclenching his fists. That's all that matters. It doesn't matter who rescues him. It doesn't matter at all. Piccolo will be going home with Grout and Nigel to the Catguts' home in Sussex. He'll be cared for by Lady Catgut. And news will be sent to Will as to how Piccolo is faring.

Will and Sid walk back along the entrance tunnel. The gladiator's body lies motionless on the ground. Next to it is a liz'oid. Blood, or is it tomato ketchup, dripping from its jaws? Sid has his RasaLasa primed to act, just in case.

A youth hurries up to the liz'oid. He kneels to put a collar around its neck. Will's eyes narrow. He recognises the youth as Innit, a Dekaydence thug. Someone he and Grout dislike in equal measure.

'I told you before, Colin, you ain't to think for yourself!' Innit is scolding the liz'oid as he picks up the gladiator's sword. 'You do what I say, Colin, and you don't touch any miniaturised man, you 'ear? You don't know what chemicals they got inside them that could harm you if you took a bite.'

Suddenly, Innit lets out a terrible howl, that's echoed by the liz'oid. He turns from the gladiator to stare at Will and Sid, recognising neither of them.

'It's me cousin!' he blurts out in distress. 'Me cousin Wassit!'

All fall silent. A new first-aid team arrives, masked and dressed in red. Sid firmly leads Innit away from the body. They stand, watching the proceedings. The team uses a selection of instruments, the like of which Will has not seen before. They scan the body, speak in staccato bursts, and make notes on their devices. Innit begins to sob, which unsettles the liz'oid as it tries, and fails, to copy the sound.

Suddenly, the gladiator stirs. He yawns and stretches. He espies Innit and leaps to his feet, hovering over the lad, his eyes dark and crazy.

'I'll be havin' my sword back, you thievin' bag of haggis dung!' the gladiator cries.

'It's me, Wassit. It's your cousin Innit,' says Innit, quivering as he hands back the sword.

The gladiator snatches the sword and looms over Innit. Sid cocks the RasaLasa.

'Whoever you are, haggis dung…' The gladiator spits at Innit. And then his demeanour changes. He ruffles the little bit of hair remaining on Innit's head and gives him a broad beam.

'Have a nice Dekaydence day, lad!' says Wassit cheerily, clapping Innit on the back, nearly sending him reeling, before he strides off with the first-aiders.

Innit looks stunned.

Will says nothing. He realises what's happened. He thinks Innit has seen it, too.

'O, my gawd,' Innit whispers. 'They've 'oided him, ain't they, guv'nor? He was my cousin Wassit. He was a gladiator. And now Wassit isn't human no more. They've turned 'im into a glad'oid. Perhaps that's not so bad. But if it happens again, what will they do next? He might become a tea-urn. My cousin, the oversized teapot.'

Colin the liz'oid emits a sound like a long, soulful foghorn. The noise frightens practically everyone within earshot. Innit flings his arms round Colin's neck and sobs. The haggoid grrrargles mournfully.

2

It comes as a shock to see the skin colour of the President of the USA change from black to brown, through yellow to pink to white, randomly and continuously.

The President of the Federation and His Overall Highness Randall Candelskin have met the American President before and witnessed the rainbow experience but they're still mesmerised by it. And now, in a meeting at No 10, they're speechless because every 30 seconds the US President's voice takes on the accent of each and every one of the 50 states.

The President of the Federation and HOH Candelskin are fully aware that they are dealing with a great and powerful man. But they've seen the label on his neck – Made by Dekaydence. They've said nothing but now they realise this man is a Dek'oid. He could be programmed to do most anything.

In fact, what is he doing now?

The President of the Federation and HOH Candelskin watch nervously.

The President of the US is staring intently at the liquid in his glass, and sniffing it.

'D'you know what you've gotten in here?' asks the US

President in a Texan drawl that will travel swiftly on to California, through to South Dakota and Florida.

'Water?' says the Federation President.

'Right – and wrong,' says the US President. 'See, you got close relatives of mine in here, Mr President.'

Candelskin and the President of the Federation appear startled.

'I can scent them out real quick,' says the US President. 'They're nan'oids. In other words, these guys are spies. They report back to you, or your appointed representative, everything I say or do or think. Now, I thought we wouldn't travel this path because we went over and agreed everything. But maybe now you think the pay-offs into Swiss bank accounts aren't big enough? Perhaps you'd have preferred a few chocolate bars?'

The Federation President is speechless momentarily as he sees money with many noughts attached escape his hands for ever.

'Mr President, I'm more than happy with your generosity,' the Federation President blurts out. 'What concerns me is the state of your poor relatives – the nan'oids. I don't know what they are or what they're doing in our water but...'

Candelskin nods vigorously, equally keen to hold on to his money.

'Forgive me, but that's a tough one to believe, sirs,' says the US President, 'because it's your Dekaydence lab that has developed them. Took an unofficial skin graft from my neck when I was asleep. Yep, your guy might've taken more had Mrs President's scream not awoken practically everyone in the State of New York.'

'I...I don't know what to say.' The Federation President flounders over his words. 'This must be investigated as a matter of urgency.'

'I think so,' says the US President. 'We don't want any of our pension funds and Swiss accounts put in jeopardy, now, do we?'

'No! Oh, no!' HOH Candelskin and the Federation President chorus vigorously.

'So, no more nan'oids?'

'No, absolutely, none whatsoever. But we do need to know exactly what they are so we can identify and expunge them. We'll get the Professor on the case.'

'No need. Our Secret Service tells me that there's a young man called Gout who did the nan'oid development. And from what I hear, Gout is one bright guy.'

'I think you mean Grout,' the Federation President responds quickly. 'Gout with an "r". Don't worry, we'll dispense with him immediately.'

'No, no, don't do that!' says the US President. 'Grout's too valuable, with or without an "r". Our guys will keep an eye on him, if you don't mind. He's the brains in this operation. But there's a smaller man, who did my neck. He's one hell of a thug. Name of Bodkin.'

'Oh, my!' The Federation President expresses surprise, which he shares with Candelskin. 'Is he one of ours, Cyril?'

'I'll have to check, sir,' his private secretary responds, with a wide-eyed innocent blink.

'We'll keep an eye on them both,' says the US President, whose accent has crash-landed somewhere in Alaska. 'Now, I'm just popping to the little boys' room.'

The butler bows as he closes the door behind the US President.

'Do you think he suspects anything?' says the Federation President.

HOH Candelskin shrugs.

'Even if he does, it's a bit late now. I checked our accounts first thing. The gold has arrived in our vaults. That's why I was able to give you the go-ahead for the fighter planes to take off for the eastern conflicts.'

'What a relief!' says the Federation President. 'Just remind me, HOH Candyfloss dear, what is it the Americans want in that wasteland?'

'Everything beneath the surface,' says Candelskin.

'But that's only rocks and sand and skin and bones, isn't it?'

'It's also packed with coltan, cassiterite, wolframite and gold. Minerals needed for consumer electronics. You name it, it's there. Black diamonds, black opals... Soon, Mr President, we'll all be as rich as Croesus.'

'Crisis, what crisis?' asks the Federation President anxiously.

17.5 SIX OF ONE, 1.5 DOZEN OF THE OTHERS

Schneek rollerblades out of Petty Master's hospital room and proceeds at speed along the corridor.

'So where do I get hot organic gluten-free porridge with a chocolate and date filling, and full-fat goat's milk, at this time of night in W6?' he mutters into his ad'um.

'Search me, guv,' the ad'um responds, before yawning and shutting down.

Honestly, Schneek thinks to himself, you'd have thought having a baby would put a stop to all this faddy food nonsense. But, I s'pose, given the circumstances...

Petty Masters is in bed, staring up at the ceiling. She appears oblivious to the dozens of white scented lilies, the cards and telegrams, the blue balloons and streamers. She's only dimly aware of her husband Hunky Doré, cooing in the corner, his many arms full of baby.

'The boys have got your beautiful eyes, honeypot,' says Hunky Doré, mesmerised by the glorious bundles he's holding. 'You are three lucky little lads, gentlemen, to have the mummy you have.'

'Mmm,' Petty Masters murmurs distractedly, still in shock at having produced triplets. 'And somehow they've each inherited your six black and white arms, HD.'

SECTION 3

*If you have men who will exclude any of God's creatures
from the shelter of compassion and pity, you will have
men who deal likewise with their fellow men.*
St Francis of Assisi (c. 1181–1226)

18 HOLY VANISHING ACT

'What do you mean, He's not in? He's omnipresent, isn't He? Always there when you want Him. It's in His job description,' snaps Randall Candelskin, His Overall Holiness (or HOHness) of all faiths, of no faith, and of the Order of Humpty Dumptys that sit on the wall, a fence, or any artefact of their indecisive choosing.

'Ye-es,' says an angelic Indian voice hesitantly, 'but…'

'There can be no buts,' insists Candelskin. 'Is it simply He's too busy to take calls?'

The angel hesitates before responding.

'No-o, not exactly.'

'Is it *my* call specifically God is ignoring?'

'No, no.' The angel sounds shocked at such a thought but then enquires anxiously, 'But might I ask how you got this number? It's not listed, you see.'

'I am Randall Candelskin, His Overall Holiness, and I was given this number by the Holy Father, the Pope,' says Candelskin haughtily. Knowing that the number actually came via Lord di'Abalo, he quickly makes a few multi-faith hand movements to absolve himself of the teensy exaggeration, better known to others as a lie.

'Oh, my! HOH! I so admire you! I was reading about you before I was…well, you know!' The angel is distracted momentarily. There's the sound of a sniffle and a snuffle before he continues.

'Look, I'm terribly sorry, I'm new. In fact, I arrived only today. My name is Bhupi and I tell you, HOH, I thought it was bad on earth but it's absolute bedlam here. Well, it would be if it weren't Heaven. Everyone's flying around in circles. The air is full of angel feathers. Quite pretty really, bit like snow on...'

'Bhupi!' Candelskin interrupts sharply, any trace in his voice of the milk of human kindness soured and gargled out by his impatience. 'Where is He? Where is God?'

'No one knows, your HOHness,' whispers Bhupi. 'No one has a clue.'

'So God moves out in His mysterious way! Disgraceful! Put me through to His number two, this instant!' demands Candelskin.

'I'd like to, your HOHness. Really, I would,' says Bhupi, 'but no one is responding on that line.'

'Great Scott! Then put me through to His number three.'

'The Holy Ghost has fled the nest, sir. Someone left the door of the holy birdcage ajar,' says Bhupi. 'Oh, and I really must apologise for the noise on the line. Heaven is experiencing a...a bit of a coup. So, is there anything else I can help you with today?'

Exasperated, Randall Candelskin hurls his ad'um at the wall and snatches hold of a pen. He starts to draft a letter of complaint and then stops, realising the highest land-based religious authority he can refer to is none other than himself.

'What in God's name...?' he mutters. He rings a bell. He demands high-speed delivery of a bottle Aconcagua 1812 and a sack of the best giant milk chocolate buttons. Once his order arrives Candelskin flicks the switch for room soundproofing and turns the volume to maximum for a few hours of Wagner. Now, there's a man, he thinks, who is a god. A reliable one, what's more.

BREAKING NEWS

Ruby Q Cooper reports from Manchester, UK for *The Daily Unigraph*.

The girl is attractive, in looks and personality. She has an infectious laugh and bright, lively eyes. She has a promising future: at the least, an estimated four A-stars in A-levels. She is also kind and popular. She helps the children who live in her street with their homework. She regularly visits an elderly woman who is alone in the world. University awaits; a career in medicine is fast becoming a realistic dream.

The girl's father sees his daughter talking to a young man of a different faith. The father tells his brother and they take to following her. They decide that she must be eliminated before bringing shame to the family.

The girl is a few days away from her 17th birthday when she is murdered.

The girl's sister and a female cousin decide to write down everything they knew of the girl and the boy, a relationship that was a burgeoning rosebud of love before it was destroyed by fear and hatred. The two young women give evidence in court against the two men, the murderers, in return for protection and rehousing.

LIVE FROM AN ILLEGAL INTERNET SERVICE PROVIDER

The police do their duty. The two men are tried and sent to prison. But still there are those in the girl's family who pursue and harass the girl's young suitor. The police step in but the two communities hunker down and keep quiet even when the young man is found bound, bloodied and unconscious, in a back street not long after his girlfriend's body is found.

We understand that all information has been sent to the human rights activist the Phoenix. He will read the reports, examine the pictures of the girl's bruised and battered corpse, bloated to twice life-size after it was dumped in the river and left to rot.

The Phoenix lives

19 'OID TO FREEDOM

The Phoenix unlocks a cubicle and out steps a machine fashioned as a luminous sylph-like blond, blue-eyed young man nigh on seven feet tall.

'Ready for action, Jojo?' the Phoenix asks.

'R-A-W! Sir!' The machine responds promptly. 'Rarin' and willin' to go!'

'Excellent,' says the Phoenix. 'And should you calculate you can't escape...?'

'R-A-W!' shouts Jojo. 'Return At Wonce! Sir!'

'Good man, Jojo.' The Phoenix chuckles, his eyes watching the eyes of the machine that are scanning the room.

'You too, sir! And, while I'm finishin' software updates, if you'd be so kind as to open the window?'

'Of course,' says the Phoenix.

The tall, lithe-bodied Phoen'oid sprints across the room and flies through the open window, up into the sky. The Phoenix thinks of Josef, the young man on whom the 'oid is based, the young man who was killed a year ago but who will now live for ever.

Good luck, Jojo, the Phoenix says inside his head. Good luck, my eternal little brother.

20 THE STAFFIE OF LIFE

North is spending a few days with his mother before travelling south for the next GeeZer meeting. He has thought much about a new campaign movement, including its name – Justice. Now he is set to meet Will face to face.

'Here are your sandwiches, pet, and your sun hat,' says his mother.

He nods.

He's like his dad, she thinks. A man of few words. Steady, ever dependable. Much of what she misses in her long-dead husband she sees in their only child. But she'll not cling to him as a replacement partner. She'll let him do what he chooses in life. She'll not point him in any direction. She'll be there, as and when he needs her. She will, however, yearn quietly for grandchildren.

He takes the bus from Beadnall to Alnmouth where he boards the train. He finds he's sitting next to the father of a boy he knew slightly at school. This Pa is a large, balding man in his fifties, fair and ruddy, as North is tall, dark, pale and brooding, like his dad. They acknowledge one another with a quick nod and return to their own thoughts. But North is distracted by Pa, who fiddles with a dog collar and lead as though they're part of a rosary or tasbih.

'Hamilton were me mam's dog,' says Pa, realising Will has been watching him. 'An old Staffie. A rescue. We loved him like a baby. Kids loved him like a grandpa.'

North nods sympathetically. He knows what it's like to lose a beloved pet.

Pa takes a handkerchief from his pocket and blows his nose.

'Had to come up, take him to the vet's for her. Not something she should do on her own.'

'No,' North agrees. 'Sounds like the dog had a good life with your family.'

Pa grins.

'Aye! If I'm to come back, I'll come back only as me mam's dog. I'll be spoilt rotten.'

North smiles as he feels enveloped suddenly in a soothing warmth, quite different from the oppressive heat of the day. He looks up. Sitting opposite is an elderly lady in a blue dress and a cape covered in feathers and bracken. She's immersed in a book.

There's a kerfuffle in the next carriage. Shouting and ferocious barking. Everyone in the carriage looks up questioningly. It becomes obvious the noise is not going to stop.

'Sommat's up in the guard's van,' says Pa, frowning.

'I'll take a look,' says North. 'Won't be a minute.'

A stockily built man is leaning against the door, preventing North from entering. North bangs on the window. The man takes a swig from a can of beer, turns and sneers, jerks a finger at North and leans against the door. North catches sight of the guard's cage, and what's inside – two powerfully built dogs are fighting, goaded by three other men swigging from bottles and cans, holding fistfuls of banknotes, shouting, and kicking the metal bars of the cage.

North whips a small axe from his rucksack and swings at the glass, which fractures and then pops loudly. There are screams from behind him; in front, the man is frozen for a moment before he makes a lunge at the door. North is too quick for him. He grabs the man and smashes his head against the door. The man shrieks and falls to the floor, his head covered in blood and glass.

North grabs hold of the other two men and smashes their heads together. The men sink to the floor. Beer-cans and banknotes fly into the air. Pa blocks the door behind him. In the far doorway a train guard arrives, assesses the scene and takes a swing at the third dog-baiter punter and knocks him senseless to the floor.

'OK, let's separate the dogs before they kill each other,' says North to Pa, who's wiping sweat from his brow.

As they go to enter the cage the elderly lady in blue emerges from the lavatory by the door.

'These should help,' she says, holding out two large, thick blankets doused in water. 'Wrap them round the dogs, tightly, and make sure you cover the muzzles.'

North and Pa take the blankets, enter the cage and quickly throw them over each dog's head, tightly enveloping their jaws and front and back legs.

'Nice work, lads,' the guard says, taking a gun from his pocket. 'Funny, I just found this thing in me lunchbox. I shall have to have words with the wife. I asked her for corned beef.'

He winks and calls ahead to Newcastle, the next scheduled stop. He needs police and a vet, he says. Ambulance? the operator enquires. No, says the guard.

'Let 'em suffer,' he whispers to North and Pa, nodding at the dog-baiters.

The men whimper and sob, like babies. The guard swears at them. Tells them in no uncertain terms that they'll get more of a battering if they make another sound. Thus, order and peace are restored. The passengers settle back in their seats, relieved, or almost.

'If you're heading for London it's not a problem, I live local,' Pa tells North. 'I'll go with the dogs. They're Staffies. The best, most loyal dog a man can have. For a man and his family. They'll have been mightily abused to behave like that. I'd like to see what I can do for 'em, long term. Here's my address, keep in touch.'

Pa stays by the cage while North goes to thank the elderly lady in blue and tell her that the police have her blankets. But she's nowhere to be seen.

21 WALKING BACK TO UNHAPPINESS

Piccolo is walking in the woods that back on to the Catguts' garden. He walks in circles, big and small. First one way, then the other. He's spoken scarcely a word since Grout and Nigel rescued him from the arena. His memories of the event are hazy, and if he finds his mind goes anywhere near them his hands start shaking. He stares at his hands as though they're alien beings. Currently, they are, as they haven't touched the piccolo since...

Everyone at the house wants to help him but no one knows how. Everyone has tried but no one can get through. There's something of a mad, wounded dog about him. Grout struggles for something to say. Nigel merges into the walls or shadows if he passes nearby. Catgut weeps alone in his study, blaming himself, as he did when his son died. Lady Catgut talks to Piccolo as though nothing's happened. She talks about the garden and the animals. Many a time she turns to find he's left the room.

There's little music in the house. More often there's a deep, heavy silence.

For the first time in her life, Lady Catgut finds herself crying regularly at the kitchen sink.

Today will be better, she tells herself on a daily basis.

Today there are visitors for Sunday lunch. Aside from their family of Piccolo, Grout, Nigel and Maria, there are friends and neighbours: Indigo (who refuses to use her royal title among friends and in the country); her cousin, Tommo; Miss Edwina Gardening-Fork (pronounced Spade) and her companion, Young Miss Burgess, and their young friend and former journalist protégée, Ruby Q Cooper who has been encouraged to invite Rallan and Elsa, her father and grandmother who aren't.

'Catty, dear, you're in charge of the drinks and nibbles today,' Lady Catgut informs her husband.

Fortunately, the warm sunny weather continues, which means lunch can be taken in the garden.

Lady Catgut is busy in the kitchen, while Catgut bustles in and out with trays, happy to be distracted from his melancholy. Grout and Indigo are locked in conversation. Piccolo is in the woods. Nigel was last seen sitting happily next to the pig, Montezuma. Rallan is walking with his mother, admiring Lady Catgut's handiwork in the garden. Unsurprisingly, Elsa is less than enthusiastic. As is Maria, who keeps to her room.

'I'm interfering, Ruby Q, but that's what I do best,' Miss Gardening-Fork announces. 'You need professional help to care for your father and grandmother.'

Ruby Q nods. She doesn't want to hear this. Besides, Mr Treasure helps out.

'And Mr Treasure is getting on in years, dear,' says Miss Gardening-Fork as though she were a mind-reader.

Ruby Q looks across at Grout. As ever, he's engrossed in conversation with Indigo. She'll try later.

The sound of a violin comes from the woods. It's Tchaikovsky's Violin Concerto in D major. The passage sounds as tragic as a lone bird searching for its lost mate. So much sadness. So much pain. Everyone is silent.

Someone screams. Above the music. Grout sprints into the woods. Indigo holds tightly on to Tommo who looks as frightened as a rabbit about to bolt. Elsa clings to Rallan's arm. Ruby Q hesitates, then hurries into the woods.

Grout is way ahead, tracking the music. He hears Montezuma, making odd sounds. But he walks on quickly, warily, alongside the fence dividing the animals' quarters from the woods. He hears shouting. It's Piccolo, ranting and raving above the music. Someone is crying. Piccolo is towering above the little figure of Nigel, sitting huddled on a tree trunk, tears trickling down his cheeks.

'What's going on?' Grout demands of Piccolo, as he kneels to check on Nigel and hands him a large handkerchief.

'None of your business!' Piccolo snarls.

For a moment Grout thinks Piccolo is going to hit him.

'It *is* my business,' Grout says, firmly. 'You are both my friends. You are both upset and I want to help.'

'You can't. No one can.' Piccolo kicks away the radio playing the music and walks off, deeper into the woods.

'You OK?' Grout asks Nigel, who nods.

'What happened?'

Nigel shrugs, and blows his nose.

'I was on the radio, it was a recording of a performance I did years ago, when I was a soloist. He came running out of nowhere, shouting at me to stop. He came up close. I was so scared...I...I've never seen him like that. I thought he was going to kill me.'

22 THE DOG IT WAS THAT DIED

The train doesn't stop at Newcastle. No one knows why. There's a brief announcement but no explanation. The guard travels through the carriages, apologising to one and all, especially those due to disembark at Newcastle.

'No matter, I'll get the late train back. It'll give me more time to get to know the dogs,' Pa says to North, gently stroking the dog that's most injured.

Word travels through the train faster than the guard and the tea trolley, which results in a vet arriving from a far carriage. She examines both dogs and shakes her head. The dog Pa is tending is so badly injured, she says, it must be put down. No, please, no, says Pa, shakily.

'Believe me, I'd much rather put down the oiks that did this,' says the vet.

Pa blows his nose. The injured dog is lying on its side, panting and whimpering, blood trickling from its mouth.

'If you hold her,' says the vet to Pa, 'you can talk to her. She'll focus on you, and she'll go with goodness and kindness in her mind and heart. You'll be giving her the greatest leaving gift that's possible. Something these monsters could never give her.'

Pa kneels down, right up close to the dog. He talks to her, so softly that North cannot hear what he says. The dog's tail twitches slightly. Pa strokes her face and carries on talking. She scarcely moves, though she's looking at him with bright dark trusting eyes. The tail twitches again. And then it is still, the brightness is fading fast from her eyes. Now they are dark, lightless and lifeless.

Pa carries on stroking her head, talking to the dog as he wipes away his tears on the sleeve of his jacket. He mops the blood from her mouth and tells her how beautiful she is. Tells her to look out for his ma's dog in Heaven. Tells her how they'll have fun together. 'Think of all those old bones to gnaw at...if you'll beg pardon,' he says, hoping the dog doesn't misinterpret his words. 'And,' he continues, 'you'll be coming home with me, if that's all right, when they've done examinations and stuff. You'll come home to our garden. It'll be your garden, too.'

The other dog lets out a horrific yowl. Pa reaches out to stroke its head but it goes to bite him. Pa backs off.

'I won! I won!' one of the drunken punters shouts to another, as they fight over the banknotes. 'My dog is the killer! So you owe me, big time!'

Before anyone can stop him Pa has leapt up and got the dog collar round the man's neck. He knots the lead to the metal bars, so tightly that the man begins to whimper, before he realises that only makes the tightness worse.

North and the guard exchange glances. The vet is absorbed in dealing with the dogs. With one look the two men agree silently that the dog-collared man is best left where he is.

For the rest of the journey, North, Pa, the guard and the vet sit in the carriage. In turn, they get one another cups of tea and biscuits. The elderly lady in blue returns and offers them slices of homemade fruitcake from her voluminous handbag.

The vet talks about environmental meltdown; how the world can and must be changed before it's too late. The guard recalls the good old days, when people looked out for one another. North argues that 'false green talk and action' has propelled business and governments into jumping on an enormous money-making bandwagon. As an example, he cites the case of wind farm turbines that do little to recoup energy and, in any event, are owned by foreign companies that pick up £500 billion in government subsidies.

How odd, North reflects. He is arguing like Will. And acting like the Phoenix.

Sitting opposite him, absorbed in a book, the elderly lady in blue looks up for a brief moment and gives North a smile. Once again he feels a wondrous sense of all-embracing warmth and serenity.

23 THE OTHER TRUTH

Piccolo never shows at lunch, which is a subdued affair. Edwina Gardening-Fork (pronounced Spade) does her best to provoke debate, expressing passionate support for youngsters worldwide who are protesting outside their parliament, big banks and corporations, cathedrals and temples, for being oblivious and/or careless of the needs of the people.

Tommo chatters and smiles away to himself like a budgerigar, which makes Grout realise that the medicine he's created isn't touching the happy-chappy effects induced by the experience in the Dekaydence White Room and that he must find a remedy.

Grout bumps into Ruby Q outside the loo.

'Have you got a moment?' she asks.

'I must look for Piccolo,' he says but then sees the anxiety in her face. 'What is it, what's wrong?'

'I've heard rumours of a killer virus.'

'Yes,' says Grout, lowering his voice. 'I'm working on an antidote.'

'That's great,' says Ruby Q. 'Good luck and everything.'

'Thanks. What have you heard?'

'That it started in the Far East and is heading this way.'

Grout sighs.

'Up to a point,' he says quietly.

Ruby Q gives him a questioning look.

'At the moment,' says Grout, 'the virus is killing impoverished people in third world countries, areas demanded for mining, building new towns, or commandeered for exclusive shopping malls.'

Ruby Q frowns.

'You mean this virus is a form of corporate chemical cleansing?'

'Spot on!' says Grout. 'Dekaydence developed the original virus, through the Professor. Now they've got me working on an antidote, simply as a precaution and as a way of making money. I thought, for once, Dekaydence was doing something honourable. How could I be so stupid?'

'Because you're a good man, short-sighted to much that is evil.'

Grout shrugs.

They stand in silence, each lost in their own thoughts.

'What next?' says Ruby Q.

'I don't know,' says Grout. 'There's a feeding frenzy among investors queuing up to invest in Dekaydence. Meanwhile, the project gets Federation grants for research and development and for creating overseas jobs. You couldn't make it up, could you?'

Obviously someone has.

'Look, let's talk again. Soon,' says Grout. 'But for now,

I must find Piccolo. He is in one hell of a bad place.'

She watches him go, realising how he's changed. In less than a year he's matured from a nervous, bullied young lab technician into a thoughtful, quietly confident, highly-esteemed young man. Fit, too. But not for her, alas; her heart has gone to another. Even though he is dead, her heart is with Jack.

24 TRAIN OF THOUGHTS

The arrivals and departures board at King's Cross railway station announces the delay of the train from Northumberland. No reason given. Will is uneasy. He buys a newspaper. He leans against a pillar, glancing this way and that across the concourse. He knows somewhere in the crowd Sid is watching out for him, just in case.

He's dressed casually, sporting sunglasses and an old hat. The Palace staff didn't appear to recognise him as he passed them in the corridor on his way to the secret exit in Indigo's room.

He walks round the concourse, and sets off again. He's on the third tour of the station when he hears a wail of sirens as police vans pull up and block the exits. There's shouting. Doors open, bang shut. Moments later, photographers and armed police race across the concourse, seemingly towards him. He turns but it's too late. He's carried into a scrum of departures and arrivals. And then Sid is by his side.

'What's happening?' says Will.

'Trouble on the Northumberland train,' says Sid.

'What kind of trouble?' says Will.

'A dog fight in the guard's van. Set up by some drunken gamblers. Luckily, some good ol' members of the British public intervened. Hence the cops and snappers.'

'Oh, my God, they've got North!' exclaims Will, seeing North surrounded by police.

'No, sir,' says Sid. 'They're protecting him from all the snappers who want the best picture 'cos your mate's the one who broke up the dog fight.'

'It's the last thing we need, a bunch of cops and camera crews.'

'That's why you've got to get out of here now. Before you get recognised.'

'I can't *not* see North. It's vital. He's made a special journey.'

Sid hands Will a key.

'OK, leave the station by the entrance on the right. The fob will direct you to my car. Wait 10 minutes. If I'm not back by then quit the car and get home quick as you can.'

'But...'

'Trust me, sir.'

Will struggles through the crowd to reach the exit. He sees handcuffed, bloodied men being marched away by the police. Press photographers busy with their cameras. Several ambulances. And a muzzled dog, struggling to escape its handler.

And there is North, imprisoned in a scenario from which he can't escape, without bringing unwanted attention to them both. Will hopes North understands he's in the same predicament.

He sees Sid approach a policeman, as another policeman hurries through the crowd, focused on him.

Will hastens through the exit. He's not aware of the elderly lady in blue until she careers into him, causing her large handbag to spill out its contents in every direction, which trips up the following policeman.

'Get going!' the old woman mutters to Will. He hotfoots it along the mercifully busy pavement. He glances over his shoulder. The elderly lady gives him a discreet nod as she engages the policeman to pick up everything that's fallen from her bag.

The policeman hesitates, scans the scene, fails to spot Will, and turns back to assist the elderly lady.

Will finds the car and waits in the driver's seat. Ten minutes pass leadenly. He's about to give up when the passenger door opens.

'Drive off, quick but not fast,' Sid orders.

Will obeys.

'Keep changing direction,' says Sid, looking in the rear-view mirror while fiddling with a device that, in seconds, changes the registration on the number plates and the colour of the car.

'What's happening?' says Will.

'They've arrested North,' says Sid.

'Oh, no.' Will's grip tightens on the steering-wheel. 'What for?'

'Seems like one of the dog-baiters is about to snuff it. They've arrested North for assault and battery. If the bastard dies, he'll be tried for murder.'

'Do they know he's North, head of the Real GeeZers?'

'Seems not,' says Sid. 'But I'm beginning to think this whole thing is a set-up. Or there's someone on the inside spilling the beans.'

'What do you mean?' says Will.

'The police believe North is the Phoenix.'

BREAKING NEWS

Ruby Q Cooper reports from London for *The Daily Unigraph*.

Two of three men have hold of the dead girl's young suitor. His legs and arms are bound tight, his eyes are blindfolded. The young suitor hasn't healed from the last attack and knows it'll soon be over for him, that he'll soon be with the girl he loved dearly. The attackers sneer as they tell him so, too.

The third man starts punching and kicking the young suitor but then, all of a sudden, the attack stops. The young suitor falls to the ground. His attacker, the third man, screams and clutches his face. He turns but can see no one to hit back. He stumbles and then is thrown into the air, and lands face down on the hard concrete. A small cry dribbles out of his throat, along with blood. He quivers in agony, and then is still.

It's over in seconds. The two assailants have watched the extraordinary events, frozen in terror. They squint into the darkness, searching for the attacker. But there's no one there. No sound. No voice. No smell. Nothing.

The two men are shivering. They look at one another and make gestures to the unseen assailant that he might

LIVE FROM AN ILLEGAL INTERNET SERVICE PROVIDER

want to have a go at the young suitor. They point at the young man, as if he were a sacrificial victim. The young suitor struggles to stand. An unseen hand steadies him and helps him to sit on an upturned box. The binding on his eyes is removed in an instant. The two men are sneaking away, along the wall, when they feel their arms grabbed tightly. They howl. They're spun round so fast that they collide head to head and crash to the ground.

A few minutes later, after a tip-off from an anonymous, untraceable call, the police and an ambulance arrive. A policeman finds a small device on the ground near the young man's feet. The device is plugged into an adservarum and the scene is replayed, although there's no sign of the invisible assailant or the film-maker.

'You know what this is, Sarge?' says one of the younger policemen, picking up a feather.

'No, but I know you're going to tell me,' says the sergeant.

'It's a feather.'

'You'll make CID yet, son,' says the sergeant.

'It's a very special feather, Sarge. It's the red and gold feather of the Phoenix. It's his calling card.'

The young suitor hears this and understands. Tears trickle down his face. He watches the film of his attack. Something makes him look up. A scattering of tiny lights,

red and gold, sparkle and shimmer just above his head.
For the first time in a long while he smiles.

'Well, I'll be...!' exclaims Sarge, scratching his head.

Justice for all

25 TEA AND SYMPATHY

Mr Treasure is making a pot of tea for the household as he listens to Ruby Q's tale of two fathers, a lost mum and an evasive aunt.

Mr T's unusually quiet. Remember, he's fond of Rallan. Tread carefully, Ruby Q, and maybe save the virus story for another time.

You're right.

'How's Mrs T?' says Ruby Q. 'I haven't seen her in ages.'

'She's travelling. Got a sudden bee in her bonnet and took off.'

Gosh!

'Gosh, how exciting!' says Ruby Q. 'Are you managing?'

'Oh, yes. Thank you,' says Mr Treasure, with a quick smile.

I'm not convinced.

Me neither.

'Er, Mr T, could you stay here for a while? It'd save you a journey and it'd help me out enormously. Dad and Grandma would love you being here, too. 'Course, you don't have to say yes.'

'I...er...' Mr Treasure stutters and then stiffens. 'That's a very kind offer, Ruby Q, and I accept. Though I hope you'll understand that I'll need to pop out from time to time. Bits of work to do here and there.'

He looks better already.

'By the way,' says Mr Treasure, 'if it helps, I'd say your father is the one who has cared for you. The one who has nurtured you through good times and bad. That's the man I'd call father.'

Ruby Q is about to thank Mr T when her ad'um rings.

It's her boss, Spiky Hair. Ruby Q needs to get to St Paul's Cathedral, a.s.a.p. A number of people, young and old, apparently peaceful demonstrators, are assembling to protest about the state of the world, human rights, freedom of speech, the disappearance from the streets of people young and old, the high cost of food and fuel, the continuing bad behaviour of schoolboy politicians and dishonourable bankers, and the apparently relentless burgeoning force of Dekaydence.

'The leader is a young man called North. The movement's called Justice,' says Spiky Hair. 'We can only hope they mean it.'

'But how do we, a Dekaydence-owned paper, do Justice justice?' says Ruby Q.

Don't expect too much, Ruby Q.

'Don't expect too much, Ruby Q,' says Spiky Hair. 'Too many people hiding too many evils will do anything to keep them secret. However, we must do our best.'

We think alike, Spiky Hair and me. So, go for it, Ruby Q! And good luck in the process!

3

The President of the Federation is visiting an army barracks in Surrey, talking to soldiers on 48 hours' leave away from the fighting in the eastern conflicts. The President has honed his sympathetic look, comprising anguished, furrowed brows, an occasional angled nod of encouraging support and eyes brimming over with concern and, if necessary, a few tears as well as some grindingly contrived compassionate smiles. The TV cameraman considers he's captured an Oscar-winning performance.

A soldier in combat gear steps forward. He is tired. He's just come off the plane after a six-month tour of duty and is thrust before the President, who asks the soldier to recount his latest experience.

The soldier looks doubtful but acknowledges the encouraging nod from the General... The soldier pulls himself up to his full height.

'We were ordered to shoot on a building where the enemy – men, women and children – were hiding,' says the soldier. 'The sensor gave me my target. I just had to line up my gun. I did what the others did. I opened fire. When we felt sure that no one was left to fire back we entered the building. I've cleared away body parts before, of colleagues and the enemy. You don't forget that. It lives with you forever...'

The General gives the soldier another encouraging nod. The soldier takes in a deep breath.

'I still think of a comrade, a brother soldier, a good man, a brave man. I held his dead hand, a hand that had once held the hand of his mother, his lover, his friend. That's bad enough, sir. But when you pick up the body of a dead or dying child, Mr President, maybe seven years old, whose body is bleeding heavily all over you, whose empty eyes stare at you...you can't forget that. Ever. She'll be in my mind when I hold my own child. When I see her born, when I see her marry, I'll recall the so-called enemy child who'll never marry, who has had her entire life stolen from her.'

'I do understand,' says the President softly. 'I pray often for comfort for souls.'

'That's not enough, Mr President,' the soldier says flatly.

The General's eyebrows shoot upwards but he nods to the soldier to continue.

'You guys at the top are all the same, telling us not to worry. That they'll get our heads sorted when we get *home. I want my head sorted now. Before it's too late to live in a normality, whatever that is. Before I hang up my uniform I want to hang up my hang-ups. Leave them all behind. Or as many as possible.*

'Do you understand that, Mr President? Imagine finding one of your kids shot to smithereens in your home. Staring into its face, knowing it has no life, no future. I weep fire and blood for the people of this world, sir. Red ice streams through my head and heart and my tears for the dead and the dying, and the living who've brought this about. Thirteen unlucky years, thirteen years of lives wasted, and still you let it go on. There has to be a better way to sort out problems, don't you think, sir?'

'Yes, yes, of course, but to find the answer, to work out a long-term solution requires patience, years and years of negotiation – it's slow progress...'

'So why throw money at foreign governments and arms dealers?' says the soldier grimly. 'We shouldn't be there, sir, swimming in blood and murder and destruction. We should be building in love and justice...for all.'

'Indeed. Good to meet you, soldier,' says the President, flashing his ubiquitous oleaginous smile as he hurriedly moves on.

In a month or so, when nine coffins arrive on the tarmac

at the military base in the UK, the Federation President, standing to attention by the Federation flag, will be reminded of, and will immediately forget, the name of the guilt- and grief-stricken soldier who told his story and who is now lying in a flag-covered coffin, having joined the ranks of the fallen.

25.5  A CHILD IS BORN

'It's a boy, Mum!' Cage almost shouts down into the ad'um to his mother, as he paces the hospital corridor outside the room where Waat, his dead brother's widow, is resting with her newborn son. 'It's a strong, healthy boy! He's got the Martin dimple, Mum, just like Jack! We're calling him Jake.'

Mrs Martin is crying tears of joy that her son Jack has given her a grandson. And tears of sadness because Jack is dead. She pulls herself together to pass on the news to her husband, her middle son Kane who is on a link in the USA, and to her two daughters, Meryl and Taylor, who are standing next to her, crying and weeping with joy for the newborn and in sorrow for his father, Jack, their beloved brother who was lost in the London tsunami.

'Mum, are you having a rave or something?' Cage shouts, his words lost in the din at home. He raises his voice. 'Mum, I'll have to go. I must get back to Waat. I'll find out visiting times and see you later. OK?'

The Martins sit round the kitchen table, tidal with mixed emotions.

'Taylor,' her mother says quietly. 'It'd be nice to drop a note to Ruby Q. To let her know. I don't want her hearing from just anyone in the street.'

Taylor nods but says nothing.

Since Jack's death an awkwardness has grown up between her and her friend Taylor, an awkwardness that neither fully understands, that neither appears able to overcome or share.

It's later, when she tries to sleep and fails, that Taylor thinks back to times spent with Jack and Ruby Q. She gets up and tries to write a letter. It becomes a card that becomes a brief note that she posts through the letterbox of the house next door where Ruby Q lives. Taylor knows how much Jack meant to Ruby Q and expects the news will hurt her. But she hopes Ruby Q won't withdraw further. She misses her friend as much as she mourns the loss of Jack.

SECTION 4

To educate a person in the mind but not in morals is to educate a menace to society.
Theodore Roosevelt (1858–1919)

26 HEAVEN'S ABOVE

Bhupi is now in charge of Heaven. He's content. The job is less pressurised than his previous one: taking endless misrouted telephone calls from irascible people around the globe, who waited hours, sometimes days, for a reroute from his tiny newsagent corner shop in Mumbai.

Bhupi finds that the Archangel Gabriel can be a problem, as he insists on doing everything by The Book. But now Bhupi has the company of his old friends the Clives (1 and 2; soon to be joined by Clive 3). They are practical, skilled and qualified men, who can turn their hand to almost anything, and here have been given the task of renovating and repairing Heaven after ages of considerable neglect. As Mother Nature told God, the back gate to Heaven is in a dreadful and insecure state. So are many boundary points.

Luckily, or perhaps not, Bhupi and the Clives have been joined by the internationally renowned interior designer who's working with, or sometimes against, them on the project. Poor Claud Canapé. He is so dumbfounded to arrive in such a well-worn, shabby place that for a few days he can't think straight, let alone speak.

But, then, to be fair, no one in Heaven speaks. What little communication there is comes and goes from within.

A message, a question, a joke, a worry or melancholic mood (yes, the parasite exists in Heaven) is passed from one spirit to another by TTT (thought-talk-transference). Everyone has a personal off switch, for extra-quiet moments. So the sounds in Heaven are confined to a number of zones for music, nature, sport and special debates, *et al*.

Oh, there are also sounds, loud sounds, in the soundproofed nursery. The amount of settling and soothing, playing and giggling that is given to the babies is, unsurprisingly, second to none. Currently, that's due in part to a young nurse, Jezza, who was Innit's girlfriend, and a young man, Jack, whose widow, Waat, has just given birth on earth to their son, Jake. Yes, it's the same Jack who continues to occupy Ruby Q's heart.

It's Jack who is asked by the Clives to inspect Heaven's far-flung boundary points, which haven't been visited for eons. It's Jack who discovers that behind a thick screen of tangled ivy is an ancient locked door. It's not on the map of Heaven. Neither is it on the celestial radar of St-Nav. The old door is fashioned from a peculiar, unidentifiable dense material. Nor can Jack translate the symbols etched on the surface. Rather than worry Bhupi or the Clives, Jack decides he'll say nothing until he discovers more.

27 MAMA MIA!

On her way to St Paul's Cathedral Ruby Q pops into a 24-hour Dekaydence mini-mall to buy a few treats for Rallan and Elsa. In her basket so far are a glossy magazine and a tin of small cigars for Elsa. She's reaching for a packet of chocolate ginger biscuits for Rallan when a hand dives into her shopping basket, takes out the cigars and returns them to a shelf.

'They're no good for you, Ruby Q,' a voice says firmly, with a hint of an Italian accent.

Ruby Q turns to admonish the busybody and stops in her tracks. She stares aghast at the tall, auburn-haired woman dressed in an elegant red suit, matching high-heeled shoes and a chunky gold designer necklace.

'It is you, isn't it? Angelica Nera? My long-lost mother?' says Ruby Q, nervously.

Angelica Nera nods but says nothing, just examines Ruby Q's face forensically.

They stand together in an awkward silence.

Hold back the tears, Ruby Q. It's shock. Let's do weeping later, OK?

You're right. I must not show my feelings to this, this... woman.

And later we'll do anger, too, but not now, if you

don't mind.

Ruby Q swallows hard.

'It's, er...a bit of a shock to meet you after so many years,' she manages to blurt out.

'Likewise.'

There's a longer pause.

'I can't hug you or anything like that,' says Ruby Q.

'I understand.' Angelica gives a curt nod.

'After all these years of searching,' continues Ruby Q, 'I think I want to scream at you. Equally, I want to walk away from you. Never see you again. And there's another side... Oh, I don't know what I want.'

Confuse the enemy with a reasonable tripartite thought process. Love it.

Angelica gives a brief laugh. The sound reminds Ruby Q of mulled wine, winter sleigh rides and tinkling bells all at the same time. People in the shop turn and smile.

'You sound like your father,' says Angelica.

Steady, Ruby Q. This could be tricky.

'That's interesting,' says Ruby Q casually. 'Because I've been wanting to ask you, who is my father? Rallan Cooper or Lorenzo di'Abalo? You're the only person who knows for sure.'

Oo-er, Ruby Quby. The jugular approach.

Angelica is no longer laughing.

Ah, the woman has adopted the iron mask look. Even then she's a stunner, for sure. No doubt. And such beautiful sleek hair.

Do you mind? Push off!

I'm not leaving you alone on this one. Even if there is a commercial break.

'I assume my dear sister Lily has spoken to you,' Angelica says, coolly.

'Yes,' says Ruby Q.

'I won't play games with you, Ruby Q—' Angelica begins.

'Given you've been playing them for years.'

Steady, Ruby Q!

'Some things are none of your business,' says Angelica, coldly. 'But it is true, Lorenzo di'Abalo is your father. If you want to tell Rallan and break his heart...'

'You've got a cheek!' Ruby Q snaps. 'You did that years ago. To him and to me!'

Stop it, Ruby Q. If you want to get to know her.'

Angelica turns on her heel and marches off to the exit.

You've done it now.

I know.

Ruby Q stares out of the shop window and sees her mother climb into a Dekaydence limousine. The chauffeur holding the door open for Angelica turns to Ruby Q and bows low, his hat falling into his hands. As he slowly unwinds his body she sees his face.

Oh, my God! There's no escape from them!

Get a grip, that's what you'd tell me.

Ruby Q turns her back on her mother, the car and the

chauffeur, who has revealed a head of thick, straggly yellow curls, a white painted face and the improbably large bright red grin of a clown.

Diplomatically, I'd give you zero for that encounter.

I don't need you to tell me that. Or that it could be another nine years before I see my mother again. Or it'll never happen.

Somehow, I think it will.

28 THE KILLING FIELDS

Grout's face is ashen. He is sure he is going to vomit. But he mustn't, he tells himself. The Phoenix is standing beside him.

Grout sits in front of a monitor, watching film clips of animals. Dogs, cats. All shapes, all sizes. Young and old. They could be sitting on your lap. In your home, knowing they are regularly fed and watered, taken for walks. Cleaned and vetted, when necessary. Most of all, they'd know that they are loved and cherished beyond words. That they are family.

But the animals on the screen have no family. Not now. They have no one who cares for them. They are stacked, packed, stuffed alive into cages, bags, sacks. They haven't been fed or watered or cleaned since…when? They are being tormented with sticks poked through the metal bars into their faces, eyes and stomachs. A dog's head emerges slowly from a sack and is swiped so hard by an unseen hand that it falls back into the sack. The faces of these animals show fear and terror. A questioning, desperate look, wondering what they have done to deserve this treatment. On many there's a pitiful look of defeat. They know what happens next.

They are skinned alive.

A large dog is tied to railings. A man grabs its tail from behind. A man with a large knife. The skinning process begins. The dog howls in fear and pain as the man works his way round its body to the face, slicing and ripping the lips from the jaw. And then the dog's live naked body is thrown on to a heaving heap of scores of others to die slowly and in agony.

Grout turns from the screen, tears of anger flooding his face.

'God Almighty!' he says, through his teeth.

'Don't expect *him* to do anything,' says the Phoenix bitterly. 'But we can.'

'What can we do?' says Grout.

'First, don't turn away,' says the Phoenix. 'This is happening on an industrial scale. Don't condemn any more animals to this fate. If you want it stopped you must know this and more. I know these pictures torture your heart and soul. Or push you into despair because you can't help everything and everyone but—'

'Give me some facts,' says Grout. 'But no more pictures, please.'

'OK,' says the Phoenix. 'Every year two million dogs and cats die. They are hanged by the neck and water hosed down their throats until they drown. Or they are bludgeoned, bled to death and skinned alive and left to die slowly in excruciating pain. The fur skinners claim it's cheaper and easier to skin a live animal that's convulsing in agony than a dead body. They say the whole skin comes off easily and in one piece.

'Thousands of animals die a different agonising death. They are loaded on to transport trucks, in stacked cages that are thrown to the ground from a height of 10 feet, shattering an animal's bones. Thus, cats and dogs, rabbits and other creatures are transported over days to fur markets, packed tightly into cages without food or water. They're scared. They fight. They're wounded. They give up. They die.

'Children are often used to round up and kill the animals that end up as gloves, hats, coats, trimmings and table-top miniatures of themselves. It takes around 24 cats or 10 to 12 dogs to make a fur coat. Some skins become drum skins. And, not unusually, imports are mislabelled to mislead customs, buyers and the public.

'And don't think it's happening only in the Far East. This is a global industry. It's happening here in London. There's a fur trader making an extremely lucrative living out of this barbarism. It is alleged he happily boasts about it.'

'So what are you going to do?' Grout asks.

'My plans are my own,' says the Phoenix. 'Have you programmed the Phoen'oid?'

'Yes.' Grout nods.

Grout glances at the pictures on the screen. He feels sick to his stomach. He must think of something else. Just for a moment. His thoughts drift to Colin the liz'oid. He yearned so to own this creature that he helped create but he comforts himself now with the knowledge that, whatever else, the otherwise detestable Innit adores the crazy metal critter as much as he does.

BREAKING NEWS

Ruby Q Cooper reports from London for *The Daily Unigraph*.
With additional reporting from T-J Jenkins

It's rumoured many millions have been spent on the wedding. And, by the looks of it, the bride's dazzling dress and jewellery have chomped significantly into that sum. The reception is being held at a chic, avant-garde London hotel serving the international cognoscenti, of which the bride's father considers himself a founder member.

It's been a long but enjoyable day for the several hundred guests. The wedding ceremony at St Paul's Cathedral. Canapés on a triple-decker river cruiser, serenaded by an internationally famous pop group, the SS. Much posing for the cameras (still, video and internet). And now hotel suites for guests to rest and adjust their attire.

Yes, a glorious occasion, especially as seen through never-ending refills of Cristal champagne. Yes, a marriage made if not in Heaven then by the bride's father's lucrative business ventures.

All now enter the grand ballroom that's decorated in apple green, with floral decorations in soft pink, peach and citrus yellow, with wafts of matching delicate scents.

LIVE FROM AN ILLEGAL INTERNET SERVICE PROVIDER

The ladies are especially pleased by the candlelight that flatters them so favourably. All are keenly anticipating a superb dinner from the internationally renowned chef.

There is much chatter, much laughter weaving in out of the music provided by the bewigged octet in their Restoration attire.

The bride is glittering, from head to Choo. The groom is swaggering as only a newly married man can. The guests are enchanted by them both, and by the tall, handsome and somewhat ethereal masked harlequins serving the meal. As for the generous table gifts – for the men, finely tooled leather wallets; for the women, elegant fur stoles.

The first course is consumed. The harlequin waiters stand ready to serve the main meal.

Someone notices a dark stain on a wall. A stain that's spreading fast. Others see it, wonder if there's a plumbing problem and attempt to inform the nearest waiter, who doesn't react. More stains appear on other walls. Some sitting close by see what the stains are. They begin to whisper and mutter that they are bloodstains. The music plays on. The harlequins stand ready.

Everyone glances at the father of the bride. He'll know what to do, the guests reassure one another. The father of the bride nods at one of his heavies to fetch the manager but the door is locked. In fact, all doors

LIVE FROM AN ILLEGAL INTERNET SERVICE PROVIDER

and windows are locked.

The FoB's men bring their considerable weight to bear to force open the doors as the sound of music is overwhelmed by a chorus of terrified screams, moans and whimpers, and bloodcurdling howls that echo around the room.

Suddenly, images appear on the bloodstained walls. Of dogs and cats, rabbits and mink. Stuffed into crates. Into bags. Of dogs and cats, rabbits and mink piled high on lorries. Of dogs and cats, rabbits and mink being hanged, beaten, drowned or skinned alive.

As one, the silent harlequin waiters remove the lids from the silver serving plates and reveal to the guests dogs and cats, rabbits and mink, writhing furless like the live raw bodies seen on the walls. To the guests they look so convincingly real that they shriek and scream and howl, sounding not unlike the dying animals on the walls.

The bride is sobbing, she's banging her fists on the table. A woman faints. People are trying to call for help on their ad'ums – to no effect. Trying to force open doors and windows – to no effect.

'Listen!' a voice commands over the sound system. The room falls silent. 'This is the work of your host! Your friend makes his money from this butchery. This "entertainment" is paid for with the blood of thousands, nay, millions, of animals, animals that could be sitting in your home, on your lap. But which have the misfortune to be at the mercy of this evil, greedy man, this despicable butcher.

'Know that your complimentary gifts of fur and leather have been ripped from the live bodies of these creatures. Read about this murderer in your revised menus. We pray compassion compels you to condemn this man and shun him and his work.'

The guests are in shock. Furious or confused. Silent or sobbing. There's renewed effort at the doors and windows where someone sees outside a mass of banners, denouncing the FoB, carried by people dressed as animals, baying and bellowing for the FoB's blood. The guests fall back from the window as a gentle shower of red and gold feathers rains down on them from the ceiling.

The bride is shivering with tears. The bridegroom is stunned and immobile. The FoB is looking for someone to shout out, threaten with legal action or, at the very least, punch. But there is no one except the musicians, who are attempting to calm the atmosphere with soothing music. The harlequin waiters have vanished. So have the demonstrators outside the hotel.

Suddenly, the doors fly open. The room is awash with police and ambulancemen. In their midst is the hotel manager, who, along with his staff, has been locked up

LIVE FROM AN ILLEGAL INTERNET SERVICE PROVIDER

by the protestors. He behaves kindly, impeccably. He is a credit to the hotel's owner, who lives abroad. Gradually, order and calm are restored. The offer of an excellent meal and overnight accommodation suits a number of guests. Others are provided with a voucher to receive the same apologetic offer at another time.

The bride and groom make a subdued departure to catch a flight to their honeymoon destination. There are hugs and handshakes, quiet words and rumbling threats between guests and the FoB, who, with his wife, decide to retire to the comfort of their own home.

The chauffeur drives at a comfortable pace as in the back seats the FoB and his wife are edgy with temper. They mutter and fume, rage and rant, sob and sulk.

They appear to settle when they see the welcoming lights of their home. The FoB recalls, with relief, that the staff have the night off. So, as the chauffeur drives off to his cottage, the FoB asks his wife for the front-door keys she carries always.

They enter the house and she goes to make a cup of tea in her refuge, the wood-panelled kitchen with its grand, welcoming fireplace and family photographs. The FoB is in the drawing room, pouring himself a double brandy, thinking of the action he'll take against the hotel, when he hears his wife scream.

LIVE FROM AN ILLEGAL INTERNET SERVICE PROVIDER

As ever, he's irritated by her interruption.

'What is it?' he shouts out crossly.

There's no reply.

He calls again. Again, there's silence.

Thoroughly annoyed, he storms into the kitchen. A barbed criticism gets stuck in his throat when he sees his wife leaning over the kitchen sink, either vomiting or crying. Or both. In an instant he feels sick at the stench of shit and more that's almost unbearable. In the same instant, he sees the reason. Hanging from the ceiling, between the chandeliers, are scores of animal bodies, large and small, dripping blood, rotting and smelling to high heaven.

'Oh, my God!' he says under his breath. 'Oh, my God!'

A thought hits him like a thunderbolt. Where's the dog? Where's the constant companion he's had for 15 years or more? The Jack Russell who's with him always, in the office or at home. Who he loves more than his own wife. Spoils more than his own daughter. Who he talks to more than his lawyer.

'Woofie!' he screams, running through the kitchen, staring up at the animals (discovered only later to be authentic-looking fakes), searching, searching, as blood drips on his face and clothes. 'The bastards have killed Woofie! I'll kill them! With my own bare hands, I'll tear them limb from limb.'

LIVE FROM AN ILLEGAL INTERNET SERVICE PROVIDER

His wife turns to him.

'They haven't killed him,' she sobs.

'How do you know?' he demands, seeing she looks as white as the hanging bodies.

'They've taken him,' she says.

'Where?' he shouts.

He cares little that she's being sick again. He runs to the corner of the room where stands an expensively crafted wooden hut labelled DOG HOUSE. On the walls behind it is a message written in blood and shit:

'Now that I know you've killed not one but millions of my kind, I can no longer live with you. I am no longer your Woofie. And I shit on your memory, bastard.'

The FoB sinks to his knees, aware vaguely of a feather, red and gold, near the elaborate kennel.

'Woofie!' the FoB cries out. 'Woofie! Where are you, baby? Please, come home to Papa.'

The Phoenix lives

MORE BREAKING NEWS

For a long time in China compassion for creatures was considered counter-revolutionary. Pet owners condemned as a luxury of the exploitative class, alien to the life of working people. By the end of the twentieth century, bear farming was being exposed and reviled. The attitude of animals suffering unnecessarily was replaced with long-suppressed compassion.

Now it appears the younger generation in China, especially the urban young, are increasingly concerned about animal rights. They are also digitally aware. Thus, via social media, a group in Beijing contacted animal-lovers and a group was able to intercept a truck with some five hundred dogs headed for a slaughterhouse.

Awareness is growing about the welfare of farmed animals and the state of public health and safety on factory farms. It appears times are changing and dramatically so.

LIVE FROM AN ILLEGAL INTERNET SERVICE PROVIDER

29 THE GRAPES OF WRATH

As he waits word from Sid about the fate of North, Will makes an unscheduled hospital visit to his boss, Cataract, head of the London accountancy firm Cataract, Cyclops and Mote that now runs the economy of the entire Federation. Following the albeit partial success of the implants of gold bars into his legs (for safekeeping), Cataract is recovering from an implant of similar 24ct gold bars into his arms.

'Where did those grapes come from? And those flowers, are they covered in chemicals from the third or fourth world?' Cataract looks suspiciously at the proffered gifts as he covers his mouth and nose with a handkerchief.

'The grapes are organic, from the Catguts' vines,' Will replies patiently. 'The flowers are from Lord di'Abalo, via Mr Killivy, the Dekaydence gardener.'

'Charming.' Cataract sniffs at the flowers. 'But we must press on with the despatch lists.'

'Despatch lists, sir?'

'Yes, boy, have you forgotten already?'

Will shakes his head.

'I don't think I know anything about despatches, sir.'

Cataract frowns and mutters to himself.

'Perhaps it was the other one...'

Will is growing used to Cataract's confusions, the blunted synapses of the formerly razor sharp mind.

'How's your father?' Cataract enquires abruptly.

'Er, he's dead, sir,' Will replies.

'Of course, of course,' says Cataract hurriedly. 'I see your great-uncle the King is developing a career as a ribbon-cutter. What's the pay like, I wonder?'

'The King has committed his entire life to serving his people, in whatever way he can,' says Will, controlling his irritation. 'And now, sir, do you have any business we need to attend to today?'

'That is kind,' says Cataract, putting a hand delicately to his head. 'But I do feel rather frail just at this moment. Perhaps, later in the week...? Best give a call, in case I'm tied up.'

'Of course, sir,' says Will. 'Anything you'd like me to bring in?'

'Dark chocolate cake. But don't let that dragon sister see it. She'll confiscate it and eat the lot herself. I know her game.'

As Will enters the nurses' office to check out Cataract's progress, he catches sight of a familiar figure walking towards the old man's bed. It's someone Will thinks is more likely to have put the old man into hospital rather than visit him. The unlikely visitor proceeds to share a high-five greeting with the old man. Will's jaw drops.

'I don't like the look of him either,' confides a nurse. 'But the old man seems quite taken with him. And now he's in here every other day.'

How odd, Will thinks, given the visitor is Innit.

30 SUNDAY CRUNCH

During the week Grout stays in London at Dekaydence HQ. He has a lot of work to do. For Dekaydence. And, secretly, for Will, the Princess Indigo, the Phoenix and Ruby Q Cooper. He also does a lot of worrying about Piccolo, who's at home on doctor's orders.

Piccolo isn't speaking to Grout. In fact, Piccolo scarcely speaks to anyone, not even Montezuma, the pig he loves, or Billy, the gentle goat. He takes long solitary walks or remains in his room, brooding, neither playing nor listening to music. Even Sir Harrison Catgut has realised Piccolo cannot be cajoled or enticed out of his deep depression.

One weekend back at the Catguts', while Piccolo is taking a shower, Grout fits a hidden camera in Piccolo's room. Grout explains to Nigel it's a safeguard and gives him a specially designed ad'um. Nigel proudly undertakes the role of official guard but makes it clear he will not spy on Piccolo visiting the lavatory.

The house feels like a landmined area, where all tread carefully and quietly as the ghost of Christmas past rattles memories of happy times for which all but Piccolo yearn.

One day, Grout wakes up feeling odd. He checks himself out and realises the unusual experience is an emotion he's not used to. Anger. And it's growing. He's angry at Piccolo for dragging them all into his personal mire of misery. He decides Piccolo is selfish, self-centred and ungrateful for all that the Catguts have done for him. Grout's fury grows.

He gets up. It's early but Lady Catgut is busy in the kitchen, preparing breakfast. She seems to read his mind.

'Piccolo's gone out. Not long ago. And without breakfast.' She shakes her head.

'I'll try and find him. It shouldn't take long. And don't worry, I *am* hungry,' says Grout, with a contrived joviality he hopes Lady C finds sincere.

She smiles and nods but she sees a rare fury in his eyes and is concerned.

Grout walks towards the woods, past the animals' paddock, where Montezuma and Billy regard him keenly.

'If I'm not back in 30 minutes, Billy, call for help,' he tells the goat.

He swears Billy winks back at him.

Grout walks deeper into the woods. A handful of wood pigeons take flight. He takes the trodden path so he makes less noise. He hears the loud tapping of a woodpecker before he sees it high in a tree. A red patch on its neck, crimson on its abdomen and under-tail coverts, as it ascends in a circular direction, tapping the bark as it goes. It flies off to another tree, another bout of concentrated tapping, another loud attempt to attract a mate.

Sunlight drips through the trees like melted honey. There is birdsong. Warmth. Take-offs and landings of squirrels, butterflies. A breeze gently stirs the leaves, creating a sound like surf on a pebbled beach. Grout feels he's absorbing a great natural peace and, for a moment, quite forgets the reason he's there.

And then a terrifying scream echoes round the wood. Birds screech and fly up into the sky. Who or what...? He feels a sickening blow to his head that sends him reeling. He staggers, tries to steady himself, but crumples to the ground.

31 GOOD, INNIT?

The nurse – a staunch supporter of Will's side of the Royal Family – draws the curtains round the bed next to Cataract, enabling Will to sneak in unseen from the nurses' office and listen unobserved.

'Haven't seen you for a day or two, Mr Innit,' Cataract is saying. 'What wickedness have you been up to?'

'I lost me cousin,' Innit says flatly, kicking at imaginary dust on the floor.

'Oh, dear. Sorry to hear that,' says Cataract. 'How come?'

'He was a gladiator. At the new arena. Then they went and turned him into a glad'oid.'

'Ah. You'll have to explain that in a tad more detail, Mr Innit,' says Cataract.

Innit does. Quite a lot more detail.

'I see,' says Cataract, who clearly doesn't and chooses to move on. 'Ah, well. Life goes on and we must proceed with haste and deal with the despatch lists.'

'Despatch lists?' Innit looks puzzled.

'Yes, yes,' says Cataract testily. 'We talked about them, the despatch lists.'

'Not with me, your honour.'

Cataract scratches his head.

'So who did I...? Oh, no matter. You'll more than do for this task, Mr Innit. And I think you'll like the pay increase.'

Innit's wide, drooling grin reminds Cataract of Gordon, his brother Wiggins's lugubrious, ever-ravenous, slavering old boxer dog.

'We at Cataract, Cyclops and Mote,' Cataract continues, playing cat's cradle with his fingers, 'manage the economy of almost every country in the Western world. Integral to that is a programme of despatch. It's the way to go, as modern parlance has it. So, we "manage out" troublesome elements in the population.'

'Manage out?' Innit repeats, curious.

'Yes. An example. The elderly. Costly, troublesome creatures, Mr Innit.'

'Smelly, too,' says Innit. 'And difficult. My friend's gran could've started a world war with her little finger. And I've picked up some ripe 'uns in the Ashcan.'

Cataract frowns. The word 'ashcan' slithers around in his brain. He knows the term but can't connect it to a meaning. He moves on.

'You'll need a dose of the antidote, Mr Innit. And you'll be supplied with protective clothing. You'll be working on your own or within a small group of people who will remain anonymous to each other. Or else.'

'OK, so when do I start? And what do I do?'

'Excellent can-do attitude, Mr Innit! Just what we need. Currently, we have areas in the Federation rife with young troublemakers attacking the establishment. They need to be dealt with. I think you should be part of the team stopping them.

'For your information,' Cataract continues, 'in these areas we're increasing air pollution and building schools and homes on chemically contaminated land. We're establishing sub-education, abolishing classes for learning to read and write. And we're close to achieving zero jobs available to youngsters in the entire Federation. We've dumped competitive sports and learning languages: don't want young 'uns talking to Johnny Foreigner, they might learn something. Or, worse, *do* something.

'Dekaydence will be taking over every NHS hospital, which should help despatch many thousands of unwanted staff and patients.'

'Sounds fun,' says Innit hesitantly.'Oh, your honour, there is one condition to my accepting this assignment.'

'Which is?'

'If I'm to do this work for you I want my best friend to have this special injection, too. And I don't want no argy-bargy 'cos he's a liz'oid.'

A memory within Cataract rises into his consciousness. It was a bridge night. His three friends boarded a bus. He didn't because he knew better. He knew better because... it was an Ashcan! His friends perished in the Ashcan. He gave up bridge because there was no one left to play with. More memories stir. The driver of the Ashcan... Wasn't it the young man standing now at his bedside? Yes! The same young man who tried to rob him of his golden legs, and whose liz'oid tried to kill him? And wasn't the tin can creature called...Colin?

Cataract's scaly eyelids are closed tight. Is he asleep, dead, or possibly hibernating?

'You all right, your honour?' Innit enquires.

Cataract opens his eyes and blinks at Innit. He says nothing for some while.

'I'm fine. Thank you for enquiring,' he says eventually. 'And, yes, of course Colin must have his injection.'

Cataract makes a mental note that Innit must be watched and monitored at all times. And then dealt with.

Innit knows he didn't mention the name of his pet liz'oid, Colin, and makes a mental note that the old man must be watched and monitored at all times. And then dealt with.

Will feels uneasy at what he has overheard. He's already unsettled by what Grout has recently told him.

'It's not just the killer virus they've created, Will. Dekaydence aims to control more than food and water. There's stuff I'm being told to research...

'It's like they're trying to control Mother Nature herself.'

32 A TALENT TO DIFFUSE

No sooner has Grout fallen to the ground than Piccolo is on him, punching him about the body, shouting at him, cursing him, swearing. It's a lifetime or a few seconds before Grout recovers and is able to catch hold of Piccolo in the groin and throw him off. Now it's Piccolo writhing in the bracken, doubled up and moaning in pain and cursing Grout all the way.

Grout moves slowly to sit up. Blood is flowing from his forehead. He sees Piccolo lying nearby, still, apparently mesmerised by the tiny egg-white clouds whisking across the sky.

Grout hesitates but says nothing.

The long silence is broken eventually by Piccolo.

'Your work-outs in the gym have paid off,' he says matter-of-factly.

Grout says nothing.

Piccolo springs to his feet and goes to kick Grout, who grabs his leg and swivels it so that Piccolo is felled and, immediately, Grout sits astride him, pinioning him to the ground.

They stare at one another for some time in silence.

'I hate you!' Piccolo says suddenly, his voice full of venom.

'I gathered that,' says Grout. 'Am I allowed to know why?'

Piccolo shrugs and turns his head to look away.

'I dunno,' he says.

'Any clues?'

'You think yourself so clever, don't you?' Piccolo sneers at him.

Grout releases Piccolo, rolls off him and sits down beside him.

'No, I don't think I'm especially clever but I know I've got a talent for creative technology, as you have a talent for composing great music.'

'Butter-mouth bullshit! I might have had. But not now.'

'Is that what's getting to you? Composer block?'

Piccolo shrugs.

'I don't care any more.'

'About music or what?'

'Anything. I don't care about anything.'

'I see,' says Grout.

'No, you don't!' says Piccolo fiercely. 'Because you're different from me. OK, yah-di-yah, we've both had the classic troubled childhood. But you've got over it. Yous getting on with your life, man. Yous got friends, people who respect yous. And admire yous. Like the fine and mighty Princess Indigo. Your life is going onwards, upwards and outwards.'

'And yours isn't?'

Piccolo shakes his head. He stares hard at Grout.

'My life is over, man,' he says softly.

Grout is shocked.

'Your life is just beginning, Piccolo. But you can't shake off the old one, can you? Maybe it's scary to let go. You saw your dad murdered by your mum's boyfriend. That's huge tough shit but you weren't responsible. You were a kid, what could you have done? You don't forget but you've got to get on with your life. Else the backpack of the past will increase, weigh you down, suffocate you. You've got to offload history, Piccolo. You've got to live for now. Not yesterday. Not tomorrow. Now.'

Piccolo's head is tucked on to his knees. He says nothing.

'How about breakfast?' Grout asks, standing up. 'Lady C does mean scrambled eggs.'

'In a minute, man. In a minute. Just leave me for a while,' says Piccolo.

Grout is reluctant to leave. He tries to think of something steadying to say.

'Tea or coffee?' he asks.

'Whatever,' says Piccolo, without looking up.

Grout walks back to the house, deep in thought.

Montezuma and Billy are standing at the gate. They look ill at ease because they are. They both sense trouble.

33 A STRANGER IN THE GALLERY

The Rare Books Reading Room at the British Library is carpet thick with a deep rich silence. At seat Number 59 Ruby Q feels as though the scores of people around her, sitting in green leather chairs at long wooden desks, are deep-sea divers searching for hidden treasures as they plunge their minds into centuries-old words and thoughts from lands near and far.

There are occasional coughs and sneezes, spectacle cases opening and shutting, the irritating clatter of computer keyboards, the click of heels, or a tinny stuttering crutch, and the rustling of a see-through plastic carrier in which readers must put their restricted goods. But as she awaits the book she's ordered, Ruby Q feels as if she's in her own personal cabin, setting out on a voyage of discovery on a glorious yet uncharted sea.

The room, indeed the very building itself, encourages this feeling with its American white oak panelling, tall white walls and columns, spacious Italian stone 'decks', brass and black leather handrails, and all its architectural homage to ships and liners.

A woman passes, wheeling a small metal trolley with several books on it. Ruby Q's heartbeat increases. She feels as if a newborn baby is being put into her care.

'Should I have brought gloves, white ones at that?' she whispers to the woman, who smiles and shakes her head.

'No, that's only for TV programmes,' she whispers back. 'A natural hand is kinder to old paper than a dry glove.'

The book is placed carefully on Ruby Q's desk. The woman and her trolley move on to make further deliveries.

Ruby Q sits and waits, staring at the room that holds so much information. She looks at the book. *Le Famiglie Nobili Italiane*, The Ancient Families of Italy. Will it be in here she will discover more of the man who is her father – Lorenzo di'Abalo?

As she carefully opens the book she catches a waft of a familiar but mildly disagreeable scent, the exclusive perfume for celebrities and royalty only – Dekaydence 3-2-1. She looks up. A man turns on his heel at the enquiry desk and is heading purposefully in her direction. Yikes, it can't be him, can it? He has a cap pulled down over his hair. He's dressed in expensive country casuals of tweed, cords and brogues, and has a rich burgundy scarf round his neck. He looks determined...

Yikes! It's him. His Overall Holiness, Randall Candelskin. What does he want?

She pulls up her jacket collar, trying to make her red curly hair less conspicuous, and focuses hard on the book in front of her. Candelskin is the last person she wants to see. She feels a tap on her shoulder and groans inwardly.

'You've got my book, Miss Cooper,' says Candelskin,

louder than the readers in the Reading Room want to hear.

Brows frown and mouths tighten, warning him to lower his voice.

'I don't think so. I ordered it a few weeks' back,' she says, firmly. 'I've got confirmation.'

She ferrets in her rucksack.

'Look,' says Candelskin, urgently, 'I've got something I want to check. If I gave you money for a lemonade or a coffee...?'

'I don't think that's allowed,' says Ruby Q. 'But how long do you need?'

'A few minutes. At most.'

Ruby Q bites her lip. He looks so distraught.

'OK.' She lowers her voice. 'Sit here, beside me. I don't need a drink, I'll look at my notes while you look at the book.'

'Thank you, Miss Cooper, thank you,' whispers Candelskin. 'I hear you're teaching yourself Italian and I wondered if you'd care to accompany me on a trip to Italy to meet the Pope.'

'Gosh, yes! I need to check the dates with my editor but I must tell you I'm only halfway through the first book in a series of nine.'

'No matter, it's further than I ever got.'

'Actually, I've just remembered something else. I've been given a device that does automatic translations.'

'Excellent! Perhaps I should have one, too, just in case.

I'll talk to your editor, get her to commission you to do a piece or three on my high-profile meeting...'

Aha! Truth will out, even from a man such as HOH Randall Candelskin.

'Will you please lower your voices and cover your thoughts?' says an elderly lady, who sits down next to Candelskin on his other side. Candelskin bows an apology. The elderly woman in blue winks at Ruby Q who smiles back and feels unusually cheerful for the rest of the day.

34 WHERE IS CROMARTY?

MacMinor senses something is wrong when MacNoodle arrives with only one yattering, howling haggoid, Ross, at his side. He's about to ask Cromarty's whereabouts but MacNoodle beats him to it.

'He's gone!' cries MacNoodle. 'Cromarty's disappeared. I've been in the sewers all night. I've left trails of empty crisp packets, offal and homing devices but...not a thing. No clues, nothing.'

'He cannae gone far, man,' says MacMinor sympathetically, even though the haggoids have recently devoured his entire stock of soft lavatory paper with added aloe vera. 'Think about it, Mr MacNoodle. He wouldnae run away from you, you're his daddy. Maybe he's got stuck somewhere.'

MacNoodle groans.

'Don't say that. I'll only worry some more.'

'Man, it's only been one morning and you're already a certainty for an Olympic gold medal in the world's worrying finals.'

'When I woke up about four o'clock this morning I discovered Cromarty had eaten the door.'

'Not again. That'll be the sixth time this month.'

'Aye.'

'He is a costly brute, MacNoodle, is he not? Maybe someone decided he's *too* costly.'

'Och, who'd want to do away wi' him? He's too cuddly for words.'

MacMinor says nothing. Cuddly is not quite the word he'd use to describe Ross or Cromarty, the wild metal Dekaydence haggoids on a constant lookout for rubbish and blood. Hasn't he got the cuts and bruises to prove it?

'Have you tried the kitchens?' MacMinor asks. 'They must have giant magnets in there, the times we've had to go and collect one or both of them.'

'MacGluten's young 'un, Goo, keeps feedin' him. He loves Cromarty.'

Ross howls.

'Goo loves you, too, Rossi boy.' MacNoodle tickles behind the haggoid's ears.

'Have a word wi' Goo. He might've seen the wee greedy hoggoid.'

'Don't call him a hoggoid, even in jest, man,' says MacNoodle sternly.

'It doesn't mean I don't love him,' MacMinor protests quietly.

'My, but there's a terrible stench coming from the kitchens,' MacNoodle remarks as they walk along the corridor. 'That happens when MacGluten is in a bad mood. Have you not noticed?'

'No, I have not,' says MacNoodle. 'I lost my sense of smell when I was a wee lad.'

'Oh, I'm sorry, I never knew that,' says MacNoodle. 'That's terrible bad luck.'

'Yes and no,' says MacMinor. 'Like now, I'm not bothered by the unsavoury.'

'Here we are,' says MacNoodle. 'And here's young Goo, on his hands and knees. My, but it's nice to have someone show you some respect.'

Goo looks up, puzzled.

'Um, there's been an accident. Bit of mess and stuff. Sorry.'

'That's all right, lad, I'm sure it wasn't of your making,' says MacMinor.

Goo nods, relieved.

'Actually,' says MacNoodle, 'I wondered if you'd seen Cromarty. The wee man got out last night and I haven't seen him since. I'm gutted, Goo. I'm truly gutted. I expect I've brought you gutting news at an inconvenient moment, too, but...'

Goo swallows hard.

'Um, yes, Mr MacNoodle,' says Goo. 'That's terrible, terrible news. I am so sorry. But I've got to go now. I'm on canapés. And if I'm late, my dad...'

'Understand, Goo. You carry on, lad,' says MacNoodle.

Goo hurries off to the kitchen with his bucket and mop.

'I smell a rat,' says MacMinor.

'I thought you couldnae...?' says MacNoodle.

'No, no, man,' MacMinor tuts. 'I mean, something fishy is going on. That lad knows more than he's saying.'

MacNoodle blows his nose.

'If they've put him in a casserole...'

'MacNoodle, get a grip, man! How many folk d'you know eat circuit boards and solid metal, with or without engine oil?'

Ross whines.

'Och, other than you, that is, wee wicked man Ross.'

4

The President of the Federation flies first class and eats deluxe on his voyage to the eastern conflicts. He transfers on to an army helicopter where the only fare is boiled sweets, one of the many things he won't touch since his uber-expensive dental treatment.

On arrival at Camp Bassard, the President shakes hands with army chiefs but his mind is elsewhere.

'Are you looking for something in particular, sir?' the General enquires, as the President glances variously into the distance over this shoulder or the other. Mostly, he watches his back.

'No,' the President of the Federation demurs. 'It's the scenery...and the, er...amazing...insects and magnificent wildlife. I mean, it's quite...er, quite extraordinary!'

The General's eyes brighten with a childlike excitement.

'I'll escort you on a nature trip, Mr President,' says the General enthusiastically. 'It is spectacular. Most people don't notice it so it's a joy to meet someone who already appreciates it.'

The President spots a fast-approaching Eye-Spy and a Dekaydence logo'd jeep. His staff are arriving. He spots a TV camera pointed at him and hurriedly puts his arm round the nearest soldier, gives a thumbs-up sign and performs a wide grin.

'Not to worry about a trip out of camp,' he says, vigorously shaking the General's hand for the next publicity shot. 'You've got enough work to do. Wouldn't want to cause you any trouble.'

'No trouble, Mr President,' says the General. 'But first let me take you to your quarters.'

'Quarters? Didn't they tell you, General? I'm not staying. Schedule demands,' says the President, dark clouds travelling his face. Some time, somewhere, a civil servant will be in deep trouble.

'That's not what it says here, sir,' says the General. 'HQ says the President of the Federation is here for three days. It's, er, it's an order, sir. From the top.'

'Why on earth...?' The President fights to rein in his anger. 'Three days?'

'That's right, sir. In any event, there's no aircraft here. They're on overhaul.'

'Then what am I doing here?' the President mutters. 'I could get...' He shudders with fear. But to back out now... He might lose him his pension and Swiss bank account.

'The US President wants to see you "get to know the men" and how you face up on the front line, sir,' says the

General.

The President of the Federation pushes his designer sunglasses from his nose to rest on his head. His skin is quite pale. He is taken to his quarters. It's a one-person tent off a larger one where his entourage – including the camera-happy PR, the hairdresser, make-up artist and bodyguard – will live for three days.

A small book lies on the President's pillow. He picks it up. It's a Bible. He puts it into the top pocket on his shirt. Well, it might stop a bullet.

He falls into a deep sleep, awakening in the dark hour before dawn to the sound of birdsong. He wonders whether to go for a walk. Then decides it's safer if he goes for a stroll. Get to know the layout. See what the chaps are up to.

He gets out of bed in the combat gear in which he somehow crashed to sleep and makes his way to the door flaps. He steps outside, looks around and frowns.

A few women in eastern attire are cooking over an open fire. Nearby, is a man carrying a Kalashnikov.

The Federation President turns to alert someone, anyone, in the next tent but they are all sound asleep. The next he knows is the feel of the barrel of a gun in his side and then the sound of the weapon being cocked.

34.5 NIGEL'S NEWS

Grout is having brunch with the Catguts. Home-laid, free-range eggs, home-grown mushrooms and watercress and home-baked bread and home-produced honey. Grout's admiration for Lady C knows no bounds. Catgut feels the same. But unusually, this morning, the two men eat little and do so in silence.

They're thinking of Piccolo. What can they do to help him? He's seen a doctor. He's on prescribed tablets. But still it appears he can't abide almost everyone in the household. What can be done?

'I've heard that an excellent therapist has moved into the village,' says Lady Catgut. 'He's retired but I think he does take the odd rare case.'

'Or in this case, the very odd,' says Catgut gloomily.

'Catgut, that's most uncalled for,' Lady Catgut ticks off her husband, who is muttering his apologies when—

The door bursts open. Nigel is standing there. His face is as grey as a raincloud, his whole wee metal-and-flesh body shakes, rattles and rolls.

'Come quickly!' he says, his teeth chattering. 'I think Piccolo's taken an overdose!'

SECTION 5

*Sometimes I wonder whether the world is being run by
smart people who are putting us on or by imbeciles who
really mean it.*
Mark Twain (1835–1910)

35 A CLAW IN HEAVEN

A howl rips through Heaven like a jagged claw. It is a cry full of pain. A noise like no other. The more so as Heaven is set to silent. What's gone wrong? The angels are fearful. God is not there to explain and soothe, and make whatever amends are necessary.

Bhupi and the three Clives examine the outmoded communications system and begin work on an upgrade.

Meanwhile, Claud Canapé is corralling newcomers to help in the redecoration. While the Archangel Gabriel is on a high, literally, with a paintbrush, he's aware of the clouds trembling beneath his stepladder. What on earth is Mother Nature up to? he wonders.

It's Jack who finds the haggoid at a small side gate just over the boundary. As the creature enters Heaven the howling is silenced. But the creature's inner distress is almost palpable. It is cowering, its thin wiry tail — partly detached from its broken body — drips oil. It watches him with its bright red eyes and, as he approaches, its nervous look changes to one of terror.

Jack crouches down, several steps away.

It's you, isn't it? Ross? No? Ah, Cromarty, he says in his head.

The creature's ears prick up.

Cromarty! Jack speaks the name in his head as if it's a precious treasure.

The haggoid staggers towards Jack, falls at his feet with a clank and a rattle before attempting a roll-over, of sorts, on to its back. Jack gently strokes its metal stomach and tweaks its leathery ears, and sees that three of its metal legs are all but detached from its body.

You're safe now, Cromarty, Jack says in his head. *A few running repairs and you'll be as right as rain and... Yikes!*

He struggles to extract his arm from the haggoid's jaws.

No love bites, old chap! And I'm not food!

Cromarty's eyes are fixed on Jack, who is thinking of MacNoodle, the Red Tartan Guard and Cromarty's handler. MacNoodle, who he knows will be searching for the creature, devastated by his loss. The haggoid starts to pant excitedly but silently, as if he knows what Jack is thinking. Equally, Jack knows someone who'll be overjoyed to welcome the haggoid to Heaven. He scoops Cromarty into his arms.

They haven't gone far when the haggoid makes it clear it wants to be put on the ground. Jack complies and, immediately, the haggoid limps off, as fast as it isn't able, heading towards the secret ivy-covered door Jack discovered. The creature flops down by the door, staring at it intently, its tail attempting to wag.

Which is odd, Jack thinks, because behind the ivy is not the boundary wall but an old door that is not on any map he can find in Heaven's vast library. Yet Cromarty, just arrived, appears to recognise it and know what it's for.

36 FIRST AID

'Get out and leave me alone! I want to die!'

Grout feels his blood run cold as he hears the anguish, anger and desperation in Piccolo's voice. How can his friend feel so bad? How can he be so loved, so cared for and yet feel so driven to want to kill himself? It doesn't make sense. It rattles the logic Grout lives by. It hurts his heart, too.

He stands outside Piccolo's bedroom with the Catguts and Nigel. A sob escapes Catgut's throat. Nigel, head bowed, is shivering. Lady Catgut stands erect, like a warrior waiting to do battle with whatever the unknown assailant brings. Inside, she weeps.

Grout catches a glimpse of the paramedics before the door is shut. He sees them trying to get a drink down Piccolo's throat, a carbon drink to absorb the toxicity of the tablets he has taken. There's a long pause before the paramedics emerge, either side of Piccolo, guiding him down the stairs and into the ambulance. Piccolo walks as if in a bad dream; his dark eyes set within dark circles appear to see nothing or everything. Catgut and his wife, and Nigel watch the proceedings in shock and fear.

The ambulance, its lights flashing, heads for the local

hospital some 20 miles away.

Aware that Catgut is in no fit state to do anything, Lady Catgut drives, following in the path of the ambulance. Catgut, Lady C, Grout and Nigel remain silent for the entire journey, too worried to talk of their concerns or to add to the distress of the others.

In the accident and emergency department Lady Catgut and the doctor talk in hushed tones before the doctor is called away. They sit in the waiting room and do just that – wait. Occasionally, Grout paces up and down or gets coffee and drinks. There's a hissy radio tuned to a rock-music channel on top of a cabinet in A & E. It drones on like a nagging toothache. Nigel grimaces and tries to bury his ears in his shoulders.

Nurses come and go, some purposefully, others wearily, as a long shift comes to an end.

The doctor returns.

'He's...'

Unable or unsure quite what to say, the doctor changes course, smiles and says brightly, 'A psychiatrist will be with him shortly.'

'A psychiatrist?' Catgut expostulates. 'Fat lot of good—'

'Catgut!' says Lady Catgut sharply. She turns to the doctor.

'Can we see him?'

The doctor hesitates.

'Please,' says Lady Catgut. 'Unless you think it'd harm him in some way.'

'One of you only,' says the doctor. 'And, at most, for a few minutes.'

But which of them can talk to a young man who feels so bad about his life that he is determined to end it?

They look at one another.

'It can't be me,' says Catgut, punching his fist into the palm of his other hand, over and over again. 'I'll upset him, I know. I always have done. Shouted at him. Bullied him. I can't lose another boy, Etti, I...'

'All right, Catty, all right. Don't fret, dearest,' says Lady Catgut soothingly.

Grout and Nigel shift embarrassedly in their seats. They know of the tragic death of the Catguts' son and the sudden disappearance of Cage after Lady C sheltered him from the police. It must seem like a recurring nightmare.

'I can't do it,' says Nigel. 'He's so nasty to me. Says my minimalist height gives him maximum eye strain.'

'What about you, Lady C?' Grout asks.

She turns to dab away a tear.

'Would you like me to see him, Lady C?' says Grout quietly.

She nods, unable to speak.

They watch Grout's departing back. Each in their own way worrying, wondering, and praying to their God, or simply into the air, that all will be well. That all will be well.

37 FACE IN THE LEAD

'I know about North,' the Face whispers to Will. 'You've got to spring him before the bassards have him done away with.'

'I do know that,' Will replies testily.

'OK,' says the Face. 'Keep your hair-shirt on, I've got something else to say.'

Will groans inwardly. He's never found it easy dealing with this temperamental woman who has lost her role in life. GeeZers quit the environmental pressure group she ran to join the more radical, violent Real GeeZers. She has few followers now. So why does she want a meeting? he wonders. She must want something from him. But what?

'Look, I haven't got much on so I thought why don't I stand in for North?'

'*What?*' says Will. 'Face, you're a peacenik, albeit an angry one! How on earth could you organise violent action?'

'Do you know, to be honest, I feel my true nature is coming to the fore,' says the Face languidly. 'Since I heard about North I've felt...the dark side of myself.'

She studies her black-limbed arm, transplanted from her brother-in-law Hunky Doré after she'd lost her own in the tsunami.

'Perhaps this did it,' she says, smiling at Will.

Will grunts.

'Let's sleep on it,' he says.

'That'd be nice,' says the Face cheekily, toying with her dark nails.

'I'm going,' says Will, and gets up.

'Oh, dear,' says the Face. 'Something I said or royal stuff?'

'I'll contact you tomorrow,' says Will brusquely.

'Before you go,' says the Face, 'you need to know something. I've spoken to East and West, among others. As far as they're concerned, I'm in charge. You're outvoted. Get used to it.'

Will fights to suppress his fury.

'OK, Face, but get this. Don't go near the Phoenix. Understand?'

'Too late,' she says, with a sneer.

Will clenches and unclenches his fists.

'What have you told him to do, you interfering, manipulative...?'

She shrugs, miming pulling a zip across her mouth.

'If anything should happen to him...' he says menacingly.

'You'll smack my bottom?' The Face adopts a childish, simpering voice.

Will makes a move towards her. She shrieks, turns to run, loses her footing, and falls to the floor. He stands over her.

'If anything should happen to the Phoenix, I'll kill you,' he says, and turns on his heel.

'Ooo!' She squeals with laughter. 'So, who do you fancy more, him or...?'

But he's gone, slamming the door behind him and doesn't hear what she says.

'...the music man, Piccolo?' she shouts out louder, and follows it with a cackling laugh.

38 VIGIL

Grout is sitting at Piccolo's bedside. He's nervous of saying anything that might upset his friend, who is staring fixedly at the ceiling.

'Piccolo, it's me, Grout. I'm allowed only two minutes with you,' says Grout. 'So tell me if there's anything you want or need.'

Piccolo hears Grout's words as a long, low monotonous noise but he has no energy to speak. His mind is immersed in old memories of bruises and blood, his father's murder, the abuse he received from his mother and her assassin boyfriend, and of broken bonds.

'We... I miss you,' says Grout suddenly. 'You've become like a brother to me. As Catgut is our second father...'

Father. The very word pierces the fog in Piccolo's mind and triggers another memory: *My father who art in Heaven, Hallowed be Dad's name, Thy Kingdom of music and love come. As it hasn't on earth...*

'I wish I'd met your dad,' Grout continues. 'He gave you love and music, Piccolo. Two things I don't really understand. Probably never will.' He gives a shy laugh. 'Yes, I think I'd have learnt much from your dad.'

My father who art in Heaven. Or somewhere, or nowhere, thinks Piccolo.

The curtain rustles. The doctor frowns and taps her watch.

'With you in a moment,' says Grout.

'I don't know about that,' says Piccolo, suddenly and clearly, his eyes focused on the ceiling.

Grout looks up. Who's he talking to? What's he talking about?

'We want you back with us, Piccolo,' says Grout. 'We need you.'

Piccolo says nothing and carries on staring at the ceiling.

The doctor returns and gives Grout a meaningful leave-now-or-else look.

Grout gets up and leaves the cubicle, glancing one more time at Piccolo. He turns questioningly to the doctor.

'It's too early to say,' she says quietly.

39 ROYAL QUESTIONS

The King is in his Counting House, one of a dozen or so old wooden summerhouses in the Royal Park that have become the Royal Family's official home. His Majesty has a view towards the Dekaydence arena, where stood his palace with the great Armageddon conservatory that he himself designed. Here, he counts his monies and blessings. The thought that it could have been his head from which he was separated rather than his home and heir has helped staunch his tears.

Nowadays, he takes pleasure, not from the rare Verdeccio in the conservatory but from the bright, exuberant, second-hand Hockney prints on the thin walls.

He is alive and he is King, just. His damaged confidence in the Rroyal Family's future is repairing itself. He sees his son, the Crown Prince, is much at ease with modern culture, people and manners. He was a troublesome child with a cut-and-paste attitude to learning. He quit school at 16 to meddle with drugs and thieving. Now he campaigns vigorously against both activities, riding out nationwide on one of his many cherished Harley-Davidsons, his young son clinging to his father's back.

On occasions the Crown Prince likes a drink or three

and the King understands that the media consider him to be a regular bloke. The more so, apparently, as he's on his third wife, a perfectly charming young woman who keeps her husband and her housekeeping in check. Well, almost.

The King is humming to himself as he sifts through his sadly diminished old record collection when there's a knock on the door.

Sinus, the butler, appears from nowhere – or was it a cupboard? – and opens the door to Will.

The King nods distractedly to his great-nephew as he puts a record, 'Singin' in the Rain', on the antique player.

Sinus moves stiffly to remove stacks of old records from a chair and then shuffles to a kettle residing on the floor. Will notices he uses one, already-used teabag to make them all a cup of tea.

'What news of Cataract?' says the King.

'He's fine, sir...a bit forgetful.'

The King snorts.

'Aren't we all? It'll happen to you one day, my boy. But my dear old schoolfriend is recovering, is he not?'

'He's working from his hospital bed, sir.'

'Excellent! On what?'

The King sees Will glance at Sinus.

'Sinus is my guardian angel and the soul of discretion,' says the King, irritated. 'You should know that by now, boy.'

Indeed, Sinus has been good to the King, thinks Will, but there's something about the old butler... He can't quite put his finger on it but... Certainly, he'd prefer not to say anything to the King but it's too late. And he does want to discover where the King stands on certain issues.

'There's talk of a new virus designed to kill people living on land wanted by property developers.'

'What?' The King's face puckers with confused stress lines. 'Have you been reading those sci-fi books your brother and father were so keen on?'

'No,' says Will.

'Do we know about this, Sinus?' the King enquires of his butler.

'No, sire,' says Sinus, serving a chipped plate of out-of-date, reduced-price biscuits.

'So what's this got to do with Cataract, boy?' says the King.

'I happened to overhear a conversation. Someone from Dekaydence—'

'You're not into drugs, are you?' The King enquires of Will. 'I know it can stimulate one's imagination. I know that only too well through years of living with the Crown Prince.'

'Perhaps I misheard,' says Will.

'Perhaps you did. I should keep quiet on matters of which you're not sure. Especially snatches of other people's conversations. Could land you in hot water. And as your star is rising in royalty ratings...'

Will says nothing.

'Otherwise,' the King continues, 'your work at CCM is progressing?'

Will proceeds to give the King an account of what's he's learning at Cataract, Cyclops and Mote. He omits everything connected to the firm's ruthless profiteering and intense infiltration into countless influential institutions and governments worldwide. Neither does he mention the humungous bonuses paid to those already on vastly inflated salaries, nor those whose work has wreaked havoc and destruction on the poor and on those tired teams of overworked warhorses, the poor and the middle class.

After Will leaves, the King sighs and shakes his head.

'Cataract and I go back a long way. Our wives are related. My brother is… I don't want that boy messing up family relations.'

'I'm sure he won't, sire,' says Sinus. 'He is a dour, humourless lad, for sure. But I believe he is a good and honourable soul at heart.'

'Thank you, Sinus,' says the King.

Later, when the King retires for the night, Sinus steps outside into the darkness for a forbidden cigarette and then whispers a code into his ad'um.

'Trouble?' says a good-humoured musical voice at the other end.

'My Lord,' says Sinus, 'the young Scottish prince knows

about the virus. From Cataract and, possibly, also from Grout.'

'No matter,' says Lord di'Abalo, with a bored yawn. 'We could bring forward our plans. Or not.'

Sinus coughs, a raw, rackingly sore sound.

'Smoking again, Sinus,' di'Abalo says sternly. 'You need to be steady and in good health – until it's all over. Understand?'

Sinus chokes up an agreement through the phlegm in his throat.

'Good man,' says di'Abalo encouragingly. 'Not long now.'

The call ends and Lord di'Abalo walks on to the balcony of his penthouse apartment and looks out over the river.

Phlegm clears his throat and steps forward with a silver goblet on a tray, and bows. Lord di'Abalo takes the goblet and drinks deeply. Then, he leans back, opens his mouth wide and, with a great roar, shoots forth a torrent of wild, spectacular flames of red, yellow and orange that fly high into the air, scorching the darkened landscape. Phlegm sighs. The sight triggers within him an irresistable desire for a cigarette.

40 ANGELICA'S SECRET

When she's not working or helping Mr Treasure care for Rallan and Elsa, Ruby Q spends her time in the Rare Books Reading Room at the British Library, searching through an old faded copy of *Le Famiglie Nobili Italiane* ('The Ancient Families of Italy').

Fortunately, the tiny automatic Turing Translating Device given to her by Mr Treasure translates 'out loud' into her head as she reads. Unfortunately, there's scant information on the Di'Abalo family. But there is something. A mention of a Di'Abalo prince visiting London and Washington. There's also a footnote on the prince having a brief audience with the Pope in the Vatican and the Papal residence at Castel Gandolfo. So brief, that it's described further in a smaller footnote as 'abrupt' and that the prince was in such a raging mood that he stormed out, leaving behind his butler, forever.

One day Ruby Q takes a lunch break in the restaurant. She queues, pays for the vegetarian option, and searches for a seat. The area is packed with people of all ages. She spots a space in a far corner that's opposite someone she recognises. It's not just the shining auburn hair or the expensive clothing that tells Ruby Q it's her mother. It's also in a memory of long ago, in the way she was encouraged to sit straight-backed, as her mother sits now.

Ruby Q hesitates, before walking through the crowded area towards the mother she scarcely knows.

Angelica Nera looks up, indicates the spare seat and smiles.

She's smiling at you, and her teeth aren't bared!

Stop it. Don't judge. Not yet, anyway.

'Hello,' says Ruby Q, as she sits down. 'This is the last seat in the place.'

'I've been here a while,' says Angelica Nera. 'I knew you'd have to eat at some point.'

'Were you waiting for me?' Ruby Q says, surprised but rather pleased.

'Yes.' Angelica Nera nods, and sips her black coffee.

'How did you...? Why?'

Angelica takes a deep breath.

'I owe you an explanation.' She stirs sugar into her cup.

'Anything in particular or every...?' says Ruby Q.

Stop it, Ruby Q! If you want to learn something.

OK, OK.

Angelica stares at Ruby Q, who wonders at her mother's beauty and feels uneasy with her own plainness.

'You are an attractive young woman, Ruby Q,' says her mother suddenly, examining Ruby Q's face. 'You have a certain *je ne sais quoi*. I can't put my finger on it but....'

Ruby Q blushes.

Angelica laughs, like a tinkle of bells. People look round and smile. And Ruby Q suddenly realises she's heard a laugh not unlike her own.

'And you blush easily, like your Aunt Lily,' says Angelica, with a smile.

'Is that it, is that the explanation?' says Ruby Q. 'If it is...'

'No,' says Angelica. 'I thought you'd like to know some family attributes.'

Try not to react. It could get nasty. As you said yourself: don't judge, not yet, anyway.

Ruby Q's back and neck are ramrod straight.

'I don't think we're ever going to be close, Ruby Q,' says Angelica quietly. 'I've hurt you too much. I understand that better now that I've met you and seen how you've grown up. You were always a determined, principled little loner. I wanted to call you Diriturra, it's Italian for integrity, but Rallan objected.'

Thank you, Dad, for getting me out of that one, Ruby Q says in her head.

'Then I realised it's not a name that would go down well in a playground,' says Angelica, with another smile.

That's for sure.

'Look, Ruby Q, there are things in my life that are personal and private, that I don't intend to share with you or anyone. I do want to tell you, and you alone, one thing that might help you understand why I walked out on you all those years ago. You're a young woman now, a woman of the world, doing well in your career, but I remember you as a little worrier, like Rallan, so I hope this helps you understand me a little better and that my leaving was not, in any way, your fault.

'I am not founded on emotion, Ruby Q, I'm sure you sensed that as a little girl. I understand numbers so much better. I'm happier around figures than people. Numbers are intriguing, fascinating and clear as water. And, refreshingly, lacking in emotion.'

'Is that it? You're excused because you're an accountant?' asks Ruby Q.

Lay off! Let her tell her story.

Angelica's eyes wear a worn, troubled look.

'Nothing to do with accountancy, Ruby Q. Nothing to do with you. The reason I left is because I found out that my father wasn't my true father.'

'Oh, my goodness!' says Ruby Q, taken aback. So, her mother has gone through the same wretched experience as she has.

Yes. But hang on a moment. What difference should that make to you?

'But what difference did that make to me? Or to Rallan?' says Ruby Q.

'When I found out...' Angelica pauses '...I felt broken, as if I'd been shattered like a mirror. I no longer knew who or what I was.'

'I do understand,' says Ruby Q, quietly, 'but...?'

'I had to find out who my father was.'

'I understand that, too, but why did you have to leave us?'

'I realised it might be a long, hard journey. I knew I had to make it on my own.'

'Did you find him, your real father?'

'Yes.'

'Can I know his name, or something about him? He is my grandfather.'

'No,' says Angelica. 'I don't want you chasing after him. He's not worth it.'

'Why not? I'm entitled to know my own grandfather, aren't I?'

'I know you investigate things, Ruby Q, but I ask you to stop here. For the sake of us all.'

Ruby Q says nothing.

'I'd best be going,' says Angelica Nera, slipping her coat over her shoulders. 'Oh, I almost forgot. These are for you.'

She reaches into her handbag and hands her daughter a tiny parcel. Ruby Q carefully unwraps the lilac tissue paper and into her hand drop a pair of glass heart-shaped earrings.

'Oh, my, they match!' exclaims Ruby Q, touching the glass heart necklace she's wearing under her shirt.

Angelica smiles.

'The set belongs to our family.'

'So was it you who came to see me in hospital that Christmas and left me the necklace?' asks Ruby Q.

'No. Your Aunt Lily came into the ward. I stood guard outside.'

'Does Aunt Lily know all this stuff about your father? Is that why she doesn't want to see me, because she doesn't want me asking her questions?'

'She knows nothing. And it must stay like that, Ruby Q. For the sake of us all.'

41 FACE ON FIRE

As the Face storms into the room her minder, Hilli, sees her face is flushing tomato red. That indicates, nothing unusual, she's in a fury. He'd prefer to say nothing but with this look he's learnt it's safer to defuse her sooner rather than later.

'What's up, boss?' he says, wondering if a hard hat on his head might protect him.

'The Phoenix has pulled out. Freakin' wimp.'

'Did he give any reason?'

'Yeah. He's going soft. Said he was concerned that I hadn't recovered fully from my arm transplant. Pigeon poo! I know it's 'cos he wants to know every detail of the plan and I'm not prepared to tell him 'cos he'd want to take over.'

'Right,' says Hilli, who's heard it all before. The Face's inflexibility and jealousy has led to a fallout with Tommo, Will, Piccolo and North. And others. Somehow Hilli survives. He puts it down to exercise, meditation and goat's yoghurt.

'I told him we're widening the brief,' the Face continues. 'Fighting to save the planet is obviously the priority. But I agree wholeheartedly with his campaign for people and animal welfare. And I reckon North is right, we've got to include human rights and sustainability and a fair deal for all if not...'

There's laughter outside the door.

'Where's Comprendo?' the Face asks suspiciously.

That's the other thing, thinks Hilli, she trusts no one but herself. She must wonder how we manage to breathe for ourselves.

'He's checking out the boys' disguises,' Hilli responds.

'Good. Then let's go.'

BREAKING NEWS

Ruby Q Cooper reports from London for *The Daily Unigraph*.

A dozen or more veiled women are walking the London streets in the cold night air. They chat among themselves, they hold a bundle of baby, bounce a toddler on their hip, or push a buggy. When no one's looking, they smoke. When they think they're being watched, or filmed by journalists, they shout, make rude gestures, and throw their long full skirts over their heads to reveal their underwear, and more. They pretend to be of a religious faith but they are not.

They're accompanied by two dozen or so children. It's difficult to be accurate because the children run about all over the place. They're not playing, they're working. Begging from anyone and everyone. Nagging people, persistently, continuously, until they feel the source has dried up. Then they move on to the next victim. Each successful 'hit' they return to one of the women, who could be their minder and/or mother.

A child in nappies toddles unsteadily towards a man using a cash point, and holds up his hands for cash. His mother-minder stands close by.

LIVE FROM AN ILLEGAL INTERNET SERVICE PROVIDER

There's a little girl, four or five years old. She darts about like a jet-propelled butterfly, as though this dirty, grubby business is a lark, a game. 'Please, sir, can I have some more?' Except, in the reality of the here and now, there's no please, no thank you. Only a sharp demand for more, or a blessing as deep as an inkwell.

It's 10 at night. Work started at 10 in the morning and continues. The little girl needs a comfort break and uses a telephone booth as a lavatory. The tired, whimpering toddler is fed weak beer or cola to keep her quiet.

There's the sound of raised voices. Along the street, outside a pub two men are facing up to one another. Each the worse for alcohol; each daring the other to throw the first punch. There's the flash of a knife. A breaking bottle. A nearby police van races over.

A young sergeant, two PCs and a WPC leap out of the van. The two drunks run off. The police watch and wonder at the women and children. They take names, addresses and mobile phone numbers. How old are the children? What are they doing on the street at this time of night? Which school or nursery do they attend?

The WPC opens the van's back doors. The younger children are curious and run over. They clamber inside as soon as they see plates piled high with sandwiches, cakes and biscuits. More follow. The WPC gently closes the

LIVE FROM AN ILLEGAL INTERNET SERVICE PROVIDER

doors and jumps into the driver's seat. The three other policemen pile into the van and the WPC drives off.

A veiled woman sees what's happened, starts shouting, and runs after the van. Not easy in a long garment. In any event, it's too late. She's joined by other women who realise what's happened and shout and scream. They call to the children. They weep, they wail. Their screams are now hysterical.

Someone calls the police. The real police.

Not many hours later 20 children are discovered in a local hospital café, one of those that sell chips with everything that's fatty and unhealthy and will be the cause of some of these youngsters returning, in time, to hospital with a lethal illness.

A few hours more and the children are reunited with their mothers. The real police are suspicious. Journalists, too. A quick investigation reveals that these women and children have entered the country illegally; they're on benefit, illegally; yet luxurious BMWs are parked on their driveways here and in their homeland. How come?

After more investigations it appears these women and their partners are sending home thousands of pounds every week to their 'employers' or families, who live in marble mansions that wouldn't shame an Arab sheikh. They use babies and young children in the front line. They use young teenage girls who should be in school, learning lessons to help their minds grow and flourish, but instead become pregnant girls sent on the streets to beg.

Who are the people who permit this to happen, by turning a blind eye to this lying, cheating and exploitation of innocents? Why do people yawn and shrug, and say, it has been going on for years? However long, something must, and shall, be done.

Justice for all

42 LOST AND FOUND

'There she is!' one of the Noteians shouts excitedly, waving his finger at the scenes on the live TV news. 'That's Maria! Among the beggar women!'

The other Noteian replays the scene, freezes and scans the face on the screen.

'Yes,' he says, quietly. 'It's her.'

'How on earth did she get involved with them?' says the first.

'I don't know, brother. What matters is that we get her away from them, fast. Before they ship her back to wherever they come from and she's lost for ever.'

'Yes, but how?'

The second Noteian is making a call.

'You recall the sister of the chap who composed music for our school play?'

The first Noteian's frown turns into a bright, sunny smile.

'Rather,' he says admiringly.

'Yes. Well, she's a policewoman now, top rank. And on-side. Ah, she's picked up.'

Not far away, the Phoenix is in a safe house, relaxing on the sofa after a long, luxurious bath. He's eating handfuls of dried fruit and nuts, and abstractedly watching the live news on TV.

Suddenly, he sits bolt upright. He grabs the control and presses the replay button. It is her. His sister, Maria. Among the beggar women who he sees on the streets near where he's staying. He watches the clip again. To familiarise himself with his own sister, hating the irony of it.

She looks dreadful, he thinks. Sick, tired, matted hair, and dirty in grubby old clothes. What is she doing with these people? Oh, God, he suddenly thinks, is the toddler she's overseeing her own? His niece or nephew?

He pulls on his jacket and rushes out into the street, missing a message on his ad'um from the Face, boasting of her success. He looks this way and that for Maria, peers into passing cars, squints into a large police van that stops alongside him at a red traffic light. He neither hears nor sees the half-dozen plainclothes policemen quietly getting out of the back of the van until they surround him and shove him into the back of the van.

43 RE-WRENDERING

It's the evening rush-hour when Ruby Q takes the Thameslink train to St Paul's. She walks along Ludgate Hill and stops to stare at the enormous cathedral dome, lit up and seeming to glow in a grey-white, magical, mystical light, miniaturising the shops and crowds in the busy high street.

It looks like a giant alien spaceship.

Right. And how many of those have you seen in recent times?

Oh, you know what I mean.

Actually, I do. I used only to see its beauty but now there's something other-worldly about it. Something's not quite right, but I'm not sure what.

Ruby Q crosses the street and walks on to the cathedral's forecourt. What follows is her report for *The Daily Unigraph*.

BREAKING NEWS

Ruby Q Cooper reports from London for *The Daily Unigraph*.

It's evening rush-hour when I visit St Paul's. Traffic on Ludgate Hill moves at a snail's pace compared with the fast-footed pedestrians weaving in and out of others on the busy, narrow pavements. Looming over it all is the huge dome of Wren's cathedral, glowing sepulchral grey-white, like a giant alien spaceship.

Despite the intense, mostly negative media coverage of Justice, the recently formed campaign movement, I'm not sure what to expect. To one side of the cathedral forecourt is a small encampment of some twenty tents, mostly one- or two-person-sized, arranged in neat rows and set on and secured to wooden pallets packed with newspaper (including *The Daily Unigraph*) to keep out the bitingly cold night wind.

Three marquees serve as a free library, a meeting place-cum-lecture hall and an information centre. And at a smaller encampment in Paternoster Square, to one side of St Paul's, there are half a dozen tents and a food kitchen. An ugly wire corridor affords access to cathedral visitors, giving the impression that this is a dangerous war zone.

LIVE FROM AN ILLEGAL INTERNET SERVICE PROVIDER

Which it isn't, at least not on the face of it.

Justice doesn't block the famous forecourt, and they leave a wide berth between the tents and the shops that, at times, might contain a few jugglers, a few musicians.

Justice campaigners don't interfere with visitors or tourists; quite the reverse. It's the tourists and visitors who flock to meet them, masked or unmasked. The mask is the face of Themis, the ancient Greek goddess, embodiment of divine order, law and custom, organiser of the communal affairs of humans, especially assemblies. Justice wear their masks not to hide but to underline the aims of their campaign.

So who listens? On one bitterly cold day when I visit again, one Justice campaigner is sweeping and cleaning as though this was her home. There are City gents, a couple of middle-aged skinheads, a mystic and a handful of elderly folk who've come for a concert in the cathedral.

The front row of tents contains campaigners skilled in listening and talking: somewhat bemused at being interviewed and photographed by an endless array of journalists, photographers, and visitors, young and old, from around the world, they nevertheless answer endless questions of varying profundity.

And people get on-side. Late one night a wedding guest drops off a dozen platters full of wedding banquet food; a group of Irish girls, office workers, asks what's needed by the 'campers' and go and get it. After a long in-depth conversation, a distinguished gentleman admits he's changed his views on Justice and donates a bundle of cash. Much of the 'village' has been formed by donations – in money and in kind, such as tea and tents.

Every campaigner I meet is opposed to violence, even some Real GeeZers who no longer believe that force is the way to win someone to your way of thinking.

'I'm a teacher,' says Dan. 'How can I go into school and expect a child not to hit someone if I've hit out?'

'If I'm greedy,' said Andy, a long-term campaigner for human rights, 'how can I argue or demand that others shouldn't be?'

Gay has just joined Justice. She's campaigned for human rights for years. She was a social worker in local government, dealing with services for young adults with learning difficulties, people with disabilities, and the elderly.

'The day centres have been closed down,' she says. 'Now there's nowhere for these people to go. They're housebound and lonely. The council says budget cuts were necessary. Then you do a bit of research and discover the pay rises of the people at the top who ordered the cuts. It's despicable, and unjust.

LIVE FROM AN ILLEGAL INTERNET SERVICE PROVIDER

'In a way,' says Gay, 'we're doing hands-on social work here at St Paul's. People of the night, who sleep out on the streets, come here for protection. And yes, there are homeless drug and alcohol addicts. These people have nowhere to go. So, of course, we provide them with food and shelter. And support, because no one else does.'

It's early days but it appears the voice and message of Justice is spreading. Worldwide, as well as on our own doorstep. But perhaps we need more on-side worldwide movements – listeners and doers.

'What are you up to, today?' A young man from the Justice movement asks me.

'I'm a conduit,' says Ruby Q. 'Like most every working day, I pass on the essence of what you are saying and doing. It's up to the individual reading or hearing those words as to which path they choose to take.'

Justice for all

44 MUSICAL THOUGHTS

Piccolo stares at the ceiling. All around is bustle and chaos. Children and elderly adults alike are crying like babies. Noise is happening inside as well as out of his head. He wants rid of it. He wants... Someone is talking to him.

'Don't give up, Piccolo,' a voice says, briskly practical. 'Your father would be very disappointed.'

Piccolo's gaze slithers down from the ceiling and alights on an elderly lady dressed in cornflower blue that matches her eyes. He stares at her vacantly. Who is this woman? What does she know about his father? How does she know his name?

'I'd be disappointed, too,' the woman continues. 'You have so much to give to others. Music is a gift to be shared. Like happiness, love and nature.'

How does she know about his music? What is she doing here? And what's she rambling on about? Is she one of the mad cronies who hang out with Lady Catgut? Or some stray religious nutcase? He shuts his eyes, feigning sleep.

She's pressing something into his hand. He keeps his eyes tight shut.

'This will stay with you for as long as you need it, Piccolo,' she says.

How does this woman know his name? There's no sign above his head. He opens his eyes a tad.

'Don't forget those who've cared for you, those who love you. Grout and Nigel. Lady Catgut. Catgut himself. Rallan. Indigo. And, of course, Will.'

He's startled to hear her mention Will's name. How does she...? He opens his eyes a tad wider but she's gone. A nurse enters, and checks the medical notes.

'Did you see the elderly lady in blue? She left a moment ago,' he asks.

'No.' The nurse looks up, puzzled.

'I must have been dreaming,' he says, watching a smile relax away her concerned look.

After the nurse leaves he opens his hand. He's holding a clear blue stone, the shape of an olive. It's warm to the touch, and that warmth seems to stroke him gently like a spring sun. He sees, scents and hears salty waves swishing backwards and forwards over a pebbled beach. He breathes in slowly and deeply and, for the first time in a long while, he senses the warmth of a smile on his face.

5

'What d'you mean, kidnapped?' demands the President of the Federation. 'I'm the President of the Federation, I'll have you know. You can't go around kidnapping me, and the likes of me. You'll have to hand me back, sooner rather than later. Else you'll be in big trouble.'

The Federation President is met by dismissive laughter from his captors, who sit cross-legged around a fire. He also faces yawns, shrugs and scornful-sounding words in a foreign language.

'Alas, Mr President, we've stumbled against a rock and hit a hard place,' says a cultivated voice belonging to a dark-haired young man in flowing robes. 'We have tried to raise a ransom for your release but, worldwide, no one is interested.'

'What do you mean?' the Federation President retorts. 'There's the US President, the Pope, the new Emperor of Africa, the King of England, Lord di'Abalo, HOH Candelskin...'

The young man shakes his head.

'According to Cataract, Cyclops and Mote, the esteemed accountants of your Federation, Mr President,' he says, 'the very, very small print beyond the very small print in the contract you signed apparently forbids you any negotiation appertaining to ransom demands.'

The President's large jaw drops, creating a wobbly turkey pouch on his neck.

'Nothing personal,' the young man continues, 'but we were in the process of trying to kidnap someone else. Someone with a higher, more popular profile, who could help revitalise this region and bring an end to this bloody conflict.'

'And who might have a higher profile than me?' enquiries the Federation President huffily.

'Someone who offered us his services as we were making final preparations to kidnap him. He is already popular here and now he's a revered hero. He's got the US President talking to our President. He's got businessmen, educationalists worldwide talking to our people. You're old but you may have heard of him. His name is Hunky Doré.'

The Federation President is shocked into silence.

'HD – he's for me! HD supports our wounded countree-ee!' sings one young man, to a chorus of cheers and an outburst of snatches from HD's hit songs.

'If you ask or research,' says the young man, 'you'll find we are fighting only because we have been attacked

*and robbed by your so-called friends and allies. I would
advise you, Mr President, be careful of them – perhaps
more than of us.*

*'Now, we await the advice of our elders as to what we
should do with you.'*

44.5 HOMEWARD BOUND?

'So, we've had dinosaurs, the Flood, numerous Ice Ages, the great darkness post-Krakatoa, the Black Plague and other assorted colours thereof, and still they come back for more,' sighs Phlegm. 'As do we.'

'Mother Nature can be monstrously cruel at times,' Lord di'Abalo reflects as he strokes the black cat. The white cat watches his actions with narrowed green eyes from the edge of the settle. 'Yet she receives so little blame. God gets it all. I've always found that most curious.'

Phlegm coughs.

'It's an addictive game, Phlegm, playing with the lives of human beings,' says Lord di'Abalo. 'It's hard to give up.'

Phlegm nods.

'You want to go home, don't you?' says Di'Abalo.

Phlegm's eyes go as misty as a damp windscreen.

'Not long now, old chap,' says Di'Abalo. 'Please continue.'

Phlegm clears his throat.

'The girl's reports are proving popular.'

'Excellent. Keeps her busy, and away from investigating us. Not that she'll find much. And it's useful for the paper to show a compassionate, investigative side from time to time. Puts us on a pedestal, out of harm's reach. It means we can progress, privately and more comfortably with more important business.'

SECTION 6

*'Emergencies' have always been the pretext on which the
safeguards of individual liberty have been eroded.*
Friedrich August von Hayek (1899–1992)

45 NEW ANGEL DELIGHTS

Heaven is being refurbished. It is a chaos of ladders, paintbrushes, dust-sheets and an unholy smell of turpentine. There are disputes in the Design department. It's the NewComers. They wear white foundation and thick glossy lipstick, have over-rouged cheeks and sport brightly coloured curly wigs. They're always arguing with each other, as well as with the establishment. Yes, Heaven is awash with dust as well as hot air. It's not good. It's not cricket. And it's not Heaven; certainly not as it used to be.

'This new tortoise design *must* be used more widely,' a NewComer says decisively, stumbling over his words in TTT (thought-talk-transference). 'Think of the potential.'

'Actually, I can't see any,' says an OldTimer fluently.

'Why can't we leave well alone?' asks another OldTimer.

The NewComers smirk behind their hands.

'Imagine the revenue from a Tort'oid TV channel!' says the NewComer, with a loud guffaw.

The NewComers clap their hands, shout and roar with laughter. The OldTimers shudder at the non-TTT noise inside their heads that they're not used to.

'I dimly recall,' says a very old OldTimer, 'that the man

who developed the original tortoise and its carapace went ahead and introduced it to Earth without the consent of the Almighty.'

'In that case, as Himself is off with the fairies for an indeterminate length of time we may as well continue in the footsteps of the ancient originator,' says the first NewComer.'

'Tread carefully,' the very old OldTimer warns. 'When He returned and saw what cruelty had been inflicted on the tortoise He banished the designers.'

'I didn't know that,' says another OldTimer. 'Where did they go?'

'To Hell,' says the very old OldTimer. 'For ever and a day.'

The NewComers exchange looks from under lowered eyelids.

'Time to move on,' the first NewComer urges. 'Next on the agenda is gold taps. Oh, and hot water. They're a must. After all, this is 'eaven, innit? What do new arrivals think when they see all them common or garden taps, and cold (only) showers?'

46 CHIPS WITH EVERYTHING

The Noteians leave the police station by a side door and bundle the young woman into the back seat of a car. She's attached to one of the Noteians by handcuffs, just in case. The other Noteian climbs into the driving seat and drives off. The sullen-looking girl is silent until the police station is out of sight.

'So, what games do you two like to play?' she asks the young men disinterestedly as she stares vacantly out of the window.

'We like to play it straight,' says Handcuffs, the Noteian attached to her.

'Cool,' says the girl in a bored tone.

'We play games from time to time,' the driving Noteian, Driver, reflects.

'Oh, yeah?' A sneer spreads across the girl's tired, grubby face.

'We do guessing games, don't we, my brother?' says Driver.

'Coo. Like, how much did it cost you to spring me from the cop shop?' the girl demands.

'Yes, except in this instance they tried to pay us to take you away. They were keen for you not to do any more damage,' says Driver.

'Why don't I believe you?' she says.

'Probably because you haven't believed anyone in a long time, Maria,' says Handcuffs.

'They didn't know my name, so how did you?' she snaps, suspicious.

'We've known you since you were a little girl,' says Handcuffs. 'You were a dear little thing, bright, funny... I remember you in a sandpit, draped in your mother's purple feather boa, giving orders to everyone around.'

Maria's jaw drops. She stares at first one Noteian then the other. She looks away, seemingly at nothing in particular but actually at much. She's reviewing the years. When she had a mother, a father and two brothers, a family, albeit creaky and dysfunctional, as well as regular contact with her brother's kindly Noteian schoolfriends.

They enter a safe apartment via a deserted back alleyway. When they unlock her handcuffs Maria flies at doors and windows, tugging at handles in a desperate act to get out. She hides in corners, behind furniture, in an ominous silence. She starts screaming. It's when she tries to climb up the chimneybreast that one of the Noteians grabs hold of a leg, drags her back into the room and pinions her to the floor. She tries to knee him in the groin. At which point the other Noteian jabs a needle in her shoulder. Her eyes become saucers full of terror before she slumps into unconsciousness.

★ ★ ★

They bathe and gently examine her. She is skin and bones, bruised and scarred. They take blood to test for anaemia and much else. They dress her in a pair of their pyjamas and put her to bed, leaving the door open so as to keep an eye on her. As she sleeps the Noteians work intently side by side at their slabs. They eat large feta salads and dunk chunky fries into tomato ketchup.

'Oh, no!' murmurs Driver.

'Don't say we've run out of ketchup? I couldn't bear it,' says Handcuffs, raising one hand to his forehead in a dramatic pose.

'They've got him,' says Driver flatly. 'The Black Tartans have got the Phoenix.'

Handcuff leans over his friend's shoulder.

'How do you know?'

'I can see what he sees, hear what he hears.'

'How on earth can you do that?'

'I put a microchip into him when he was laid up with us, after the tsunami. I didn't tell you 'cos I wasn't convinced it'd work,' says Driver.

'I hope you discussed it with him.'

''Course I did,' says Driver.

'So, have you got anything? Like how he is? Or where he is?'

Driver's eyes are fixed on the screen.

'They've needled him. He's unconscious.'

'So we've lost contact.' Handcuffs can't keep disappointment from his voice.

'Not exactly,' says Driver.

'What does that mean?'

'His brain has been sending out messages since he was captured. The signal is weaker now that he's unconscious but—'

'Do you know where he is?'

Driver anxiously taps his foot on the floor.

'What is it? What's worrying you?' says Handcuffs.

'I don't know exactly where he is. I suspect it's Dekaydence because this new software identifies each scientist's voice and the Professor's voice is among them. They're conducting tests on him that I recognise but I'm picking up some kind of undercurrent, a vibe, if you like.'

'What does that mean?'

'Given his position, it's perfectly normal for the Phoenix to feel worried and/or frightened. But there's something else, something different. I can't explain it fully but it's like he's a clairvoyant. It's like he can see something in the future and I can't.'

'So why isn't he telling you what it is?'

Driver shrugs.

'I don't know. I created a secret chamber for his secrets that we can both access. Now it appears he's created an area that I can't get at, whatever I do. He's either cunning or desperate.'

'Or maybe both,' says Handcuffs.

47 THE TOWER OF EDEN

A thick white meringue of mist hovers above the garden and around the marquee, while the orchestra of birdsong grows denser. The early morning light tiptoes through the kitchen window where Lady Catgut has been cooking for several hours for the launch party of her secret project.

She's looking forward to the arrival of the four beautiful, talented young sisters from the next village who'll help her with the preparations for the buffet. Their two tall, handsome brothers will arrive soon to set up and run the bar. Later, all six will give a concert to a diverse crowd of people Lady Catgut sees as like a varied bunch of glorious flowers.

The Princess Indigo is a guest, having worked with Lady Catgut and Grout on the project. Nigel will attend; Piccolo won't. Indigo will bring Tommo. Ruby Q Cooper will bring Rallan and Elsa and half a dozen acquaintances from Justice. Hunky Doré, Petty Masters, the triplets and Schneek will come. HD is really keen to hear the band perform. The Face may come, which worries Petty because she'll bring her mouth with her and that can only mean trouble.

But before then...

Grout and Nigel are setting up tables, chairs and lighting in the marquee.

Edwina Gardening-Fork (pronounced Spade) and Young Miss Burgess are laying the tables with plates, cutlery and serviettes, filling vases with home-grown flowers and generally decorating the marquee.

Catgut will stay indoors with his music, tea and macaroons until he is summoned.

Piccolo remains in his room, reading. Only Lady Catgut is allowed access. She takes him food and beverages that she's pleased to see he devours hungrily, if somewhat abstractedly.

Guests begin arriving in the late afternoon when the sky is still bright and warm with sunshine. By 6pm everyone has arrived and every guest has a drink in their hand.

Catgut leads the way to the back of the house where, next to the kitchen garden, stands a 36ft-high tower wrapped in a haze of deep purple shot through with golden ribbons and bows. The excitement is palpable and grows as Catgut switches on the mike and calls for hush.

'Dear friends, old and new,' he says. 'Welcome. We are gathered here today to launch a dream that has been imagined and developed into a reality by my dear wife, Henrietta, with the help of her friend, Indigo, together with Grout, one of the three talented and beloved young men who have kindly taken on Etti and me. We're equally grateful to our sponsor, Lord di'Abalo, without whose generosity, help and support...'

There is a round of applause and Catgut continues.

'Etti's dream is a simple one – to grow good, unadulterated, healthy food that's available for all, throughout the year. And to show that it can be done for a family, friends, even a community. So, without further ado, allow me introduce to you – the Tower of Eden!'

Catgut punches the air with a triumphant clenched fist as, somewhere close by, Grout presses a button.

The purple haze and golden ribbons dissolve instantly to reveal a 36ft-tall, 50ft-wide circular tower made of solar panels and plithanium that glints in the sunlight and moves slowly, slowly on a rotating pedestal as it follows the axis of the sun.

The crowd cheer and applaud and, enthusiastically, join a queue to climb the staircase that entwines the building, to peer inside, while referring constantly to an informative pamphlet produced by the gardening journalists, Edwina Gardening-Fork and Young Miss Burgess.

Suddenly, Catgut runs across the garden and leaps on to a podium. He taps the music stand with his baton. There is coughing, shuffling and then a bar of silence at the end of which the music starts. The Summer movement from Vivaldi's 'Four Seasons'.

Curious, guests crane their necks to see if they can hear more. (Don't try this at home without a sensible child present.) Others see and hear, and draw nearer. The sight that greets them makes them catch their breath. Some leave the queue and draw closer to the beautiful sounds created by an orchestra of miniature and marginally larger musicians from the Imperial Orchestra of the Union. The soloist is known to many of them – it's miniaturised Nigel, playing as if inspired, a beatific smile on his face, his eyes closed as if in a heavenly dream.

Even those remaining in the queue – admiring the Tower's summer crops of sweetcorn, peppers, tomatoes, potatoes, beans, salad, grapes and kiwi fruit growing inside – stop to listen.

When the music ends Catgut leads the applause for the orchestra and cheers for Nigel, who has tears running down his face. Fortunately, Lady Catgut has created and treated him with a herbal gel to prevent his wet metal face from rusting.

In the interval people head for the buffet in the marquee. They pile their plates with home-made quiche, fish pie, baked potatoes and fresh salads. They return for seconds and/or thirds, as well as trifle, cake, and pudding. The young helpers refill glasses.

The music continues, as does the conversation. Members of Justice talk enthusiastically with Lady Catgut, Indigo and Grout, Edwina Gardening-Fork and Young Miss Burgess. All learn much from one another.

Later, as they watch fireworks fizz and crack and shoot colourful sparkling stars into the sky around the Tower, Indigo leans across to her friend Grout.

'I'm so proud of you,' she whispers.

'It was a team effort,' says Grout, blushing slightly. 'And we couldn't have done it without financial support from the anonymous benefactor who must remain so.'

'Yes,' says Indigo, giggling. 'Lord di'Abalo must never know what I've done.'

'I won't tell,' says Grout. 'But he might have guessed already, given you and Lady Catgut are so close.'

Indigo shrugs.

'Grout,' she says, slowly, 'I have a serious favour to ask.'

'Ask away.'

'My grandfather wants his throne, and heirs, to be secure,' says Indigo.

'Ye-es,' says Grout slowly. 'Is this a genetic or an engineering question?'

'Both.' She smiles at him sweetly, and lowers her voice. 'I want you to father my child.'

'What?' Grout, taking a long refreshing swig of his drink, starts coughing uncontrollably.

Indigo pats his back while several guests nearby tsk and tut and direct severe frowns at him. If they were in his place, he thinks, they'd fully understand his reaction.

'I want it done technologically, using test-tubes or whatever,' says Indigo. 'I don't want it to get personal and messy and interfere with you and your life. But you are brainier, stronger and kinder than almost everyone in my immediate family, so...'

'Indigo, I think this fruit cordial might be a tad strong for you,' Grout says, attempting to take the glass from her hand. 'Look, I am flattered by your unexpected offer but I think you ought to give yourself a few years before you decide what you do with your life and body.'

'I have thought long and hard,' says Indigo, imperious and regal, 'and I realise it is my duty to my grandfather and to my country. I have decided as I see fit. And equally, even though you don't appear to know it, Grout, dear, you are rather fit.'

She grins a wicked grin. Grout blushes geranium pink.

'Pretty soon, Indigo,' he says, in a voice he hopes is serious without sounding patronising, 'the queue for you will stretch from here to Timbuktu. I'm the last person you'll want then.'

He hears someone close by cough discreetly. He turns. It's Lady Catgut, her cheeks unusually flushed with...? Distress? Anger? Certainly, it's not drink, but what is it?

'A man has arrived from the local council,' Lady Catgut announces, crisp and cross. 'He says we have more glass in the Tower than is allowed by law. Unless we can prove him wrong the Tower of Eden will be demolished at the end of the week.'

48 LOSING A FRIEND

Piccolo remains beyond the fringes of the party. He keeps his door locked, opening up only to collect and return food trays left outside his room. On no account can he bump into Will. But when someone knocks on his door and calls out his name, he opens the door, knowing it'll be Rallan. He's shocked to see that the great bear of a man is now less than half the size he was when they were both prisoners underground in Dekaydence.

'How are you doing?' he mouths carefully to the deaf man, and draws with his hands the shape of the big stomach he once had.

Rallan mimes strenuous weightlifting and a stance based on a yoga exercise.

Piccolo laughs.

'How are you doing?' Rallan points to Piccolo, with a thumbs-up sign and a questioning look.

'Come in and see,' says Piccolo, taking Rallan by the arm.

Piccolo shows Rallan the pile of books by his bed.

'Music therapy?' says Rallan questioningly.

Piccolo nods.

'I can't do Dekaydence any more,' he confides. 'I can't take the pressure. I came so close to...'

Rallan nods understandingly.

'You've had big trouble in your life, Piccolo. Big pain is to be expected.'

'I see this chap,' says Piccolo. 'Ted's a retired psychotherapist, highly regarded, and he's come to live around here. The Catguts begged him to take me on... and, after some thought, he did.'

'The Catguts are kind people,' says Rallan.

'Yes, they are,' says Piccolo. 'I realise, more and more, how lucky I am. How things could have gone wrong for me. But didn't.'

'You have good friends.'

'Yes, and you're one of them. And now I want to use music to help others. Can I pick your brains?'

'Sure, but they won't be around for long.'

'Oh! You off on tour or something?'

Rallan focuses on folding and unfolding his fingers.

'I am going away but not on tour.'

'So, where are you going?'

Rallan stares into space.

'I've no idea where I'm going, Piccolo. Or when. I haven't told Ruby Q but I've been diagnosed with dementia.'

Piccolo feels his innards somersault. He doesn't know what to say. He wants to hug the man, hold back whatever it is that is damaging him. Rallan was like a father to him and now he's losing this gentle, kindly man, a real father figure.

Piccolo looks at Rallan and wonders how he must be

feeling. How is he coping? He thinks of Ruby Q. How will she cope when she hears the news?

'I shall look out for Ruby Q, as you looked out for me,' Piccolo blurts out. 'And wherever you and your mind go, however far away from me you travel, you will be in my heart and head, always.'

The floorboards creak outside the room. The door is ajar and Piccolo spots the laden tea tray on the floor, with two cups. Lady Catgut must have seen them together, he concludes, wondering how much of their conversation she overheard.

In fact, Lady Catgut heard none of it. But the person she asked to carry up the tea tray did hear what Rallan Cooper had to say. And that person was his daughter, Ruby Q. At some point, much later, she will talk about it with Lady Catgut. For now, she walks down to the river and cries.

49 JUDGING TIMES

Schneek mutters to himself as he pushes the large bespoke pram containing the baby triplets. He didn't sign up to be Petty Masters's personal assistant to become a nanny. He wanted to be in the fashion business, travel the world, meet interesting people, have his finger on the fashion button and buttonhole.

The three young boys are adorable but they are a handful. And here he is, pushing a heavyweight pram up and down the streets in Smithfield's, wondering how much longer Petty will be in her meeting in the tiny old pub with some tall, ancient man in a dark suit while he, Schneek, is desperate, simply desperate, for a hot strong coffee. Perhaps, he sighs deeply, perhaps it's time to look for another job.

Inside the dark, secluded pub the respected judge, Wiggins, listens thoughtfully to his luncheon guest, who's on her second family tin of cream crackers.

'So are you persuaded to the cause?' says Petty Masters.

'I've never needed persuading,' Wiggins replies, with a smile. 'Even before my children got at me. Before others, including your good self, put forward the arguments, I decided that politics is far too important to be run by politicians. That society is moving in the wrong direction. And that we're heading for a social lemming suicide, if you ask me.'

'But you've done nothing to stop the decay,' says Petty.

'I have done a few things. Behind the scenes.'

'Such as?'

Wiggins smiles.

'Well, let me think,' he says. 'Ah! North is free.'

Petty's eyes widen.

'How did you...?'

'It wasn't exactly difficult to prove North isn't the Phoenix. And, luckily, the presiding judge is an avid dog lover who applauded the behaviour of North and Pa, his fellow "get-stuck-in" passenger. He got the court to award them both a goodly sum of money, which the two men decided to donate to two dog charities, one London-based and one national.'

'So you do support Justice?'

'Indeed. And here's my cheque, by the way, to pass on to them. I take it you are aware of the subversive elements within the movement, as well as the Dekaydence spies.'

'We have one or two people under surveillance,' says Petty. 'But now, with North back on the case...'

'And the Face off it?'

'Yes, much to the relief of us all,' says Petty. 'The Face suffers badly with foot and mouth disease. Seemingly, there's no cure and no other role for her, at least within the GeeZer movement.'

Wiggins nods understandingly.

'I think my dear brother suffers from a mild form of it,' says Wiggins. 'It seemed to develop when he went to work in the City.'

An ad'um rings. Wiggins apologises as he takes a call that's soon over.

'Speak of the devil,' he says with a grin, scooping up his coat.

'Nothing wrong?' Petty asks.

'On the contrary,' says Wiggins, beaming. 'My brother Cedric asks that I fetch him home immediately.' He chuckles as he glances at his ad'um. 'Thing is, any moment now he'll receive a surprise present. Something he can never resist, a chocolate cake. I ordered it a few days ago from the 2-2 Divine Dekaydence range to cheer him up. He could well have finished it by the time I get there.'

'I hope he saves you a piece.'

'I jolly well hope he doesn't,' says Wiggins. 'Courtesy of a prank conducted by my dear brother, I haven't touched chocolate cake since I was a knee-high to a sugar mouse.'

50 GOLDEN OLDIES

Grout has completed trials testing the safety of the antidote to the killer virus on mini-test'oids he's created. Lord di'Abalo orders the trials continue immediately on injured glad'oids and other creatures imprisoned underground in the arena.

Grout is working all hours to ensure everything is safe and in order. On this project as well as others. He is under pressure and senses his boss, the Professor, is increasingly put out by his protégé's scientific and technological prowess and his progress within the company. For once, it appears Di'Abalo's admiration of Grout hinders rather than helps.

There are large glass partitions between the laboratories, which means while Grout is busy making notes he fails to see that Innit and Bodkin are where they shouldn't be – in the next room.

'I gotta get Wassit out of the arena, and fast,' Innit confides in Bodkin. 'Given the reconstruction job they're doing on glad'oids, by Tuesday week he could be rebuilt as a teapot. And I'll never recognise him. He'll be gone. I can't bear to think of him not being around, Bods. I can't cope with another loss, not after my Jezza.'

Bodkin ignores the reference to Innit's girlfriend, Jezza, who died in the London tsunami.

'Even if you did get him out, what then?' says Bodkin.

Innit nods at the window.

'I get Grout to work on him. Grout'll get him back to normal. No problem.'

'I don't reckon even Grout could do that, In,' says Bodkin.

'Wanna bet? How much d'you think he'd charge?'

Bodkin snorts.

'In, I doubt he'd charge. Grout is weird like that. But think on it, In. Wassit would need constant medical attention. And if he did recover, he couldn't live anywhere that's been Dekaydence'd, could he? They'd get him, and then what?'

'If only I'd been quicker in the tsunami I could've gotten hold of old man Cataract's legs.'

'I don't think they'd look quite right on Wassit,' Bodkin ventures.

'No, Bods!' Innit snaps, irritated. 'Cataract has golden legs.'

'What d'you mean? As in running and medals? At his age?'

'No, Bods. He hid his money in his legs, didn't he? They replaced the bones with his gold bars. I reckon that's why he's in hospital now, he's had his ruddy arms done as well.'

'Coo-er,' says Bodkin. 'He's a real Golden Oldie, then,

in' he, In? But he's been good to you, ain't he, getting you on some nice little earners?'

'Yeah, he's been good to me.' Innit nods, thoughtfully.

Bodkin wonders if he didn't just catch a glint in Innit's eyes. Bods tastes joy. At last, his friend is returning to form.

'Bods?' says Innit, softly, backing away from the lab window. 'Can you reach out your hand to the rack on the table and lift out that solitary test tube?'

Bodkin's eyes widen dramatically.

'The one labelled "virus"?' he says nervously.

'That's the one, Bods,' says Innit brightly. 'Gently does it, old man. Gently does it. It's got a good home to go to.'

Bodkin gulps, finding his shaking hand has communicated its unsteadiness to his knees.

51 A RIGHT TURN

Years ago, not long after it was built, the concrete car park by the river was voted one of the ugliest car parks in the country. Privately owned and managed, it was then privately disowned and unmanaged. No one admitted responsibility for it. But all had ideas aplenty as to its future.

Knock it down. Sell the land for development. Keep it as an example, a warning even, as to how ugly four concrete storeys can look, even if they do sit on the north bank of the river, facing south. Arguments raged on. Several lawyers purred contentedly, as the process saw their children through private education over a number of years.

One day the town awakens to find the area is cordoned off by tall fences and sharp railings. The car park itself is wrapped in something like a dense crepe bandage with large lettering on it declaring: 'JUSTICE – working to make things better'.

Days progress into weeks; 'facts' grow out of rumours. Transit vans come and go, day and night. Some claim they've seen deliveries of rolls of black carpet, numerous panes of glass and loads of trees. Others have heard banging and crashing, cursing and drilling. There's talk the car park is about to become a detention centre for young offenders. Or a new shopping mall. If the council knows anything, it's saying nothing. Instead, it puts up pages of official jargon on lamp posts that no one understands.

One morning, as people pass by what they now call The Bandage, they find the perimeter fence has gone. The Bandage itself remains wrapped but now there's a moat around it, a drawbridge at the main entrance and gardens beyond, one for each season, with seats for picnics and play areas for children.

People start to sit out contentedly in the sunshine, reading, watching their children play, or feeding the ducks on the river.

Time moves on but The Bandage remains a mystery.

One day in the early hours when the dawn chorus is at full throttle, a group of men and women arrive wearing masks of the Green Man, the spirit of nature and rebirth. They arrive with Justice banners. They hand out leaflets and talk with people about the importance of local communities, local produce and recycling, re-use, bartering markets and local governance.

Someone blows a horn, the crowd quietens and the bandage round The Bandage dissolves. The car park is revealed. There is a stunned silence. In place of grey concrete there is soft gardenia paint. The long bleak open slits that let in rain, hail and sleet now have plithanium windows that let in light and warmth. The roof area is awash with blossoming fruit trees; the south-facing wall is covered with vines of black and red grapes and kiwi fruit.

There are cheers and enthusiastic applause. What exactly is going on? Could this be a new garden centre? Well...yes and no.

Men and women from Justice, some wearing legal wigs dyed the colours of the rainbow, take groups of visitors round the building, reminding them to be aware of small tractors collecting or delivering to each floor.

Visitors discover parking bays by the walls have been turned into raised beds for growing vegetables, salads, herbs and fruits, corn, chilli, peppers, potatoes, tomatoes, eggplants and beans. Mushrooms happily relish their residence in darker, danker areas. Chickens and goats are living summer outside and will winter within, providing compost as well as eggs, yoghurt, cheese and milk. An apiary and tea bushes thrive in poly-tunnels. An irrigation system runs on all floors, fed by a collection of water butts and tanks, and the river.

Yes, behind the new drawbridge a new market flourishes in London, a two-acre farm on four storeys to which come household cooks and acclaimed chefs, having heard about the new Tower of Eden. There is a café on the roof, selling refreshments made from in-house produce. Seeds and seedlings are sold in the ground-floor farm shop, alongside produce and helpful literature. There are talks and courses on what and how to grow, nurture and reap, held in lecture rooms sited in the centre of the second and third floor, lit by harvesting gas from the sewers.

Lady Catgut and Indigo take turns in managing this city farm and training new managers. They are delighted at the interest from schools and colleges, teachers and young people, who feel they want do something similar with their own local neglected or abandoned land and buildings.

Catgut eagerly awaits the new Tower's red wine. The Crown Prince himself has ordered several cases for personal consumption.

Indigo is thrilled that part of her mother's inheritance money has gone to good use, and hopefully news of the project will spread far and wide, and other Towers of Eden will germinate countrywide.

BREAKING NEWS

Ruby Q Cooper reports for *The Daily Unigraph*.

The young man lives a few doors from a couple renowned for their magical work in TV and film. As a child he'd pop by to see what they were creating in model, computer or sculpture. His favourite was a model black and white cat with green twinkling eyes that followed him around the room.

A few years on, the woman modeller is preparing for her daily trip to the hospital to see her dying husband. The boiler packs up. Her boilerman is away. She finds a company a few towns away that'll do the job that day for cash.

Within the hour three men arrive in a large, battered white van. She lays out tea, coffee and a packet of biscuits that are, or were, her husband's favourite. She tells them she'll be back at the day's end. As she closes the front door she hears the men's feet echoing in the loft where the old boiler is.

She returns to find the men packing their toolkits into the van. The house is warm and she gives them the cash. Call if there's a problem, they say. The boiler packs up in the night. In the morning she calls them but there's no

LIVE FROM AN ILLEGAL INTERNET SERVICE PROVIDER

reply. After a week, the young neighbour, now at college studying design, uses his computer to discover the 'firm' has disappeared, along with the men and van.

The woman loses her husband. The funeral comes and goes, the memorial service, too. Someone else fixes the boiler. She cries. She thinks. She finds work in a local school. She visits friends and makes new ones. Several years pass.

She receives a party invitation from the young man. 'I want you to meet my friends,' he says, adding excitedly, 'And someone very special.'

She decides to dress up for the occasion but can't find her jewellery box. She calls the young man and asks if he'd look in the loft.

'Should I look under the floorboards?' he calls down to her.

'No, we liked things above board, as it were.'

'Well, there's nothing here. Except an empty biscuit wrapper.'

The memory nearly knocks her over.

'I remember,' she says. 'We put everything up there. Our old work, my jewellery box. I forgot all about it until...the boiler had to be replaced. They took my money and vanished. Police never did find them.'

The young man gathers information that's forwarded

to an independent judicial reform group, established and empowered by the King himself who is persuaded by measured arguments from Will and Wiggins.

The young man is sent a camera, the size, shape and colour of a table tennis ball, which is covered in tiny bumps. In the loft he follows the instruction: rub in hands for ten seconds then gently open hands. The bumps blink, as though adjusting to the lack of light. The camera flies from his hands and begins scanning the loft, every inch, including photographs on the wall of the missing sculptures and jewellery, including the blue necklace and matching earrings, a gift from her husband on their silver wedding anniversary.

The young man quietly closes the loft door behind him.

The information provides fingerprints and DNA that produce identities leading to three neighbouring addresses. A second report delivered to the reform group is considered and approved.

The Phoen'oid is focused not on the smart new estate properties but on what's inside. Software accesses the first home, neutralises alarms and cameras, and renders all life unconscious for 30 minutes. The location of the stolen goods is pinpointed. The Phoen'oid enters as a streak of lightning, flies direct to the handful of models and sets a program that dissembles them and then reassembles them in the widow's loft.

The same procedure happens in the second house.

In the third house the Phoen'oid finds a woman, collapsed mid-vomit in the bathroom, wearing the blue necklace and earrings. Again he sets a program so that the jewellery reassembles on the widow's bedside cabinet.

The Phoen'oid's software detects what goods are important to each of the three men, and destroys them all.

When they awake the next morning the three men can't stop sneezing as showers of tiny red and gold feathers fall about their faces. The feather shower happens whenever they go to buy, borrow or beg money to get a replacement for what's gone missing. In time, the feathers, the sneezing, happen so often the men give up and move to Spain. They get sun on their faces but mostly it's feathers. No one has a clue where they come from.

The widow weeps with joy on the recovery of her treasures. She knows it's down to the young man. The woman sells the sculptures, save one, and wears the necklace and matching earrings to the young man's party. At the end of the evening she presents the young man with a gift. He unwraps it and grins. His girlfriend claps her hands with delight. The widow smiles.

'You're sure you're not too old for it?' she asks anxiously.

'Never too old for this,' says the young man, gently stroking the model black and white cat with its green twinkling eyes. 'I hope our children and grandchildren feel the same way.' He smiles at his girlfriend, who smiles at the elderly widow and says, 'How can you not love this dear, handsome little face?'

Justice for all

52 RELATIVE VALUES

'It's been a long time since we met up, Catty. Far too long,' says the King, sitting in a small hospital lounge with Cataract, who's dressed, his travel case by his side, eagerly awaiting Wiggins to chauffeur him home.

'We're both too busy with business, Maj.' Cataract smiles. 'You with your Crown. Me with my European half-crowns.'

'It can't be easy, looking after so many different economies.'

Cataract shrugs.

'I enjoy it. As you, I believe, enjoy your work.'

The King nods in agreement.

'I work to keep the Crown secure for my son and his heirs. To maintain a strong backbone within the country.'

'Even though Di'Abalo forces you to live in reduced circumstances.' Cataract shakes his head. 'With only a part-time butler in the Royal household.'

'It's not so bad,' says the King, in what could be termed, unwittingly, a cavalier manner. 'I miss the Armageddon conservatory but there's much for which to be grateful.'

'Is there?' says Cataract dryly.

The King ponders.

'I have a son, two grandchildren. I have duties. Oh, and...' The King lowers his voice. 'Every day Di'Abalo sends me a secret supply of Dekaydence puddings.'

'Really?' says Cataract, suddenly and keenly alert. He lowers his voice. 'What do you get, Maj? Can it really be better than what we got at school, at dear old Note?'

The King rolls his eyes in ecstasy. Cataract watches. Saliva dribbles from the King's mouth. He comes close to swooning.

'Hang on a minute, I'm forgetting my manners,' says Cataract, sitting bolt upright. 'And my chocolate cake.'

With an elegant movement of his hand he indicates a dark, luscious-looking chocolate cake on a side table close by.

Both men stare at it, in awe and wonder.

'Alas,' says the King. 'I am full to the brim of my Crown and the breadth of my waistcoat with Dekaydence treacle tart and custard.'

'In which case,' says Cataract, 'I shall rein in my desire and have a slice after you depart.'

The King says nothing, but continues to look, admire and desire the cake.

'Cut yourself a slice, Maj, and have it later with your tea,' says Cataract.

'Jolly decent of you, old thing,' says the King, leaping up to cut and wrap for himself a singularly large helping of cake. 'When I visit you at home I'll bring you a treacle tart.'

'With hot custard, Maj!' Cataract commands eagerly.

'With hot custard, dearie!' The King agrees readily. 'With or without lumps?'

'I don't care, Maj!' Cataract says, cavalierly. "You choose.'

'Do you remember our Noteian midnight feasts?' the King says dreamily.

Cataract's eyes glaze over with joy.

'Oh, what fun they were.'

'D'you recall the night we hid a pillowcase full of Easter eggs in young Wiggins's bed.'

'Rather!' Cataract giggles. 'It was bitterly cold, wasn't it? Then the heating came on unexpectedly, boiling hot. When Wiggs climbed into bed and, by mistake, into the pillowcase...'

'Got covered in the stuff! Stuck like glue to the sheets!'

'That's right, Maj! Got banned from the tuck shop for the rest of term and has not touched chocolate from that day to this.'

'Hah! That means all the more for us, my dear, does it not!'

'Indeed, Maj,' says Cataract. 'Indeed!'

'We must do this again, and soon,' says the King, rising from his chair and kissing the top of Cataract's head. 'Call me when you feel settled at home and I'll pop over. We'll have a PPP – a Private Pudding Party. Just the two of us!'

'Great Wallop, Maj! See you at the end of the week!'
'You're on, dearest. The end of the week it is!'

6

'What d'you mean, kidnapped?' the US President demands of the General over the wire. 'He's the President of the Federation. You don't go about losing a President. Globally, it doesn't look so good. So, whosoever has got him, you gotta force them to hand him back, immediately, if not sooner. Else you and your soldiers are in big trouble. It's dereliction of duty, man.'

'Yessir!' the General responds. 'Problem is, Mr President, there's no definite clue as to who took him or why. It's not easy to track down this unknown, unnamed group asking for a ransom but communicating only via a mailbox in Bognor Regis.'

'Bognor who?' demands the President impatiently.

'It's a quaint old seaside town in Britain, sir,' says the General. 'And the leads go in every direction, except straight. The only identities we've managed to trace to a mailbox are a handful of doddery old men who once worked as circus clowns.'

'So, out there, in the wild terrain of the eastern provinces – fightin' going on all around – you're tellin' me a bunch of old British guys – with a strange, worrisome habit of dressing up as clowns – go kidnap the President of the Federation and hole him up in some rundown seaside joint in Merrie England for a crumpet and scone and an ice cream or two?'

'I know what you mean, sir,' says the General unhappily. 'But, at present, we got nothing much else to go on.'

'Try putting your feet on the ground, General, before I get to thinking you belong in it.'

'Yessir,' says the General, nodding miserably.

The US President cuts the phone line on the General. He ponders for a few moments and then makes a call.

'We're in a spot of trouble.' The US President speaks softly into the tiny ad'um fixed under his Presidential badge of office.

'Yep, the story's just broken on the news,' the President of the Dekaydence World Bank & Federal Reserve responds. 'Do we have any idea where the poddleypoo is? Or who's got him?'

'Nope,' says the US President, deciding it better not to mention The Bognor Regis Clowns Theory.

'The media's having a field day, Mr President. Blaming us and baying for our blood, and trying to canonise the widowed poodle,'specially now they've spotted his new, much-rehearsed limp.'

'We should make a move on the gold. Get it back, pronto,' says the US President. 'We got friends in the vaults, have we not?'

'It's in hand, kid,' says the President of the Dekaydence World Bank, with a deep chuckle. 'Man, have we got some high flyers on this job. They're in their own league.'

'Great stuff!' says the US President.

'Yeah!' laughs the President of the Dekaydence World Bank. 'I shouldn't be telling you this, it's beyond tip-top secret, but I've had a few beers and...' He chuckles. 'These guys are strongmen, in all ways. But they're clever and cute. They travel with a funfair, do strongman stuff and keep well fit. When they're off site, as it were, they're in disguise. You'd never give them a second look.'

'How come?' says the US President, intrigued.

'They become respectable old men, with sticks and frames. They look so frail and respectable that in the subway people offer them their seats. But on their real job they dress up in wild wigs, bright lipstick and big pyjama bottoms. They become clowns and never the same one twice. And, strangely, as they work and get their goodies, they never ever get caught on camera. No matter how good that camera is. Anyways, I'd best get going, Mr Pres. I need another drink. Talk soon, y'all.'

The US President puts down the phone. You couldn't make it up, he thinks as he searches the web, curious about the attraction of Bognor Regis.

52.5 SEEDS OF CHANGE

The council's building inspector arrives, confirming glass must be removed from the Tower of Eden.

'How much exactly?' asks Lady Catgut, intervening before Catty loses his temper.

'Every pane of glass down one side,' says the inspector, making notes. 'You can decide which side.'

'How remarkably generous of you,' says Catgut. 'I'd never have thought—'

'By the way.' Lady C speaks firmly over Catgut. 'For health and safety's sake, I must tell you none of the windows is glass. I did inform your colleague, they're solar panels. And to remove them would defeat the object of the exercise of this revolving greenhouse.'

'Greenhouse?' the inspector repeats, making more notes and watching the edifice turn slowly on its revolving base. 'Odd sort of design. Thought it was some kind of folly.'

'Spot on!' exclaims Lady C. 'It's a grand folly where we grow food for our community and beyond.'

The building inspector's face lights up further. He makes more notes, a smile not quite reaching his eyes.

'If you're selling produce, madam, that turns the greenhouse, or folly, into commercial premises, and a different, higher rate of council tax.'

'Ah, but we don't use money, we use goods and services as payment.'

'So you're conducting business under the wire?' The inspector's eyes glitter as he quickly writes more in his notebook.

'I have yet to come into contact with any wires,' says Lady C. 'We are conducting ourselves as people have done worldwide for centuries, before the corrupting pollution of money arrived. What we're doing is legal. In fact, we have supportive documents from Justice, signed by the Lord High Justice Wiggins himself. Would you like to see them?'

The inspector is somewhat taken aback as he examines the documents. He returns the papers and accepts Lady C's offer to taste her home-produced cheese and orchard pears, home-made elderflower cordial, oat and honey flapjacks and macaroon pyramids. His mood is so much improved that he promises to revoke the council's order and offers to return the following weekend to do some gardening – all in exchange for a bagful of vegetables for which he insists on paying with several hours of his labour.

SECTION 7

If you're going through hell, keep going.
Winston Churchill (1874–1965)

53 THE INVADERS

Bhupi is having a tough time with the NewComers and has called an assembly.

'There have been complaints,' he begins in TTT (thought-talk-transference).

The NewComers begin a chorus of loud, affronted noises, definitely not in TTT. Bewigged heads are tossed, in the manner of an outraged Regency dandy or a regular turkey.

'Despite warnings,' Bhupi continues, 'NewComers continue to contravene the strict dress code of this place that demands clear skin, bare feet or flesh-coloured socks, and a white cotton nightdress. Instead, you wear lipstick, false eyelashes, wigs, baggy pyjamas, orange and purple socks and clumpy black "bovva" boots.'

Someone blows a farting whistle. Another a raspberry. A third a lugubrious horn.

Giggles and outrage explode around the room.

'And that's another thing,' says Bhupi. 'We have received innumerable complaints of bad and inappropriate behaviour.'

The farting whistle repeats itself. The horn plays a high-pitched staccato laugh.

'That's it! Inappropriate behaviour!' says Bhupi, sorely

affronted. 'There are banana skins everywhere. You bring party poppers, screeching whistles and whoopee cushions into meetings...'

An orgy of real noise emanates from such items.

Bhupi tries to raise his soft voice.

'...when you know full well that noise is strictly forbidden in this place. So I hand you over to Jack and the three Clives, who'll inform you as to what will happen next.'

'After lengthy discussions the committee has made a decision,' says Jack briskly. 'NewComers are to be held apart in soundproofed accommodation on the outskirts of Heaven.'

'Not on your nelly button!' is among the more polite utterances hurled out loud into the air. The place is in uproar. Jack waits for the noise to subside.

'Those wishing to live by the rules of Heaven will undergo schooling and training for a year and a day. Those refusing to live by Heaven's rules will be returned forthwith to their former place of residence.'

The uproar continues. Jack and the three Clives exchange glances. They all know that forthwith might easily become fifth-with or even fiftieth-with as no one has any idea how the clowns entered Heaven or how they can be removed from it. It appears the clowns are able to come and go at random. There are no security checks. No guards to prevent them. Jack and the Clives sit down to discuss a plan. Unusually, the NewComers say nothing. They're too busy smirking behind their squeaky hand glove puppets of famous leaders, which include the President of the Federation.

'Where d'you get them gloves?' one clown asks of another.

'A little shop in Bognor Regis,' replies the second clown. 'I'm surprised you don't know it.'

'Oh, but I do,' the first clown muses. 'I'm just surprised you got hold of what was a special order. For me. So, best hand 'em over, *now*! or they'll be trouble.'

54 NORTH TO THE FORE

'How do we do this?' North asks Ruby Q, when they meet in a London pub.

Ruby Q smiles.

'I ask questions. You answer them. I write up the interview. If the editors like it, it gets published in *The Daily Unigraph*.'

'Right,' North says uneasily.

Ruby Q laughs.

'I've had it on good authority that it *is* less painful than having a tooth taken out.'

North manages a nervous half-smile.

'OK, let's go.'

'Let's start with your beginning and background.'

'OK.' North nods. 'My parents were teachers passionate about education. I went to a "problem" school full of "problem" children. I was one of them. I did stupid kid stuff and got into trouble regularly. At some point I realised I was wasting my life. I changed my behaviour to see if things improved. My folks were supportive. I found something I wanted to learn. Now I'm a fully qualified science teacher working, by choice, in "problem" schools with "problem" kids, hopefully helping them overcome their problems by introducing them to different opportunities.

'Trouble is, education standards in this country are collapsing. One school told me that students had to cut and paste exam answers from textbooks. I told them that's not teaching. And you don't, you can't learn in that way. "It gets results and that's all that matters," was the examiner's response. Apparently, that's all the government is interested in.'

'That's a shocking story in itself,' says Ruby Q. 'I'd like to pursue it at some point.'

'I've plenty more stories like that,' says North. 'People in government must be made aware of what's going on and wrong, on the cheap. That's what Justice is for.'

'So, what next?'

'I'm thinking of moving to France because they value education.'

'But...?'

'I'm frustrated by the system here, Miss Cooper. This country is deep in trouble and debt. Why? Because we've been encouraged into it by government. We shouldn't be cutting spending because we'll be making thousands, no, millions of people unemployed, many of them young people. So, say we cut all, or maybe 90 per cent of taxes. Cut control. We fire up manufacturing industries because they form part of a country's engine and drive.

'We should slash the government's annual budget, and taxation. Do rigorous auditing – of politicians, councils, health and education authorities, *et al.* Let's insist that politicians fulfil their job description – to protect the constitution and, thus, we erase whips to ensure all politicians have free votes. They can speak from their hearts, not the party song-sheet.

'But I suspect none of the above will happen. We no longer live in a democracy, Miss Cooper. We exist in a demockrazy, a shallow, loony entertainment industry that drugs people into lethergy. So this country fast becomes the new third world, soon to be run exclusively by the Company of Dekaydence.'

North has much more to say. And at the end of the interview he has a question for Ruby Q.

'Do I get to see this before it's published?'

'Not usually, no,' she says. 'But because I want to be sure I've understood what you're saying, I want you to read it before I submit it.'

'Do I have to have my picture taken?' asks North.

'No,' Ruby Q replies. 'Someone on the train got a good shot of you intervening in the dog fight. Bizarre thing is, in the background you get a glimpse of an elderly lady in blue who used to be our cleaning lady before she moved on.'

They're both silent for some moments.

'I 'd like to drop those dog-baiting men and others like them into a deep pit,' says Ruby Q. 'They can fight all they like. They don't get out until they're carried out, dead.'

'Wow.' North takes in a sharp breath. 'Tough talk, Miss Cooper.'

'If they don't understand what they're doing and can't be retrained, how else do you stop these people and their evil ways?' says Ruby Q. 'How long must animals as well as people have to suffer in this wretched god-forsaken world?'

55 GOLDEN MOMENTS

Cataract is devouring a large slice of chocolate cake – his sixth since the King left an hour ago before – when his younger brother, Wiggins, KC, enters the hospital lounge.

Wiggins smiles indulgently.

'I can see you're back on form, old chap,' says Wiggins, bending to kiss his older brother on the top of his head.

Cataract's eyes glitter.

'*Absolument, mon brave.* On my sixth slice. Warming up for the seventh. You couldn't have sent me a better going-home present. Thank you, dear boy. Thank you.'

'Glad you like it.' Wiggins chuckles happily. He sniffs the air discreetly. What a relief: his brother no longer smells of fish and urine. But, wait a second, there is an acrid smell. Perhaps the scent of an embittered elderly man? He wonders.

'Wiggi, dear,' says Cataract, his eyes suddenly dazed and unfocused. 'I feel a tad sick. Might need a bowl or something. Could you call for the nurse?'

'Maybe too much cake, old chap. Just take a few deep breaths. I'll get someone.'

Wiggins can't find anyone so he presses the alarm bell inside the lounge door. He turns round to check his brother. Cataract is slumped in his chair, his eyes blurred and blinking fast, as though he's trying to expel dust or some other foreign body.

'Cedric! What's the matter?' Wiggins moves swiftly across the room to sit next to his brother.

'Beluga,' whispers Cataract, with a sob. 'Beluga.'

'It's OK, dearest,' says Wiggins, wondering why Cataract is thinking of a childhood pet. 'Deep breaths. You'll see pusscat when you get to Heaven. But you're not going there yet. I won't hear of it. Anyway, you can't go because I suspect they don't do a chocolate cake anywhere near the high standards you demand.'

The Royalist nurse bustles in, and quickly examines Cataract.

'He's had quite a bit of cake,' says Wiggins. 'He thought he was going to be sick. But this is different, isn't it?'

The nurse frowns.

'Stay with him until I return with the doctor,' she says, briskly quitting the room

As if he would leave his old brother when he's obviously not well, thinks Wiggins.

He leans forward and takes Cataract's hand. It's unusually hot. Gently, gently, Wiggins strokes it, talking softly to his brother, who appears to be drifting into sleep. It's odd, he thinks, Cataract's skin is dry and rough to the touch. This isn't normal, he knows. His brother has always had very soft, smooth skin.

Wiggins examines Cataract's hand. The skin is oddly

scaly. And the scales appear to be spreading. Across his face. Around his eyes. Cataract is looking less human, more like...a reptile.

Wiggins wants to shout for the nurse but doesn't want to leave his brother's side. He strokes his brother's head and is startled to see the pupils in his terrified eyes focused on him, sharp and bright, not plain pupil black but as fiery red and orange as burning coals. Wiggins drops Cataract's hand, and runs to press the alarm bell when...

Cataract emits a terrifying scream as flames burst forth from his eyes.

For a split second Wiggins is frozen with shock. The fire alarm sounds. The noise is deafening and relentless. Wiggins scans the room for a source of water, a fire blanket, anything. He seizes a soda siphon and starts spraying his brother's face, at which point flames erupt from Cataract's body.

Wiggins cries out his brother's name as he throws his heavy-duty coat over Cataract's body, trying to staunch the flames. He runs to the door. He won't leave his brother but he must get help. Immediately. At once. He shouts, he shouts again, only louder.

He turns to tell his brother that help is coming but... his brother is no longer there. Only the chair, with the remains of the coat. Wiggins stares in disbelief. He looks around the room. Behind the curtains. Inside a tall cupboard. Under a dining table. Nothing. No one. No smell of burning. No smell of burning flesh. No Cataract. Only a strong, acrid smell of carbon.

Wiggins's pulse is racing, though he's shivering and his hands feel like ice. Where is Cataract? He stares at the chair in puzzled disbelief. Gingerly, he lifts up his smouldering coat with a pair of tongs he grabs from the grate. Odd. The chair is not in the least bit singed. There's a coat button on the seat, another on the floor. Then he sees four golden ingots, two short ones under the arms of the chair, two longer ones on the floor.

Wiggins is shaking. He's conscious that the little boy inside him desperately needs his older brother. He wants the clever, bossy, difficult control freak to reach out and comfort him, tell him it was all a bad joke, a nightmare. As he did when they were young.

56 THE TAMING OF THE SHREWD

The two Noteian doctors bring Maria to the Catguts' home in Sussex. Lady Catgut is appalled at her deathly pallor and the needle marks on the girl's arms. She's saddened that such a young girl should be so listless, so indifferent to everything and everyone about her. She doesn't speak and her eyes appear permanently glazed.

Lady Catgut shows her to her room, with its en suite bathroom. She explains the workings of the TV and the shower. How to make herself tea or coffee. How she's welcome to partake of the home-made biscuits and cordials in the mini-fridge.

Lady Catgut is about to talk about mealtimes when she realises Maria is staring out of the window, her hand clutching a grubby old plastic bag containing, Lady Catgut supposes, her few possessions. She probably hasn't taken in a word I've said, Lady Catgut thinks to herself.

'Come down when you're ready, Maria,' she says, gently touching the girl on her shoulder. Maria spins round, grabs tight hold of Lady Catgut's wrist and throws it from her body.

'Don't touch me!' she snarls, her voice echoing down the stairs and beyond.

★ ★ ★

Maria walks past the table where all are seated, having lunch, and heads for the fridge. She takes out a large quiche and a bottle of wine, and returns to her room.

She's swigging from the bottle when there's a knock at the door.

'May I come in?' says a voice.

She doesn't answer.

The request is repeated. So is the silence. The doorhandle turns, the door opens, and Grout enters. He sits at a distance from Maria, who ignores him and carries on eating, dropping lumps of cheese and pastry from her mouth on to the bedspread and the floor.

'I wanted to say that if you need to talk, any one of us here is a good listener. And we're discreet. And the Catguts are amazingly kind and gentle people.'

'That's it,' he says, and gets up to go. 'I hope we can help.'

Maria burps. Other than that she's silent.

As he reaches the door she speaks.

'You don't think I'll fit in, do you? You think I'll mess it all up for you little boys in your little country idyll?'

She takes another swig from the now near-empty bottle.

'If you're anything like your brother, you're a fighter,' says Grout. 'Someone to admire and live up to.'

'Yeah, well, I wouldn't know. I was a kid the last time I saw him,' she says, with a sneer.

Grout senses her despair.

'If you like, if you can cope with it, I can tell you about the three of us who live here. To show that you're not alone in living with despair.'

She shrugs.

'Suit yourself. If it makes you feel better, evangelising, go for it. Just don't expect me to join in.'

And with that she curls up on the bed, yawns and falls asleep.

Grout sits for a few moments and then quietly clears up the girl's mess. He picks up the carrier bag beside her hand and is putting it on the floor when he catches sight of the pistol inside. He checks it and returns it to the bag. There is no ammunition to be found. Did she have any? If so, has she hidden it in the house? And what sort of life has she led that's made her feel the need for a gun?

57 WHAT IS MARIA DOING ABOUT MARIA?

'What am I doing here in this dump?' Maria demands with a waking yawn and a sulky look at Grout.

'That's up to you,' says Grout, from the chair opposite, as he pockets his work notebook. 'You can enjoy good food, with the company of nice people. You can walk in the gardens. Help Lady Catgut with the animals...'

Maria snorts. 'Smelly beasts? I don't think so.'

'Forgive me, but you don't smell that good yourself.'

'You cheeky...!' she snarls. She looks ready to erupt but instead bursts into laughter that dissolves into the hacking catarrh-filled cough of a long-term smoker.

Grout pours her a glass of water.

'Here.'

She takes a deep gulp, and wipes her mouth with her hand.

'Ta.' She examines Grout with interest.

'So why are you here?'

'I had nowhere else to go.'

'What about your folks?'

'Given they didn't notice me when I was there, it's likely they haven't noticed that I've left.'

She gives a cheerless laugh.

'Cor! We must be related.'

'Anyway, I like it here,' Grout continues. 'This is my family. I love coming back here after a working week.'

'Aren't you the lucky one?' she murmurs sadly. Grout is about to reply, to remind her that she is now family, but realises she's stopped listening. She's far away, though her unhappiness fills the room.

58 LOVE BUGS

'Someone told me you were a singer,' says Piccolo, sitting at the piano, nervously watching Maria walk around the soundproofed room, examining everything, saying nothing.

He senses the young woman is wounded inside and that, like a wild distressed animal, she could attack at any moment. It reminds him of home, of the abuse and fear he suffered for years. So it's a comfort to him to know the Noteian doctors are on the other side of the mirror. Just in case.

'Monitoring us, are they?' she enquires, sticking out her tongue and making a rude sign at the glass.

Before he can say anything she utters a terrified cry that turns into a long shriek of agony.

There's no time to think. Piccolo hits the keys with force, echoing the loud dissonant noises she's making. She stops; he stops. She begins again, jumping up and down the scale at random; he echoes her with his keyboard. It's an abstract duet and a fierce battle. It's energy, passion, fear and anger, a huge creative force. When it's over, when she stops singing, both are sweating and exhausted.

There is a gentle knock at the door and Lady Catgut

enters with a tray of tea and cordials, sandwiches and cake.

'Thought you might want some refreshment,' says Lady Catgut, and leaves as quickly as she came.

'Why does that woman keep skivvying about for others?' says Maria angrily.

'Love,' says Piccolo. 'I think she wants more than anything to heal and mend wounded people and to see them grow through love.'

'Blimey, what are *you* on?' she says sarcastically.

'Love,' says Piccolo, with a shrug and a grin. 'Watch out, it can be catching.'

'Not for me, Sunny Jim, I'm immune,' Maria says firmly, piling a plate with sandwiches and taking them up to her room.

'Same time tomorrow?' Piccolo calls after her, but there's no reply.

BREAKING NEWS

Ruby Q Cooper reports from the Federation for *The Daily Unigraph*.

There are farms, with hundreds of acres and thousands of pigs. Everything appears to be fine—health and safety, animal welfare, quality of the meat. All boxes appear to be ticked; all paperwork is in order. And then animal welfare campaigners go in undercover. Armed with cameras.

The videos appear on illegal websites and go global. They show men beating pigs across the body and the face with iron bars or wooden planks. Kicking piglets with their heavy boots. Smashing the heads of animals against the concrete floor. Using them for rifle practice.

The film moves on to another farm. A man boasts of killing millions of pigs. Millions, the Boaster repeats proudly. He kicks the big pigs, swipes them across the face, tearing open eyes here and there, sticks knives into the animals' flesh so they bleed, and stuffs an anus with a clothes peg or worse. He hurls them by the leg or any means over a wall into a pile of thick deep wet mud or concrete. The lamed, injured animals struggle in their agony to stand up. The Boaster throws piglets at walls, and when they fall to the ground he watches, sneering or

LIVE FROM AN ILLEGAL INTERNET SERVICE PROVIDER

laughing, as their bodies go into convulsion. That's when he steps on a leg to break it or a neck to suffocate it.

Pigs, remember, are sentient beings. Cleverer than most animals, certainly much cleverer than humans such as the Boaster.

The man, if you can call him that, is tried in court and found guilty. He receives a sentence of nine months.

59 THE PHOEN'OID GOES INDEPENDENT

The Phoen'oid, on charge overnight in his cubicle, catches the pig videos on the illegal websites. He computes. He is a prototype, on trial, and reckons he can easily handle this on his own. He is juiced up and raring to go. He compiles a checklist that he checks. He unplugs himself, contacts the Boaster, whose suspicions are quickly soothed by the mention of a 'significant' contact and the high price offered for a job. The Phoen'oid makes his exit through a window.

He takes a car that his computer brain reads has sufficient petrol and arrives, as planned, at the Boaster's house, in the dark hours and driving rain, dressed in a long, hooded raincoat and thick waterproof gloves. The Boaster is ready and waiting, and wary. The Phoen'oid hands over a thick wad of high-value notes. The Boaster eyes it greedily, checks the money and stuffs it deep into his coat pocket.

'Remember, the animal must be disposed of so it's visible, but not too much so,' says the Phoen'oid. 'The owner wants to claim on insurance.'

'Must be a pretty valuable beast to go to all this trouble,' the Boaster says.

The Phoen'oid reads his calculating mind.

'I reckon I'll need help,' the Boaster suggests casually.

'There's a truck on site,' says the Phoen'oid. 'And a chap who'll help you for a few backhanders.'

The Boaster nods.

'So, you're not from these parts,' says the Boaster, relaxing in the comfortable heated seat.

'No, but my contact told me since your release you were doing this work on the side.'

'Had to do sommat after I were sacked,' said the Boaster testily.

The Phoen'oid nods. He pulls the car off the country road and travels along a potholed track that leads eventually to a large, partly converted barn.

'Here we are,' he says, getting out of the car.

'Can't hear no horse welcoming you home,' says the Boaster, following.

'Had to drug it,' says the Phoen'oid, nonchalant. 'Otherwise they'd have heard it in Timbuktu.'

The Boaster gives a leery grin.

They enter the barn.

'Through here,' says the Phoen'oid, leading the man into a large overheated room.

'So where's the beast?' says the Boaster, wiping his brow and hanging his coat on a stray chair.

'It's in the stable attached to this room,' says the Phoen'oid. 'All the gear's there and there's a choice of weaponry.'

'No, ta. I got my gun,' says the Boaster, a nasty glint

in his eyes as he reaches into his pocket. He cocks the trigger. 'It's foreign, ancient, stolen and untraceable.'

'I don't want it shot,' says the Phoen'oid. 'As I said, everything necessary is in the next room. You've got a choice of an iron bar, wire, builder's boots, clothes pegs, a knife and a few concrete statues. And there's a huge steaming bath. Hence the heat.'

'You some kind of perv?' the Boaster asks.

'What makes you think that?' the Phoen'oid asks.

'Seems like you're getting me to do what I got sent down for doing.'

'That's right, up to a point,' says the Phoen'oid. 'Except I can reassure you there are no pigs. No horses. And soon there will be no you.'

'What do you mean, you...?'

It takes a moment for the Boaster to work it out.

'You're a stinking animal rights bassard, aren't you?' the Boaster shouts out as he fires the gun.

There's a click as the hammer hits an empty chamber. And nothing else.

The Boaster stares at the gun in disbelief.

The Phoen'oid rattles his closed hand, then opens it to reveal six bullets.

'How did you...? You firkin'...' shouts the Boaster, and throws his big, hefty weight at the Phoen'oid. But the Phoen'oid is made of faster, lightweight stuff. In an instant he is behind the Boaster, shooting a RasaLasa directly into him.

The Boaster's body is immobilised instantly. He stands like stone. His voice alone is free.

'What's this about?' shouts the Boaster. 'What have I ever done to you, perv?'

'A prison sentence is not enough punishment for your actions. And I'm reliably informed that since your release you've continued your foul ways. So, as you have killed or tortured pigs and other animals, old and young, in many horrific ways, you will die by the same means. Time now for you to choose which way.'

'What if I say no to them all?' says the Boaster, disbelieving and cocky.

The Boaster feels his body rise up. He is moved by an unseen force that carries him horizontally across the room and into the next room, where he hovers above a large steaming hot bath. He fights against an unknown, unseen force before he is dropped low enough for his buttocks to skim the surface of the scalding water.

The Boaster screams. He has seen this from another point of view. When he lived abroad. He was part of it, securing the pig so that it could be dunked live into boiling water He was part of it, hearing the other pigs screech in fear as they understood fully that they would be next. Then he'd thought nothing of it. Or just laughed at their suffering.

Now he is turned over so his nose and cheeks skim the boiling water. He screams again, louder.

'Take back your firkin' money and let me go. I won't

say nuffin', I swear!' The Boaster screams.

'If you won't make the decision, I'll make it for you,' says the Phoen'oid.

The Boaster hears a running tap, feels the steam's heat surround him. He sees the knives, a coil of rusty wire and several heavy iron bars lying on the floor close by. And then he sees fully the face of his assailant before him—or at least the face of the mask the Phoen'oid wears under his hood. It is the face of a pig, bleeding, bruised and bashed, and dead.

The Bruiser screams, shouts and beseeches the Phoen'oid and God for mercy. Neither answer.

The Phoen'oid disposes of the Boaster's body parts and clothes in an incinerator that is then destroyed. The room is cleaned and sterilised. And having sterilised himself, the Phoen'oid returns to the lab. Via the Boaster's ad'um he uploads the film footage under the name Renegade and returns to his cubicle. Within the next 12 hours, the film is watched by millions. The reactions are mixed— shock, disgust, disbelief, as well as much support for the Phoen'oid's action.

There is one who is outraged at what's been done. And in his name. It's the Phoenix himself.

'This is not the way to behave or win support!' he shouts at Grout, in a fury. 'I can*not* allow this Phoen'oid, or any other, to behave in this way. JoJo must be shut down and exterminated immediately.'

Behind them in the cubicle the Phoen'oid overhears everything.

60 ASHES TO ASHES

And that's all that remains of Cataract, thinks Will as he looks into an old oak display cabinet in Wiggins's London flat and stares at the golden femurs, tibias and fibulas, humeri, ulnas and radii, and two buttons from Wiggins's coat.

Will and Grout have crossed the river to Southwark to offer condolences on the death of Wiggins's elder brother and Will's former boss.

'There was also this. It must've fallen down the side of the chair,' says Wiggins, taking a small aged tin box from his pocket. Gently, he opens the lid and shows them the contents – a lock of black hair.

'His wife's hair?' Grout asks.

Wiggins gives a quiet smile.

'I couldn't give it to the police. You see, this is not about someone, it was something. Something my brother Cedric loved above all else. His cat, Beluga. The little creature would've followed him to the end of the universe.'

'Maybe now they're reunited,' says Grout.

'I'd like to think so,' Wiggins says, 'but I don't believe in that stuff.'

'Have the police got any idea what happened?' says Will.

'After eliminating me as a suspect? No.' Wiggins shakes his head.

Will clears his throat.

'Lord Wiggins, I brought Grout with me because as Head of Innovation at Dekaydence I thought he might learn something new that'd give us a clue as to what happened exactly.'

'I've told the police everything,' says Wiggins.

'If you wouldn't mind, could we go through it again?'

'Of course,' replies Wiggins promptly. 'It is most kind of you and your colleague to try to help. Please, thank Lord di'Abalo for allowing you time off.'

'He doesn't know, sir,' says Will.

'In that case I've already forgotten your visit and, indeed, who you are,' says Wiggins briskly. 'But if I talk to myself, feel free to listen in.

'My brother phoned me,' Wiggins continues, 'telling me to pick him up and take him home, immediately. I left my meeting, got to the hospital and was delighted to see him, chirpy and keen to get home. He was devouring a 2-2 Divine Dekaydence chocolate cake I'd sent him. He seemed on top form. He was sitting in a chair, his suitcase ready and waiting, like himself, to be discharged.

'Then he said he felt sick. Too much cake, I thought. A nurse went to get a doctor. I held my brother's hand and looked into his eyes and...'

Wiggins swallows.

'It was his pupils, mainly.'

'What do you mean, sir?' asks Grout.

'They had this fierce look, red raw and angry as a raging inferno. The next moment flames shot forth from his eyes... He screamed. Oh, God, the pain, the fear in that scream, I shall never forget it.'

'And then?' asks Grout swiftly.

'I sprayed him with a soda siphon that was to hand. Then his whole body erupted in flames. I ran to the door to raise the alarm. I turned back into the room and he... my brother Cedric was gone. Literally, in a flash. The only things left were his golden bones and two buttons from my coat.'

Wiggins takes a handkerchief from his pocket and dabs his eyes.

Grout looks at Will, who shrugs.

'Nothing else, sir?' Grout enquires.

Wiggins looks at them, one after the other, as he appears to ponder.

'There is something. And it may be nothing.'

'Which is?'

'It must be the chocolate cake, don't you think, or some stray drug?' says Wiggins. 'The police examined the cake but forensics found nothing.'

'Do the police still have the cake?'

'Yes, as far as I know.'

'I doubt we'd get it back, even if we asked nicely,' says Grout.

'Wait, I'm forgetting,' says Wiggins. 'I have a slice my

brother gave me. It's in a box in the fridge.'

'I'd like to take it, if I may,' says Grout.

'Of course,' says Wiggins.

'One thing, sir,' says Grout. 'Did you take a bite of the cake? Even a few crumbs? Or a bit of icing?'

Wiggins shakes his head.

'I haven't touched chocolate since I was knee high to a grasshopper. A schoolboy jape of Cedric and his best friend, the King, put me off it for life.'

'I am sorry for your loss, sir,' says Grout, 'but I think you've had a very lucky escape. The symptoms your brother suffered are identical to those associated with victims of the new virus that's hit parts of Africa and the Far East.'

'The new killer virus?' Wiggins frowns. 'That's in all the news bulletins?'

'Yes, sir,' says Grout.

'What the stories don't tell you,' Will intervenes, 'is that this virus is designed to kill off "troublesome" people living on prime development land around the world. Dekaydence is moving on from media and sweets to murder. It appears that activity makes more money.'

'What kind of man is this Di'Abalo? And how on earth did my brother get involved with him?'

'We need to do forensics on the cake but I'd rather Lord di'Abalo doesn't know what I'm doing,' says Grout.

'I quite understand,' says Wiggins. 'I'm grateful for your kind concern. And if I can help you in any way...'

'Best thing is, sir, don't tell anyone else what's happened,' says Will. 'Should the papers get to hear of it...'

'Quite understand,' says Wiggins. 'I'll fetch the cake and, if you prefer, you can make your departure discreetly via the fire exit.'

61 HEARTBREAKING NEWS

Ruby Q is in Spiky Hair's office at *The Daily Unigraph* when news comes in that there's been an accident. All three lanes on a section of the M25 motorway, south of London, are closed. Traffic is gridlocked. An air ambulance is on its way to the scene.

'Sounds serious.' Spiky Hair sighs. For a moment the two women share a silence and a concern. Someone at some point will be told that the accident involves a member of their family, a close friend, a colleague, an acquaintance, an admired celebrity. A somebody or a nobody. It's still a human being or an animal that's been lost.

Spiky Hair channels the conversation back to where they were: discussing the growing prominence of North and the global spread of the Justice movement.

'Interesting times,' says Spiky Hair quietly.

'Yes, but will it change anything?' says Ruby Q. 'We're up against forces that we can't fight.'

'How did you get North to agree to putting the dog-baiting footage on an illegal website?'

'He's as passionate about animal welfare as he is about the Justice movement,' says Ruby Q. 'He wants people to be aware of what's going on, what's going wrong in the world.'

'Good... Now, next on the agenda—'

Jarvis, the deputy news editor, knocks on the door and walks in. His hair and tie askew, his face ashen.

'Sorry to barge in, *mon capitaine*, but...' Jarvis stops to blow his nose, suddenly overcome by what he has to say.

'What is it, Jarvis?' says Spiky Hair.

'The motorway accident,' replies Jarvis. 'It involves members of the Royal Family.'

'Oh, God,' says Ruby Q, and prays in her head for Will and Indigo's safety.

'We haven't had confirmation as to who as yet...' says Jarvis.

'We'll know soon enough,' says Spiky Hair grimly. 'Pull the front page.'

'Yes, *mon capitaine*.'

The door is flung open and the news editor enters.

'The Crown Prince's son is dead,' he announces abruptly.

Ruby Q involuntarily covers her mouth with her hands.

'What happened?' says Spiky Hair, thinking of the young prince, the King's grandson, about the age of her own son.

'We don't know all the details as yet, other than he was a passenger on his father's motorbike.'

'And the Crown Prince?' asks Spiky Hair.

'That's the odd thing,' says the news editor. 'The police

have searched everywhere but they can't find him or his body. They got a call from a man in a motorway lay-by. He saw a man clamber over the barrier and weave and stagger his way across the lanes. The caller said the man was covered in blood, ranting and weeping and beating himself about the head with an empty bottle of champagne. The caller realised the man was the Crown Prince and offered him help. But the Crown Prince screamed at him, tried to hit him with the bottle, and ran off.'

7

The only sounds in the tent are from the fire in the brazier, cackling and spitting, popping and hissing. The men sitting close to it stare into the bright apricot, red and yellow flames that dance around and through one another.

Despite his proximity to the fire the President is shivering. He feels his body is shutting down while chill and fear seep through his flesh and penetrate his bones.

He shudders.

What is going to happen? he wonders. Shouldn't it be like the movies? The Americans come barging in to rescue him at any moment? But he doesn't hear helicopters. Or jeeps. Or American accents. Why isn't the General on his case?

His nose leads him astray. He breathes in the smell of baking bread.

A young lad enters. He spreads a large tablecloth over a rug. The President is presented with a copper basin and a beautiful pot filled with clean water. The young lad attends each dinner guest, pouring water over their hands, offering them soap and a dry cloth. Then the food arrives: naan bread with chutneys and pickled fruit such as peach and lemon. Then rice and meat dishes, salads, relishes, yoghurts and locally grown nuts, and local fruits such as pomegranate.

The President's stomach yodels loudly with joy at the sight and scent of the banquet. The men laugh and tell one another jokes that the President knows involve him. They raise their glass to him. He smiles nervously and raises his glass to them.

The President is tucking into the delicious food and beginning to relax when he feels a spot of water land on his hand. He looks up at the tent roof. A drop falls into his eye. He moves his hand to the ground and feels it suddenly clamped by a set of determined teeth. The men chuckle. The President stares at the clamp, which looks back at him with large soft and loving dark eyes. It's a black woolly puppy, looking longingly up at him and down at the food.

The men indicate that the President must not indulge the dog.

'You have a dog at home?' asks the dark-haired young man.

'Yes,' the President responds quickly. 'Well, I did have but not now.'

The young man nods in sympathy.

'He died, your friend?' he asks.

'She did.' The President replies quietly, lowering his face, giving a quick nod and shutting his eyes. He cannot admit that he killed the dog and all her newborn pups. He cannot tell them his reason. That he couldn't stand the noise or the mess or the smell in the house. He cannot tell them that his eldest son saw what he did, showered him with abuse and then silent disdain and left the family home...breaking the heart of his mother before her own husband killed her and her younger son with a bomb. Oh, the never-ending consequences that have brought the President to this place.

Oh, God, not finally, please, make not this my final resting place, he pleads vehemently inside his head to the Being for whom he normally has no time.

He is aware of a silent tension in the tent. Everyone has stopped eating and is staring at an elderly man standing in the doorway, who nods and smiles to all within. A burly guard stands beside him, holding a large wooden box that is placed on the floor by the edge of the tablecloth.

The old man sits down by the President.

The President attempts a friendly look but senses the old man with his sharp, knowing blue eyes can see straight through his facade.

He looks back at his food. He's lost his appetite.

The dog is on its back, at his side, fast asleep, all four paws up in the air.

Like a baby, thinks the President, stroking the dog's belly. The dog opens its eyes and stares at him, then clasps tight the President's lower arm with its four paws and gently clamps hold of the President's hand.

The President shrieks in anger, goes to strike the dog, which runs howling into a corner of the tent.

There is dark muttering in the group. The dark-haired young man slowly approaches the dog, gently fussing and reassuring it.

The President stands up.

'Time for bed,' he says, yawning and stretching.

'Alas, no. We move on tonight,' says the old man. 'Security reasons. And remember, please, our orders are to shoot if you attempt to escape.'

The President shudders. He wishes the gas uncomfortably trapped in his gut would expel him up, up into the air, knocking out all those on the ground and returning him at speed to the American base.

61.5 SPECIAL DELIVERY

Taylor thinks she hears a knock at the door and goes to answer it. But it's not a knock. Someone has pushed an envelope through the Martins' fiercely uncooperative letterbox. Taylor opens the door and sees Ruby Q disappear from view.

She closes the door. The two girls haven't spoken for... Who knows how long?

Taylor picks up the envelope. It's addressed to the family so she opens it. It's a card congratulating the Martins on the birth of Jake. Signed by Ruby Q, Rallan, Elsa and Mr Treasure. She puts it on the table.

Later, when Mrs Martin returns home from work she discovers a note on the back of the card advising her to look in the dustbin cupboard, where she finds a bunch of sunflowers and a home-made blue teddy bear.

That evening, tears are shed in both houses, mostly by Ruby Q in her room. And then another note is delivered. To Ruby Q from Taylor. It's a note of thanks and much more. And though it's night time Ruby Q feels that she's received a shaft of warm sunshine. She rereads the letter and *knows* she has.

SECTION 8

I have just three things to teach: simplicity, patience,
compassion. These three are your greatest treasures.
Lao Tzu
(born and died during the Zhou dynasty [1046–256 BC])

62 A HEAVENLY UPROAR

The NewComers are herded into the new extension – a huge grey cumulus cloud, the size of a colossal ocean-going tanker, that's in dry dock as it awaits a deluge of rain refill. The NewComers are fractious, partly because they are being corralled and sung to by a chorus of cherubs, armed with bows and arrows, partly because they are on the receiving end of that spiteful streak that cherubs share, and can be seen in Renaissance paintings. Oh, but they knew a thing or two did the likes of Masaccio *et al*.

The NewComers glance sulkily at the noticeboard. Lectures. Talks. More lectures on rules and regulations governing Heaven. TTT classes morning, noon and night. Tests. Exams. Yes, amidst the raspberry blowers there is much dark stuttering and muttering.

'It's an insult to our intelligence!' says one.

'And our right to free speech!' says another.

'Free and *loud* speech!' squeaks a third.

With difficulty and a few physical tussles, the NewComers are ushered into a vast hall within the cloud. When the lecture turns out to be on dress code there's a stampede for the doors as clowns jump, somersault and catapult themselves one over another. HaHa (Heaven aid and Health aid) has never had to mend so many broken red noses and torn curly wigs.

Bhupi arrives with Jack and Cromarty. He tries to hide his tears at the mayhem. Cromarty, his broken body still in the mending process, growls huskily and rustily in TTT at the NewComers.

'Ooo, get him!' says one NewComer. 'Dead scary! Best I go and hide in me hairnet.'

The NewComers roar with laughter.

'Wasn't he a tin of tuna tin in his previous life?'

There is raucous laughter.

'OK,' says Jack firmly. 'If we release this cloud you could be drifting about for all eternity in Purgatory or Limbo.'

The NewComers emit a wave of alarmed squeals, screeches and groans.

'You couldn't,' whispers one nervously.

'You wouldn't, would you?' says another.

'Oh, yes, I would!' says Jack, firmly.

'Oo-er,' say some, while others simply think it.

A murmuring in voice and TTT sweeps around the hall. There are whispers and nudges. Someone is pushed forward as a spokesperson. It's Spaghetti Sureshi, a strong, compact, dark-skinned NewComer, his face covered in sweat and glitter, his great curly wig as bright as lime soda. He dabs his face and bows to Jack.

'I must apologise for the behaviour of some of the NewComers,' Spaghetti Sureshi says to Jack, as he hears the rustle of rebellion amidst the swelling ranks behind him. 'We must all try to be patient and keep calm.'

Jack scans the crowd of NewComers. It's going to take time to settle this, he thinks. Certainly much longer than the six days it took God to create the world. Invasion and revolution are on the march in Heaven. Has it ever happened before? If so, what was done? If only He was contactable to give advice, thinks Jack.

63 DUST TO DUST

The King is sitting, woebegone, holding on to a box of treacle pudding, a large flask of custard wedged between his knees. As promised, he is taking the pudding to his dear old schoolfriend, Cataract. But the taxi is late, held up somewhere by a motorway incident. His Majesty is stuck, as is the news of his old friend's death, which'll reach him too late. Sinus suggests tea; the King perks up. The Princess Indigo arrives unexpectedly; the King perks up even more.

They sit at a small table and play a word game. So far the Princess leads five games to two. And between you, me and Heaven's gatepost, she gives the King three games.

'You are a bright girl,' says the King, considerably cheered. 'Who else could make words out of three letter Es, two Ds, a Y and A, K, N, C ? But you're still a girl, Indigo, more's the pity. And we can't have that, can we? A girl on the throne. I mean emotions and all that. And then you'll likely choose some unsuitable chap as your partner and—'

'Grandfather,' Indigo interrupts sternly, 'this is irrelevant because, as I've told you before, I do not want the throne. But I must remind you that we have had some excellent queens on our throne. Queen Elizabeth the Second—strong and regal, diplomatic and discreet, and a film star to boot. And there have been excellent foreign consorts, such as Prince Phillip of Greece, Queen Elizabeth's husband. You, of all people, would've liked him. He always spoke his mind.'

'Precisely,' huffles the King tetchily. 'You simply can't beat a good man.'

Indigo reins in a tart response as Sinus carries in a tea tray.

'Sinus, I'll have Mr Cataract's cake with my tea,' says the King. 'You could cut off a crumb for the Princess Indigo. A very small crumb. Or rather a crumb almost invisible.'

Indigo laughs.

'You are incorrigible, Grandfather. But so am I. Must be in the genes. So I'll settle on a tiny wee crumb, if I may, Sinus.'

'Sinus, when you're done,' says the King, 'please telephone Mr Cataract to say I'll be a tad late.'

Sinus bows, continues with the tea ceremony. He takes the slice of cake from the small fridge in the corner and hands it to His Majesty.

'Are you quite sure, Indigo?' says the King, the cake hovering close to His Majesty's mouth.

'I'll have a literal crumb to see what I'm missing,' says Indigo, with a grin.

Sinus delicately places a small crumb on a small saucer and His Majesty swallows his slice in one kingly gulp.

Indigo laughs, and claps her hands.

'Mmm, 2-2 delicious!' says the King, warm colour displacing the pale woebegone look.

Indigo smiles. She's reaching for her crumb when there's a knock at the door. She puts the crumb and saucer on the table and turns round expectantly. Nowadays, the King seldom receives visitors.

The visitors are Lord Lorenzo di'Abalo and HOH Randall Candelskin who acknowledge the King with a slight bow.

'I'm sorry to arrive without warning,' says Di'Abalo. 'But I'm afraid I have bad news.'

'No more secret puddings?' says the King warily. He winks at the Princess, who is perturbed to see how horribly flushed the King's face has become.

The King belches, drops his plate, and with trembling hands attempts to take hold of the arms of his chair. He gives a horrific screech as he stares in raw fear at Di'Abalo, flames suddenly shooting forth from his eyes.

Indigo screams. She jumps up. The saucer drops to the floor. The four of them grab any cold fluid they can find in the fridge and throw it at the King's body, which is now erupting into a forest of tiny flames growing larger and fiercer until...his entire entity is consumed in fire.

It's over in seconds. No one can speak. The King is nothing but a pile of ashes at the foot of his chair.

Candelskin kneels at the chair and begins to pray fervently. The Princess Indigo stares at the ashes. Sinus hesitates as he hovers with a dustpan and brush.

'I've read about self-combustion but never seen it, or anything like it,' Di'Abalo says quietly to Indigo. 'I am desperately sorry, Your Royal Highness. You are too young to have to bear witness to such a strange, shocking tragedy. And, alas, I have more bad news. There has been a car crash. Your brother is dead. Your father is missing and, by report, has possibly gone mad.

'It would appear that you are now Queen, Your Majesty.'

He bows his head.

Indigo hears the news but it doesn't sink in. It won't for days. Only later will she begin to realise what she has lost and what she is about to take on. Already she yearns to speak to Grout. For now she appears perfectly calm and serene, as if returning from another place, another world.

The moment the flames had appeared, she'd felt that she, too, would be consumed in the fire. At the same time she saw a tall dark muscular creature leap forth from within Di'Abalo. It sprang towards her, shielding her from the flames. A young athletic man whose skin glowed like polished ebony, who stood encased in a sparkling bright light of lily white. He made her feel safe, so that when he departed she was left with a deep and rich feeling of peace and happiness, and strength.

64 THE FUTURE

Will deals with the police, as well as the officials organising the combined funeral of the King and his grandson. Indigo, meanwhile, sits at her brother's side in a room in the funeral parlour where vases of artificial flowers attempt but fail to heal broken hearts.

The young prince looks as though he's asleep, a bud of teenage youth about to blossom into handsome manhood. A draught of air ruffles his thick fair hair that's alight with rays of sunshine that flood through a small high window. It's like a final encounter, between life and death. Here, death is already the conqueror.

Indigo takes hold of her brother's hand. It is heavy, cold and limp, his fair skin now paler than parchment. She feels a peppery attack behind her eyes and sees her tears fall on to his skin.

She goes to wipe them off. He mustn't go to his grave with her tears, only with her love. Then she realises that within her tears is her love, as well as an eternal message of how much she'll miss him. The little boy who teased her mercilessly, not in the least interested in her life and doings; the young teenager always keen to be off with their wayward father. Who, nevertheless, regularly brought her fresh flowers and excruciating jokes. Her darling baby brother. Who always will be that. She buries her head in his chest and sobs.

Later, she sits in the garden within the ruins of St Dunstan in the East, with its remaining tower and nave walls. In the Middle Ages it was a place of execution. Now it's a quiet place where City folk sit on stone benches amidst trees and shrubs, eating their sandwiches, perhaps under the fig tree planted on St Patrick's Day, 1937, which, she recalls from her family history lessons, was the coronation day of a forebear, King George VI.

She sits, remembering her grandfather. Even though she was a girl, she knows he cared deeply for her. In fact, he was like a father to her, which her own father couldn't be. She is relieved that the King died before knowing what happened to his son and grandson. For sure, the news would have killed him. But what was it that actually did kill him? She wonders. Was it an assassination? If so, what was the reason? And if it was self-combustion, how did it happen? Should she be scared?

Of one thing she is certain, it was a shocking experience and while she feels sure that though the memory of it will haunt her for ever, she will be glad always that she was with the King at his end. That he hadn't been alone. Someone from the family had been with him. Albeit a girl.

65 THE CHOCOLATE KILLER

Will is furious: a trace of the killer virus is found in the chocolate cake that killed Cataract and in the slice that Cataract, unwittingly, gave to and killed his childhood friend, the King.

Grout informs Will that a test-tube of the killer virus has gone missing, most likely from the R&D laboratory next door to his.

'You do realise, Grout,' says Will, angrily, holding his thumb close to his forefinger, 'that Indigo was this much away from the same fate as the King and Cataract?'

'No, I didn't know,' says Grout miserably. 'She didn't tell me; I didn't think to ask. If I'd known... But it sounded so...'

'Weird? Like a conspiracy?'

'I don't know what you mean?' Grout says, surprised.

'Have you not heard the news?'

Grout shakes his head.

'The King's grandson has been killed in a motorbike accident and the rider, his father the Crown Prince, has apparently gone mad and AWOL.'

Grout stares at Will, dumbstruck.

'Trust me, Grout, conspiracy, backstabbing and lies — they're happening all around us,' says Will. 'So, even more than before, you and I must ensure Indigo's safekeeping.'

'Of course,' says Grout.

Will nods, only partially satisfied.

'So, what did you do with the renegade Phoen'oid?' he demands.

'Nothing,' says Grout quietly.

'Grout!' says Will, his anger re-ignited. 'The Phoenix told me that he ordered you to destroy it.'

'I believed I could make suitable amendments.'

'That wasn't your brief. I hope you've put it well out of harm's way.'

'You're not going to like this,' says Grout. 'The Phoen'oid has escaped.'

'*What?*' cries Will.

'He escaped. I don't know how and I don't know where he is.'

'But he's got embedded tracking devices to tell you his exact whereabouts.'

'It appears he detected and deleted most all of them.' Grout answers quietly.

'We must get to him and stop him, Grout. Who knows what appalling acts he'll commit next?'

'First, I think you ought to listen to this,' says Grout. 'It's a recording he left for the Phoenix. I don't think he knows that the Phoenix was imprisoned after trying to rescue his sister from the streets.'

'Not many do know, thank goodness,' says Will.

'Before you do anything, before you say anything to the Phoenix or anyone, just listen to this,' says Grout. 'It's a recorded message from the Phoen'oid to the Phoenix.'

Grout presses his ad'um. The Phoen'oid speaks.

'Sir, I hope you'll forgive me for what you might see as my "overstepping the mark" on the last assignment. I know you wanted me destroyed and I foresee that day as not long off. But I have been constructed to serve, to help humanity rediscover its respect for this world, its people and creatures. Equally, I find I operate on a moral code based on the Old Testament rather than the New. So I can change little.

'Sir, you named me after your beloved younger brother, killed by a Dekaydence bomb. I would be honoured if you allowed me to keep the name of Jojo for the time I have left to do my work. I wish you well, sir. I feel, yes, I now feel that our bodies may be of a different composition but that our hearts are equal in their power to care and love. Farewell, my brother in Alms.'

Will frowns.

'Do you know yet where the Phoenix is being held? And by whom? And why? And where the Phoen'oid might be?'

Grout shakes his head.

Will clenches and unclenches his fists.

'If the Face is involved in either kidnapping, I won't be answerable, Grout.'

Grout says nothing. He wonders when or if Will might

see the similarity between himself and the Phoen'oid or the Face or even Cromarty, the wild haggoid. Or whether he ever considers any similarity between their genes or programming. And then it occurs to him. Are the experiments in the White Room to do with genetic engineering? He has come across and kept secure documents he'd found left lying about in the next-door lab, presumably by Bodkin. The trials and tests appear to show tests on three levels – alpha, beta and gold. Like the three stages in IT development. But what does it mean? And what on earth is Di'Abalo searching for?

66 THE CHASE

The part-time guards working in the Royal household, all two of them, have been sacked. They'd attempted to follow the Crown Prince but, as usual, hadn't been able to match his speed on the motorbike. Di'Abalo dismissed them. It's a useful snippet to pass to the media and it's a diversion. Now there's immense pressure on police forces countrywide to find the Crown Prince.

'We don't want another dead body,' says the Deputy Commissioner, chairing a national committee meeting via satellite and airwaves. 'So, come on, let's go. Let's find him.'

'It'd be far easier if the prince were dead,' mutters a senior policeman, getting up from the table.

'No, it wouldn't,' retorts a senior policewomen. 'We'd never hear the end of it. TV and history books, now and for generations to come, would be pointing an accusatory finger at us.'

She shudders.

'For now, they'll probably fine us. Sack us. And/or cut our pensions.'

'More likely, they'll be replacing us with the new police'oids.'

The others mutter in low voices. That time will come, they know. And soon.

★ ★ ★

The Phoen'oid is lying on a large branch in an old oak tree. He's programmed himself to be on sleep/alert, so he'll hear any unusual noises. He is woken by shouts from all sides, birds calling alarm and a rustling and snapping of branches pushed back by insistent passing traffic. It's the police, he suspects, and remains still and quiet. The noise retreats.

He senses something else in the woods. Beyond the thick, delicious delights of the dawn chorus he scents a wounded animal in distress. An animal close by. An animal... He turns, knowing what he'll see. Yes, it's a man, filthy, bloodied and angry. With too much alcohol in his system, and fear at how high he's climbed. And then to find a stranger on the same branch...

The man is about to say something but the Phoen'oid puts a finger to his lips. The man shuts his mouth. Luckily, they're encircled by an embrace of dense foliage.

The noise in the woods rolls back and in from all sides, stays for a while, and then as quickly moves on.

The man relaxes.

'You're not from these parts?' says the man, unsure of what to say to this young stranger whose face is chiselled and deathly pale, like a mask.

'I am from many parts,' says the Phoen'oid, chuffed as he realises he's cracked his first ever joke.

The man nods an understanding he doesn't have.

'Are we both on the run?' he asks.

'Seems like it,' says the Phoen'oid.

'Will you be going home?' asks the man.

'No. You?' says the Phoen'oid.

'Never,' says the man.

'Odd, because you have family commitments,' says the Phoen'oid.

'I've killed my young son,' says the man, and starts to cry.

'Was it intentional?' the Phoen'oid asks quietly.

'No. But I feel I must kill myself. As a punishment for being careless with his life. The truth is I'm a coward.'

'It's not often cowards kill themselves. Equally, it requires bravery to carry on and try to live through one's pain and guilt.'

'Is that what you're doing?'

'I killed a man who tortured animals.'

'In which case, I salute you,' says the man.

'I went too far,' says the Phoen'oid. 'My anger got the better of me. I executed him by a barbaric method he used on animals. But we can't go back. We must move on.'

'You know who I am, don't you?' says the man.

'Yes,' says the Phoen'oid. 'You are the Crown Prince.'

'And you knew that I'd be here?'

'Yes,' says the Phoen'oid.

'Did they send you to arrest me or murder me in the way I murdered my son? As I deserve?'

'No one sent me. I came to listen. To offer comfort and

support. You will live with guilt till you die. Perhaps you can get through in life by helping others in need.'

'Do you feel guilt?'

'I understand the meaning of regret but I don't feel it,' says the Phoen'oid.

'I knew you weren't from these parts,' says the Crown Prince. 'Will I see you again?'

'Unlikely, alas, there are forthcoming events over which I have little control. But I wish you reunited with yourself. Failing that, I wish you peace.'

'It's been a privilege to share time and this tree with you,' says the Crown Prince.

He puts out his hand. The Phoen'oid hesitates before he takes it.

The man feels in the handshake both an ice-cold strength and a warm heart.

The Phoen'oid removes his hand. He's curious: he's never experienced a handshake, or any physical proximity to a human. He admired Grout and, of course, the Phoenix but now...He's aware of a peculiar sensation in his body and mind. He sets his brain on search. But before it responds, the answer dawns on him – for the first time he knows he has feelings, deep feelings.

67 I ONCE MET A GIRL CALLED MARIA

Given Maria's mercurial moods and temper, the others in the Catgut household decide it's better not to tell her that her brother, the Phoenix, was taken prisoner by unknown captors as he attempted to rescue her from the streets.

Everyone is relieved when she says she wants to join Grout on his weekend visits to the gym. He suggests she take lessons from one of the trainers but she's adamant that she wants him, and him alone, to show her what she should be doing.

'First thing is, cut out the smoking, drink less, and eat more organic food,' says Grout, as they step on to neighbouring treadmills. 'And go easy on this machine, you don't want to lose weight. You're all skin and bones as it is. You need some meat and muscle on you.'

'Will that make me more or less attractive?' Maria enquires coyly.

Grout laughs but doesn't register the affected innocence in her voice.

'I've no idea,' he says. 'I'm thinking of your health.'

'Boring,' she retorts loudly.

Grout introduces her to a range of machines and exercises and she notices how many people, men and women, young and old, going in and out of the gym, stop for a few words with the quiet, friendly, fit young man.

She won't go to the gym during the week. She does a bit of running, a bit of wobbly cycling, or walks into the village to get a magazine and a packet of cigarettes that she smokes on the quiet, but perhaps more sparingly than in earlier days. Mostly, she keeps to her room, except at weekends when Grout is about.

'Fancy a walk?' she asks Grout one Saturday night.

'Sorry,' he says, his head in some hi-tech magazine, 'I'm meeting up with Will and Indigo in an hour.'

'That gives us plenty of time for a quick brisk walk. And it's so lovely now the rain's stopped and the birds are singing and—'

'OK, OK,' says Grout, putting down his magazine and getting up. 'A quick brisk walk and then I need to wash and brush up.'

'Shouldn't you do that *before* you take me for a walk?' she says.

'You are incorrigible,' says Grout, with a dry laugh.

The dog walkers are out and once again Maria notices how many of them and others stop to chat with Grout. And how much he does the listening or advising.

They walk along in silence. From time to time she glances at Grout from under her lashes. He's not a great looker, she decides, but there's something about him. He's certainly fit. He has a quiet strength, a steadiness, honesty, compassion and kindness about him. He helps her over a stile; he warns her of an obstacle on the ground; he listens to her. He is the complete opposite of all the men she's known over the past few years. And there have been a good, or rather a bad, few. She shudders. And he notices.

'Are you cold?' he asks, with concern.

She shrugs.

'Only with memories.'

'Want to talk about them?'

'No,' she says, firmly. 'Thank you, but...'

'But what?' says Grout.

She turns to face him. Her eyes are awash with tears.

'Would you mind putting your arms around me?'

''Course not,' he says, gently, stepping towards her, opening his arms wide.

She collapses into him, sobbing. He enfolds her in an embrace, his head resting on the top of hers.

He has no idea how long they stand like that. But at some point she throws back her tear-stained face and looks at him.

'I know now why you come back to this place,' she says.

He looks at her questioningly.

'It's corny,' she says, abruptly, 'but you're right, it's full of love.'

He sweeps her up in his arms and laughs. He is relieved and overjoyed at the breakthrough they've achieved with this wounded, abused and aggressive young woman.

Maria laughs, too. She throws her arms round Grout's neck and kisses him full on the mouth.

'I love you, Grout,' she shouts. 'I love this place and I love you!'

Grout is suddenly confused. What is she saying? And what does she mean?

Before he can decide anything he hears someone cough. Still holding Maria, he turns and there, before him, stand Will, Sid, his bodyguard, and Nayr, bodyguard to HRH the Princess Indigo in both her official and personal capacity.

'Best we press on,' says Indigo, loudly and firmly, sweeping past Grout, her nose in the air, without a second look at Grout as he lowers Maria to the ground.

Acutely embarrassed, the three men nod at Grout and follow Indigo.

Grout and Maria follow along behind. She tries to link her arm through his but he resists. They walk back in silence. Cheered by Grout's physical closeness, she is charmed by what she takes to be his shyness. Meanwhile, he feels an idiot for not seeing what was coming, where Maria's behaviour was leading. Unhappy at her desperate need for love, he is devastated more by the thought of the pain he has possibly caused Indigo, and at such a dark time in her life.

Later, at some point, he'll explain it to her. She'll understand, he tells himself, while a voice in his head shouts, "You moron! Indigo has just lost her grandfather and her brother. And now, seeing you larking about with Maria, she will feel she has lost you, too!"

Grout stares fixedly and quietly at the ground, while experiencing hot flushes of shame and embarrassment. Surely Indigo will see it all as nothing. He would, wouldn't he? He finds he can't answer himself; the torturing flushes continue.

BREAKING NEWS

Ruby Q Cooper reports from London for *The Daily Unigraph*.

Think about a teacher who inspires you. A current teacher; maybe a teacher of decades ago. There is nearly always someone who inspires within you a hunger to read, to write, to paint, to build, to care, to play ball, to create. Or gives you a lifelong hunger to learn. The list of what these committed, inspirational teachers can do is endless and amazing – for pupils and society. So why do some teachers desperately want to leave the education system? It's not only the bureaucracy, the focus on achieving high grades at the expense of growing a 'rounded' person.

Let's take the example of Mr X.

Mr X has taught A-level mathematics for more than two decades in several 'good' schools. Unusually, his classes tend to have seven students more than average; pupils stay the course; their exam results tend to be As and a few Bs. He gives extra coaching, teaches pupils on exclusion orders. He teaches but despairs of the growing number of youngsters whose parents ignore their offspring's complete lack of enthusiasm for mathematics, law or medicine but still force them along these paths. (Ah, but

LIVE FROM AN ILLEGAL INTERNET SERVICE PROVIDER

here's another problem, another disaster, personal and national, that's waiting to happen.).

Mr X is proud of all his students, including the disinterested youngster 'lost' in the education system who takes to maths sufficiently to get the grades to win a place at an Oxford university college.

Oh, yes, Mr X is an inspirational teacher. But now he wants out. Why?

He's experiencing bullying and harassment.

One year and, not unusually, Mr X's pupils get excellent grades. Unusually, the new head of department decides to take over Mr X's class for the following, final year. Why, you might ask? Leave well alone, you might say. Mr X did good. Then you learn that in the second, final year good results are added to the current teacher's 'score' sheet. But the group, under the takeover teacher, get noticeably poorer results. The pupils are rubbished and blamed for not working hard enough; Mr X's teaching skills are also rubbished and questioned despite his outstanding history of A results. The head-teacher appears blind and/or oblivious to the situation, and to the frustration of the pupils who could get great grades.

Mr X takes a few weeks off work to be with his dying mother. After her death, and in the school holidays, he decides to run a month of study and revision to make up for his enforced break and ensure his pupils are fully prepared for and confident about the forthcoming exams. He doesn't charge; he takes no payment. Word gets around. Pupils from other classes attend, and ask if they can bring friends. Mr X makes all welcome. All of which leads to him being reprimanded. And advised not to do it again.

Then he discovers the teachers are using his notes, taken without permission from his desk. While his pupils have to listen to other teachers bad-mouthing their respected teacher.

The undermining and bullying of Mr X continues. His union is of no help. The reason? Mr X joined after the trouble started. Durr, we chorus. So what? A good teacher is in trouble now! Isn't that reason enough to help? Apparently not. There are rules and regulations. Get a grip: action helps, red tape stifles help. Eventually, Mr X's doctor strongly advises him to leave his job on health grounds. Hu-bloody-rrah! But what does Mr X's head of department say? 'Glad you're getting help at last. Call me if you need anything.' Odd that, given he hasn't spoken to Mr X for a year or more.

After a holiday Mr X is set to embark on a new career. He is talented and resourceful and will do well. He will be a world away from teaching, and he'll probably move abroad. He relished teaching A-level mathematics and will miss his pupils, he says sadly, but this experience has worn him out. And so the education system and our children are deprived of an inspirational teacher. Alas, Mr X is not alone. This is wasteful, distasteful and wicked – for all concerned. For Mr X, his pupils, and wider society.

Where in Heaven's name are the people cherishing good tutors and retraining or, if necessary, sacking the incompetents? And if there is no one there to do this, why isn't there? To nurture the young must be a priority for a healthy society for all.

68 GOO HOO-HA

Grout wants desperately to talk to someone about the lost phial but who to turn to? Will is still furious with him for losing the phial, angry at the potential risk to Indigo, and distraught at the whereabouts of the rogue Phoen'oid.

The Catguts are busy establishing more organic garden towers. Piccolo is absorbed in his work with Maria and, although Grout accompanies her less frequently to the gym, she is the last person he'd confide in. He is fond of Ruby Q and grateful for the kindness she's shown him but he knows she has enough pressing problems of her own. And now Indigo won't answer his calls.

It's late at night and Grout is sitting in his Dekaydence lab, at his ad'um. He's trying to distract himself with work. Certainly, he's got enough of it. But he worries about the lost phial of the deadly virus and frets about the possible thieves, Innit and Bodkin. How and why did they get hold of the phial? How and why did they know of its deadly contents? And why on earth did they want to use it on Cataract? Did they know about and expect to retrieve the gold bars from his limbs?

He hears a noise, lifts his head and through the window sees a shadow flickering in the next-door lab. He slides quietly off his stool and moves to the door. He slips into the corridor, along to the next lab, and flings open the door so it hits the wall. Simultaneously, he switches on the lights.

The shadow gives a muffled scream and stares at Grout in terror.

'Goo?' says Grout, startled to see before him the young son of MacGluten, Dekaydence's head chef. 'What are you doing here? How did you get in?'

Goo says nothing but continues to do a passable expression of a lemur caught in the glare of headlights.

He holds up a key and Grout takes it.

'Who gave you the key to this door?' he asks.

Goo's eyes enlarge further.

''Snot my fault,' he says, quivering.

'Goo, I don't know what you've done so...'

'I ain't done nuffink,' wails Goo. 'My dad told me to return this bottle to the lab. And I'm here, returning it.'

He hands the phial labelled 'Virus' to Grout.

'Thank goodness,' says Grout, breathing a sigh of relief.

'It's not the same stuff in there now, Mr Grout,' says Goo. 'My dad took the stuff wot was in it. And replaced it with water and brown sauce.'

'Oh, no,' Grout groans. 'Do you know what he did with the stuff?'

'Oh, yeah,' says Goo cockily. 'But I can't tell you.'

'Goo, it's a matter of life or death.'

'Yeah, it will be for me if I tell you. And my dad finds out.'

'We don't have to tell him, Goo.'

'So what's in it for me?'

'Nothing, but you need to know we're talking a double, potentially a triple murder here.'

'What?' says Goo, goggle-eyed.

'The news hasn't broken yet but the King is dead. So is the Federation's chief accountant. There could have been more, including the Princess Indigo.'

Goo's eyes have trebled in size and fear.

'Are you saying that my dad...?'

'Possibly, probably. You'll need to tell me what you know, Goo, else you might get arrested for treason and murder.'

'OK, OK,' says Goo. 'But it was the 'aggoid wot started it. Belongs to a Red Tartan guard. It was always finding its way into the kitchen from the sewers, looking for scraps. It shat metal, crisp packets anything, everywhere. It drove my dad insane. The guard couldn't control it and my dad tried everything but...in the end, he heard on the grapevine you had some powerful killer stuff and he asked someone to get it. A Black Tartan lent that someone the key.'

'Do you know who that someone was?'

'Yes, but ain't telling you. They'd get me for it, you know that, Mr Grout.'

'OK,' says Grout, trying to remain calm. 'What happened then?'

'My dad gave some of the brown stuff to the haggoid, greedy thing wolfed it up, and it worked. The haggoid sort of keeled over and then disappeared, right in front of us. Never seen it since.'

'Did it go up in flames?' asks Grout.

'No.' Goo shook his head. 'It went kind of inward on itself, in one almighty metallic fart.'

'What did your dad do with the rest of the liquid?'

'He put some in a cake for a man he said owed him.'

'Do you know who the man was?'

'Yeah. He slagged off my dad big time. His name's Cataract.'

'Oh, and what had he done to your father?'

'Spat out all his food at some posh do. Shouted for all to hear that the food was chemicalised garbage when it should be organic. My dad couldn't get a job for years until Dekaydence arrived in town.'

'And so...'

'A special order come through for Cataract to receive a special chocolate cake. My dad said it was too good an opportunity to miss.'

Grout hesitates. There's something about Goo that reminds Grout of himself as a boy. Alone within a fractious family set-up, and abandoned. Grout knows he can't take in every waif and stray home to the Catguts' but...

'Will you do me favour, Goo?' he asks.

'What kind of favour?' asks the boy suspiciously.

'That we keep this meeting secret, between ourselves.

For the time being. And possibly always. Agree?'

The boy nods.

'You won't tell my dad nuffink, will you, Mr Grout?'

'No,' says Grout, 'definitely not.'

He offers Goo his hand, which the boy takes tentatively.

'It's a deal, then, Mr Grout,' says the boy, looking over his shoulder, just in case.

'By the way,' says Grout, casually, 'you said your dad used *some* of the stuff in the cake. That implies there was some left over.'

'That's right,' says Goo. 'But I ain't telling you where it is or who's got it. I don't want to die young.'

'Or be imprisoned for life, or sent to the White Room...'

'Awright, awright!' says a panic-stricken Goo. 'The one behind all of this, the one who's got the phial is Bodkin.'

69 MISCARRIAGE OF INJUSTICE

Maria is lying on the bed in her room. She's shivering as she clutches a hot-water bottle to one side of her lower abdomen, which is painful and cramping. She is curling into a foetal position when she becomes aware of an involuntary flow of warm fluid from her vagina and pain in her shoulder blade.

There's a gentle knock at the door.

'Who is it?' she strains to call out.

'Only me, dear,' says Lady Catgut. 'I've brought you some tea.'

'Hang on, I think I've locked the door.'

As she eases herself up and off the bed Maria feels light-headed. She grasps the bedside cabinet to steady herself. She feels another stream of fluid flood from her body. She makes it to the door and turns the key, when she's aware of another rush of fluid soaking through her underwear. She sees it on her trousers before she drops to the floor in a dead faint.

'Are you all right, dear?' Lady Catgut calls anxiously from the hallway, her hand hesitating on the doorknob. Getting no response, she opens the unlocked door.

She nearly drops the tea-tray when she sees Maria on the floor, out cold, patches of blood on the girl's trousers, the bedspread and the carpet. She checks the pale-as-icing-sugar girl, hands her a warming mug of sweetened tea and dials the emergency services for an ambulance.

Maria groans as she experiences a sudden sharp pain in her abdomen.

'I don't need hospital, Lady C,' Maria begs weakly. 'Really, I don't. I just feel a bit sick.'

'Maria, dear,' replies Lady Catgut, gently but firmly, 'I believe you do need the hospital. And I'm coming with you. Trust me, if only this once.'

Catgut, Grout, Piccolo and Nigel stand aghast in the hallway as the paramedics carry out Maria on a stretcher, her face the colour of ice, her eyelids closed to the world.

'What's wrong with her, Etti?' Catgut demands quietly of his wife.

'I may be wrong,' Lady Catgut replies, softly, 'but I think she's in the process of miscarrying.'

Catgut gulps. He nods understandingly. Inside, he feels as helpless as he did when years back Lady Catgut experienced something similar, if not the same. He scolds himself.

He must be strong for the sake of Etti and Maria. He'll explain the situation to the boys, who he knows will react with kindness. His heart aches with sorrow for Maria, and for the loss of his own son and the miscarried baby. But there is also much room in his heart that feels pride and joy for their three adopted, nicely maturing, caring boys.

70 COOKING UP LIES

'What news, Mr MacCavity?' Di'Abalo asks the head of Dekaydence Security.

'The Black Tartans are helping police with their enquiries, my lord,' says MacCavity. 'Police say they can't do much forensics wi' a tiny pile of ash. But, they add, the trail keeps leading back to Dekaydence.'

Di'Abalo nods thoughtfully.

'If you don't mind my saying so, sir,' says MacCavity, slowly. 'I think we should dispose of MacGluten.'

'Could present difficulties,' Di'Abalo says. 'Just because he made the cake it doesn't make him the poisoner. Although...'

'I'm convinced that—' says MacCavity.

'Conviction does not make you right,' says Di'Abalo. 'I wonder if we're better off making a celebrity chef out of him. Give him his own TV programme. The mantle of fame will protect him, and us.'

'Brilliant, if I may say so, my lord.'

'You may, Mr MacCavity,' Di'Abalo says. 'But I'm not so sure. Perhaps we first get him to compile a book – a collection of allegedly secret Dekaydence recipes for cakes and puddings, perhaps with no mention of chocolate cake.'

'Pity the King died earlier than we planned,' says MacCavity. 'He could've written a wee foreword.'

'Now, that is odd,' says Di'Abalo, leaning forward conspiratorially. 'I have a copy here of a draft foreword His Majesty wrote and gave me but a few weeks ago. Did I not give it to you to read?'

Di'Abalo lifts one quizzical eyebrow.

'Och aye, now that you've jogged my memory, my lord,' says MacCavity deliberately. 'I thought at the time what an excellent idea you had for a Dekaydence cookbook by Mr MacGluten. And how beautifully crafted and from the heart, as well as the stomach, were the King's words.'

'How right you are, Mr MacCavity. The only problem is to find a replacement for Cataract. He was the perfect man for the job. He was one of us, if you understand me.'

'Yes. So, who will be Mr Cataract's replacement, my lord?'

Di'Abalo sighs.

'It had better be his young helper, Prince Will. It might take his attention away from saving the planet and any other lost cause he's collected along the way.'

71 A ROYAL FUNERAL

The weather is biblically ark-wet and cold, and has been for weeks: a daily diet of torrential downpours and angry hailstone showers, in between a few short, sharp sunny breaks. And there are continuing hiccups of earth movements, felt most keenly in the Federation, China and the USA.

Thus, crowds lining the streets are only one or two deep but thick with blustered, flustery umbrellas, as everyone attempts to catch a glimpse of the coffins of the King and his grandson, the son of His Mediumness, The Crown Prince, who is still on the missing list.

Each lies on one of two horse-drawn gun carriages that leave Westminster Hall after a three-day lying in state, heading for the funeral service at Westminster Abbey. Each coffin is draped with the occupant's personal Royal standard and surmounted by the occupant's own crown, as well as a wreath of gardenias and bluebells from the remaining members of the Royal Family.

As the procession sets off the first in a 41-gun salute is fired, one salvo fired every minute from Green Park. There are royal salutes, guards of honour and music from the massed pipes and drums, including popular songs from his adolescence, which the King had been wont to sing.

Behind the gun carriages walk the new Queen Indigo and Prince Will, each deep in silent thought, together with the Crown Prince's widow, his third wife, who is happily booked to return later that day to her home town in Sweden. Meanwhile, the Dowager Queen, widow of the old King, knits away as usual as she walks between her nurse and a lady-in-waiting, who carry backpacks full of wool that are linked to the Royal knitter.

And now they have proof the Royal Family is not only mad but Irish, thinks Will as other dignitaries from home and abroad follow, including the multicoloured US President, whose ears are changing from emerald to shamrock green to indicate his pride in his Irish inheritance.

The procession stretches for half a mile and involves 1500 servicemen and -women. There are also countless Black Tartan guards – their eyes and much of their faces hidden behind red tartan sunglasses – weaving in and out of the crowds, dignitaries and servicemen.

The coffins are met at Westminster Abbey by HOH Randall Candelskin and carried by the bearer party through the Great West Door and along the centre aisle to the catafalques in the Lantern. The service begins. When it ends the wreath is taken off the coffin of the King's young grandson and placed by Indigo, the new Queen, on the Tomb of the Unknown Warrior, as a lament is played by the massed pipes and drums.

The coffins, surmounted by their crowns, are each

placed in a hearse that sets off for the final resting place
– St George's Chapel, Windsor Castle – as ten dark, sleek
Euro-bombers, shaped like giant arrowheads, cloud the
sky in a fly-past over the new Dekaydence arena and the
Royal Family's old decaying summerhouses in the Royal
Park.

72 THE LOST BRAIN

'You must be exhausted,' says Driver, leaning back in his computer chair. 'Do you want a drink or a salad? Maybe some chips?'

'Yes, yes, yes, and yes,' says Handcuffs, collapsing into a chair. 'Oh, and add to the final three yesses, please.'

'Give me a few moments,' says Driver, tapping furiously on the keyboard, while scanning the monitor.

Handcuffs stands up and makes his way to the kitchen, returning with two glasses of red wine.

'Here, square eyes, feast your eyes and gullet on this instead,' Handcuffs says, putting a hand on his friend's shoulder. He sips his wine and glances at the computer. 'Is it my imagination or has the screen been jammed like this for weeks?'

'Hang on,' says Driver, leaning in closer to the screen. He types, he looks up, he checks, he waits and watches. Then he picks up the wine glass and takes a long slug.

'Oh, but that tastes good,' he says. 'Thanks, although I should be waiting on you.'

Handcuffs, slumped in a chair, chuckles.

'Look at us, we're like a couple of old prize boxers before the nurse comes to tuck us up for the night.'

'We work too hard,' says Driver, studying the screen.

'What are you working on? I can see it's a brain but you never tell me anything until you know the finishing line's in sight.'

Driver continues to study the screen.

'You'll make yourself ill,' says Handcuffs, dragging himself to his feet.

'You're a doctor, you can heal me any time,' says Driver, immersed in the screen.

'Physician, heal thyself, but first look at this.'

'So the end is in sight?'

'It depends what end you mean.' Driver sighs.

'Do we know the owner of this brain?'

'I thought it was obvious,' says Driver. 'It's the brain of the Phoenix.'

'You mean he's dead, and you didn't tell me?' Handcuffs sounds aghast.

'No, he's not dead. Thank your God,' says Driver, 'but as near as. He's unconscious while they download his mind.'

'What?'

'Don't say it's not possible. Grout has begun to crack it but is going slowly, on purpose.'

'So this is Dekaydence, behind closed doors?'

'Yes,' says Driver. 'They want his mind, memories, what he sees, what he thinks, what he likes, what he wants and feels...' He hesitates.

'God!' Handcuffs exclaims. 'What's happening to the Phoenix now, this minute, can you tell?'

'They keep exploring his adolescence. But whatever it is they're looking for they haven't found it.'

'But they've got Grout, can't he tell?'

'I don't know. And I won't know for a while. Grout doesn't know as yet, but he's about to be suspended until he decides definitely who he's working for – Dekaydence or us. It's Di'Abalo's decision, although the Professor wants him back immediately and at any price.'

'Poor Grout.'

'Poor Phoenix. It's not healthy for him to be in this state for long. But one thing's for sure...'

'Which is?'

'They can't get hold of his secrets.'

'Why ever not? You can't separate them off. And how would they know...?'

'Grout cracked that, too,' says Driver.

Handcuffs scratches his head.

'So, when you told me some time back you'd inserted...?'

'Yes, I'm sorry, I should've told you everything then but...' says Driver. 'Look, the Phoenix, Grout and I agreed this months ago. It was going to be a trial. We designed a code-blocked wall around anything the Phoenix thought should be secret. Luckily, we also agreed to trial a download of the entire contents of his brain, to keep it safe, in case...'

'In case of what?'

'Who knows for sure?' says Driver. 'But he is the

President's son. And the way the President is behaving...I reckon he's going to go for a dynastic claim to take over the Federation. Or even the Crown. And as he hasn't got that much dynasty left to pass it on to...'

'Have you forgotten,' says Handcuffs, 'this is the President who condoned the murder of his own wife and young son? And given the Phoenix is a constant and considerable thorn in his father's side...

'We need to pray, my brother,' Handcuffs continues. 'The Phoenix needs any god who can help us get him out of Dekaydence. Even if you have given up on your god, I shall pray to him and also to mine. It matters little whose god is asked, and which answers. The Phoenix needs just one to answer the call, to save him.'

8

Ruby Q has a new commission from her editor, Spiky Hair. She's to write a series about bereaved families whose soldier sons and daughters have been killed while fighting wars on the eastern front of the Federation.

Ruby Q sits in the lounge of a small, neat and tidy semi-detached house in a northern suburb of the Federation. There are potted plants on the window ledge and on the mantelpiece photos of a young man from newborn to first day at school, university graduation, and in army uniform, standing proudly with his mates. In the last photo he's grinning at the camera, his arm protectively round his fiancée's burgeoning waist.

'He was a lovely boy and he grew into a lovely man. He'd have been a great dad,' says the young man's mother, who blows her nose, which triggers more tears.

Ruby Q swallows hard. She mustn't cry, she scolds herself sternly. Her job is to write about the effects of a war that is bringing death into households throughout the Federation. A needless war begun by a power-hungry president – rumoured to be on the payroll of a foreign power – that brings needless deaths and destroys families.

Psst... Psst... Psst... Psst... Psst...

'He didn't want to go back this time,' the woman muses. 'He was unhappy with the kit. Vehicles designed for terrain quite different from the land where he and his mates were fighting. And he'd just lost his best friend. He and Gary went to primary school together. And Gary was to be his best man and godfather to the baby.'

The woman swallows a sob.

'She's a nice girl, his fiancée. Too young to have to cope with this. She'll find someone else one day, I'm sure. I hope she does. She mustn't go through the rest of her life mourning and being a widow. She needs someone who'll take care of her and the baby.'

The woman stares into space.

'But what if she moves away, Miss Cooper? Goes abroad? Then I've lost them both. He'll be lying in the earth, forever alone. No visitors, when I'm gone. No flowers. No tears. Nothing.'

She puts her head in her hands and sobs bitterly.

'What was it all for?' She pleads for an answer. 'Do you know, Miss Cooper? Do you know what this war is about, really about?'

'At the end of the day,' says Ruby Q, quietly, 'I think it's about greed. Power and greed.'

The woman nods.

'I got a note from the President of the Federation,' she says, fetching an envelope from the letter rack on the sideboard. 'Look at it, Miss Cooper. One sentence comprising 24 words, and the wretched man misspelt my son's name. One sentence comprising 24 words so he should've got it right. It's the least he could do, don't you think? Out of respect. Out of humility. Because he sent my son, aged 24, to his death. And in return he sent back a word for each year of his short life. And got his name wrong.'

'But we're not going to let him get away with it,' says Ruby Q.

'I don't know there's much we can do, Miss Cooper. I hear and applaud your intentions, don't think that I don't, but the obstacles they'll put in your way. The bullying, the threats they'll make... They'll do anything to stop you. We both know that they're capable of anything.'

'Yes,' says Ruby Q. 'That's why it's important to challenge them. We may not win but it doesn't mean we can't try. This is for your son; it's also for your grandchild. For a better future for us all.'

Ruby Q travels to the other side of town. The flat is small, neat and tidy. She sits in the front room and sees on the mantelpiece amidst the flowers and a few cards the same photograph of the happy, smiling soldier with his arm round his fiancée.

A young pregnant woman enters the room with a tray of tea and biscuits.

'He'd done three tours of duty. He didn't want to do a fourth,' she says. 'He'd lost three of his mates, including his best mate, Gary. I think he'd had enough. He was hiding something from me. He wouldn't tell me what it was. I think he wanted out of the army but was too ashamed to tell or to ask.

'But why couldn't he tell me, the one he loved, the one who was his partner in life?'

'He could've been trying to protect you from his troubles,' says Ruby Q.

'Maybe,' says the young woman, with a defeated shrug.

'I walk near his home most every day. His mum is lovely. I feel dead mean not calling but I can't go in. Not yet. I wrote to tell her why. She wrote back. She was very understanding. I need a bit of time before the funeral next week. I've got to get used to the fact that he's not here. He's not there. He's not anywhere.'

The girl stares into space.

'Did his mum tell you? She spoke to him on the phone, just half an hour before... He was in his barracks. Then she rang me, asked me to call him. Said she could hear in his voice that something wasn't right. She thought he'd tell me what was wrong. But I got no answer when I rang. No answer when I rang later. It was when I rang much later that someone picked up the phone and told me the news.'

'And then?' asks Ruby Q, quietly.

'This chap, I forget his name, told us he'd hanged himself and they'd just found him. I...I couldn't believe it. We'd been talking about marriage. About the baby. He had been happy. So, why? Why did he do it?'

'Did he write a note?' says Ruby Q.

'Yes,' says the young woman. 'They sent them on. One to his mum and one to me. He told us how much he loved us. Thanked us for all we'd done for him. That we weren't responsible in any way for him wanting to die.

'Some of his mates wrote to me. It was very kind of them. And it helps to know...how much they thought of him. That he was a top guy. If only he'd known that, or, better, believed it.'

She starts to cry.

'It's such a waste of life. I loved him so much. And we

had so much to look forward to.'

Gently, she strokes her bump.

'I think about what he did out there. What did he achieve —for himself, or anyone? It's criminal, all these young people, men and women, dying unnecessarily.

'They're given the wrong protective clothing, the wrong vehicles. Because someone sitting behind a desk, someone with no experience of life or war gives the command and says go!'

'That's why we must challenge them,' says Ruby Q. 'We may not win but we must campaign for your child. For a better world. A world your child, every child, deserves.'

72.5 HOLY RECYCLING

'He's a miscarriage,' Jezza says in TTT. 'He'll need extra care and attention.'

'There's no one better than you to give it,' replies Jack.

Jezza blushes. Childless on Earth, in Heaven she has a nursery of dead newborns to tend.

'Do we know how and why?' asks Jack.

'The mother is in her late teens. Her mother and her young brother were killed in the explosion at Number 10, Downing Street. Rumour has it that the perpetrator was her father, aiming for a massive sympathy vote to get himself elected President of the Federation. Her brother is the Phoenix.'

'So, this is the child of Maria?' says Jack, peering into the baby's face.

'Yes, Maria was living on the streets. She suffered much. And now this, another loss. But she is in good and kind hands. She will mourn and she will recover. She will never forget but she will move on.'

'And this little one?'

'You know the form, Jack.'

'Yes, but I never tire of hearing you tell me.'

Jezza smiles as she cradles the baby, which begins to wriggle and giggle in her arms.

'He has led a number of lives. And when the time is right he will return. He will be someone else. He will be born again. And again. Until he is perfected and becomes an angel.'

'And us?'

Jezza shrugs.

'There are rumours of us all being recycled, but none of us knows that for sure. Our fate is in the hands of God.'

'A god who has gone missing. So where does that leave us?'

'Carrying on, Jack. Doing God's work and carrying on. We have no option.'

Jack says nothing but he's not so sure.

SECTION 9

Friendship improves happiness and abates misery, by the doubling of our joy and the dividing of our grief.
Marcus Tullius Cicero (106 BC–43 BC)

73 HEAVEN ON RED ALERT

'How many NewComers d'you think want to remain in Heaven?' Bhupi asks the NewComers' spokesperson, Spaghetti Sureshi.

'It's impossible to say, Mr Bhupi.' Spaghetti Sureshi responds hesitatingly in TTT. 'NewComers play such a complex game of bluff and counterbluff that I doubt they themselves have any idea which way they'll go until the very last moment.'

'Oh, dear,' sighs Bhupi, who is keen to create a flock of NewComer angels.

'There's also the problem of vertigo,' Spaghetti Sureshi continues. 'Most of them live on flatlands. They're not used to heights so here, they can't look over the edge of a cloud without being sick.'

'And that's costing us a fortune to mop up after them, let alone the cost of acquiring innumerable recyclable sick bags.' Cataract sounds exasperated.

'You talk of where *they* come from,' says Jack. 'So where do you come from and how did you end up here, Mr Sureshi?'

'I've lived high and low. But the night I died I'd been at a fancy-dress party. I awoke to find I was in a large, mixed bunch of clowns. Someone told me we were in Purgatory.

And then, suddenly, we were all fast-tracked through the gates into hell,' Spaghetti Sureshi says sadly.

'What rotten luck,' says Cataract.

Spaghetti Sureshi nods.

'I went through The Seven Stages of Red Tape to try to prove I was down to come to Heaven but the documents kept getting mislaid and the call centre in India was always so busy...'

'I am so sorry,' says Bhupi. 'The call centre problem is down to a distant relative. He began using the communication cables in his works of art. He made a fortune. Luckily, the Archangel Gabriel has said he'll visit him in a dream and make him promise to use some of his wealth to replace the cables.'

'That is very reassuring,' says Spaghetti Sureshi. 'But I am in Heaven now. And here I shall happily remain while trying to do good, helping people on Earth, where I'll call myself Clarence, after the dear old angel in *It's a Wonderful Life*.'

'Such a lovely film,' muses Cataract. 'But I heard tell you play bridge. D'you fancy a rubber some time?'

'I'd like that,' says Spaghetti Sureshi. 'Thank you, Mr Cataract. But for now I must warn you there are NewComers here, working undercover. For the Other Side.'

'We know that,' says Jack. 'But do you know what it is they want?'

Spaghetti Sureshi nods slowly.

'They want to destroy Heaven.'

'Oh, my God!' says Bhupi.

'Precisely!' says Jack. 'Where is He? We're facing an emergency, a 999 red-alert crisis, and we've no way to contact Him. It's so ludicrous it reminds me of...of...life on Earth!'

74 BROTHERLY LOVE

Wiggins enters the crematorium chapel near the river in the old village. Two members of staff cross the room and speak to him in hushed voices. They inform him that the Order of Service sheet is on every one of the 100 seats in the room.

They relieve Wiggins of a memory stick of music, a photograph of Cataract's cat, Beluga, and a carrier bag containing the small casket of his brother's ashes, which is placed on a table near the lectern. They go to stand outside the doors to the chapel, ready to usher in the mourners.

Wiggins sits in the front pew, alone in the chapel. He's glad his wife chose not to come. She had no time for Cataract; thought him a smelly old tyrant. Which he was, Wiggins concedes silently. Equally, Cedric Cataract was his brother, whom he loved and who loved him. Who is no longer available for a companionable brothers' dinner. No longer working all hours. No longer dreaming of living by the sea. Who suddenly *is* no longer.

He looks around the room and sees no one. Outside, in the chapel garden, he spots a large black bird in a tree, seemingly watching him through a wall of window as it fidgets and twitches its wings as though adjusting a tiresomely itchy cloak.

Wiggins drifts into memories: sitting on a little wooden bridge over a lively bright stream where he and Cataract sat together watching birds, fish, water-boatmen and floating twigs. He recalls shock at finding an adder in the grass, climbing trees and getting stuck in one until their father came to their rescue. Cycle rides along the lane on to the moor. Catty as a fit young man in red pyjamas herding an escaped bull from the croquet lawn and back into the farmer's field – returning unscathed, much to the relief of his anxious mother.

Wiggins sighs. Fifteen minutes have passed and the chapel remains empty but for himself. He makes a sign to the undertakers at the door to start proceedings. He has been told there is a queue of funerals after Cataract's. And now HOH Candelskin has introduced fines should a funeral service overrun... He shakes his head in sorrow. All is rush in life and now in death.

Gene Kelly is crooning 'Singin' in the Rain'. Wiggins smiles, remembering the school production in which Catty took Kelly's role. A true hoofer, with a chocolate cream voice, Cataract had been a happy young man before... Wiggins gets up and begins to dance and tap. He had been the understudy. And now?

The song ends. Wiggins makes his way to the lectern. He looks out across 100 empty seats and is surprised to see two young men, hovering at the back of the chapel, looking awkward. The taller one is wearing a crisp white shirt and a smart dark suit and tie. The stocky one wears an ageing ill-matching suit with sleeves too short and shirtsleeves too long. Wiggins has no idea who they are but gives them a welcoming smile and indicates they can sit anywhere. The two shuffle into seats closest to the door.

Wiggins clears his throat. He had a speech prepared for a crowd of Cataract's friends, family and colleagues. Now he decides to speak from his heart.

'My dearest brother, Cedric...'

The two young men exchange glances. So, this man is Cataract's brother?

'...we had good and bad times. You were the very best of brothers and, occasionally, among the naughtiest. I hope you knew that, regardless, I loved you, Cedric, and shall love you always and for ever.'

Wiggins looks towards the casket.

'Today, dearest brother, you are free of this mortal coil and later today I shall cast your ashes into the river by which we grew up, the river we both loved that will take you into the ocean for which you pined, to the shore on the other side where, I pray, we shall meet again, as brothers, as friends, as soul-mates for ever. Amen.'

'Amen,' the tall young man in the smart suit repeats firmly, his head lowered, before he blows his nose, making a noise so loud that it causes his stocky friend to jump, visibly. Wiggins feels touched by the hidden support in these sounds and actions of apparent distress.

'You all right, In?' whispers Bodkin, hoping his friend

isn't about to lapse again into grief and good deeds. It was bad enough after his girlfriend Jezza died.

Innit gives a flicker of a smile.

'Thanks for coming with me, Bods. You're a real mate.'

Bodkin is aware suddenly of something odd in his chest. It feels very warm and, actually, he admits to himself, rather nice. It's a sort of glowing feeling. This was what Innit was talking about on the journey down, having bumped into some mad old dame on the street.

Firkin' hell, Bodkin thinks, *firkin' Innit is doing this! Making me feel good and stuff. I'll have to watch him. We got work and business to do, and money to make so I can retire when I get to my twenty-first birthday.*

Wiggins looks out of the window. The big black bird has flown away. The two young mourners have departed, unnoticed. Such a shame, he thinks. He would've so liked to know their connection to his brother. He feels Cedric has flown away, too. Like his beloved children who have left home to make their way in the world. He feels a black hole of emptiness inside him fast expanding.

75 MACBANGERS AND BURGERS

'MacGluten wants a ghostwriter to do the Dekaydence cookbook,' MacCavity informs Di'Abalo. 'He's also demanding eighty per cent of takings from sales.'

'So, he's from Aberdeen?' Di'Abalo enquires, with a wry smile.

'Aye, how did you guess?' says MacCavity. 'But he is some thug.'

'Isn't that part of the Dekaydence job description for thugs, Mr MacCavity, that our thugs should be thugs?'

'Aye,' says Mr MacCavity. 'But he goes beyond the pale.'

Di'Abalo ponders.

'Anyone else of any talent in the kitchens?'

'Och aye, and some,' says MacCavity. 'There's two young lads worth watching. Goo, MacGluten's son, and a young Chinese wonder, MacSoya. I'll get the kitchens to send up some of their dishes.'

'Hot dishes,' says Di'Abalo. 'Phlegm likes especially hot dishes.'

'Right you are, my lord. What d'you want to do about MacGluten?'

Di'Abalo looks out of the window.

'The sun is shining. It's just the weather for a barbecue.'

'Yes, sir, but...' says MacCavity.

'Sausages,' Di'Abalo muses.

MacCavity frowns.

'My lord?'

'Nice, crisply burnt sausages, Mr MacCavity. With a Dekaydence hot chilli ketchup.'

MacCavity swallows hard, bows and leaves the room. He never did like MacGluten but...

76 A MOTHER WRITES ...

Ruby Q receives a sealed letter from her mother, with a covering letter from her mother's lawyer, which she reads first.

Dear Miss Cooper,
Your mother, Mrs Angelica Nera Cooper, has asked me to forward to you the enclosed sealed letter. She asks that you contact me should you need any assistance in any area.
Yours sincerely,
Wiggins QC

PS On a personal note, may I add how much I admire the bravery and honesty that shines through your reports in The Daily Unigraph, *and earlier still the fascinating music stories about Stanley Halls and the Dipstick Five in* Shed Monthly, *to which I was introduced by my children.*

Ruby Q opens the sealed envelope, takes out the letter from her mother and begins reading.

Dear Ruby Q,

Apologies, I write in haste. Very soon I shall be off on a long journey for an indeterminate time. Don't come looking for me, you won't find me. No one knows where I'll be or how long I'll be there. Wiggins, the lawyer I have instructed for years and to whom I have entrusted this letter, knows nothing of my destination or purpose. He knows only that it's likely I won't return.

So, on a practical level I have left money for you in a bank account, the details of which are held by Wiggins.

Don't mourn for me, Ruby Q, I trod the path I wanted and have had a good life. Don't mourn for what we didn't have as mother and daughter. We love in different ways, each is incomprehensible to the other.

I can see strength in you, Ruby Q. A courage that I like to think you get, in part, from me, in part from Rallan. You have a mystery that draws others to you – as happens with your biological father – and a compassion and kindness that comes from the good man who raised you. These are great gifts, Ruby Q. You haven't had a regular family life (whatever that is) and I think it unlikely you'll have a family of your own. I doubt that'll be news to you. But you have gifts sufficient to make good the rest of your life and, in our brief encounters, I feel confident in the belief that you'll have friends who'll love you always.

Sincerely,

Your mother, Angelica Nera Cooper.

Don't cry, Ruby Q. I'm getting wet and soggy. Look, I mean... Hang on, what do I mean? There is good stuff in your mother's letter. Reread it and see. I think it shows that deep down, in her own way, your mother is concerned about you, Ruby Q, and, yes, in her own way I think she's saying she loves you.

Ruby Q shakes her head. She feels she is drowning in tears and unhappiness.

Sorry, Ruby Q, I don't come with a handkerchief. And my shoulder to cry on is, alas, metaphysical. And for now I'm right out of jokes, inappropriate or otherwise.

That night Ruby Q has a dream. Her mother is sitting in the garden where Ruby Q lives. It's early evening, the sun is like a ball of tangerine fire and Angelica's auburn hair shines like polished copper. The birds are feeding and singing, loud, bright and determined, to ensure others are warned about who owns this territory.

Mr Treasure comes to sit next to her mother. They talk but Ruby Q can't hear what they're saying. Mr Treasure brushes feathers—or is it crumbs?—from his trousers. He takes from his pocket a handkerchief – shaded all the colours of the rainbow – and hands it to Ruby Q's mother. She smiles. So does Ruby Q.

Later, Ruby Q has another dream. She's following her mother, secretly, at a distance. They travel along a corridor. Out of a thick grey mist emerges a huge ivy-covered garden wall. She watches her mother run her hand across sections, as though searching for something. And then appears an old door.

Her mother looks over her shoulder. Ruby Q sees the scowl on her face before Angelica disappears through the door, which shuts smartly behind her. Ruby Q runs to the wall but the door has disappeared. Try as she may, she cannot find it. Neither can she find any other way through.

She wakes up sobbing. She finds she is calling out for her mother, as she did when she was a little girl, after her mother had walked out of her life.

Maria is recovering from a miscarriage. She makes no mention of it and Piccolo doesn't ask. But they both feel that their sessions together are progressing well. Maria enjoys screaming and shouting and banging away on drums, cymbals, chimes and bells. At times, hearing Piccolo mimic her noises on the piano, she is reduced to tears of laughter. Sometimes, it's tears alone. Sometimes, she can emerge cleansed, with a small fresh smile. Sometimes, she sits in dumb silence, her head in her hands, staring into space. Once she threw a book at Piccolo, which straight away he threw back. Once she stormed out of the room but turned up next day for her appointment, with an apology in the shape of a bunch of flowers from the garden.

'So what's your story?' she asks Piccolo one day when they're sitting outside, relaxing in the warm-as-a-blanket sunshine, enjoying tea and a slice or two of Lady C's home-made apple cake.

Piccolo hesitates.

'It's only fair,' she says. 'I've told you mine and you've seen a bloody bit of it.'

'I don't find it easy to talk about it.' Piccolo shrugs, looking at his shoes, and trying to imagine how Maria is feeling about the loss of her baby son.

'Get a grip!' she commands, with a dollop of gentleness in her voice.

He smiles.

'How can I resist you?' he says.

'Is that an offer...?' she asks suspiciously.

'No!' he says emphatically.

She swallows hard.

'Sorry,' she says. 'I don't know how to tell any more. I mean, what normal people do and say. I think I've lost it. It's not only reading between the lines, it's understanding what the lines themselves mean.'

'It'll come back. In time,' says Piccolo, thinking she needs to hear this.

'Come on, then, tell me your story. Please,' she says.

Piccolo takes in a deep breath.

'I saw my father murdered. I saw them do it. My mum and her boyfriend. She helped him,' he says. 'I was a little kid, watching them through a crack in the bathroom door. Too scared to say anything, let alone do anything. But I wish...I wish I'd tried.'

'Hey,' says Maria. 'That's easy to say now. Now you're grown up. But back then... Look, if you'd tried to intervene they'd have killed you, disposed of you because you'd been a witness. Your dad didn't see you, did he? No. So, I bet he died praying and believing you were asleep in the next room.'

Piccolo shrugs.

'Didn't the police investigate?' she asks.

'No.' He gives a hollow laugh. 'A neighbour rang them. My mum told them the neighbour was a busybody and that my dad had walked out on her. She lied to the social, too. Every time someone came round asking why I wasn't at school, why I was so thin, my mum had a different excuse. She could've won an Oscar for each of her performances. She and her boyfriend locked me in the bathroom. Mostly, I lived in the bath. Ate soap to stop the hunger pangs. Usual stuff.'

Maria is quiet, clutching her knees to her chest, rocking to and fro. Once upon a time she would've asked Piccolo more questions. But not now. She has little energy to take on the sorrows of others. Anyway, her focus is elsewhere.

'What happened to Grout?' she asks.

'It's for him to tell you,' says Piccolo.

Her face turns sulky.

'Well, he won't, will he?' she snaps.

They are silent for a moment or two before she sighs.

'Maybe mixed-up people shouldn't mix with mixed-up people.'

'Mmm,' says Piccolo. 'That could lead to a dramatic crash in the population but...' He blushes at what he's said, that it might open a healing wound.

But Maria just laughs. It's a raucous sound like a squabbling duck in a pond fight, but there's a wild warmth in the laugh that makes Piccolo smile.

They hear voices. The Catguts have guests for lunch: Edwina Gardening-Fork and Young Miss Burgess. Maria flinches. She can't work out whether or not she likes or loathes the two old biddies. But they obviously adore and feel protective of the Catguts and Maria finds she is touched by that, and just a little jealous.

But the person who comes round the house to the back garden isn't either of the elderly ladies.

Piccolo jumps to his feet and is off but Will is too quick for him, heading him off before he reaches the back door.

'Why?' Will demands. 'Why must you keep running away from me?'

'I've made a promise,' says Piccolo, shaking himself free. 'It's to keep you safe. Now leave me alone. And don't come after me. Please. I'm doing this for you.'

Piccolo takes off. Will hesitates. He looks round and sees Maria. She's watching him. She looks vaguely familiar but he can't recall where or how or why.

She's rocking to and fro on her chair.

'It's none of my business,' she says, 'but there's enough mess in this world without you two adding to it. So, I tell you this for nothing: neither of you appears to realise it but you two love one another. So why not just get it together?'

If only he could, thinks Will. But what can he do when, every time they meet, Piccolo runs away from him?

78 OUT-DEK'D?

Grout is staying in London seven days a week. He has much work to do at Dekaydence, as well as secret 'stuff'' for friends. He wants to avoid bumping into Indigo, who calls often on Lady Catgut to discuss the organic greenhouse movement sprouting up countrywide.

One night, after catching a few hours' sleep, Grout returns to the Dekaydence laboratory in the early hours. Almost immediately there's a knock at the door and, without waiting for a reply, in marches a Black Tartan guard, his eyes hidden by red tartan sunglasses.

'The boss wants to see you,' the guard says sharply.

'At this time? What on earth for?' says Grout, uneasy.

'Och, that's between you and him, is it not?' says the guard.

Phlegm opens the door to Lord di'Abalo's penthouse apartment in Dekaydence HQ. For a moment Grout is taken aback: he was sure someone told him the old butler had died.

'Tea and sympathy?' says Phlegm. 'Or something stronger?'

'You tell me,' says Grout, espying the gold and mosaic egg-timer on Di'Abalo's desk, the black sand abundant in the lower phial. For something, or someone, he thinks, time is definitely running out. He shudders. Could it be him?

Di'Abalo enters the room.

'Dear boy, you look utterly exhausted. Best you sit before you fall down,' says his lordship, indicating the densely comfortable cream settle on which are sleeping a black cat and a white. Di'Abalo sits down beside them. Phlegm hovers unobtrusively.

'Now, Grout,' says di'Abalo. 'You know how much I admire the work you do for Dekaydence. I have backed you and financed you for some time and I don't resent a penny that I've spent on you. However, I do wonder if the time has come for a parting of the ways?'

Grout's eyes widen.

'But...?' he begins, nervously.

'I think you know why,' says di'Abalo quietly.

Grout nods.

'Because I work for other people?' says Grout, his voice almost inaudible.

'Indeed,' says Di'Abalo. 'I've no overall problem with the concept of freelance work. And I know you don't take money from anyone else, which is noble, or, in my personal opinion, foolish. But I see, increasingly, there could soon be a serious conflict of interest. So I want you to go away and think about the direction you want your future to go in. I'll give you 72 hours to make a decision. Now, get some sleep, dear boy.'

Grout leaves the room. His head and shoulders hang heavy. With fatigue but, more, with what he feels to be an almighty dilemma.

'So which way do you think he'll jump, sir?' says Phlegm.

'He's on the horns of a dilemma, is he not?' says Di'Abalo, with a short laugh.

Phlegm smiles.

'The old ones are the best, sir. I have missed your humour.'

'Not cross with me, then, for bringing you back to the land of the living?'

Phlegm shakes his head.

'How many times does that make?' Di'Abalo frowns.

Phlegm shrugs.

'I lost count, sir, circa AD164.'

'Good man, Phlegm,' says Di'Abalo. 'If you don't find that term too insulting.'

79 INDIGO TO THE RESCUE

Piccolo decides to cycle to Indigo's house. It's some dozen miles away and the weather is suddenly providing a few glorious days of warm sunshine. And, at any time, the Sussex countryside boosts his spirit into the stratosphere.

He cycles past remote cottages wrapped in soft pink clematis and pale lilac wisteria, where tiny holly blue butterflies cavort around potted plants. He cycles along deserted lanes, under magnificent old trees, oak, wild ash, copper beech. Hockney hawthorns are exploding in a froth of gently scented creamy white blossom while the dreamy lacy acers with their tiny delicate leaves wave to him as if they were fairy hands. There is courtship all around, from the tiniest insect to the jumbo-jet-sized pigeons, and now here he is, too, is on a mission of Cupid's making.

One day, he decides, on another glorious day when time stretches before him like a vast undulating roll of carpet, he will translate these feelings, this beauty into a symphony to remind himself and others of the natural world in which they live, and to inspire people to care for and nurture it.

★ ★ ★

Piccolo shows his ID medallion to the policemen on the gate. They recognise him and salute as they let him through. He gets off the bike and begins the long walk up the driveway. The heat has suddenly become more intense, despite a frisky breeze that chases itself in and out of the trees.

When the big old country house, bought by Indigo as a working family home, comes into view so too do the numerous vehicles on the forecourt. Piccolo groans inwardly. Why didn't he stop to think? There's a coronation in a few weeks' time and loads of extra people must be involved in the organisation. He imagines Indigo rushed off her feet, round the bend with details and nerves. Aside from the grief she must be feeling at losing two close members of her family, with another gone missing.

He's been so entrenched in his own problems, his own depression, and now the worries of trying to study to improve his teaching skills and to help heal Maria and assist her to find herself.

He could kick himself. Instead, he kicks out at the gravel pathway, creating a cloud of desert dust.

'What's up?' says a voice behind him.

He turns to see Indigo emerge from the shrubbery.

'Sorry, I should've rung you. I forgot all of this was going on.' He nods in the general direction of the cars. 'I'd better leave you in peace.'

He's mounting the bike as she steps forward and puts

her hand on the handlebars.

'It'd be awfully nice to have a chat with someone normal,' Indigo says ruefully.

He laughs.

'Should I take that as a compliment?'

'Yes.' She smiles. 'Definitely, because, currently, I'm submerged in red tape and historical protocol. I could do with coming up for a breath of fresh air. And the company of a Young Person.'

'I'll try to oblige, man,' says Piccolo.

'Thank you. So, let's put the bike in the shrubbery and go down to the river. Away from prying eyes.'

They hide the bike and walk a path unseen from the house.

'How is everyone back at the ranch?'

He hesitates. Should he mention Grout?

'Everyone's fine, thanks.'

There's a moment of uneasy silence.

'So, why did you want to see me?' she asks.

'Grout,' he mumbles.

He sees anger in her eyes and flushed cheeks.

Oh, God, he's no good at this, he thinks.

'He's not well,' he blurts out. 'Not at all well.'

He relaxes. Her anger is replaced by anxiety. What should he say next? Oh no, he thinks, she's gone all frosty again. He opens his mouth but—

'He has a new friend to care for him,' Indigo says haughtily.

Piccolo wishes he read the problem pages in the women's magazines that Young Miss Burgess collects. They're ages old but so is the problem.

'He was right, he is too old for me,' Indigo says firmly.

'I don't think he is,' says Piccolo. 'Anyway, I don't think age comes into it.'

She goes to speak but he continues.

'Look, it's none of my business but you two are my friends. You get on so well I don't like to see your friendship in trouble. 'Specially over something that didn't happen.'

'You're just trying to cover up for your friend,' she says, her tone sharp.

'No, I'm not,' he retorts emphatically. 'OK, Maria was making a play for Grout but he's a chap – we don't see things in the same light as you. He was as shocked as you and me about what happened. He's gutted that you got the wrong end of the stick. He is truly gutted. Believe me, and now he's been sacked...'

'What?' she demands.

'Di'Abalo has found out about the freelance work Grout does for you and the others. He's got an ultimatum to decide what to do. Stick with Dekaydence, with all the support, financial and otherwise, that goes with it. Or go it alone with no job, no money, but on the side of good.'

'What's he decided?'

'I don't know,' says Piccolo. 'For what it's worth, I don't think he's got a choice. He needs paid employment.

And given his skills he should find a job, no problem.'

'Given the current economic climate, I'm not so sure,' says Indigo thoughtfully. 'Where is he now?'

'Unusually, he's at home. Or he was. Sitting with Billy and Monty, the three of them staring into space.'

'I'm coming over,' says Indigo.

'Fantastic!' says Piccolo. 'Oh, but I've only got my cycle.'

'Not to worry, I'll have it sent back tomorrow. For now, I'll call Nayr as I'm supposed to have a security guard with me 24/7. He can say he's accompanying me on a walk and then meet us with a car in ten minutes at the river-gate, where no one will see us.'

80 MAKE-UP TIME

Grout is startled to see Indigo marching towards him across the field where he's sitting with Montezuma and Billy.

'What's all this I hear about you being sacked?' she demands, standing before him, hands on hips.

'It's not quite like that,' says Grout.

'How is it, then?'

'Hello, Indigo, kind of you to pop round and interrogate me when you've ignored all my calls,' says Grout acidly.

'I've been busy,' she snaps back. 'I'm about to undergo a coronation, if you'd forgotten. I'm still in mourning, if you'd forgotten. And on top of all that, I'm not sure I've forgiven you.'

'That's fine,' says Grout, 'because there's nothing to forgive. We're a bunch of broken people in this household and the aim is to help one another mend. Maybe you should abdicate and join us.'

Indigo gasps at Grout's unusually brusque manner but says nothing.

'Look, I'm sorry for all the stuff you're going through,' says Grout, speaking more kindly. 'Truly, I am. It's not fair. You're too young and there's too much pressure on you. But if you think for one moment that I'd do something to hurt you...'

He shakes his head as he gets up to leave.

'Grout,' she calls after him. 'I'm sorry, too. I so miss your friendship. Please, please, can we still be friends?'

There's silence for a moment, from them both.

''Course, Indigo.' He shrugs. 'I've missed your friendship, too.'

'And I really do want to know what's happening at work,' she says.

'Indigo,' says Grout firmly. 'Listen to me. Whatever you say, I've made up my mind. I'm staying with Dekaydence. And you can*not* persuade me otherwise...'

'But what about all your freelance work, doing good stuff out there for Justice, for us all...?'

'I know, I know. My plan is to leave Dekaydence as soon as I can find a decent job working with honourable people. One that enables me to have more time to do free, freelance work for Justice, for Will, the Phoenix, Ruby Q and for you.'

'Sounds like a plan. Well done, dearest Grout. Just make sure you get a good pension plan!'

Grout smiles. Indigo smiles. They high-five and walk on together.

As they reach the end of the field they see in the distrance Nayr, accompanied by two Black Tartan guards. She recognises another man who's approaching, HOH Randall Candelskin in a flowing white, purple and green cassock.

'Oh, no,' Indigo groans, 'this is how my life is going to

be, Grout. Surrounded and suffocated by security guards, protocol and HOH Randall Candelskin in multicoloured frocks. I can't do it.'

'Yes, you can,' says Grout gently. 'There are very few who could do the job but you can, Indigo. You can and will. And I promise to be there for you, if you need me, every step of the way.'

BREAKING NEWS

Ruby Q Cooper reports from the Middle East for *The Daily Unigraph*.

Additional research by T-J Jenkins

The dictator who ordered the murder of four dozen children under the age of 12, along with their parents, has young children of his own. Today, in one town, he has killed more than a hundred people in total, families, old and young, and the unborn. Well, given his average day is thirty or forty gunned down or throats slit...

The dead eyes of the murdered children stare back lightless and lifeless into the eyes of a peace-keeping force that think of their own children, safe and sound back home. Or they reflect on the years of life and living they've been given, years that have been stolen from these young souls lying before them in pools of drying blood and flies.

The eyes of one boy, nine or ten years old, appear to ask gently but plaintively: Why?

There's no answer that makes sense because there is no question that what was done is anything other than wicked and brutal, a sickening insight into the cruelty of man. Along with stomach-curdling fear and panic, this

LIVE FROM AN ILLEGAL INTERNET SERVICE PROVIDER

would've been the last impression these young children had of life and adults.

What did these children know or care of religious differences? Of political manoeuvring intent on winning at any cost? Of foreign powers gorging on massive payments from an impoverished country on the brink of civil war, with roots deep in terror, blood and death? These young ones, just setting off on a voyage of discovery – climbing trees, playing chase, hide-and-seek and football, and discovering the joy of friendship. Mown down like frail and irrelevant blades of grass.

The Phoen'oid watches the video footage, takes in the information, and is startled to feel a prickling sensaton behind his eyes. He blinks. He wonders. Nothing happens.

They might have been tears, he decides. Whatever, they are of no use. They will not bring back the dead children or their families. No, it's time for the guilty to be punished. It's not long before he has an idea and works on it for long hours. Only then does he set forth.

The Phoen'oid is in Paris. In the Rue du Faubourg Saint-Honoré, one of the most fashionable streets in the world, which contains almost every major global fashion house. The dictator's wife visits regularly. She's here now, moving from shop to shop, her security guards and chauffeur on hand to pack the boot of the long limousine with dozens of boxes of acquired goods.

The Phoen'oid is in a car across the street, ready for action. So, when she steps out of – is it the ninth or tenth shop? – pondering where to go next, he fires. She rubs her forehead as if to rid herself of a piece of grit or an irritating insect. She thinks nothing more of it, and moves on. As does the Phoen'oid.

He travels to the capital of the dictator's land and is able to repeat the exercise on the dictator himself who, similarly, tries to brush away an irritant from his forehead and moves on.

The Phoen'oid books into a hotel and awaits night.

The results come through in the early hours of the morning. The Phoen'oid's aim was perfect. The nano-cameras fired into the dictator and his wife start producing excellent results. The pictures the Phoen'oid is watching show the dictator and his wife tossing and turning, and muttering and shouting in their sleep.

The wife is the first to awake. She screams at the top of her voice, shouting the names of her children. Her husband awakes and also shouts out the names of their children. Guards and servants come running. The dictator's wife pushes past them all and runs along the corridor to the children's bedroom. She pushes past the guards on duty at the door and falls upon her children, who sit up in bed and stare wide-eyed with shock and terror at the noise their mother is making. Then, seeing their father, equally wild and distraught, behind her, they begin to sob.

Later, back in their bedroom, with lemon tea brought by the servants, the dictator and his wife talk in whispers. What was it that disturbed them in the night? A dream, a nightmare. So vivid, they agree. They lower their voices.

'The dead children,' says the dictator's wife. 'There were so many of them, bloodied and bruised, and cut about with knives and ripped open by gunfire... All of them had...'

He completes the sentence she cannot bring herself to do.

'...the faces of our children.'

'Yes,' she said, startled that in his sleep he has shared her nightmare. 'Every one of them had the face of one of our children. Everywhere you looked, there was one or other of our children. Dead.'

'We shall tell no one about this, habeebee. No one.'

She nods, and then glances at her watch. She must hurry. She must be at the beautician in a few hours.

The Phoen'oid files a short report in his memory bank.

★ ★ ★

LIVE FROM AN ILLEGAL INTERNET SERVICE PROVIDER

The nightmares continue night after night. As does the screaming on awakening. The dictator and his wife grow increasingly uneasy. Nervous of sleep and what it will bring. Wine, parties and designer jewellery don't block out what's happening to them. They bicker. Their children shy away from them and cling to their nannies and guards.

Now the dreams come during the day as well, when the dictator is in meetings with his generals; when his wife is in shopping therapy or at the beautician. The children, with the faces of the dictator's children, spring to life. They scream at their parents to stop what they're doing. To stop the fighting. To work for a civil peace rather than a civil war. The children point at the horrific wounds and injuries their young bodies have incurred. They shout at their parents, calling them child murderers. Pouring the lifeblood of their country down the drain.

In their daytime nightmares the dictator and his wife, who is close to a breakdown, watch as the blood of the children – who have the faces of their own children – drips into the sewers and soaks the very soil and soul of their mauled homeland.

Justice for all

81 QUEENS TOGETHER?

'Do you want my job?' Indigo asks Will, who reckons this is the third time he's been brought on, or nearly, as a substitute. 'Many people believe the crown is yours by right and I'm happy to abdicate.'

'Och, no,' Will says. 'Thanks, most kind. But I'm a Scot, remember. I'm not here to become King of England. Besides, I think it politic to stay with Cataract, Cyclops and Mote. I owe it to the old man, bad and mad as he was. I learnt much from him. And if I qualify in one of the top accountancy firms in the world, I can pass on information that'd help Justice.'

'Is this what you want in life?'

'Kind of. But not really,' says Will. 'It'll have to do for now.'

'What would you *like* to do, Will?'

'More than anything? Be at home in Scotland. Running the estate, giving my mother a break. Reading in the library that my father built. Boating on the loch with Tommo, seeing his big broad grin at my incompetence as a sailor.'

'Where does Piccolo fit in?'

'Mind your own business.'

'You're my cousin, I want to see you happy. I know you love him and—'

'We'll drop this subject, if you please, Your Majesty.'

'Don't start that. You're my cousin. We are Will and Indigo. And with a fair wind, who knows? We could rule neighbouring countries. Think, Will, then we'd be queens together.'

'You cheeky monkey!'

'It's in the genes, kid!' she says, adopting an American accent.

Will laughs as he throws a cushion at her.

9

The President of the Federation stumbles along in the darkness, through densely wooded areas and an underground maze of tunnels. Since his son, the Phoenix, shot him in the leg he's had a few falls. They serve to win him more votes, he knows, but the injury is infuriatingly inconvenient. Especially when he sees men older than himself with boundless energy and the agility of a monkey.

Several men in the party offer him one of their meagre snacks. He acknowledges their kindness with a nod and what passes for a smile, while grimacing at the offerings behind their backs. Colleagues in his political party, as well as the opposition, have described the smile as the grin of an expectant vampire. Some swear they've seen blood dribble from his mouth. Stalwart friends say it's the result of a recurrent gum infection.

As he meanders by foot and in thought the President decides he'll return home and write a book about his experiences in this godforsaken land. It should bring him in a tidy sum. And more votes. Maybe a film role? Talking of which, where did he stash his camera? His hand reaches into a pocket and withdraws instantly: his hand is sticky with a lump of squashed dates. That mischievous child in the camp who pretended to want his autograph!

He glances down and bolts down a scream. A goat, saliva dribbling from its jaws, has in its mouth a piece of fabric from the sheep's wool thawb, the long flowing garment he's wearing to keep out the cold.

Another local incident for the book, he reminds the inner author.

Beware of the camera flash, an internal voice responds, it could cause problems.

Great! says the President. More colour, more drama, so much the better.

The President focuses the camera on the goat staring mournfully at him and a bright flashlight explodes over the travelling party.

Guns go off from vantage points in the surrounding hills.

'Oh, my God! Oh, my—' shouts the President, as the dark-haired young man rugby tackles him to the ground and covers the President's body with his own.

'This isn't a day trip to Bognor Regis,' the young man hisses in the President's ear.

'What d'you know about Bognor Regis?' the President splutters through a mouthful of dry sandy earth.

'My great-grandfather was born there,' the young man whispers. 'Keep your head down, pray to your god, and I shall pray to Allah. Then follow me quickly, on all fours. We must crawl into that tunnel over there. Then we travel underground, heading for that hill over there.' He gestures.

'That hill is miles away and there's an armoury out there.'

'Yes, and there's also a cave known only to a few. If we are separated, go left and up a bit from the tall tree. We hide there for a few days. Then we'll get you out.'

'You must come out, too. You can advise me on all the native background stuff for my book.'

The Federation President sees the white grin in the creamy coffee-coloured skin.

'That'd be fun,' says the young man. 'But my wife would have a fit and—'

A hail of bullets ricochets round the valley.

The Federation President scrabbles to dig his body deeper into the ground but the weight of the youth is suffocating him. It's a struggle to move. He berates the young man for being a deadweight.

Someone grabs him by the wrist. It's an older man, who drags him out of the dirt, from under the youth who topples, face upwards. Only then does the President realise that the dak-haired young man who shielded him is dead. He reaches for his camera. A dramatic shot for the book. The older man gives him a look like thunder.

'He died trying to save you, Mr President. In his memory, let us continue his work, bravely and honourably, to help get you rescued,' he says crisply, nodding towards the hill and the hidden cave. 'We must get there before the sun rises. Before our brother here gets to the doors of Heaven.'

The President stares at the young man lying on the ground before him as others appear from nowhere and continue the digging. The body is laid to rest in the ground. Words are spoken quickly, and quietly.

The President's heart is in his mouth. The fighting sounds harsher than before. When will they quit this wretched place? He frets. He wants to shriek at everyone: I came here to help you rebuild your country and economy. I'm trying to make a film about you and your plight. You could be in it if you stopped shooting every one of us... You've killed a young man... Can't you stop fighting for one bloody moment? I must have—

'Silence!' The President shrieks with frustration, and without thinking. (Well, he's always been good at that). He soon realises what he's done.

Spotlights scan the hills and the valley. The shooting starts and stops.

The older man punches the President in the face, knocking him to the ground.

The other men hoist the President to his feet, hand him his stick, and help him into the network of underground tunnels.

'You did the best and only thing, my son,' the elder says to the older man. 'That man is a fool. Why do they have him as their President? He has caused the death of a good man, one of the best. And we know it's not the first time and probably will not be the last.'

'He was a good man, your nephew,' the elder continues. 'If he had lived he would have become the Pathfinder for this tribe. As it is, we shall give the torch to his young son, in memory of his father, and in the hope that he will learn the skills necessary for such an important role in this tribe. And let us hope also that the boy forgets the dreams of his father to go on a pilgrimage to Bognor Regis.'

81.5 HOME FROM HOME

Indigo has a difficult decision to make. She doesn't want to part with Tommo but she's concerned that the house she lives in — expanded now by dozens of staff to look after her and state affairs as well as the house and gardens — will no longer be a suitable home for Tommo. However kind people are, they have work to do. What would he do if she were to be away for any length of time? No, Tommo needs to live in a caring, stable family environment. She talks it over with Lady Catgut.

'I like to think a family environment is what we have here,' says Lady Catgut. 'Piccolo, Grout and Nigel. And now Maria. All of them have problems but over time they draw strength from one another. And build friendships.'

'Has Maria recovered from her operation?' Indigo enquires politely.

'I think it'll take time but this is a safe haven, a good family environment for the wounded in heart and spirit. I'm sure Tommo would be happy here. In time, Maria, too.'

'It'd mean a lot more work for you, though of course I'd pay for someone to help you,' says Indigo.

'I wouldn't hear of it,' says Lady C. 'I wonder what I did before the boys came along. They give us back so much, especially to Catty. They are a joy. And I think Tommo would fit in very well. He'd enjoy the garden and the animals...'

'That's for sure.' Indigo sits back, relieved, and smiles. She'll discuss it later with Will, though she's sure he'll be happy with the idea. 'Now, please don't be cross, Lady C, but I shall be contributing to the housekeeping.'

Lady Catgut starts to protest.

'No, I'm not arguing or debating,' Indigo declares forcefully. 'Otherwise I'll have to issue some kind of proclamation or whatever.'

Lady Catgut laughs.

'I'm sure you'll get the hang of the job pretty quickly, Indigo. Don't ever forget you've got helpers – your cousin Will, and good friends such as Grout, Piccolo and Nigel, the Fork and Young Miss Burgess. And Maria, in time.'

'Grout thinks I'm just a kid,' says Indigo, ignoring the reference to Maria. 'Will does, too.'

'That's not what I hear,' says Lady C. 'Grout and Will say you're an incredible young woman, feisty, full of spunk, common sense and fun. Piccolo and Nigel adore you. For them, you are a role model.'

Indigo says nothing. Her sixteenth birthday isn't far off but she's thinking: perhaps she is too young for Grout, who's coming up for his twenty-first.

SECTION 10

Every great clown has been very near to tragedy.
Margaret Rutherford (1892–1972)

82 HEAVENS ABOVE

'You murdered me, you complete and utter ars—!' the King shrieks at Cataract in TTT, as he struggles to retrieve first one, then the other, large white sleeve of his Heavenly gown, which constantly slips from his shoulders.

'Maj! Why on earth would I want to kill you? You're my best friend!' Cataract retorts.

'So I thought! But then I remembered. You made your first attempt to murder me at Note when we were 11-year-old schoolboys!' says the King, in a fury.

'That is true, Maj.' Cataract's tone is as spiky as railings. 'But you had eaten the entire contents of my autumn tuck box, including my mother's home-made chocolate cake. I simply sat on your stomach to empty it to get back what was rightfully mine.'

'With half the form joining in!' retorts the King.

'Exaggeration, as ever, Maj. It was a job-share between me and Bradley, who was the size of an emaciated mouse, and Woolgar, who kept wandering off to listen to classical music on the radio. In any event, you ignored us. You had your head in a comic.'

'So, why did you want to kill me this time? Not enough for you, ruling the Federation? Wanted my crown, did you? You wouldn't be the first. Or the last.'

'What nonsense bumbles about in your head, Maj, crashing into all manner of other idiotic detritus before...'

Cataract stands silent, staring into space.

'Seeing the error of your financial ways at last?' says the King scornfully.

Cataract turns to the King, who sees something akin to panic in his friend's eyes.

'The cake!' Cataract blurts out, his face whiter than his garment.

'You didn't manage to bring it with you, did you, Cedric?' says the King excitedly. 'Because I'm getting tired of reconstituted ambrosia. And it was a cake to die for. Er...well, you know what I mean.'

Cataract struggles for words.

'I've just recalled. That cake was a special get-well gift from my brother, Wiggins.'

'Catty, dearest,' says the King seriously. 'Wiggi is the last person on God's earth, if you'll forgive the metaphor, to raise a hand against you. What we need to know is from whom or where did he get the cake?'

Cataract's blurred thoughts clear for a moment.

'Dekaydence,' he says flatly. 'It was a '2-2 Delicious Dekaydence cake!' A Dekaydence extra-special order.'

'Bastard!' the King shouts.

Even though this conversation is taking place in their heads, Cataract jumps.

'Damn di'Abalo!' cries the King. 'Knocking off people

left, right and centre because he deems them no longer useful. That's his method, isn't it?'

'Yes, but I don't think—' says Cataract.

'You were his right-hand man, Catty. And his left. God only knows why he bumped you off.'

'He didnae,' interjects a deep, growly voice. 'I did.'

The two old men turn to see a tall, well-built figure in a chef's apron emerge from behind a Canapé column.

'And you are, sir?' King says crisply.

'Name's MacGluten,' says the man. 'Head of the Dekaydence kitchens. Or was. I've just been bumped off and barbecued as a string of sausages.'

'Oh, my goodness,' the King says, shocked. 'It's that man again, isn't it? That diabolic Di'Abalo. Why on earth did I ennoble him?'

'Money, Maj,' says Cataract, his heavenly heart fluttering fast as he recalls a memory and shudders: MacGluten is the chef he derided loud and long, many years ago.

'My name is Cataract,' says Cataract quietly. 'I think I owe you an apology, Mr MacGluten.'

The King is taken aback. He has never in his life heard his friend apologise.

MacGluten shrugs.

'Och, no, Mr Cataract. The final order came from on high.'

'Di'Abalo?' Cataract enquires.

'Aye.' MacGluten nods.

'Damnable man!' exclaims the King. 'We've all died too young. And there was so much I needed to pass on to my son, the Crown Prince, and to his boy.'

'Before you go any further, sir, there's something else you need to know,' says MacGluten.

'And what's that, Mr MacGluten?' says the King.

'There's no way to make this easy,' says MacGluten. 'But your young grandson has just died in a motorcycle accident. And your son, the Crown Prince, is missing, presumed mad with grief and guilt at being the cause of his son's death. I am truly sorry for your loss.'

The King cannot speak. He stares wide-eyed into nothing.

Cataract watches him anxiously. Whatever's happened between them, the King has been his best friend since childhood. A good friend. A loving one, too. Cataract's marriage was childless but that doesn't mean he can't understand the feelings of those who have lost a child. Or, in this case, possibly two.

'The boy,' the King says, suddenly and slowly. 'The poor young boy. He so loved his father. And his father so loved his boy.'

'You'll see him soon, Maj,' says Cataract, patting the King's shoulder.

'Oh, God,' says the King, burying his head in his hands. 'I don't want him here. I want him back home. Both of them should be back home, on solid ground.'

'I hear the Almighty's gone missing, too,' MacGluten

whispers to Cataract, who shakes his head despairingly. He so dislikes disorder.

'Oh, God,' repeats the King, uncovering his face. 'I've just realised.'

'What?' says Cataract. 'What have you realised, Maj, dearest?'

The King grabs hold of his friend's hand and clasps it tight.

'Catty! This could mean the Crown will go to the Princess Indigo.'

'Yes, dear,' says Cataract soothingly. 'That's right, Maj. Your granddaughter.'

The King looks at him, exasperated.

'She's a child, Catty,' he says. 'And what's worse, she's a woman!'

'If you recall, Maj,' says Cataract, 'your dear wife is also a woman. I spotted that quite early on.'

'So did I,' says the King. 'And the way they can't do things the way we men can. They don't think in the same way as men. Indigo is a good girl but, like most women, she's made of water, emotions and strange, unsettling and changing passions.'

'Possibly,' says Cataract slowly. 'But that could be all to the good, Maj.'

'Aye,' says MacGluten. 'Give the lassie a chance, sir. Not that you've got the option not to!'

The King stares into his memories and his dreams.

'After all I've worked for. All the years. All the

deprivation. All for nothing. It's over. All to put a girl on the throne. Whatever next?

'And after the girl...' says the King despondently, staring at a passing grey cloud. 'Look! That's the very lot that will inherit the earth!'

Through a rift in the cloud, Cataract and MacGluten catch a glimpse of a large jest of clowns laughing wildly, mooning, and making rude noises and ugly gestures. Many wearing crowns made of silver foil and shiny gold paper.

'It's as if if they know their time is coming,' the King whispers sadly.

'Rubbish,' says Cataract. 'I have it on good authority from Spaghetti Sureshi that the clowns have put in a plea to return to earth as politicians. They claim they are much better qualified and more professional than the current amateur clowns allegedly in charge. And they insist they make better jokes.

'That wouldn't be hard,' the King mutters.

BREAKING NEWS

Lavender Blue reports from New York for *The Daily Unigraph*.
Additional research: Al Farr

'Ladies and gentlemen, you are here today to share what will be a secret between us until I say otherwise,' says the President of the Dekaydence World Bank & Federal Reserve, glancing admiringly at his sparkling fingernails buffed up that morning at great expense with rare salts from the small puddle that is all that remains of the once-magnificent Dead Sea.

'As you know, we've been in discussions with a number of countries that have, or seek to introduce, Dekaydence shopping malls and products in their nation. We have also made certain arrangements that include extensive discounts should armaments be bought and sold on through us.

'So, partly as a result of these actions, the Company of Dekaydence is to launch a new global currency.'

There are gasps of shock, admiration and excitement, and some nervous applause from the Dekaydence WB&FR presidents and deputies of the five continents seated at a table in a meeting room on the 333rd floor of a New

LIVE FROM AN ILLEGAL INTERNET SERVICE PROVIDER

York skyscraper.

There's a silence. No one is prepared to put a foot, or a trillion-dollar pension and bonus package, at risk.

The President emits a deadly smile that infects his eyes with a mean sense of danger. The memories of several bankers recall the look only too well, and shudder.

'In six months' time our global currency will be...' says the President, lingering over his words to boost the suspense. He sits – smilingly, knowingly – inviting the young man on his right-hand side to take over. The sharp young man with a sharp haircut and sharper suit jumps to his feet, sharply.

'Thank you, Mr President!' the Sharp Young Man cries enthusiastically. 'Yes, in six months' time Dekaydence will have a new global currency that'll be beyond sweet because it is...'

He turns to the President, who smiles, calmly and coolly, before announcing:

'Strawberry Jam!'

One president crashes to the floor and doesn't get up. A stroke? A heart attack? The on-call medics enter and swiftly exit with the limp body. The jaws of several presidents remain gawpingly open. It's lucky that no bird flies at this altitude.

Most presidents and their deputies search surreptitiously

LIVE FROM AN ILLEGAL INTERNET SERVICE PROVIDER

for the eyes of others that might offer an explanation. Is it April Fool's Day? Has the President gone mad (they all know he's an 'oid, fashioned by Dekaydence, and thus not above quirks in the works). Worst-case scenario: could they be the only ones who don't understand what's happening?

A distinguished-looking elderly gentleman, a deputy who has secured his pension in gold and property, raises his hand.

'I don't understand what's going on, or why,' he says. 'Why didn't we stick to gold? Solid food, not fluids?'

The President gives a cavalier smile. 'As it is, money in today's markets is churned out in cheap metal alloys and bits of colourful paper valuable only to wipe one's bottom.'

'And Strawberry Jam will change that?' the elderly gent enquires. 'If so, why not...raspberry? Or gooseberry? Or quince?'

One look from the President silences the few sniggerers he won't forget.

'We're on the make, man.' The Sharp Young Man speaks patronisingly to the elderly gent. 'And Strawberry Jam is a game in which we'll all be winners.'

'What fun!' an elderly lady in a blue dress cries out, clapping her hands. 'Do tell us the rules and what we must do.'

The Sharp Young Man smiles. Who is this old bat? He manages a nonchalant glance at the seating plan. Ah, a last-minute substitute for the deputy to a deputy's deputy. He bestows a patronising smile in her direction and moves on.

'Basically, ma'am, Strawberry Jam is a currency used in digital transactions by tablets, ad'ums and the like, and can be stored digitally and virtually on your computer. We issue Strawberry Jam credit and debit cards and tokens that can be used internationally in Dekaydence stores and wherever you see the sign of the Strawberry.

'Strawberry Jam offers a competitive monthly bank charge; huge savings at Dekaydence stores worldwide; and regular "jammy" prizes of Dekaydence vouchers, goods, VIP travel and jam.'

The President picks up the story.

'Dekaydence, as you know, is now the lead player in many areas of daily life. The move into currency was a natural progression, conceived by the company's distinguished accountant, Cedric Cataract – recently and sadly deceased – who had called it originally a "Chocolate Cake" currency, which, for reasons we now know, has had, out of respect, to be dropped.

'We like to think Mr Cataract would approve of our rebrand as we make Strawberry Jam the new gold. A must-have at any price. Yes, a matching asset and a great jammy publicity add-on.'

'And to achieve that goal,' the Sharp Young Man continues, 'Dekaydence has bought up all significantly sized strawberry farms worldwide. There are a few remaining in private hands but not to worry, they're small and won't last long, you can be sure of that.'

'Sounds as if people and their businesses, perhaps even some countries, could go bust,' says the elderly gent sadly.

'Yes, rather!' says the Sharp Young Man. 'Essential part of the Strawberry Jam game. But not to worry, we bail 'em out and make more money through Strawberry Jam loans and insurance cover.'

There's silence.

And then...

'Could get horribly messy, if not sticky,' says the woman in blue. 'Things could so easily go pear-shaped, or, in this instance, strawberry-shaked.'

'I doubt it,' says the President. 'Remember, our company's priority is driven by a remit. To extort for those of us here seated, from any source, the best monetary package of pay, bonus, pension, lifelong family, house and pet insurance, as well as a dozen cases of Strawberry Jam to lay down every year. Otherwise, life for us just ain't worth living, is it?'

A pot of Dekaydence Strawberry Jam is put before each person seated at the table.

'The new gold,' The young man whispers reverently.

'Mmm,' mutters the elderly lady seated beside him. 'You don't think there's a chance it might be fool's gold?'

The man laughs.

'Not many fools round this table, ma'am. No paupers neither.'

83 TEARS AND RAGE

Ruby Q – back from a brief assignment in New York following the jam story – has half an hour before leaving for the next job. She sees the Taylors' black cat, Baghilde, under the dining-room table. Feathers and down tumble over the floor, over traces of blood. Ruby Q shouts at the cat, which drops the baby thrush in its mouth, only to pick it up again. The bird makes a squeaky noise, like the growling device you press in a teddy bear's stomach.

The cat drops the bird and shoots out the open back door, with a backward glance of disdain. Ruby Q bends down. The little bird is alive. Just. Its tail feathers flutter like a lady's fan. It opens and shuts its beak soundlessly. Its legs have no strength. Its eyes – like large shiny chocolate raisins – stare. Is it in terror or beyond fear? Is it wondering about the next torture? Should she leave it to its own devices? Or rush it to the vet's? Would it have been kinder to let the cat finish the job? Might it recover? There's no time to consider this life-and-death decision.

Gently, she scoops up the bird into thick sheets of newspaper. The bird blinks. Gently, she carries it into the garden. It is a sunny, warm day. Where to put it so it's protected from heat and cat? There's a bench under the roof of the summerhouse with a soft blanket on it. Gently, she places the bird at the shadier end. She brings it a saucer of water, hoping it might take some succour. Instead, a drop of blood falls from its beak.

She kneels, talking softly to it, when its tail feathers suddenly spread, its wings beat fast, whirring like an engine. Her heart sinks. She knows what will happen, though she holds her breath and prays fervently, to a god, any god who might be listening. The bird lifts its head. Its eyes grow bigger. Does it know? The neck drops. Everything collapses.

She places the bird – on its bier of newspapers – on a large garden pot filled with violet flowers. It is sheltered, yet supported. The eyes are all but closed. She picks a flower and places it at the bird's breast, whispers a few words and leaves.

On the bus she weeps silently behind her sunglasses.

When she returns the bird is still there. No longer plump with life but now empty, vacant, a void of feathers and bones. Eyes shrunken, almost white, staring into the beyond. She kneels down beside it.

'What is it, Ruby Q?' says a familiar voice behind her.

Mr Treasure follows her gaze and sees the dead bird.

'Bloody God!' she shouts out, startling Mr Treasure. 'What does he think he's doing, creating a beautiful creature that will sing his praises? No, it has to be programmed to kill or be killed. It is utterly sick. If God truly had compassion, if He had any real love, it wouldn't be like this, would it? You wouldn't create a world like this, would you, Mr Treasure?'

Mr Treasure stares hard at His ancient sandals.

'I am sorry, Ruby Q,' He mumbles to the ground beneath His feet.

'No, I'm sorry, Mr T,' says Ruby Q, a sob in her voice. 'I'm not shouting at you, it's those ancient, deaf non-interventionists in the sky. Here's a young bird, killed before its time. After the terror and suffering it's had to endure. For what? Any god who claims omnipotence should be able to do something about all this – this unnecessary suffering.'

Mr Treasure nods slowly, sympathetically.

'I'm afraid it's not in my hands, or my contract, Ruby Q.'

Ruby Q nods, feeling tears fighting her to be released.

You appear to possess great reserves of inner rainfall.

Where you've been in all this time?

Never mind. Leave poor old Mr T alone. It's time you got going. You have work to do.

84 BUSY BUZZY

Grout is becoming a keen gardener, learning much from Lady Catgut, who one day shares with him her distress at the plight of the honeybee.

'They're dying, Grout. All over the world, they're dying,' Lady Catgut says, halfway between tears and fury, a state neither he nor Indigo has ever seen her in.

'Worldwide bees are being poisoned, malnourished, overworked and stressed by the thousands of miles they're forced to travel to pollinate farmers' crops. Why, in China, they were beekeeping three thousand years ago. Now there's a bee-less area that has to employ manual labour to pollinate the fruit trees. An operation that's difficult, expensive and time-consuming. And unnatural.'

'If bees are wiped out it's curtains for mankind, and the planet,' says Indigo, giving Grout a book.

He's absorbed by the book, *A World Without Bees* by Alison Benjamin and Brian McCallum. He reads of the discovery that in about 2400BC the ancient Egyptians became the first beekeepers in history. How bees were sent to the colonies in America to enable new immigrants to pollinate their crops. How there have always been severe losses of bees and how no one is sure what is happening and why. Or what can be done. The more he reads of the industrious little worker the more he realises that he too, like Lady Catgut, has an internal place he never knew existed that stores his tears and anger. It makes him think and that leads him back to his own dry land – research.

He talks to beekeepers nationwide, in villages and cities, and abroad. He examines pesticides in the lab and listens to the thoughts of specialist scientists. He collects and examines the bodies of dead bees. He sits and thinks in the garden, Billy, the goat, and Montezuma, the pig, never far from his side.

Mostly, he works in secret deep into the small hours in the Dekaydence lab.

85 FUTURE IMPERFECT

Wiggins leans back in his chair, watching the electric fire in the grate. It's taken time to look at flames, even if unreal, without recalling his brother, his terrible demise and the dull cocktail of the jagged, relentless pain of bereavement.

Now he welcomes the happy childhood memories that call on him. His father, who devoted so much time to his two boys, reading to them, talking with them, playing croquet and tennis, swimming, learning woodwork, holding barbecues and bonfire parties – even though his father had a tough job as head of the Bank of England. Their father sought in his staff, and his children, good and honourable behaviour. Any staff member with the remotest hint of greedy, grasping ways was removed from office. Wiggins wonders what his father would think of today's world, as well as the work of his elder son.

Wiggins knows Cataract sailed close to the wind in many deals. He did not approve. But how do you tell your older brother how to behave? And if it's the path he's chosen, beyond an exchange of views, does a brother have a right to interfere?

How come Cataract strayed from the path their father subtly showed them? How come all the love they experienced in childhood desiccated in the adult Cataract? Was it working long hours in the City? Cataract's work was his life and certainly his home life suffered. His wife did her own thing, as they say, which could mean anything. And maybe did, or maybe didn't.

Wiggins considers the deep mystery that is life. It's like being an amateur juggler, he decides. You learn just enough before you drop the sticks or they drop you.

While his wife is involved in charity work, Wiggins gives his time, for free, to the Justice movement. He senses worrying developments within society and the state. He has read and researched innumerable cases of serious misdemeanours, money-laundering, Libor-ing, lying and cheating. And of the abuse of children, partners, strangers and animals.

Something must be done, thinks Wiggins, otherwise society and perhaps the whole planet will go under. A better system has to be in place to educate and to protect. And there has to be effective punishment. Especially for the likes of Di'Abalo.

86 COUNTRY COUSINS

Will accompanies Indigo on an official trip to the West Country, travelling the southern coastline from Bournemouth to Penzance, returning via the northern coastline from Tintagel to Bristol.

Wiggins joins them. He's good company, as well as wise and informative. Equally, the two young people want to help lift his bereaved spirit.

They admire the vast coastline from the Bournemouth Balloon and are enchanted by the candles lit at dusk in the Lower Gardens. They visit the Royal National Lifeboat Institution HQ at Poole and hear the Bournemouth Symphony Orchestra play Elgar and Delius, which reminds Will of Piccolo. Wiggins is fascinated by Exeter's Guildhall, with its probable 12th-century hall, said to be the oldest municipal building in England that's still in use.

In Plymouth, from where Sir Francis Drake sailed to circumnavigate the globe in three years, and from where in 1620 the Pilgrim Fathers set sail for the New World, Will thinks of his brother Tommo and how, were he fit and well, Tommo would fill his lungs and heart to bursting with sea air and sea history.

Indigo feels magic in the air at Tintagel Castle, as though

King Arthur were still in residence in his castle and Merlin were in his cave. In Bristol they join a crowd to watch the International Balloon Fiesta, and Wiggins recalls with an ache in his heart how he and Cataract had come to watch the last flight of the beautiful, extraordinary supersonic aircraft, Concorde. Grounded out of existence, on groundless negatives, in the view of Wiggins and many others.

They are greeted everywhere by cheering locals. The friendly enthusiasm touches Will, so that his wave becomes easier, his smile true and genuine. They will be remembered by each and every one in the crowd for their lifetime.

If only his great-uncle, the King, could see him now, Will thinks.

Indigo is thinking the same thing.

'We're lucky, aren't we?' she says dreamily. 'We live in a beautiful country, with hordes of lovely, loving people.'

'Aye, though never forget Scotland is better,' says Will teasingly. 'And always remember there are people intent on destroying these lands and its people. Among them, and at the top, is Di'Abalo.'

'I'll fight them all,' says Indigo.

She sees him nod a look of quiet disbelief.

'Don't think I won't, Will.'

There's a ferocity in her voice and eyes that makes him smile.

'Don't mock me. I'm not a child any more, Will. I'm

nearly 16. Still young. Still much to learn. But I shall fight for my country. And, if necessary, die for it.'

Will nods his support. He hopes it never comes to that but... There are dark clouds on the horizon, metaphorically as well as literally.

87 DIABALOIC MUTTERINGS

'Why am I doing this?' says Di'Abalo tetchily, as he and Phlegm walk over a small wooden bridge that leads into the Catguts' garden.

'It makes you look good,' Phlegm says casually, watching the guests eating and drinking in the garden.

'Oh, yes. Such a irritating, difficult task,' says Di'Abalo gloomily. 'See that man over there, talking to Prince Will? It's Wiggins, Cataract's brother. Keep him away from me. He's a real goody two-shoes. I might have to be sick all over him.'

'Right-ho,' says Phlegm, wondering how a man of his lordship's stature and experience can be so...well, ill at ease in certain company.

'I need a smoke,' Di'Abalo mutters.

'My, you must be in a bad way,' says Phlegm, taken aback because this has *not* happened before. 'Do I get one?'

Di'Abalo produces two cigarillos that he lights from sparks produced by a snap of his fingers. He hands one to Phlegm. They both inhale deeply and smoke to the end in silence before shoeing the stubs into the ground.

Phlegm has a nasty spasm of coughing.

'I told you, centuries back, to give up smoking,' says

Di'Abalo. 'But you wouldn't listen. Now you've got this interminable ruddy cough!'

'Watch out!' Phlegm manages to gasp.

Candelskin is rushing across the garden towards them, as much as he is able. He's dressed in a sleeved, floor-length white silk gown that he keeps hoisting above his knees so he doesn't fall over or get grass stains on the material.

'Oh, God!' says Di'Abalo.

'Nearly, but not quite,' says Phlegm.

'What *is* he wearing?' Di'Abalo stares in amazement.

As Candelskin gets closer they see the religious symbols and gold thread that have been woven into the fabric of his cassock.

'Wretched woman and her wretched pins,' snaps Candelskin, nodding in the direction of Petty Masters. 'I'm a literally bleeding wreck under all this because she must pin up everything, including—'

Before they learn precisely what 'including' means, Lady Catgut appears with a tray of home-made cordials, sandwiches and cakes, and calls to them all to join her for tea.

At the far end of the garden Indigo and Petty Masters are too engrossed to hear the call, or the second. They're focused on books, bales of cloth and a giant trolley stacked with flowers and plants under the charge of Killivy, Di'Abalo's gardener.

'It's going to be a disaster,' Candelskin says, shaking his

head. 'The Princess Indigo has decided she'll be dressed in the Coronation robes only after she arrives at Westminster Abbey.

'She wants to walk to the Abbey, dressed casually. Can you imagine? I suppose that means Petty Masters's specially torn jeans, ancient trainers and an old torn T-shirt. What will the crowds lining the streets of London, let alone foreign visitors, think?'

'It's what is inside a person that counts,' says Lady Catgut briskly, as she bustles by with her tea tray. 'Whatever people think, it doesn't matter. It's not the end of the world.'

'Not yet, alas,' says Phlegm, darkly, as he helps Lady Catgut with the plates. He glances questioningly at Di'Abalo.

Di'Abalo gives him a stern look.

'Soon, Phlegm,' he hisses. 'Very soon.'

88 A MUSICAL REQUEST

As Petty Masters helps Schneek feed the triplets and a delighted Killivy is taken on a conducted tour of the Tower of Eden by Lady Catgut, Indigo saunters across the garden to join Piccolo and Grout. The trio sit together under a large old umbrella that bows as if it, too, is made drowsy by the hot sun.

'I have a favour to ask,' Indigo says casually to Piccolo.

Piccolo looks up from a book; Grout remains immersed in his ad'um.

'I should've asked you before,' says Indigo, 'but with everything happening so fast...'

'Ask me what?' says Piccolo.

Indigo shades her eyes from the sun and smiles what Will calls her irresistible honey-spider smile.

'I want you to compose a piece of music to be played at the Coronation.'

Piccolo looks startled.

'What?'

'I'll pay you, of course,' says Indigo, 'with my own money. Probably have to knight you as well some time afterwards. But I'll check the protocol on that.'

She records a memo on her ad'um.

'Hang on! Hang on!' says Piccolo. 'Are we talking about the Coronation in which you're the lead performer in about three weeks' time?'

'Yes, that's the one,' says Indigo, slightly huffy. 'I didn't realise I was in some kind of Coronation queue.'

'There's no queue, man,' says Piccolo, 'but a few weeks isn't anywhere near enough time to do something like that. I mean, what type of music do you want? What length do you need?'

'I don't know.' Indigo shrugs. 'What about a symphony?' She registers the horror on Piccolo's face. 'OK, a sonata? That's shorter, isn't it?'

'Yes. But what exactly do you want this indeterminate length and style of music to say?'

'I want it to be a celebration of all that is good and great in this country. When people become familiar with the opening bars I want their spirits to be lifted. I want it to be like sunshine appearing unexpectedly after weeks of dreary days. Like a welcome shower of rain after a dusty day. I want my grandfather to hear it in heaven and cheer with pride.'

'You could do that for six quid, couldn't you, Sir Piccolo?' says Grout, glancing up briefly.

Piccolo stares at Grout, and then Indigo.

'You're both crazy,' says Piccolo, shaking his head. 'I recognise that because I am, too. So the answer to your ludicrous request, Your Royal Madness, is "Yes!"'

Indigo shrieks with delight, and runs to plant a kiss on

Piccolo's cheek.

Will looks up at the sky. And just in case anyone is watching, he winks.

89 TRAVELS WITH MY DOORKEY

'You can't possibly compose a symphony for a Coronation in three weeks' time,' Catgut remonstrates with Piccolo. 'I mean, how many symphonies have you composed so far?'

'None,' says Piccolo. 'But Indigo doesn't want a symphony. At least, not yet. She wants a short piece, about the length of a sonata.'

Catgut shudders.

'Indeterminate length and subject matter,' he says. 'I don't like it. Been there before. My nerves can no longer take the pressure.'

'That may or may not be the case, dearest,' Lady Catgut intervenes, before Catgut undermines Piccolo's confidence. 'But Piccolo is young, and so are his nerves. What do you think, dear?'

Piccolo shrugs.

'I've decided to do a bit of travelling, Lady C. Stimulation and stuff.'

'You're sure you're well enough?' asks Lady Catgut.

Piccolo nods.

'Yes, thank you. And I think it'll do me some good.'

'I think you might be right,' says Lady Catgut, reaching into a drawer in the sideboard. 'This might help. And there's to be no arguments.'

Piccolo stares at a chequebook, which has his name on it. He opens his mouth but Lady Catgut speaks first.

'We've done this for all of you – for you, Grout, Nigel and Maria. You've each got the same sum of money that'll be topped up every six months,' says Lady Catgut. 'It's not much but we hope it helps. We've no heirs. No close relatives. And you three boys and Maria are our joy, even if you do decide to leave us at some point.'

'I've no intention of leaving you, ever, Lady C. Neither has Grout nor Nigel. I think Maria feels the same,' says Piccolo. 'The food here is far too good.'

'I'll second that,' says Catgut.

Lady Catgut laughs but in her heart she knows that sooner or later a departure time will come from one and all.

Piccolo travels the country, west to east, south to north. Village to town to capital, country to seaside, in what is a swelteringly hot summer interspersed with torrential, relentlessly long downpours and strange occasions when Piccolo is convinced the earth has hiccups.

At times he feels like a wide-eyed tourist in his own land. At times he feels connected closely to the land and to the water more than the people. Mostly, he feels disconnected. Where is his homeland, England or Jamaica? And what of his family? He knows only that his mother's parents arrived in London from Jamaica in the 1950s and separated when she was a little girl. And that his father never spoke of his family. Anyway, how do you trace a family of Smiths?

But now, with a stable home life, improving health and the company of friends, Piccolo is realising how lucky he is. How much he is loved. And, more, how much he loves back. The beautiful mysterious Bianco may have disappeared from his life but his deepest feelings remain for someone who is often at a fingertip's distance.

He thinks of Indigo. Of the family she has lost. The situation she is in. The burden she has inherited as Queen. Yes, he must compose for her something uplifting.

He sits on the rocks in the sea at North Berwick; he stands on the beach at Beadnell, at Anglesey, and at Land's End, watching the wild, rumbustious sea. He senses the water's soothing calm, as well as its power and energy.

He walks a short length of Hadrian's Wall in the mist and rain; and, on a hot and humid day, a stretch of the Pennine Way. Another day he scales the steep slopes of the Seven Sisters at Eastbourne. He joins a guided tour of the City of London, breathes in its rich history, from the grinding poverty of the past in its dark alleyways to the untold wealth within the modern glass and concrete constructs, and the power, on earth as it is in Heaven, of the Church and the City, represented by St Paul's Cathedral and the Bank of England.

He goes east to Heacham in Norfolk, walks beside acres of lavender through a heavy, drowsy scent that acts like a thick pillow of comfort for the myriad busy buzzing bees. He visits the Riverford organic farm at Buckfastleigh in Devon, and eats food as mouthwateringly delicious as Lady Catgut's dishes.

Travel is increasing his taste for more. Equally, he hears threads of tunes in his head that he wants desperately to weave together. Yes, it is time to sit down and pull it all together. He will create a tableau of music for the Queen, and elaborate on it over time.

Before he travels home to Sussex he wants to sketch out his thoughts in peace and quiet. But where to go? Maybe, just maybe... Many of the shops are boarded up but there is one with an 'Open' sign. He stocks up on bottles of water and chocolate bars before continuing his journey to London Bridge.

He walks the streets until the summer twilight draws in like sitting-room curtains. There are no lights in the street, or in the houses. It's difficult to tell whether they're inhabited or not.

This time, fitter than before, Piccolo scales the ivy-clad wall comfortably. There's plenty of stubborn ivy embedded in the bricks to help him climb. He squints into the twilight but can make out little detail. There used to be bushes and nettles just here, he recalls, and so he throws down his rucksack, takes a breath and jumps. This time he lands softly. In gooseberry bushes. Red gooseberry juice is squashed all over his clothes. Delicious. But how did they get into the cemetery?

He waits a moment, catches his breath and looks around. It's different. Very different. For a start, it's tidy. The gravestones have been cleaned and polished, fruit and vegetables grow around the graves. The cemetery is becoming an allotment.

Slowly, he makes his way to the shed. The door is closed and bolted. He sits down, leans his bag as a pillow against the shed and closes his eyes against the coming night and a deep hunger.

He feels something rushing, brushing past him and then he's engulfed in the scents of hamburger, fried onion and coffee. His gnawing hunger feels satisfied.

'Bianco?' Piccolo murmurs, as he opens his eyes and feels his heart soar with joy. 'Is that you?'

But the only sound that replies is that of the trees rustling in the breeze.

He lies down to sleep. He doesn't hear the key in the locked gate, or the footsteps, or the sound of a watering can being filled at the communal tap. He awakes with a start, feeling something prodding him gently but persistently in the chest.

'What we got 'ere? An 'ardy perennial?' says a grizzled voice.

Piccolo blinks himself awake. Light is breaking through and the dawn chorus is already up and at 'em.

He finds he is staring into the bright blue eyes of an

elderly man with a well-furrowed face, ancient sandals and a gnarled walking stick.

'I don't recall planting you,' says the elderly gardener. 'What are you?'

'A composer,' says Piccolo, stretching either side of a sleepy grin. 'I wanted somewhere quiet to work and I remembered this place. I haven't damaged anything. Oh, hang on, I have. I landed in the gooseberry bushes. Sorry.'

'They weren't in the best of health,' says the old man. 'You planning on staying long?'

Before he can respond, Piccolo's ad'um beeps.

'Excuse me,' he says as he answers it.

'Hello Piccolo, it's your step-daddy here,' says a voice with a dark sneer. 'Yous owe me, boy. Yous stole money from me. And your ma. Remember? And now you're in the money it's payback time. So I thought I'd pay a little visit to that nice old Sussex house you live in with the doddery old folk.'

The line goes dead.

'Anything I can help with, young man?' the elderly man enquires.

Piccolo stands numb.

'No, er, thanks,' he says, his mind racing. He snatches up his rucksack. 'I'm sorry, man, I don't mean to be rude. But I need to get home, fast.'

The old gardener nods.

He unlocks the gate and Piccolo is off like a greyhound.

It's getting darker. The streets are deserted. He'll text Grout when he's on the way. But for now he must run to catch the train. He runs and runs but he can't escape the pictures in his head. The wild, bloodshot eyes of the Big Bloke, his mother's boyfriend. The man who beat his father to death, egged on by his mother. The man who is now threatening him and his adopted family. He must reach home before...

The gardener watches him go before brushing a few crumbs and feathers from his trousers.

BREAKING NEWS

HOME | **NEWS** | MUSIC | VIDEOS | DIARY | BLOG

Babies and young children are dying, at the hands of their carers, be they a parent or partner. These innocents die wretchedly, in pain, starved of food as well as love. They are beaten and tortured. Locked in a bedroom with only the floor to sleep on. Or kept in a dark cupboard. Or simply dumped. Young children are abducted, abused sexually and killed. Young women, boys and pre-teen schoolgirls go missing.

This is not a perfect world but if a joined-up system was in place – connecting schools, social services, police, and neighbours – surely the lives of some of those most vulnerable could be saved.

LIVE FROM AN ILLEGAL INTERNET SERVICE PROVIDER

90 MURDER MOST FOUL

'What provokes someone to kill a child?' North asks Wiggins.

'Many things,' Wiggins replies quietly. 'Significant or otherwise. Alas, it has happened since time began.'

'Then there is no god,' says North. 'No deity worthy of the name would permit such a thing.'

'Is god necessarily the creator or judge? And if he is the creator of an artist, a builder or a pilot, must he dictate the way to paint a picture, design a bridge or fly a plane?'

'No,' North replies. 'But if, by some accident, I created a potential child murderer I would rework it and, should all else fail, I'd erase it.'

'And in the real world?' Wiggins raises a questioning eyebrow.

North ponders. And recalls his anger towards the Phoen'oid.

Neither speaks for a few moments.

'When such a thing happens, some people want action. A life for a life,' says North.

'I wonder what they hope to achieve,' Wiggins sighs. 'Destroying the guilty doesn't bring back the innocent.'

'No,' says North. 'But doesn't it save taxpayers hugely

costly court case; save payment of board and lodgings for their decades in prison? And it may serve as a deterrent to others.'

'I doubt it'd make a scrap of difference,' says Wiggins sadly. 'Tragically, people do things in the heat of the moment, and any thought of the consequences doesn't appear on their radar until it's too late.'

'So we sit back and wait for the next murder and the next?' says North.

'No, we strive to reach youngsters and adults, to educate them, to support and inspire them. So they grow to understand the importance of doing good in the world, not bad. So they understand the importance in life, one's own as well as others, of philanthropy. Caring for others.'

'Perhaps you should take over as God?' says North.

Wiggins chuckles.

'Not me, guv,' says Wiggins, adopting a Croy Polloi accent. 'But I do know a number of people who I think should have a go at reorganising and re-creating society.'

'You know some inspirational angels, then?' says North.

'Yes. They're working angels. Several children's librarians, some civil servants, a handful of lawyers, doctors, nurses, teachers, a few plumbers, physios, electricians, a plasterer, a tennis coach, some journalists and the odd politician. Between them they could pull it together, and do it well. But for myself,' I believe "He moves in a mysterious way, His wonders to perform." One day, we may find out more.'

North nods. He doesn't agree but he will never shake the faith of those who have it or those, himself included, who don't.

91 ONE DARK NIGHT

It is said that God hears everything. Certainly, He heard Piccolo's stepfather threatening to turn up at the Catguts' house in Sussex. Rarely – but as and when and now and then – He decides to get involved. The young composer has had enough to cope with, without another encounter with his father's murderer, so...

Normally, He'd ask someone in the Red Alert team to sort out the problem. But now He's alone. No assistant. And He can't get the wretched ad'um to work.

He stares at the thing. It's been upgraded so many times and each time He finds it gets more complicated and He gets more irritated.

At any one time, the ad'um details the names of the disciples, all 36 of them. At another, it tells him there are three commandments. From where or from whom does this misinformation come? He demands to know. No one can tell Him. Because no one is there to tell Him. He is incensed and frustrated by it all, and aware that His memory is also taking a holiday break, separate from Him.

Usually, Mother Nature would grab hold of the ad'um, impatiently press a few buttons, and hand it back to Him in full working order. The ten commandments and

12 disciples would be restored. At least temporarily. But now is not usual times: Mother Nature has left His side. So what can He do?

There's only one thing.

On the train Piccolo texts Grout, warning him of the impending arrival of the Big Bloke.

Arriving home late after transport delays, Piccolo finds the household outside. Grout, Nigel, Maria, Tommo, Catgut and Lady C, together with Erik, the man from the council who now helps out every weekend at the Tower of Eden. They're all working in and around the garden to install security lighting before nightfall.

But as twilight thickens into night, the outside lighting stubbornly refuses to work. The distant streetlighting is off, too, while the indoor lighting is ablaze and refuses to be switched off.

Furious at this waste of money, Catgut shuts himself in his study to work out how he can best protect his family from the Big Bloke. He contacts Edwina Gardening-Fork, advising her to stay inside and lock all doors and windows, and tells her why. He decides it's too late to call a neighbouring farmer who owns three enormous bombastic dogs and whose tiny wife is more terrifying than all three animals.

Lady Catgut prepares a buffet supper, though no one is very hungry, except Erik. Everyone, except Catgut, hangs around the kitchen, where Lady Catgut bustles about cooking, half listening to BBC Radio 4, and wholly worrying.

All is relatively quiet and still until the early hours.

It's about two in the morning when they hear a single gunshot. The noise triggers a riot of shouts and barking dogs. And then come the sounds of revving engines and vehicles screeching on to the roads and across the countryside. Later, there's a horrifying shriek. Was it man or beast? No one knows. No one wants to go outside to see.

Piccolo shudders, feeling ice in his stomach.

A wind picks up and rattles the windows. A shutter bangs against the wall. An owl hoots.

Grout, Piccolo and Nigel tour the house, checking doors and windows. Grout checks and peers out of every window but it's too dark to see anything.

Lady Catgut, making tea and toast, realises she hasn't seen Catgut for hours.

All at once, the sound of the door knocker resounds around the house, startling all.

'I'll see who it is,' says Grout, standing up.

'I'll come with you,' says Piccolo.

'I'll come, too,' says Nigel, heading for the door.

'Has anyone seen Catgut?' says Lady Catgut.

'He was heading for the attic. Said he was getting his great-grandfather's First World War cavalry sabre,' Nigel says over his shoulder.

'Oh, my goodness!' cries Lady Catgut, rushing from the room into the hallway. She's halfway up the stairs on her way to find Catgut when she stops as Grout opens the front door to a large uniformed man standing in the shadows on the doorstep.

10

Will, Sid his bodyguard, MacMinor, Bodkin and a young Black Tartan guard called Boston form the rescue party to unkidnap or rekidnap the President of the Federation. They enter the eastern territories to attend an official trade mission.

Will recognises his role as quaint young foreign pin-up Scots prince, with a few grey cells. That MacMinor is there because of his natural warmth and deliciously thick-as-double-cream accent that charms almost everyone. That Sid and Boston are there as the just-in-case strong-armed guys. And that Bodkin is present, much to Will's distaste, to demonstrate and explain technical issues in order to hustle and boost arms sales, through Dekaydence.

The Professor was due to join them but circumstances beyond his control...

The President of the Eastern Provinces signs up for a Dekaydence mall and a Dekaydence bank for his new capital city, bought with the money and loans he's been paid for handing over the country's many and rich strawberry farms. He signs deals with Dekaydence to turn a beautiful stretch of coastline into a vast tourist attraction. And then he and the commander of the armed forces drool jointly over the Dekaydence arms and security products.

They buy dozens of Eye-Spys, Orbies and all manner of surveillance equipment, as well as a half-dozen liz'oids.

It's when they assemble in the blue, green and gold mosaic salon for pre-dinner drinks that Bodkin takes the commander of the armed forces to one side.

'I've got something you might be interested in,' he says, in a whisper.

'Have we not seen everything?' enquires the highly decorated commander, a querying eyebrow stretching up towards the exquisite Verdeccio ceiling.

'Step this way,' says Bodkin, with a wink and conspiratorial smile.

The commander looks over his shoulder, catches the eye of his president, who grants permission with an intuitive nod and another conspiratorial smile .

Bodkin leads the commander along the corridor to where Boston stands to attention outside a door.

'All quiet on the eastern front?' Bodkin enquires.

'We've just had 15 minutes of intense activity, sir,' Boston replies. 'So...'

Bodkin smiles.

'So we've got a 15-minute window of opportunity?'

Boston winces.

'Better make it five, max,' he says.

'OK, forget the safety gear,' says Bodkin.

Boston demurs but Bodkin ignores him and talks in a hushed voice to the commander, which gives the Black Tartan guard time to clothe himself swiftly in a plithanium helmet, gloves and leg guards. He looks like an actor from a B movie.

Boston opens the door. All three cautiously enter a small library-cum-dining room. Two gasp with horror at the sight; Boston inhales a deep, deep breath.

Bookshelves have been upended, book covers and bindings are in shreds, so is the wallpaper. Pages of books are everywhere, some still cruising to the ground like feathers. Curtains are off the rails. And listing like a sinking ship is a large wooden table, three of its four legs up in the air, gnawed through.

'Marvellous!' exclaims the commander, in thrill and awe. 'What devastation!'

'Indeed,' says Bodkin, affecting casual pride. 'Now watch this.'

Within a minute the scene is restored to normal.

'This is a new upgrade, you see.'

'I can tell,' says the commander excitedly. 'I'll start

with three. See how we go.'

Bodkin's eyes are glinting.

'Good idea. As I said, this is a new model, developed by a new company. An offshoot of Dekaydence that specialises in hi-tec and 'oids.'

'Oh,' says the commander, instantly perturbed. 'An offshoot...?'

Bodkin nods enthusiastically.

'Yes, an award-winning company. Got this year's Smobaigh Award for Innovative Industry. Obviously, the company has access to Dekaydence contacts worldwide. This model is all but sold out. And the third model won't be available for some three years. Or more.'

A look of panic crosses the commander's face.

'Three years! Right, then I'd better order a dozen.'

'I would if I were in your position,' says Bodkin, 'and—'

There's a clanking, grinding noise, much whirring and...

'Duck!' Boston shouts out the command as a pair of bright blue eyes peers above the edge of the table, accompanied by a rumbling, grrrittering sound. Then from an open jaw of jagged metal teeth a shower of woodchips and spittle comes flying across the room. And a creature appears that reminds the commander of the old haggoid except...

This metal 'oid has a headful of beautifully coiffed blonde hair, a blue diamanté-encrusted collar round its neck, and a beaky aristocratic nose and jaw from which drips thick black oil.

'Yah!' the creature emits in a well-bred accent, hurling a handbag that winds the commander as it hits him in the ribs.

'Oh, my word,' says the commander admiringly, as he hugs his bruised ribs. 'She reminds me of my dear old mother. But...what's that terrible smell?'

The commander holds a handkerchief to his nose.

'It's a minor fart,' says Bodkin, with a proud smile. 'On a higher setting she can emit a powerful gas that covers thirty square miles and kills the enemy.'

The creature turns its back on Bodkin and emits another, longer fart.

'Cover your faces! It's a poison gas!' shouts Boston desperately.

'Amazing!' says the commander, rooted to the spot with wonder.

'Yes,' Bodkin mumbles from behind his handkerchief. 'They say the female is deadlier than the male. That's why she's called the Maggoid! Oh, and... Aaaggghhh!'

'Fantastic!' the commander exclaims, mesmerised as

Boston tries to prise the Maggoid off Bodkin. To no avail.

'Amend my order to nine dozen, and despatch direct to me A.S.A.P., Mr Bodkin,' cries the commander, delirious with excitement.

'As agreed, I'll pay you in cash and Strawberry Jam,' shouts the commander over his shoulder as he leaves the room.

'It's cash only, sir, Dekaydence orders,' Bodkin shouts out, a rictus grin stuck firmly on his face. Only later does the doctor confirm the rictus is rab'oidism, caught from the Maggoid's bite. Luckily, he's told, it's a mild case, so the grin should last only 24 hours.

But, as we know, 'should' is an indeterminate, vituperative and stubborn little word.

91.5 JAM'D UP THINKING

The President of the Dekaydence World Bank & Federal Reserve smiles reservedly as he receives a majority vote, minus one, from the Dekaydence WB&FR presidents and deputies of the five continents seated at a table in a meeting room on the 333rd floor in a New York skyscraper.

The President is glancing at his diary to check the time of his next appointment when the software implanted in his head sends him a red alert. It has identified a dangerous troublemaker, a potential terrorist, in the room. The one person who didn't vote for him. The lady in blue. Her name, he is informed, is Eva O'Mega.

The President looks up from his papers and frowns. The chair of the woman in blue is empty. She is not in the room. His hands and underarms begin to sweat. A word to the Sharp Young Man sends him swiftly to consult with the guards outside. No, they say, no one has left the room.

'But something strange happened a few moments ago,' one guard says.

The other guards laugh.

'He's the only one who saw it!' says one.

The Sharp Young Man quizzes the guard.

'What? What did you see?'

The guard blushes.

'It was probably nothing,' he mumbles, embarrassed.

'I'll be the judge of that,' the Sharp Young Man snaps.

The guard swallows before answering.

'It appeared, just above my head. For a few seconds. A small rainbow. Bright, glittering in the sunshine, stretching from the corridor here, through the far window into the open air. I reached out to touch it and it disappeared. But I had this amazing, warm glow of...I s'pose you'd call it happiness.'

The other guards laugh under their breath.

'And he only drinks water, sir!' says one.

'Yeah, that ghastly stuff that comes out of a tap!' says another.

The Sharp Young Man turns on his heel and returns to the committee room. He'll sack the mad, flaky guard but first the search for the woman must be extended. She can't be far away. One moment she was sitting next to him; the next she was gone.

She might scupper the plan or, worse, reveal it to the Press, the President warns the Sharp Young Man. She must be found at all costs. His conduct and success (or lack of) will show on his career projectory. He contacts Security, Reception and a detective agency the bank uses frequently, alas.

The meeting room is scoured but no devices are found. No one thinks to examine the pens and pencils on the table. Why should they? Even if they had it's unlikely anyone would discover how such a simple tool could transmit the entire proceedings and thought processes to a third party, who relays it direct to a journalist whose editor decides this piece be published under a pseudonym. So it is that Ruby Q Cooper becomes – on an occasion such as this – Lavender Blue.

SECTION 11

I believe that at the end of the century the use of words and general educated opinion will have altered so much that one will be able to speak of machines thinking without expecting to be contradicted.
Alan Turing OBE (1912–1954)

92 BEWARE THE HAGGOID

Jack is repairing the boundary area in Heaven. A few feet away, near the old locked door hidden behind dense shrubbery, Cromarty dozes contently, his head resting on his two front paws. A summer sun shines – yes, even in Heaven – and the place heats rapidly. Jack wipes sweat from his forehead and, from time to time, Cromarty opens his eyes, yawns and starts to pant, his thin black tongue hanging from his mouth like a piece of melting liquorice.

Time passes slowly but neither notice.

And then Jack hears in his head the sound of Cromarty growling softly. Yes, of course, in TTT. Automatically.

'What's up?' Jack says and gets by reply a menacing growl.

He puts down his secateurs and wanders across to the haggoid, which is now standing unsteadily near the hidden door, whining pitifully.

'You're not to worry,' says Jack, sitting on his haunches to pat the short, stocky metal creature. 'There's nothing there. I'd show you but the door's locked and I don't have a key that—'

He stops, mid-sentence. The door is opening slowly, grindingly and grumblingly, revealing a thick mist of cloud.

Cromarty yaps crossly.

Something clatters to the ground. As Jack bends down to give Cromarty a reassuring pat on the head he sees a hazy image of a tall, slender figure, clutching the doorframe for support. It rests for a moment and then slowly, slowly, removes its oxygen helmet. He watches sleek red-gold hair tumble about the shoulders of a woman. A thought suddenly occurs to him...

The woman utters a deep sigh as she subsides slowly to the ground. Jack runs to kneel beside her, convinced that this is Ruby Q's mother, Angelica Nera.

Her pulse is faint and her staring, unblinking eyes tell him she is elsewhere. He knows she could soon be joining them in Heaven but it's worth a try... He sends an SOS to 0.5 (the Halfway House) and awaits the emergency response that will check the records to see if this woman is down to join the dead in Heaven or Hell or should be rejoining the living on Planet Earth.

Angelica Nera is muttering but he can't decipher her words. She doesn't see him, though she appears to see much else beside and beyond. A ray of sunlight pierces the cloud and shines down on her and Jack is transfixed by the translucent beauty of her face.

But how did she get here? And how was she able to get through a long-locked secret back door that no one in Heaven knew about? And why is she here? He spots something on the ground. Something she dropped on her arrival? He bends down to pick up an old metal key. It fits the lock. He'll come back another time to try it out, he decides.

93 ROUGH JUSTICE

'Sorry to disturb you, sir,' says the senior police officer, showing Grout his ID card; his colleague follows suit. 'Wondered if you'd had any trouble hereabouts or heard or seen anything out of the ordinary?'

'We heard a gunshot at a distance and kept inside,' says Grout. 'Nothing's happened, as far as we know, but we did get a warning that a dangerous criminal might be in the area.'

'We've got some developments on that warning,' says the policeman. 'May we come in?'

Grout opens the door wider and the two uniformed officers are ushered into the kitchen.

'What exactly was the warning?' asks the senior policeman, looking askance at Nigel's minuteness.

Grout and Nigel look at Piccolo, who stands silent and impassive.

'Tell him, Piccolo,' Maria urges. 'If you want justice for your dad, you must tell him.'

Piccolo shuts his eyes tight. Grout and the policeman spot a lone teardrop in freefall on his cheek.

'Maybe it's better we leave you together,' says Grout.

The policeman says nothing but Piccolo nods and Grout and the others leave the kitchen.

Piccolo sits down, opposite the policeman, whose colleague stands behind him.

'So, what happened to your dad, Piccolo? If I may call you that?'

Piccolo nods and hesitates. The memory of the murder of his father has sat within him for so long he feels uncomfortable exposing the wound that has festered deep within him. But if he does want justice for his father...

'My dad...' he begins haltingly. 'My dad was a good man. He was a postman, didn't earn much but he worked hard. He was a guitar man. Loved playing and in his spare time he did gigs to earn extra money. One night my mum brought home a Big Bloke who moved in, there and then. And that night the Big Bloke killed my dad.'

'Did you see him do it?'

'Oh, yes. I saw it all right. Big Bloke kept hitting my dad about the head, over and over again. He and my mum were so busy screaming and swearing at my dad they didn't notice me peering through the gap between the door and the doorframe. The music was up loud in the sitting room and the old lady upstairs was banging on the ceiling, shouting at them to turn it down. They knew she wouldn't come down 'cos she was crippled.'

Piccolo is silent for a moment. Lost in his memories. The policeman pauses.

'Anything else you remember?' the policeman asks.

'Yes,' says Piccolo. 'I watched my dad slip slowly down

the back of the bath. I crept back to my room and was sick out of the window. I got into bed. I felt as if I'd died in that bathroom, with my dad. I was so frightened, too. I was just a kid. There was no one to turn to and I had no idea what to do. I wondered if it might be my turn next. I put on my headphones to listen to music. The next day, in the bathroom, there were plastic bags, dripping blood, everywhere. I think they cut up my dad and put him into recycling bins.'

'Did you talk to anyone about what happened? A friend at school, perhaps?'

'No, man. I told you, there was no one to talk to. They didn't let me go to school. Except for that night, I was mostly locked in the bathroom. They beat me up, stubbed out cigarettes on my body. Starved me, abused me. You probably got a list of all this stuff that people do to kids.

'A list too long, and all too familiar,' sighs the policeman. 'Go on, lad.'

Piccolo takes in a deep breath.

'I was told to keep my mouth shut when social services came round. My mum fed them a pack of lies about me. The social believed every one of them. I did escape, once, but the police found me and took me home. I got well beat up for that. So I planned and waited till I was older and bigger. So that one night when they were drunk and drugged I stole their money and made a run for it.'

'You were brave,' says the policeman quietly. 'And now here you are, a successful young composer, with a kind, loving family. Your dad would be proud of you and happy for you.'

Piccolo sighs.

'Man, I hope so. He didn't get much happiness at home. He never had much spare cash. But he saved up enough to buy me what I wanted, a wooden piccolo.'

'That's nice to remember him by,' says the policeman, putting his large arms on the table. 'Now, if you don't mind, Piccolo, I want to show you some pictures. They're not pleasant but I want you to tell me if you recognise any one in them.'

He pushes a handful of photos across the table.

Piccolo sifts through them and before he reaches the end he stares at and separates out two photos from the pile.

'That's him!' he says, prodding the photos. 'That's the Big Bloke who killed my dad!'

'You sure it's him? You're sure it's the Big Bloke?' the policeman asks.

'Oh, yes. No mistaking. Even if he does look completely out of it.'

'He is completely out of it, now,' says the policeman. 'He's dead.'

Piccolo looks up, eyes wide and questioning.

The policeman folds his hands together.

'The shot you heard came from the farm opposite. The Big Bloke walked into the farmhouse, helped himself to drinks and valuables before the farmer heard noises and went to investigate. The Big Bloke went to attack him with a cudgel and the farmer shot him in the leg. Somehow, maybe because it was dark and most of the lights hereabouts were out, the Big Bloke got away. When we got to the scene we used powerful searchlights. Blood on the ground showed he'd staggered across the road and come on to your property before falling into a ditch.'

'Did he break his neck? Or what?'

The policeman hesitates for a moment.

'We can't know for sure, Piccolo, until we get the results of the autopsy but he'd been drinking heavily and in the fall he hit his head on a rock. It so happens the ditch he fell into is next to the pig's pen. And your Monty's a big 'un, isn't he? And like most pigs he's always on the lookout for food. So, it appears Monty broke out of his pen and made for his meal. Leg of Bloke, Arm of Bloke, etcetera. The Big Bloke may have woken up or not, or slipped into unconsciousness then or before or later. But given he was full of drink and had already lost a lot of blood...'

Piccolo is speechless. They had heard screams but had thought they'd come from fighting wild animals. Given what they had been expecting, no one had dared go out exploring in the darkness.

'Rough justice, some might say, sir,' the policeman's colleague mutters to the room at large.

'You won't need to kill Monty, will you, to explore the contents of his stomach or whatever?' Piccolo asks anxiously.

'No,' says the policeman. 'We've got the technology to do all that without killing your Monty.'

Piccolo says nothing but nods in relief. He needs time to take in the news.

'I want you to know, Piccolo, if you don't know already,' says the policeman, 'the Big Bloke had form. He's killed before. And, undoubtedly, he would've killed again. We've been searching for him for quite a few years. A wily devil. Would you like to know more about him, like his name, before it hits the news?'

Piccolo shakes his head.

'Not for now, thanks all the same.'

The policeman nods.

'Do you want news of your mother?'

Piccolo hesitates.

'I don't know. I... Is she alive?'

'Just. But to be frank, I think she'll have passed on before any case comes to court. Too much alcohol, too many drugs.'

So be it, Piccolo thinks. Not once had she behaved as a mother to him. She'd given him neither love nor care. How could he undergo the hypocrisy of a bedside plea for forgiveness? No. He has received more love, more care from strangers – the Catguts, Grout, Nigel, Indigo, Maria, Bianco. And Will. Oh, to be with Will.

94 WHAT'S INNIT FOR INNIT?

Innit hesitates as he stands outside the offices of the Dekaydence publishing house in Fleet Street. He has an appointment with Mr Jarvis, the recently appointed deputy editor of the Dekaydence *Daily Unigraph*. But...

'Go on, In,' Bodkin urges him. 'You don't want to be late. You can't miss out on this one. It is a real biggy for us.'

Innit swallows a belch that's sitting in a rare build-up of gastric acid.

'OK, I'll see you later in the Olde Cheshire Cheese,' says Innit.

'Make sure you get cash, and in a brown envelope,' says Bodkin. 'A big one.'

Innit is already at the top of the stone steps. He doesn't look back.

Bodkin rubs his hands together and grins greedily into space as he walks towards the old pub whose sign boasts 'Rebuilt in 1667'.

'Landlord,' Bodkin calls out confidently. 'A bottle of your finest champagne, to be put on ice, for two young gentlemen celebrating a big win at the races.'

The landlord scrutinises Bodkin and then his note-packed wallet, which persuades him to take the risk.

Bodkin settles himself at a corner table. He scans the

racing pages in the day's paper and rings his bookie.

'Ah, Mr Innit,' says a tall handsome young man with a broad smile, bright blue eyes and a smartly cut head of thick blond hair. He offers Innit his hand. 'My name's Jarvis. Do step this way, sir.'

Jarvis leads Innit through the newsroom bustling with reporters, young and old, who sit within a colony of humming computers.

'You completely idiotic machine!' shouts out an elderly man, punching the computer in front of him. 'Why in heaven's name can't you do what I tell you to do?'

Jarvis flashes Innit an apologetic grin. 'Oakes is an adorable man, really, and immensely talented. Just can't get him to understand modern technology.'

Jarvis ushers Innit into a small room where pots of hot coffee and tea, soft drinks and biscuits sit ready and waiting.

'Please, help yourself,' Jarvis says, and leans back in his chair as Innit pours himself a strong tea. 'Now, you said you had something very important to show us.'

Innit takes a paper wallet from his jacket, hands the contents to Jarvis and watches the young man's handsome tanned face turn pale and serious.

'How did you come by these?' says Jarvis, thumbing through the photographs for a second time.

'That scumbag Solomon called me to the house,' says Innit. 'He'd forgotten who I was. But I knew him. Nasty piece of work. I had a gut feeling what he was up to, that's why I had a camera hidden in my cap. And then...well, I went back to the house a few times. Did some watching and listening in. Then I called you.'

'Anything else, other than the hacking?'

'There's a memory stick in there. It's got what the old man said on the phone to me at HQ. That he wanted the girl done away with 'cos she was trouble.'

'Do you know who the girl is?' Jarvis asks.

'No idea.' Innit shakes his head. 'Should I?'

Jarvis studies the photo, then looks up at Innit.

'I'd prefer you told no one.'

'OK, if that's your rules,' says Innit. 'I just hope she's OK now. She looked like she'd been treated rough. So who is she?'

'She's the daughter of the President of the Federation.'

'Blimey,' Innit replies, shocked. 'So the photos will be worth a lot?'

'I imagine so, yes,' says Jarvis, slowly. 'But not to us...'

'Oh!' Innit sounds surprised. 'If the quality's not good enough I can...'

'No, it's nothing to do with the quality, Mr Innit. It's a matter of principle.'

'What's that mean, Mr Jarvis?'

'We try to ignore the fact that we're a Dekaydence newspaper, and that our boss, Lord di'Abalo, is friends with the President of the Federation. We focus on our work. Until now, no one has knowingly captured this young woman on film. I look at these pictures and am concerned about the possible consequences, should this story break. The girl has been missing for years. She's lived rough, and beyond rough. Put it this way, I wouldn't want to be responsible for causing her to break down completely or even worse...'

He hesitates.

'Listen, Mr Innit, we hold her secrets close. As I trust you can do.'

Innit nods slowly.

Jarvis sighs.

'After the death of her mother and younger brother,' says Jarvis, 'she tried to kill herself.'

'Blimey!' says Innit. He says nothing for some time. His mind is running in parallel – recalling deeds or actions he has taken in the past but would prefer to forget. Thinking of the fragility of a young, abused girl, a young girl about the same age as his Jezza.

'You could go to a tabloid paper or to a celebrity website,' Jarvis speaks slowly, and almost against his will. 'And they do have money to burn.'

Innit nods but says nothing.

'You know, when I saw that girl,' Innit says reflectively, 'she reminded me of a trapped, wounded bird. So vulnerable. I wanted to help her. Put mileage between her and that pervy cleric...

'See, she reminds me of my girlfriend, Jezza. She was

killed in the tsunami. She was strong and yet vulnerable. And I realised too late that she loved me, really loved me, and that I really loved her. I wish I could've saved her, Mr Jarvis. Maybe that's what I was trying to do that night, save the girl 'cos I couldn't save my Jezza.'

'You wouldn't be the first person to try to make amends,' says Jarvis quietly. 'I doubt you'll be the last.'

'So where should I go from here?' says Innit, as much to himself as to Jarvis.

'It's up to you,' says Jarvis. 'You could go to the tabloids and get a tidy sum. Or you could go to the police, give them your evidence and see this man go down for a long time. And that might well save another life, or even more. Let me tell you, my police contact says they're within a millimetre of nailing him. Your stuff could do it.'

Innit feels his stomach begin to unknot.

'That sounds like a plan, Mr Jarvis. Thank you.'

'For what?' asks Jarvis.

Innit gives an embarrassed shrug.

'I've not been what you'd call a decent chap. Then came the tsunami and Jezza... I reckon I'm different now. Not quite sure in what way but...if I do something I think is nice or good for someone, I get this odd, no, this lovely warm glow. I got it first when I helped this little old lady in a blue dress across the road. She was a twinkly one, she was. I told her if she was younger and I was older, I'd have asked for a date. We both laughed and...'

Innit tries to smile through tears.

'Sorry, Mr Jarvis.'

'No problem, Mr Innit,' says Jarvis, with a smile. 'My uncle, a vicar, believed there is good and bad in us all. And that sometimes it's difficult to determine the path to take. So, take time out to think. Maybe even pray for guidance. Here, Mr Innit, take the police officer's name and number. Oh, and I've put your photographs in this brown envelope. Keep tight hold of them.

'As you showed some concern for the girl, Mr Innit,' Jarvis continues, 'you might like to know that she now lives in a very caring, nourishing environment. Among others who have been rescued, among others who nurture and encourage new life from old wounds. It's a joy to see her flourish, Mr Innit. A real joy.'

Bodkin sees Innit walk into Ye Olde Cheshire Cheese, and waves him over. The landlord of the pub opens the bottle of chilled champagne and brings it across with two crystal glasses.

'That'll be £1640, thank you, gentlemen,' says the landlord, pouring champagne into the glasses.

'Don't look at me, he's the banker,' says Bodkin, nodding at Innit.

'Bods, I haven't got any money on me,' says Innit.

Bods's eyes widen. The landlord's, too.

'What? Have they given you a cheque?'

'No, Bods. I didn't sell the story. I haven't got any money.'

The landlord clears his throat.

'What? Um...Is there a bank nearby?' Bodkin enquires of the landlord.

'A few doors down,' says the landlord.

'Hang on, then. I'll just pop out and rob it. Shouldn't take too long. I'm only after getting my own money back!'

'Go for it man!' shouts someone at the bar. 'They've robbed us all of enough!'

As Bodkin storms out of the pub, he hears encouraging cheers from a number of patrons ringing in his ears.

The landlord eyes Innit warily. Innit doesn't notice. He's thinking of the old lady in blue, the young girl in the old green mac, and of Jezza. And of lost happiness. He wonders if there's any way to grow it.

BREAKING NEWS

HOME **NEWS** MUSIC VIDEOS DIARY BLOG

There are so many problems in the world it's understandable that a young boy returns home from school and throws his satchel across the room, declaring he can't cope any longer. And even if the planet is in meltdown, what can he do about it?

Should this young boy surf the internet and look over the waters to the Middle East, he'll find there is one young man who has done much. He promises to do more, even as he pursues his dream to become an archaeologist or a professional golfer.

This young man – let's call him Cameron Oliver (after all, that is his name) – launched a campaign when he was 11 years old to save the camels in Abu Dhabi, where he moved to with his family from South Africa. Camels are dying excruciatingly painful and prolonged deaths after eating the plastic bags, cans, plates, ropes, tyres and other garbage thrown by tourists on to the desert sands or carried there from towns and villages by the wind.

Cameron visited a camel farm, rode a camel, and had his ear adopted temporarily by an affectionate baby camel before reading an article in the local newspaper that said one in every two camels died from eating litter dumped in the desert.

LIVE FROM AN ILLEGAL INTERNET SERVICE PROVIDER

Cameron was horrified. He decided he wanted to do something to stop these terrible deaths. He wants his own children to see camels alive and active, not just read about them in books as stories about a quaint but extinct species.

Cameron's first thought was to hold an exhibition at his school, as an opener to an active campaign. He did his research. He visited experts at home and abroad. He learnt that every year hundreds of camels, and numerous other species, die in the desert, in seas, even in cities, as they try, and fail, to digest plastic. They choke to death or their intestines become blocked and they suffer protracted deaths.

Cameron produced a website, posters and flyers, caps and T-shirts, and anti-litter-dropping stickers to put on the bumpers of cars and taxis. He encouraged friends to join him in litter-collecting outings into the desert. The group grew. And grew some more. As did the stories in the newspapers of his work.

And then Cameron was declared a community hero and received the prestigious Abu Dhabi Award for his remarkable contribution to society, presented to him by General Sheikh Mohammad Bin Zayed Al Nahyan, Crown Prince of Abu Dhabi. Cameron was one of eight 'heroes' chosen from 42,536 nominations and became the

LIVE FROM AN ILLEGAL INTERNET SERVICE PROVIDER

youngest person ever to receive the award.

'This campaign is not about me,' says Cameron, 'it's about saving the camels. When I grow up, regardless of whatever else I do, I will carry on with the campaign. I have made that promise to the Crown Prince.'

The Phoenix lives

95 ROME ALONE

Ruby Q, MacMinor and HOH Candelskin are boarding the flight from Gatwick to Rome. The trip has had to be cancelled several times because of Candelskin's close involvement in the impending Coronation. So as they board the plane, Ruby Q and MacMinor can scarcely believe they're on their way.

Then Candelskin picks up a text message.

'Oh, no-o-o!' he groans, and buries his head in his hands.

'Can I get you something?' a stewardess enquires.

'Yes,' says Candelskin. 'Get me off this plane, immediately. Preferably sooner!'

'Oh, but you can't get off, sir,' the stewardess replies, with a smile.

'Young woman, I am His Overall Highness, Randall Candelskin. I can do anything. Kindly inform the captain. And give him this.'

The woman rushes off to the pilot with Candelskin's ID card. There's an announcement and apology from the pilot. The plane taxis along the runway and into a parking bay.

'What's happened?' Ruby Q whispers, her mind filling with disaster scenarios.

Candelskin leans over MacMinor's stomach to hiss at Ruby Q.

'My right-hand man at the Coronation ceremony has been arrested.'

'Oh, my goodness,' says Ruby Q. 'But I forget, who is your right-hand man?'

Candelskin looks around, expecting ears and mobiles to be hanging on his every word. Disappointingly, though fortunately for him, he is mistaken. The muttering passengers are busy being confused, angry and/or frustrated. Candelskin pulls a newspaper out of the rack in front of him and leans across MacMinor to whisper to Ruby Q, while jabbing at a photo on the front page.

'It's this blighter,' he says.

'Och, no! That's the new Bishop of the City of London!' cries MacMinor, catching the headlines. 'But what's that red feathery thing round his neck? Is it a new Petty Masters dog collar or what?'

Candelskin shudders.

'Hush, MacMinor! You and I must disembark immediately, and without fuss. Miss Cooper, you must journey alone to Rome and explain and apologise to the Holy Father. I'm relying on you.'

'But...' says Ruby Q, unconvinced that the Pope will want to see a minion and realising that she'll miss the Coronation.

Candelskin isn't listening. He's getting his hand luggage from the cabin above his head. He's soon aware that everyone *is* now staring at him. Or rummaging in the magazine rack for the day's newspaper and then staring at him. He focuses on the task at hand. He realises too late that he really shouldn't have decided to wear the lime and tangerine-coloured cassock covered with the numerous church badges that he's collected on his many foreign trips.

96 THE WOMAN IN BLUE

After a morning of grey skies and heavy rainfall a warm sun emerges as a group of 20 people, men and women, young and old, enter the Vatican Gardens in Rome. The group is counted in one by one as they go through the museum door. As they exit at the tour's end each will be counted again.

Paolo, the tall, slender young tour guide, with rather good English, cares for and herds the group like a mother hen. He wears a backpack and is himself packed with information, historical, botanical, social and ornamental, Papal and Roman.

The tour starts at a grey/white marble statue of a young woman that early gardeners named The Spinster. Centuries old, stripped of her pre-Renaissance colouring, she underwent body surgery to make her complete once more. So now the slender young woman with a delicate, poignant face has the enormous hands and feet from what must have been a gargantua among male statuary.

'As if that young woman isn't troubled enough, without enduring mismatching cosmetic surgery,' a middle-aged woman in a blue denim trouser suit mutters to Ruby Q.

'You're right,' replies Ruby Q, glimpsing a bracelet the woman is wearing that shows ever-changing faces, young and old, smiling, laughing, gurning or waving at an unseen camera.

'What a clever device. I've never seen anything like it,' says Ruby Q admiringly.'Are they *all* your family?'

They can't be. Half the world must feature in that bracelet.

'Extended, adopted, gleaned over many years,' says the woman. 'I wanted a large family but I've always worked long hours so I have a son and an adopted one. Adorable little angels they were. But I rarely see them now.'

'Oh, dear,' says Ruby Q. 'Pressure of work?'

The woman nods.

'One is no bother. The other is gifted at making things difficult – for himself, as well as others. He believes he's not as clever as his father. And for some reason he prefers to put a distance between himself and me.'

'Oh, dear,' says Ruby.

They move on with the group. Through the English Garden, in reality a small wood. Up a long road to the statue of Mary with her lit crown, a memorial present to a dead pope from his appreciative home town, Genoa. Through the gates into the French gardens, across a small square, past the Grotto of Lourdes, and past the Papal landing strip, where sits a white OrboBubble, being washed by a sudden downpour.

The group shelters under the trees and several brollies. The woman frowns at the sight of the Orbie and then turns with a smile to Ruby Q as the sun comes out.

'So, what about you, young woman. Any family plans?'

'I'm a workaholic, like you. And given the state of the world... And a complicated set-up at home.'

'Aha,' says the woman understandingly.

'Don't know what I'd do without good friends,' Ruby Q continues.

'They probably feel the same about you.' The woman smiles. The sun appears warmer.

They walk on, past Marconi's radio station, to admire the Jubilee Bell of 2000 and the more spectacular views of the Vatican Dome that appears like a vast imperial crown rising into the blue summer sky, watching over its admirers and visitors alike. Indeed, watching everything.

They double back, and look over the immaculate Italian Garden with its long parrots' nest high in the trees. The woman and Ruby Q splinter off to look at the fountains and then saunter back to join the group. As she returns to the path Ruby Q looks through the trees to the sky.

'It's a rainbow!' she exclaims excitedly.

'Yes, the promise of hope,' says the woman.

Ruby Q stands enchanted. She turns to say something to the woman but she's no longer there. She's far ahead at the front of the group. Ruby Q hears someone shouting, with urgency in their voice. She turns.

An elderly gardener is running towards her, shouting and waving.

'*Scusi! scusi!*' he says breathlessly. 'The lady in blue

dropped this.' He holds out his hand which contains a metal key.

'Thanks,' she says. 'I'd better try and catch her up. It might be her hotel key.'

The elderly gardener nods, too breathless to respond. He watches Ruby Q run on. He can see the woman in blue is about to go back into the museum. He watches her for a moment, a sad smile on his face, and then returns to the garden.

By the time Ruby Q is counted through, she sees the woman in blue denim disappearing on to the street.

With the dense museum crowd there's no chance of catching her up. Ruby Q looks at the key. There's no hotel name on it. But there's an inscription on one side in tiny lettering.

She reads and puzzles the words.

'"Beware: I unlock dreams and nightmares."'

She examines the key. Why is it familiar? Then she realises: it has the design of the crossed keys of Simon Peter in the emblem of the Papacy.

97 CROWNING GLORIES

It's the day of the Coronation and, although it's early morning, the temperature is already hovering around 30°C. It hasn't stopped enthusiastic crowds gathering on both sides of the riverbank at Windsor to cheer and applaud, and to wave their Federation flags when Indigo arrives to board the Royal Barge.

Newly bedecked in white, green and gold, the barge will take her to London, to the Embankment, where she'll be taken by carriage to Westminster Abbey.

Indigo is both excited and nervous. She is not, as Candelskin had dreaded, wearing designer-shredded jeans or outrageous boots, hair or make-up. She is dressed in smart white cotton trousers and top, and an elegant blue and white striped fibrene silk jacket (designed by Petty Masters and Schneek). She has a fine gold and pearl necklace at her throat and wears but a touch of eyeliner and mascara, her skin already aglow with the day. Her straw-coloured low-heeled shoes match the neat straw trilby sitting tilted back on her long dark shining curls so all can see the smile on her face and in her eyes, and understand also that here is a young woman who means business, not frills and froth.

'You look beautiful, Your Majesty,' says Will, as he

waves to the crowds on both riverbanks.

'Thanks,' says Indigo, with a quick grin. 'I just hope I don't make any mistakes.'

'Aye, well, you're bound to make loads but I wouldnae worry about it. People will find it endearing.'

'Maybe, but I'm not doing this job to be endearing.'

'Och, I forgot. You've plans to be a dictator.'

'Someone has to sort out this country, Will. The GeeZers, Real or Original, haven't achieved much so far, have they?'

'You're right, of course,' Will sighs.

'Keep your voice down,' Indigo whispers. 'There are bugs as well as Black and Red Tartan guards on this boat. Oh, and check out our blackbirds.'

Will glances up.

He's seen something like it before. They're not birds, they're flying cameras inside beautifully crafted mechanical but realistic-looking birds, except that their bodies are covered in some two score of eyes that click continuously, like paparazzi shutters. They fly over the boat and the crowds, watching, listening, recording – almost everything.

The flag-waving crowds on the Embankment are even greater in number, and even louder at roaring cheers, as the Royal Barge comes into view and proceeds to its mooring.

'I'll have to do more weights to keep my arm strong for

this game,' Indigo mutters to Will, as she waves.

'And for arm-wrestling Di'Abalo,' Will mutters back.

'I'd laugh but for the fact I know that'll come.'

'Remember you have support everywhere you look. Even though you must do this next bit on your own.'

'It's a big bit, too,' says a clown, packed into the clouds of Heaven with hundreds more, all intent on the Coronation pictures on the wide screen.

'Nine outfits! I should be so lucky! Tho' some of the old stuff weighs as much as three of us. And there's all the ceremonial bling and metalwork she has to have and hold.'

'At least the crown's been thinned down,' says the King. 'The old one was so heavy one would have to practise wearing it on the morning of a State Opening. One would wear it while bathing the grandchildren and one would sit with it on one's head while one had one's boiled egg at breakfast.'

'Was that before or after one had used the heated rollers?' the clown asks.

'One is blessed,' the King retorts with a supercilious sniff. 'One's hair is naturally curly.'

Indigo goes below deck. Lady Catgut and a lady-in-waiting help her change into a simple gown, the Robe of State of crimson velvet and the ermine cape, decorated with gold lace.

As she is dressed Indigo wonders how many times one can stand up to such a man as Di'Abalo before he decides whether you live or die. Now, at the back of her mind there's doubt over the demise of her grandfather and Cataract. She fears that 'they' (Dekaydence) may have taken her father hostage, assessing him (perhaps rightly) as a loose cannon not fit for the throne.

Indigo disembarks from the Royal Barge.

Will and Lady Catgut are driven to the Abbey.

Indigo sits alone in the four-ton Gold State Coach, drawn by eight horses wearing the red morocco harness, postilion ridden in pairs.

She smiles and waves at the crowds on the roads as the Gold State Coach proceeds at a smart but dignified pace along the Strand, passing Nelson's Column in Trafalgar Square before turning into Whitehall and heading towards Parliament Square and Westminster Abbey.

'How is she doing?' Grout asks Lady Catgut as she settles into her seat.

'She's doing fine,' replies Lady Catgut. 'She's a brave and feisty young woman.'

'Aye, she is,' says Will. He thinks of the various ways she has quietly and secretly supported and protected him over the years. And his blood runs cold as he recalls how close he came to killing her in the old graveyard just a few years ago, thinking her to be an assassin.

★ ★ ★

Indigo enters the Abbey to a fanfare. She sees the reality of some eight thousand guests packed inside, of which she thinks she knows about thirty. She is taken to her seat on the Chair of Estate and six dignitaries headed by the Garter Principal King of Arms go to the east, south, west and north of the Abbey, where HOH Randall Candelskin calls out to the people at each side to acclaim their Sovereign.

Indigo breathes a sigh of relief as she hears the loud and positive feedback from the crowd. Otherwise, she thinks, it could've been hugely embarrassing.

She takes the Coronation Oath in an exchange with HOH Randall Candelskin, accepts a Bible from the Moderator of the General Assembly of the Church of Scotland, and Holy Communion is celebrated with a break and Parry's 'I Was Glad', with the resounding 'Vivat!' shouted repeatedly by the Westminster Scholars.

The new Queen moves to King Edward's Chair for the sacred anointment, which is screened from public gaze, as the Sovereign's hands, head and heart are anointed with consecrated oil.

There's more robe changing and the Queen is presented with the spurs, representing chivalry, the Sword of State and Crown Jewels. Then the Orb, with its cross, representing Jesus' rule over the world, which is immediately returned to the altar; and a ring, representing the Sovereign's marriage to the nation. After the Sceptre with the Dove and the Sceptre with the Cross are received by the Queen,

HOH Randall Candelskin places St Edward's Crown on Indigo's head and all shout 'God Save the Queen!' and cannon at the Tower of London fire their salute.

There is more ceremony before Queen Indigo leaves St Edward's Chapel dressed in the Imperial Robe of purple velvet, wearing the Imperial State Crown and holding the Sceptre with the Cross, and the Orb, with all singing the national anthem.

As she proceeds towards the Abbey doors, with the congregation's cheers resounding in her ears, the new Queen hears music that stops her momentarily in her stride. She smiles. The music weaves together and evokes the sounds of water and fire, earth and wind, and the power of love and compassion. This is the sonata Piccolo composed for her, 'Music of the Elements'. She drinks it in, as does the congregation and the crowd outside, who listen to it on the speakers. It seems to fill Indigo with a strength and awareness that's new to her.

She steps out of the Abbey and curtseys to a crowd that roars its approval. She waves to all sides and is walking towards the Gold State Coach when a shot rings out. She's thrown to the ground and covered protectively by someone, the crown falling from her head and rolling across the ground. Someone whispers reassuringly into her ear. It's Will! Will is protecting her.

'What's happening?' she cries out to him. 'Is someone trying to kill me?'

'Ach, no, dearest, no one is trying to kill you,' says Will, as guards and bodyguards rush to their aid. 'The shot was directed at someone on the rooftops. No one is after you so don't—'

There's another shot. Another scream. A brief horrified shuddering silence that's replaced by a deep, dark hum within the crowd as surprise and shock surge into panic among some, inside and outside the Abbey. Luckily, calm officials filter people into the outer streets.

Sid helps Indigo to her feet. Nayr rescues the crown and returns it to the Queen with a low bow.

What Will doesn't tell Indigo — until immediately after the Coronation banquet — is that two shots were fired at a suspected terrorist, running amok on the high buildings close to the Abbey. He also tells her later that the 'terrorist' suffered a minor flesh wound but was in a very disturbed state and turned out to be none other than her father, the Crown Prince, missing, presumed dead and now in hospital, sedated and under guard.

98 THE PHOENIX IS FADING

'Oh, God!' the Noteian, Driver, cries out.

'You must be desperate, calling out to someone you no longer believe in,' the other Noteian, Handcuffs, shouts from the kitchen.

'I am, brother, I am,' says Driver.

'What is it? What's the matter?' says Handcuffs, hurrying into the room.

'Look!' Driver commands, indicating the monitor.

'Oh, God!' says Handcuffs.

'He might listen to you,' says Driver. 'He certainly doesn't listen to me.'

'Why is this happening?'

'I don't know exactly,' says Driver. 'What I do know is that slowly but surely they are killing the Phoenix.'

'God, he looks weak.'

'He's slipping in and out of unconsciousness,' says Driver.

'What can we do, brother? We have to do something!'

'I don't know what to do, brother.'

'Problems bring out the best in you. You must have some idea what to do.'

'OK, OK. I am trying to communicate with him without them knowing.'

'How on earth do you do that?' Handcuffs asks.

Driver sighs deeply.

'I've become a taxi driver.'

'What?'

'Not literally, but I use the airwaves as if... Look, I send coded messages that in a lucid moment he should hear and understand. But I don't know how many lucid moments he's having. Or when. You're not to worry, I've layered the airwaves so there is no way they can track us down.'

'*Alhamdulillah.* God be praised. What are you saying to him?'

'Bits of news about this and that. Anything to keep his mind stimulated.'

'Why don't they kill him outright? What's their game?'

'They want to get everything that's in his mind. The open areas and the ones I've locked securely.'

'Do you know what they're looking for?'

'No.' Driver shakes his head.

'So they'll go on looking for whatever it is?'

'Yes. I think their aim is to weaken everything, so cracks emerge and spread, and everything is open. They'll take what they want and then kill him.'

'God in Heaven, we must get him out of there.'

'We can't,' says Driver. 'Not until... I've just discovered that Dekaydence is going to bring him out.'

'I don't understand.'

'It's part of the post-Coronation celebrations in the arena. The Phoenix will be on display with a huge reward for the person who cracks the code to get into his brain.'

'Ah. I get it now. You're going there to rescue him, aren't you?'

'Something like that.' The Driver shrugs.

'You are brave as well as bonkers. And I am proud and honoured to be your friend. Can I help in any way?'

'Keep talking to your god, my dearest friend.'

99 A BEDSIDE FAREWELL

Indigo sits at her father's bedside in a small private room in a London hospital. Armed guards and police stand outside in the corridor and at the front and back entrances of the building. As if this sick, wounded man could make a run for it, she thinks.

'Look after your mother,' the Crown Prince mumbles, as he looks at his daughter with eyes that are weary and blurred.

'Yes, of course,' she says, rather than remind him that her mother departed years ago to return to her Scandinavian home. A pattern repeated by his two other wives.

'You're a treasure,' he says, slurring his words. 'The King is proud of you.'

'Yes,' she says, wondering, Does he not know that the King is dead, as is his son?

There is a long silence. Strangely, she draws comfort from being alone with him, something that has happened rarely in her life. But in the silence grows a fear of him leaving her for ever, alongside panic, guilt that she wants it over as quickly as possible so she can escape the pain by focusing on trying to get on with her life. She can't imagine the size of the wound of bereavement, only that it will hurt for a long, long time, and may never fully heal.

Her father tries to speak but what she hears is an impenetrable sticky jumble of sound.

The Crown Prince falls silent. His eyes glaze over, his eyelids flicker and close. She asks if he can hear her. He doesn't respond.

Suddenly, his legs take on a life of their own. Are they drawing in or kicking out? One is an indication of life, the other of impending death. But which is which?

Her heart beats fast. She takes hold of her father's hand, and strokes it.

'Dad,' she says, leaning into him. 'You've been a wild man, and a fun, untameable father. My brother worships you. And I love you. Not one of us is perfect, but I think I am lucky to have inherited the best of you. I shall miss you so much but you will live in my heart always…'

She looks into his face. He has stopped breathing. He is still.

'Dad!' She is shaking. Now she knows there will be no answer.

She rushes to the door.

'Call a doctor! Quickly!' she commands, and returns to the bedside.

Two passing nurses bustle in and check the Crown Prince.

'His Royal Highness has passed on, Your Majesty,' says one softly.

'But he will hear you for a little while longer,' says the other. 'Talk to him, Your Majesty. Let him pass on happily and with peace. Call us back when you are ready.'

They leave as quickly and quietly as they came.

Indigo sits, holding her father's hand, and talks to him. She lists things that she knows he loved and tried to share with her. Music. Machines, though they were more her brother's interest. The wildness and wonder of nature. Perhaps it wasn't much but she feels as if the attributes mix well with what's she inherited from her mother, and her grandfather, the King.

She watches the colour drain from her father's face and hands. She considers the stillness of his body, the quietness, the change. He is there but... Her lively, vital father is becoming a corpse, closer to cold stone than full-blooded life. She kisses his cheek, lets go his hand and walks to the window overlooking a few acres of fields.

A honey-coloured horse with a wild white mane looks up, appearing to watch her. She stares back at it. It doesn't seem real and yet... She presses her face against the window, watching the horse canter across the grass towards her. Suddenly, it rears up on its magnificent hind legs and whinnies, its eyes still focused on her. And then, all at once, the magnificent golden beast takes off into the sky and disappears.

She pinches herself to ensure she's awake and can feel. She knows full well that she has just lost her father. Equally, she knows she has not lost her sanity. That she is in a painful, emotional place but is not hallucinating. She hasn't been drinking, neither does she do drugs. She can tell fact from fiction, reality from fantasy. So she knows, without understanding but with no doubt, that the horse is carrying away her father. His soul, his essence, whatever it is, has been taken by the honey-coloured horse with a wild white mane. It's not a Harley-Davidson, she thinks, but a spiritual, equine equivalent.

She whispers a farewell and slowly turns back to the bed and to the corpse. She knows her father is not there. But why has she been shown something she doesn't understand? Is it to show her that death always wins? Or that there is comfort in the vision she saw? Or what?

She sits alone within her thoughts. For some while no one comes into the room. No one pops their head round the door. No one knocks. Even her own tears remain at a respectful internal distance.

100 GROUT, BEE-WARE!

The Red Tartan guards appear not to have been told that Di'Abalo has banned Grout from the place so they nod and allow him in. They ask no questions; he tells them no lies. And time passes quickly and quietly, and without incident. Until...

Late one night he's startled by a voice behind him.

'How's your bee-witching work coming along?' asks Di'Abalo softly, drawing a stool closer to Grout and the workbench.

Phlegm stands by the door.

Grout looks deflated, as if he's given his all in a marathon and come last.

'I wasn't sure you'd approve of what I was doing, else I'd have asked your permission,' Grout says dejectedly. 'But the more research I do the more I realise that this is one of the most important projects I've ever worked on. It could be the best thing Dekaydence has ever done. To save the honeybee means to save the planet... I'm working on an 'oid...'

Di'Abalo's smile is strange. Is he bored or benevolent?

'Put the bees on hold, dear boy,' says Di'Abalo. 'Because, first, as a matter of some urgency, I want this copied. Twice. The spare is to go into a locked cupboard in my office.'

Grout frowns at the picture.

'I don't understand,' he says. 'This is the President of the Federation.'

'Yes,' says Di'Abalo. 'He's gone missing on foreign soil. At a most inconvenient time. He should be here with all the other heads of state for the Coronation celebrations, as well as the official press photographs and, later, the futile discussions. So he must be here, Grout, if only to soothe furrowed brows.

'Professor Zola will give you the blueprint for the US President. You can adapt it accordingly. Prof will assist you, should you need help. But let's be clear, Grout, this matter will be discussed with no one else. No one.'

'I understand,' says Grout.

'Later, you can return to your bees,' says Di'Abalo, and pauses. 'Strange that you have hit on a creature that is my mother's favourite. She wheedled their care into my consciousness, I suspect from birth or even before.'

'Mankind depends on them,' says Grout.

'So my mother told me, over and over again.'

Di'Abalo walks to the window and stares out into the dark overheated London streets.

'It's the old strings that pull at you, don't you find, Grout?' says Di'Abalo.

'No, not for me, they don't,' says Grout firmly.

Di'Abalo's eyebrows arch quizzically.

'Why is that, then?'

Grout shrugs.

'Something wrong with my parenting and genes, I suspect,' he says.

'There is nothing wrong with your genes, dear boy,' says Di'Abalo. 'And I should know.'

'How come?' says Grout, taken aback.

Di'Abalo fixes Grout with his twinkling eyes.

'How come?' Di'Abalo teasingly repeats Grout's question. 'Because, Grout, I am your father. Your real father.'

'What?' says Grout. 'I...I don't understand.'

'It's quite simple, dear boy,' Di'Abalo says languidly. 'These things happen all the time. It's the birds and, of course, every time, the bees. You see, you've inherited my scientific bent and, if I might say, genius, and now you're also following in the footsteps of your dear grandmother.'

'What? I can't take this in,' says Grout, more to himself than to Di'Abalo.

'That's what they all say,' Di'Abalo muses.

'D'you mean what I think you mean, that there are others like me?' says Grout.

Di'Abalo stands up and moves to the door, which is held open by Phlegm.

'First, Grout, create our 'oid. You have less than twenty-four hours. We'll talk again another time.'

Alone in the lab, Grout studies his hands and realises they are shaking. Much like his stomach. He wishes there was a door inside his head so he could slam it hard, blocking out thoughts and confusion. He can't take in fully what he's been told. And he's scared to even try.

On the other side of the door Di'Abalo leans towards Phlegm.

'Study the boy's work on bees, Phlegm,' Di'Abalo says quietly. 'Copy it and pass it to me and to the Professor. If Grout has found the cure I want my name on it as the inventor. For once it'll win me some points and get my mother off my back.'

Phlegm nods understandingly.

'You look tired, Phlegm.'

Phlegm gives a small nod.

'Bear up, man, soon be going-home time. Soon be going-home time.'

How many times has he heard that promise? Phlegm reflects. There aren't numbers enough.

101 A ROMAN MORNING

Ruby Q is asleep in a hotel room that overlooks the elegant 1920s terracotta-faced Palace of the Holy Office. This is home to the Congregation for the Doctrine of Faith that oversees Catholic Church doctrine, known better in the 16th century as the Holy Inquisition, which held tribunals against witchcraft and heresy.

In her sleep, Ruby Q is aware of a noise close to her head. A mosquito? No, louder. Air-conditioning? No, she remembers switching it off. Whatever it is, it's growing louder.

She stirs. The noise is coming from outside. Bleary-eyed, she stumbles out of bed. She pulls back the heavy green and cream drapes at the window of the small fifth-floor room. The sky is lit up by the lights on St Peter's dome, just visible, like a magnificent crown nestling between the buildings. But the noise...?

She discovers how to open the window.

The noise is deafening. She looks up. It's a white Orbobubble, a Dekaydence anti-gravitational Orbie, with a Papal emblem, descending, presumably to land on the Orbo-Pad. For a moment her eyes are level with the Orbie and she sees the figure of the Pope, clad in his white robe. The Orbie drops out of view. Moments later there is silence. It has landed.

She breathes in the warm night air, and watches the few dark figures below walk briskly in the shadows across the cobbled street. She is shutting the window when the noise begins again. Now the Orbie is rising up into the sky, and before it heads westward she gets a glimpse of the cockpit. Two pilots. No one else.

Ruby Q frowns at her ad'um. It's 3am in the morning. What was His Excellency doing out at this time? Has he forgotten their 6.30am appointment?

Perhaps he's run out of coffee.

Yes, of course, silly me for not thinking of that. But... Listen! Is it coming back?

Ah, then it's espresso coffee he was after.

102 PAPAL SUMMIT

Light is creeping into the night sky, furtive as a late arrival at a play. Soon the heating will be on full blast when the sun rises in what the Romans call a bronze October.

Already, from her bedroom window, Ruby Q sees a flock of young, high-spirited clerics hurrying towards the Vatican, the swishing skirts of their black cassocks moving like elegant gowns at a grand ball. In their various uniforms, nuns from the world over are also showing an eagerness to get to their destination. Bishops and cardinals employ a more sedate step, she observes, as they, too, head towards a synod that is aiming to modernise the Catholic Church.

There are also beggars, among them actors and cheats. But who can tell the difference? An elderly South American woman in yellow and green shakes an empty mug at one and all. A woman with nothing approaches everyone for alms. Hawkers try to sell scarves and handbags. All beggars are ignored. Ruby Q wonders how Christ or anyone could tell the difference between the poor, the needy and the cheats.

Ruby Q is hungry. It's too early for the hotel breakfast and there's no facility in the room to make a hot drink so she raids the tiny fridge and consumes a small packet of biscuits, a packet of salted peanuts and a bottle of sparkling water.

She joins the growing throng on the cobbled street outside the hotel, which is seconds from St Peter's Square. She walks towards the square, turns left, and sees two Swiss Guards in a doorway, hastily and indiscreetly stubbing out their cigarettes.

They check her Federation ID and indicate she follow them. One knocks at a door, which is opened immediately by a large older man with an authoritative air and forensically assessing eyes. He nods, the guards salute and fall back and Ruby Q follows the Large Old Man through the door.

Large Old Man leads her through marble hallways decorated with colossal vases of luscious, scented flowers. Large Old Man gives her a brief résumé of the most precious works as they pass huge oak-panelled doors, walls dripping with paintings, and numerous displays of statues and antiques. Along one corridor an unruly choir of ticking clocks is busy chiming as if in a race to get there, or wherever, first.

Large Old Man opens a door and they step inside. They're in a large room, with one wall made entirely of frosted glass. In a corner a scribe sits at a desk with a tablet. In the opposite corner is a man she takes to be a detective. Large Old Man indicates Ruby Q stand next to him.

She is wondering the significance of it all when a dark

shadowy figure appears behind the frosted glass door and then...

The room becomes an explosion of bright light. It's so bright Ruby Q is blinded. She can't see the walls, the floor or the ceiling. She loses her balance and falls to the floor.

How much time passes she does not know but, shielding her eyes, she can just make out a tall, lean man wearing sunglasses and a flowing white robe, a light surrounding his entire body like a halo.

Either you're alive, in which case this is the Pope. Or you've passed on and this is God.

Oh, so you're back now. How do you know all this? It could be Hell.

There's no fire or brimstone, that's how I know.

Right, so you've been to Hell?

And back. It's known locally as another Dekaydence mall.

The man in white stretches out his hand to help Ruby Q to her feet. She sees him gesture to the scribe and the detective to leave the room.

'I do hope you are not hurt, Miss Cooper,' says the man, sounding concerned. His English is heavily accented.

'I'm fine, thank you,' says Ruby Q, deciding she won't attempt the curtsey she's been practising, just in case... Because this, she decides, is the Pope.

The Pope smiles and Ruby Q feels herself embraced in warmth.

'I must apologise for the dramatic entrance,' says the Pope, 'It's a new idea being developed by our IT and marketing department. But we can't have people falling over in droves, can we?'

Ruby Q smiles and the Large Old Man nods in silent agreement.

'By the way,' says the Pope, addressing Ruby Q, 'did you feel an embrace of warmth?'

'I did, actually, yes,' says Ruby Q, somewhat surprised. 'It was very nice.'

'At least that works. But what about the lights? How did you find them, honestly?' the Pope enquires.

Ruby Q pulls a face and screws up her eyes.

'Very, very, very bright. Disorienting. And dangerous.'

'I couldn't agree more,' says the Pope, relieved and triumphant. 'Hence the sunglasses. I've been telling them in IT but they won't have it. They are too used to working with the Federation President, who can never get enough light or drama.'

Ruby Q nods sympathetically.

'I have taken the liberty of ordering refreshment,' the Pope continues, 'as I expect your hotel restaurant doesn't open for a few hours.'

'That's very thoughtful. Thank you.'

'You're welcome,' says the Pope. 'While we're waiting, I wonder if we might discuss the letter that Mr Candelskin was to deliver but which you kindly brought in his place. Have you read it?'

'No,' says Ruby Q. 'It's addressed to you.'

'Have you any idea what is in it?' says the Pope.

'No.'

The Pope nods slowly, and stares reflectively into space.

'Do you think Mr Candelskin knows of its contents?'

'Why, yes. I thought he wrote it?' says Ruby Q, surprised.

'I don't think he did,' says the Pope. 'It seems to me that it was written by your employer, Lord Di'Abalo.'

'Does it make any difference?' says Ruby Q.

Ruby Q stares into the Pope's extra-dark sunglasses.

'Have you had a falling out with Lord di'Abalo, perhaps?' the Pope enquires. 'I know he's not an easy man, for sure.'

Ruby Q hesitates.

Don't say anything, Ruby Q. Please don't...

'After years of believing a good man to be my father,' says Ruby Q, 'I have discovered recently that my real father is a crook, a cheat and a murderer and that his name is Lorenzo di'Abalo.'

'Aha!' says the Pope, taken aback.

'What do you mean by "Aha"?' Ruby Q asks.

'I have been wondering whether or not to tell you. And I've concluded it is much better to warn you.'

'Warn me of what?' says Ruby Q. 'Forgive me, but I really don't understand what you're talking about.'

The Pope rests his head wearily on his hand.

'I suppose it could be worse,' the Pope says. 'Lord di'Abalo asks that I get a signed agreement from you, in which you state you'll go on-side with Dekaydence.'

'I can't do that,' Ruby Q protests.

'Oh, but you must, dear girl,' says the Pope firmly. 'If you don't, the letter says you are to be destroyed. Accidentally, of course.'

11

'Good news!' says Wiggins, serving tea in his London apartment to Will, who has just arrived. 'The ICC in The Hague has read through our documents and the case goes ahead. Of course, if we could retrieve the President he'd be cross-examined in person but that looks unlikely. So, if there's a verdict of guilty, he will be convicted in absentia.'

'It's a pity you can't conduct the case,' says Will.

'As Lord Protector, I cannot. But I have every confidence in my son, Gerald, who's taken on the case. He has the forensic skills of Sherlock Holmes and the tenacity of Godzilla. As has his sibling, my daughter Daphne, which, as judgement rather than luck would have it, has led to her being in the same team.

'I shall remain here, on call, should I be needed.' Wiggins taps his ad'um.

'Have you heard that someone is paying the kidnappers to keep hold of the President?' Will asks abruptly.

'No!' Wiggins exclaims. 'Who told you that?'

'The Suit, a journalist friend of Ruby Q's boss.'

'Do we know who that someone might be?'

'We do now. It's Dekaydence.'

'Oh, my. How did you find that out?'

'After I heard the Suit's story I went into the office later that night. No one said anything; loads of CCM-ers work late and weekends. I went up to the fifth floor, the company's secret hub. The day he died, Cataract hinted that odd things were going on and he wanted me to investigate. He got me a special pass and I went digging in IT. I discovered Dekaydence covertly hires Cataract, Cyclops & Mote to manage a small company that receives unusually large sums of money, via circuitous routes, that end up in an account in the bank next door to the small company.'

'Is this some Swiss or far-off offshore transaction?'

Will laughs darkly.

'Not unless Bognor Regis has moved on and declared independence.'

'Bognor Regis?'

'Yes.'

'What on earth...? What does the company do, by the way?'

'It's a fancy-dress and joke emporium, with a huge internet following and worldwide internet sales. It's patronised by clowns globally. One room boasts over the door: "We sell anything that makes rude or loud noises."'

'If this should get out...' says Wiggins.

'Ach, I wouldnae worry,' says Will. 'We'll track down the President of the Federation and put him before the court.'

Wiggins smiles.

'Anything else?'

'I saw Bodkin and the Professor coming out of a room on the fifth floor.'

'Not surprising,' says Wiggins, sadly. 'Any idea what they were up to?'

'I can only imagine they're up to no good. I'll keep an eye open.'

'Good,' says Wiggins. 'I'll have a word with old Mote at CCM. Tell him what Cataract advised about moving you upstairs. Bizarre, I'm having lunch in the country today with Professor Zola. My brother's diary reveals they met regularly and I thought I might learn something more about him. It's a foolish whim but it's too late and too impolite to pull out now.'

'You'd regret it if you didn't go,' says Will. 'And from what I know, you're honoured to get an appointment with the Professor. He's not the most sociable being. He's interested only in his own experiments.'

102.5 JUSTICE AND JAM

North travels the country, talking to people, young and old, about the Justice movement and holding classes and seminars to explain how a community can become self-sufficient and independent of government control. It's a slow process but North finds he is inspired by their enthusiasm as much as by the thoughts and actions of the young people they talk to and work with.

Meanwhile, Will watches the movement of money, and Strawberry Jam, within the Dekaydence corporation. Much jam is being bottled and stored, more is coming in, much more is due. Will worries that many companies are gambling too much on jam and that their businesses are at risk of going into liquidation and defaulting to Dekaydence. Worldwide, the earth itself is hiccuping, with storms long and torrential. Not the weather for strawberries, for sure. Maybe for sitting ducks...?

SECTION 12

The whole aim of practical politics is to keep the populace alarmed (and hence clamorous to be led to safety) by menacing it with an endless series of hobgoblins, all of them imaginary.

H. L. Mencken (1880–1956)

103 GOD RIDES OUT

God walks through His stables, wondering which of His many trusty steeds He'll take out on this special night, the once-in-10,000-years experience that He'll enjoy savouring until the next outing in 10,000 years' time.

He spots the shiny little olive-green Vespa with its matching sidecar. How could He forget this one? He used it on His first date with Mother Nature, before it had been invented, courtesy of one of His collectors that travels back and forth through time.

He goes to dab away a tear, and then recalls He's on empty.

No, the Vespa must stay at home. It wouldn't be the same without Mother Nature. And now that she's gone... He admires the first self-propelled road vehicle, Cugnot's military tractor with its Brezin steam-engine of 1769; the first electric carriage made in the 1830s by Robert Anderson of Scotland; the 12-cylinder scarlet Ferrari F12 berlinetta and a 1925 6.5-litre Bentley.

He walks past racers of metal and of flesh and comes to Modestine, the little donkey Robert Louis Stevenson described as 'patient, elegant in form, the colour of an ideal mouse, and inimitably small'.

God strokes the donkey behind the ears, feeding her an

apple or two.

'It's time you had an outing, and some fun, Modestine. So I'd like to invite you to be my date for the night,' God tells the donkey. 'Is that acceptable?'

Modestine whinnies, throwing her head back in a gesture as magnificent as any stallion could perform.

God smiles as he leads the little donkey out from the stable.

'It'll do you good,' Jack tells Jezza, who is hard at work in the children's nursery. 'You need a break. A bit of excitement.'

'We're in Heaven, Jack,' says Jezza. 'It can't get better than that, can it?'

Jack shrugs.

'It'll be such a wild experience. You can't turn down a once in a life... Or whatever. 'Cos we don't know exactly what'll happen to us next.'

'I don't like flying, Jack,' says Jezza. 'But what's more important, who would look after the children?'

'The King has commandeered scores of young doctors and nurses who've arrived recently in Heaven from various battlefronts on earth.'

'The poor souls will need a rest.'

'They'll get that. And then they'll be revitalised by some good strong doses of love and laughter from the children in the nursery,' says Jack. 'So, how about it, Jezza?'

★ ★ ★

The King is pacing the length and breadth of the clouds in Heaven, peering out, watching, this way and that, for the arrival of His son, the Crown Prince, who is currently in a long-term Waiting Room.

The Crown Prince is sobbing his heart out, knowing his name is on the list for Hell. Will he ever see his Harley-Davidson, or his boy, or family, again? He is consumed with sorrow. He tries to steady himself by thinking of the Man in the Tree, his steadfastness and kindness, and wonders if he can learn from the Tree Man's brief teachings. He must think how he can endure with his heavy load of grief and guilt.

Meanwhile, his son waits impatiently in an anteroom for someone to take him to his father and grandfather.

'Sorry about the wait,' says a passing angel. 'Clown troubles. Wigs and make-up everywhere. And absent Archangels. I'll be with you shortly.'

A hundred Heaven's Angels are flying in space, far above the earth. Should people look up they'll see lights that they'll assume are meteorites or stars in their final days. Even the strongest telescope cannot detect the figures riding and flying through dark space.

God leads the flight path on Modestine. He is followed by the Pope and others... Jack and Jezza are with the beginners, under the tuition of the Archangel Gabriel. Jack grins at Jezza, and give a thumbs-up sign. She returns the grin but, as yet, cannot let go the handlebars of her motorbike.

Then she sees them, over Jack's shoulder. Hears them, too. A riotously colourful bunch, laughing and shouting, and revving the engines of their huge black riding machines.

'Turn left and foot down!' Archangel Gabriel yells the orders. 'Hell's Devils advancing from the right flank!'

Heaven's Angels jump at the command and stream off left.

Jezza turns to Jack but he's no longer at her side. She glances over her shoulder and cries out.

'What is it?' Archangel Gabriel enquires, flying to her side.

'It's Jack,' she shouts out anxiously. 'He was trying to protect us by luring away the Hell's Devils but now they're chasing him! Look! How do we get him back?'

Gabriel turns to check Jack's position. It's too late, he concludes sorrowfully, to get him back. But if he informs the girl, he knows she'll chase after her beau and follow his fate. They'll both go to Hell and be lost for ever.

Suddenly, a shower of fireworks, bangers and crackers and rockets explodes like dynamite over their heads. And another. And another. Each brighter, fiercer and louder than the last. Sparks fall on to their clothing and sting their souls.

'Keep moving!' Archangel Gabriel orders. 'Remember, they can't abide the cold. Pretty soon they'll be charging back to Hell.'

Gabriel flies alongside the angels, urging them on. So intent is he on his work that he fails to spot Jezza race off in the direction of the Hell's Devils and Jack.

104 SEEING IS BELIEVING

The Pope positions his fingers together in the way a child builds a digital bridge or roof. Occasionally he fidgets with the gold ring on the third finger of his right hand, the fisherman's ring of St Peter fishing from a boat, with the Pope's name in Latin surrounding the picture.

'So, Lord di'Abalo would have me killed simply because I disagree with him?' says Ruby Q, her face paler than pale.

The finger bridge divides for a moment before re-forming.

'I shall pray for you, my child, and do my utmost to protect you,' says the Pope quietly.

Does that mean you'll be forever followed by a holy Eye-Spy and a few dozen holey-cheese Swiss Guards?

'What is wrong with the man? And why is he involving you, Your Holiness?'

The Pope throws up his hands in despair.

'My dear, Lord di'Abalo had a very troubled early life. He confided in me once that he was proud of his high-flying parents but they were always too busy to attend to him.'

'That doesn't entitle him to go round bumping off people. Me included,' Ruby Q retorts. 'Sorry, I don't mean to be rude but...'

The Pope nods, slowly and sympathetically.

'You're right, Miss Cooper,' says the Pope. 'How much do you know of this man?'

'He's my boss,' says Ruby Q, and pauses. 'He's also my father.'

His sunglasses hide the Pope's reaction.

'Are you sure about that?' he asks.

'Absolutely. My mother confirmed it. So did my aunt. There's no reason for either of them to lie.'

'And your mother is...?'

'I doubt you'd know her. She works for Lord di'Abalo. Her name is Angelica Nera.'

She sees a Papal eyebrow twitch.

He knows her.

'So, you do know her?' Ruby Q persists.

'I don't think so. Perhaps I may have met her briefly on some occasion but...' says the Pope, hesitant. 'In my line of work I meet a lot of people.'

He's lying.

About the number of people he meets?

No! About meeting your mum. He's covering up something. Or, as we say: he's lying

The Pope doesn't lie. It's in his articles of association.

I don't believe you.

'But I can't recall the occasion,' the Pope muses, rubbing the bridge of his nose, perhaps trying to stop a tiresome itch, when, suddenly and unexpectedly, his sunglasses shift sideways across his face.

Oh, my God!

Oh, my God! Ruby Q echoes internally as she catches sight of the Pope's eyes, the mesmerising Caribbean colours of sapphire blue and emerald green. She knows at once: these are the cruel but utterly captivating eyes of her father, Lorenzo di'Abalo.

105 THE QUEEN'S PROMISE

Indigo arrives at the TV studios in a Dekaydence limousine. She is surprised to see a crowd of cheering well-wishers at what is a supposedly top secret visit. She is greeted by the studio's owner, Lord di'Abalo, whose alluring smile fires the twinkling magic in his blue-green eyes.

The young head of studio is unsure how to greet the teenage Queen. Aware of his nervousness, she smiles as she offers him her hand.

'The rumours are wrong, I don't bite,' she says calmly. 'At least, not often.'

Those who hear what she says relax, laugh or giggle, and wildfire the jest through the crowd. The jest arrives on the evening's websites and the front page of the next day's tabloids: 'Our new Queen doesn't bite!' An enterprising freelance produces a photo of a young Indigo biting into a sandwich, enabling a few papers to continue the jest with another headline: '...Or does she?'

Make-up applied, Indigo sips warm water to ensure her vocal cords do not dry out. A microphone is attached, the speech is before her on the table as well as on auto-cue. She commands silence from her stomach and nods to the studio manager, who counts her in. Heart pounding, she begins.

'I'm not here to present an idle manifesto of false promises to lure you into supporting me,' she says. 'But I have ideas and strong beliefs that I want to share with you.

'I know enough to recognise that I have much to learn. I am fortunate to be tutored by some of the best and I learn much from you, the people, who live and work in this country, some of whom I've been privileged to meet. I am also fortunate to have by my side, until I come of age, Lord Wiggins, now Queen's Counsel and my Lord Protector.

'We see that our land and its people and, indeed, the wider world are in need of much tending, mending, and change. While young people strive to save the planet, to improve animal welfare, attend to our crumbling social structure, and strive to find paid employment.

'Reform will take time. So I prorogue ceremonies such as the State Opening of Parliament, including the Queen's Speech. Why? Because politics is too important, and currently too enfeebled, to be left to politicians, many of whom, for too long, have ill served and undermined this nation, as they seek to replace democracy with autocracy.

'Currently, our politicians, locked in the Palace of Westminster for nigh on a year, are failing us — spectacularly — by not producing enough hot air through their enfeebled speechifying to run the National Grid. Strange, when cameras, journalists and the sofa interrogators are absent politicians go awfully quiet. Hopefully, a cut in wages, pensions, meal and drinks allowance can swiftly sort out that problem.

'Here are some of my suggestions. I'd add that full details appear in today's media. Feedback on our blog is welcome. There, that's the commercial over!

'So, first off – no one can enter politics until they've served their country honourably for at least five years in blue- or white-collar work, business, academia, hospitals, welfare, the armed forces, etcetera. Anyone working in marketing for more than two years will be barred for five years from entering politics at any level. Successful applicants will be trained, serve for five years and receive a set income and pension. They can expect no other honour or reward, except under exceptional circumstances.

'We wish to abolish income tax to boost spending. I have personally given to the Bank of England five billion pounds' worth of gold on the promise that printing paper, using "air or virtual" money or Strawberry Jam are a fundamental threat to our national security and must be reconsidered a.s.a.p. Our ultimate aim is to have a basic exchange system of goods and services.

'Hospitals and care homes, within the NHS and the private sector, will be run by experienced health officials and medical staff. They will not be sold on or leased to profit-led businesses. Heavy fines and imprisonment face the guilty. Those discovered to be incompetent or unsuitable in their work, through poor training or impaired language skills, will be dismissed.

'Schools, academies and technical colleges will be organised similarly and the bullying of staff as well as pupils will lead to expulsion. The cut-and-paste school of "learning" will be banned.

'Lord Wiggins and his Justice committee are compiling like-for-like punishments for those who break the law. The committee also suggests regular and rigorous audits on promises made by any official, including myself. Any discovered *uber*-bonus will be confiscated and put immediately into a central fund supporting educational, sporting and artistic ventures.

'There is more to be done. I do not want this country to go nuclear. Not until someone comes up with a way to get rid of the waste that will not affect future generations. Might I suggest a better source of energy that's free – the sun. Much research has been done on this by renowned scientists, much has been discarded because huge numbers of the usual "interested" finance-focused parties realise they cannot make money from it.

'At the end of the day we are considering the introduction of cantons nationwide, so that big issues really are decided by you, the people, issues such as the Federation, from which I wish to resign this country while continuing to trade with it.

'Rest assured, I hope and pray never to lead you into war. War is costly, causing massive and expensive disruption as well as death and bereavement. And always ends in peace talks. So my war policy is simple. We start with the peace talks. As soon as there is disagreement, heads of state are imprisoned in their conference room until a solution is achieved. Then, and only then, a rainbow of coloured smoke will be emitted from disabled guns to show people the results.

'Finally, may I wish you peace and contentment, happiness and love through what may well be turbulent times for us all. You have such energy and passion to give to this country and make it great again. For that I humbly thank you.'

The studio manager gives the thumbs-up sign. There is enthusiastic applause and cheers from the young men and women in the studio.

Indigo blushes.

The cameras are off. Lord di'Abalo, slow-handclapping, approaches her.

'Your Majesty didn't read my speech.'

Indigo nods.

'And you didn't let me read the speech that you just gave,' says Di'Abalo.

'You'd have shredded it. Taken out everything I believe in.'

'Your Majesty and Lord Wiggins hold the titles but, in reality, it is I who operates those titles,' says Di'Abalo. 'I control the movement of money and Strawberry Jam. I am your adviser, your unofficial but actual Lord Protector. I have the final say. This incident will not be repeated, Your

Majesty. I alone can condone, or not, all that you say or do.'

'Then needs must I give you the Crown,' says Indigo challengingly.

'Don't play the silly girl,' says Di'Abalo, the look in his eyes steel hard. 'It doesn't suit you.'

'What suits me is *not* to play at being a pawn in your game,' says Indigo, with a toss of her head. 'Unlike you, I want to bring this once great country back from the brink, not send it into the Dekaydence meltdown you seem to want to achieve.'

Di'Abalo smiles, a smile of dry ice, cold and yet burningly hot.

'Don't ever forget, Lord di'Abalo, I am a fighter,' says Indigo. 'If need be, I'll fight you all the way.'

'I look forward to it, Your Majesty,' he says crisply, and walks away. He has an appointment to keep and he must not be late.

106 FANGS AIN'T WOT THEY USED TO BE

'What's a beautiful young angel like you doing up 'ere in the back of beyond in outer space?' says a Hell's Devil, pulling his bike away from his crowd of mates to ride alongside Jezza. 'By the way, my name's Fang.'

Jezza tries not to stare at the young man's elongated molars, long black fingernails and heavily bloodshot eyes.

'I fancied a change of scenery.' Jezza shrugs, trying not to draw attention to Jack – about half a kilometre ahead of her – who is being nudged by a dozen Devils in the direction of quite where or what she has no idea.

'So, you got separated from your Holier-Than-Thou bunch,' Fang persists. 'Or are you after retrieving your boyfriend?'

Jezza tosses her head.

'I told you, I wanted a break,' she says sharply.

'Ooo, get you, Missy Nose-Up. So you're a free angel? How about a ride around the block? I got the biggest, fastest bike in the universe.'

'That is kind but, no, thanks,' says Jezza, and puts her foot down. The bike hurtles forward. But Fang's supersonic bike is in a different league. Fang punches his fist into the air and gives a broad grin, revealing even more of his stained and cracked tombstone teeth as he roars past her and returns to his gang of racing Hell's Devils.

Jezza breathes a sigh of relief. Then she realises her bike has been lassoed. So has Jack's. All at once they are both hurtled into a black hole. And there they dangle, staring at hundreds of identical doors in a skyscraper of floors. Each door an exact copy of the old ivy-covered door in Heaven that he uncovered, Jack notes.

Jeers and insults rain down from the gang of Hell's Devils above them, who, without warning, drop the lasso. Jack reacts fast. Revving his engine, he grabs hold of Jezza and her bike and rides full pelt to the nearest floor of the skyscraper. Somehow he manages to toss and tie the lasso on her bike to the railings so she can scramble over.

He revs the engine some more, hovers the bike closer until he is lined up and able to land in the nearest corridor.

'What do we do now?' says Jezza.

'Try a door or two. Maybe sing a few carols?' says Jack.

'Do you think the angels will come and get us?'

Jack shrugs. He doubts it but he won't say anything to Jezza. He puts his hand in his pocket and is surprised to find the old key that Angelica dropped on the floor of Heaven. He recalls the inscription: 'Beware: I unlock dreams and nightmares.' He feels he has experienced the dream and now here they are... How could he have done this to Jezza? He studies the key and looks up at the thousands and thousands of locked doors. What are the odds the key will work on any one of the doors?

107 UNHOLY FATHER

Ruby Q blinks as, in a sudden blinding flash of light, the elderly Pope in his white robes disappears. And now, sitting on the papal chair of red, yellow and gold is a tall middle-aged man in an open-necked white shirt and blue and white striped designer jacket and blue trousers.

The man has a frosty smile, the look in his eyes is icy, matching the look she's getting from the black cat and the white cat sitting at his feet, swishing their tails.

She stares back at Di'Abalo with undisguised disgust.

'What's with these idiotic party tricks? Why are you pretending to be the Pope? And telling me your own sob story? And what's with killing me off because we don't agree about something? Because – if you've forgotten, and I am bitterly ashamed to say this – I am your daughter.'

'We've both drawn the short straw, haven't we?' says Di'Abalo with an exaggerated sigh as the black cat jumps on to his lap.

'Strangely, I don't think of myself as a short straw,' says Ruby Q.

Steady, Ruby Q. No need to adopt fight mode. Not yet, anyway.

'I took you on at the *Daily Unigraph*, an ancient and prestigious organ that's required reading for almost everyone in high places. And I allowed you your head,' says Di'Abalo coolly. 'But over time it has become horribly apparent that you have lost your neutrality and have chosen to write from and for the enemy camp. I cannot condone that.'

Ruby Q frowns.

'So, because I believe in the "rightness" of what you call the other side, I must be eliminated.'

Di'Abalo tuts, raising his eyes to heaven.

'I'm sacking you, and you'll never again work for me, until and unless you change your mind and your perverse socio-political perspective,' says Di'Abalo, 'but I'm not likely to kill off my own daughter, am I? What kind of man do you take me for?'

'Aside from a murderer? I'm not sure. But I do know I'd have preferred to have as my real father the one who behaved as if he was. Who cared for me, had time for me, who brought me up to understand the importance of principles and the value of kindness.'

'You were lucky,' says Di'Abalo cuttingly. 'My parents chose to abandon me to pursue their careers. And their arguments. That's what Grout and I have in common. As well as a good brain. I don't think you and I have anything in common, do we?'

'No, we don't. Certainly, I haven't inherited your murderous tendencies.'

'Could you desist from this kind of talk?'

'Why? Isn't blood and murder what you get up to in

the White Room? I saw it, remember. I saw a young girl scream for mercy before she was shoved into a glass box and wired up. She emerged a smiling, happy-clappy idiot.'

Too far, Ruby Q.

'That's something else you've misinterpreted. Labelling me as some kind of Frankenstein.'

'What about Tommo, Prince Will's brother? Have you seen the effects the White Room experiment have had on him?'

Di'Abalo says nothing, distracted by the white cat, which has jumped on to the arm of the chair.

Ruby Q frowns crossly.

'I'll put it more simply: you have turned a nice, bright young man into a simpleton. I'd say that amounts to murder.'

'For your information, the experiments in the White Room will be of great benefit to mankind, most especially young teenagers,' Di'Abalo says sharply. 'Yes, I admit, there have been mistakes. And they are deeply regrettable. But the information we have gleaned will help many more teenagers than it will hurt. But I think you are too narrow-minded to appreciate that.'

'I think you're lying,' says Ruby Q. 'Why don't you come clean? Why don't you tell people about your great scientific advances?'

'Because I prefer to act more discreetly. HOH is a better performer than I. And he will perform soon. That gives me time to work on the bigger picture.'

'Which is?'

'Bigger than you can imagine.'

'And better?'

'Yes, definitely,' says Di'Abalo with a knowing smile. 'Infinitely better.'

'Strawberry Jam better?'

Di'Abalo laughs.

'Yes. Strawberry Jam and Sticky Rock Cafés better in all ways.'

'What exactly does that mean?'

Di'Abalo smiles.

'One global currency. One global social networking system. One global set of laws for the rich, for the poor and the suckers in between. One religion – to be decided. One police force. One government. That's what it means, Ruby Q, order. Order and control. That is what this world needs and will soon acquire.'

'And one army that is yours?'

'Oh, my. How did you guess?' says Di'Abalo, feigning surprise.

'A world dictatorship,' Ruby Q says, in stunned disbelief.

'Indeed,' says Di'Abalo.

'And that means you?'

'Indeed.' Di'Abalo smiles.

'And what if people don't want a world dictatorship?'

'There'll be no one who doesn't want such a thing.'

'You mean you'll kill anyone who disagrees with your plan?'

'You still don't understand me, do you? No, disagreement means re-education, because it's for the good of everyone. And one day everyone will see that.'

'And what does that mean?' Ruby Q begins, and then stops. It's too enormous for her to take in.

'Isn't it time you went?' says Di'Abalo, stifling a yawn. 'The Orbie awaits. It'll take you direct to the arena. I thought you'd want to see some of the Coronation celebrations. I'll see you there. You'll miss breakfast, of course. I thought that for you to eat here, with me, might've troubled you. Although, had I felt tempted to poison you, Phlegm would have forced me back on to the road of righteousness. Isn't that so, Phlegm?'

The butler gives a small cough of agreement.

'Thank you for the offer, but I prefer my meals Dekaydence-free,' says Ruby Q, standing up.

'Enjoy them while you can,' says Di'Abalo waspishly. 'Very soon, everything you eat, drink and wear will be Dekaydence'd. Every place you go will be Dekaydence'd. Every way you travel will be Dekaydence'd. Every drop of fuel, water...every mineral that is taken from the earth will be Dekaydence'd. And everything that is written, filmed and created into toys and computer games will be Dekaydence'd.'

'I get the picture,' says Ruby Q, walking to the door and turning to speak to Di'Abalo for the last time.

'You may be my biological father but from all that you've said today I know for sure we have nothing in common. Luckily, I've inherited more from the man who is not my father than I have from you. Goodbye, Lord di'Abalo.'

She closes the door behind her. Two Swiss Guards escort her to the Orbie pad. Even at this early hour, long before most people's breakfasts, the heat is intense. But Ruby Q gratefully breathes it in, relishing the way the sun wraps its warmth around her. It's a warmth that seeps into her body, into her very being.

Coo-er, Ruby Q! That was telling him! I wonder will happen next?

I've no idea, we'll have to see. But I do know one thing.

What's that?

Today I've come face to face with the realities of my so-called father. It has made me realise fully that Rallan, the man who has been my dad in my life, will always be my dad. And somehow, what's happened today has enabled me to understand better the frailties of my mother as well as appreciate, for the first time, her strengths and her determination, as well as her kindness.'

108 STRAWBERRY JAM GOES INDY

'So, my strawberry jam is not up to Dekaydence standards?' says Indigo, with feigned indignation. 'Such a disappointment. But more...a relief.'

'It's nothing to do with Dekaydence or any other standards, and you know it,' says Will grimly.

Will is now, reluctantly, in charge of the Strawberry Jam account at CCM and knows that Dekaydence has bought out every strawberry farm of any size worldwide. Dekaydence's global on-line banking system is backed by Strawberry Jam, while Dekaydence gold, property and oil reserves remain secure and gaining hugely in value. But it's only a matter of time...

'My jam has been rejected, too,' Lady Catgut sighs dramatically.

'Count yourselves lucky, Lady C,' Will retorts.

'Oh, but we do,' says Indigo. 'Our output is small, enough only for local consumption.'

'Don't forget,' says Will, 'you are overlooked for purely political reasons.'

'And we know full well, from experience, that might change,' says Indigo. 'We're not stupid, Will.'

'Well, I think this is a cause for celebration,' says Grout cheerily. 'May I, Lady C?'

'Of course, dear. There's one in the fridge,' says Lady Catgut.

Indigo fetches the glasses as Grout opens a bottle of Lady Catgut's home-made elderflower bubbly.

'A toast to rejection?' says Will, thinking of Piccolo working in the music studio and knowing his friend won't come out until he has left.

'No, Will,' says Indigo fiercely. 'A toast to independence!'

'Bravo!' says Grout.

Lady Catgut echoes his cry.

'A toast to independence!' all shout out, including Will, who manages the merest glimmer of a smile.

It's only a matter of time, thinks Will, before Dekaydence allows the markets to peak before fixing a sudden, unexpected crash. So, while Dekaydence makes millions, worldwide investors and businesses go to the wall, and men, women and children struggle to survive. How he hates his job. How he hates Piccolo. How he longs to be back on tartan turf with his own kind.

109 WHAT'S UP, NORTH?

'What's up?' North's mother asks, while she's cooking his favourite meal: fish pie, made with local fish and a thick creamy topping of home-grown potatoes and spinach, with an extra-large spoonful of home-grown peas.

'Nothing's up, except the temperature,' North replies, wiping sweat from his forehead. 'I've never known a summer this hot, and so much rain in between.'

'Nay, lad, it ain't the weather that's bothering you. You've met someone. I can tell,' says his mother, a big warm triumphant smile spreading across her face and into her voice.

'Mother!' says North. 'I don't know where you get your crazy ideas from but you can send them straight back and demand a refund. 'Cos you're wrong.'

'You can't fool me, lad,' says his mother smugly. 'I'm your mother.'

North decides not to argue. It's a long time since he's seen his mother this happy so, even if her thoughts are delusional, he knows that she'll find out what he's up to soon enough when she's read her weekend newspaper: it's her son's work that's exciting him. And, for the moment, he has no eye or time for anything or anyone else.

The Queen's Speech has stirred a new energy, a new

force within a young generation who, a few years back, would have been sent and lost to war but are now, more than ever, focused on saving the planet and providing food, clean water, health care and education for all that live upon it.

North, Will, Indigo, Grout, Ruby Q and others, including the teenage eco-warriors, the GeeZers, recognise that much needs to be done, given the world is facing global climate change. Irrespective of whether it's wholly or partly man-made. A worldwide economic downturn as well as the prospect of a finite supply of minerals and cheap energy becoming even more finite in our lifetime.

And youngsters, worldwide, together with committed adults, are working with their neighbours to grow a community that has a low-energy future. They work to help people turn around their lives and their communities worldwide.

'We're talking community-supported agriculture, urban orchards and reskilling classes.' North is sharing his enthusiasm under the wire with Will.

'As Lady C and Indigo are doing, even as we speak,' says Will.

'Yes,' says North, warming to his topic. 'And these groups are doing or exploring shared transport, local currency, seed swaps, tool libraries, energy-saving clubs, draught-busting teams... Do you know one of the greatest things I've learnt?'

'That I was right?' says Will.

North laughs.

'I did get there, eventually. It just took me longer. No, what's so interesting is the realism. These people know they haven't got all the answers. That what they do is just the beginning. And they accept that they don't know how it'll all work out.'

'Like most things in life,' says Will, more to himself than North.

'Ideas are spreading, Will,' says North. 'Even local governments want to learn how to run their buildings as efficiently as local communities. More young people worldwide are finding ways to improve the lot of many. They are helping youngsters get funding for their education. They help mothers in Africa ensure their children get an education as well as daily food and health care. There are young doctors going on the streets in rough areas of the Federation teaching youngsters how to deal with emergencies such as gun and knife injuries...

'Change is happening, here and now, Will! It's happening! Indigo is re-igniting the fire and passion we all felt years back. The desire for change is intense and growing.'

Will smiles. It's good to hear North's enthusiasm but, at this moment, he is consumed with melancholy, loneliness and depression – about the state of Dekaydence, the world and his broken relationship with Piccolo – and is too overwhelmed to react.

He checks his ad'um. He must get a move on. He has work to finish before the Coronation celebration at the arena. Organised by Dekaydence, in honour of Queen Indigo, and, as her cousin and only close relative, Will is her escort for the event. He is also her protector should Di'Abalo decide to conceal his urbane side in exchange for the nasty and unpleasant.

And then news come in under the wire. The strawberry jam market has crashed. Strawberry jam investments are turning to mush...

110 BABY BLEW IT

Cage and Waat shuffle along in the long, dense queue to get into the arena to join the Coronation celebrations. It is boiler-hot, and most everyone is using some kind of home-made fan. Baby Jake, a large sunhat on his head, is asleep in a papoose on his Uncle Cage's back, opening his eyes occasionally to watch the people around him and smiling, the Martin family dimple forming in his cheek.

'You can't take that in,' says the young Dekaydence Guide at the check-in.

'If you mean the papoose, I can fold it up,' says Cage.

'No, it's the *baby* you can't take in,' says the guide firmly. 'We have special facilities for babies and children under 10 that operates until 30 minutes after the entertainment concludes. You simply sign this care agreement, leave the baby with us and enjoy the show with no worries.'

'Ooh, you lovely jubbly. Come to auntie, coochy-coo,' says another young guide, reaching out to extract the baby from its papoose.

'I don't want to do this, Cage,' Waat says, quiet but firm, stepping between the guide and Cage's back to ensure it is she who takes Baby Jake from the papoose.

'I'm none too happy about it either,' says Cage. 'This is Dekaydence.'

'There was nothing about in on the website,' says Waat.

Cage nods. He's watching men and women on either side, signing up, happily surrendering their children and eagerly heading off to take their seats.

''Urry up!' says a man behind them, and others beyond echo his words. 'This is a once-in-a-lifetime spectacle! And we'd kinda like to see it in our lifetime.'

'I'm happy to go home and watch it on TV,' says Cage.

'We won't get our money back. And the tickets weren't cheap,' says Waat anxiously.

'No matter,' says Cage. 'The bottom line is neither of us wants to leave Jake. So let's go home. Let me carry him, Waat, he's getting to be a heavyweight.'

Waat smiles at Cage, and happily lets him guide her through the crowd.

A pock-marked youth in pink shorts and T-shirt rushes up to them.

'If you ain't goin' in, mate, how much for your tickets?' the youth asks Cage.

Cage pulls the tickets from his pocket.

'Here,' he says, handing them to the young man.

For a split second the youth stands there, wide-eyed, his jaw hanging open. Then he grabs the tickets and runs off, turning to call out, 'I'll pay you back, mate! Promise!' he shouts, using his T-shirt to wipe away the sweat from his face and dripping nose. 'I'll come find you!'

'Do you know him?' Waat asks.

'No,' says Cage. 'To the best of my knowledge I don't know anyone who wears bright pink shorts and T-shirt, let alone red and orange spotted socks.'

Waat laughs.

'Yes, you do. You're holding him.'

12

After the armament show almost everyone who's a buyer or a seller is in a good mood and moves enthusiastically to the banqueting hall, where elaborately decorated tables are loaded with food, wine and Dekaydence puddings. Salivation levels are high.

Bodkin and Boston slip away with the commander to a limousine that carries them to an elegant house surrounded by a tall wall. The armed guards at the gate wave them through.

A man in a white coat hurries Bodkin to an upstairs room. Boston follows at a distance and waits. But not for long. Bodkin emerges and he and Boston are returned to their hotel, into the company of Will and MacMinor. This procedure continues thrice daily for about ten days, at which point the commander passes to Bodkin a bundle of notes and a suitcase on wheels.

'Here,' says Bodkin, holding out some notes to Boston. 'Treat yourself.'

'No, thank you,' says Boston. 'I get a decent enough wage.'

'Suit yourself,' says Bodkin, with a shrug. 'I've got 'alf a million here, if you change your mind.'

'I won't, thanks,' says Boston. 'But I appreciate the offer.'

Back at the hotel, Will is fretful, despite MacMinor's valiant attempt to distract him with numerous Scottish jokes.

'How much longer?' Will asks Bodkin.

'We can leave now,' says Bodkin, with a nonchalant shrug.

'We can't leave without the President.'

'He's, er, at the airport already,' says Bodkin airily.

'That wasn't the plan,' says Will with suspicion.

'No, it wasn't,' says Bodkin. 'But circumstances beyond my control forced a change that the commander kindly fixed for us. We arrive in the Hague in about six hours, in time for a rest before the court's final summing-up.'

Will looks unsure. Bodkin is up to something, he knows, but what …?

110.5 HIVE OF INDUSTRY

There are no fairies at the bottom of Lady Catgut's garden, as far as one can tell. There are hives. Five of them, each some three metres' distance from its neighbour. Each facing east to catch the early morning sun. Each hive is home to some 30,000 bees or more (in summer), about 5,000 (in winter). The drones, slender and paler than a wasp, hang about, waiting for a possible dalliance with the queen before they expire, horribly and dramatically. The female worker bees set off for work every morning at 6.30am. They travel up to seven miles to find floral sustenance and pollen for the hive. If successful, they return home and perform a dance that communicates to the others the exact spot where nectar can be found.

As far as Lady Catgut is concerned, the fight is on to save the bee. There may not be fairies at the bottom of her garden but she believes there is an angel who hovers in the vicinity. She knows him as Grout and for his first save-the-bee project he has created a bee'oid – acceptable to the bees – that can detect and eliminate killer varroa and nosema mites as well as pesticides that find their way into a colony. About bee-time!

SECTION 13

Our peace and prosperity can never be taken for granted and must constantly be tended, so that never again do we have cause to build monuments to our fallen youth.

HRH Queen Elizabeth II (1926–)

111 GOD'S STAND-IN

By a show of many hands, Bhupi finds himself elected temporary replacement for God. Humbly, he accepts the honour but declines the privilege of the Upper Case. His first decree is that all must pray for the safe return of the Almighty. (Non-believers are asked to hope, strongly.) Bhupi's second decree is that Heaven is a multicultural place and all religious and non-religious venues must be open to one and all and must teach and encourage compassion and kindness to one and all.

The clowns are outraged. They object, bitterly and loudly (in and out of TTT). They argue that their aim in life (and death) is to tease and abuse their nearest and dearest, as well as complete strangers.

'I'd say your main problem,' Spaghetti Sureshi tells Jack, 'is that your central prayer says "Thy will be done, on earth as it is in Heaven".'

'What's wrong with that?' says Jack.

'With due respect, Jack, it's contradictory,' says Spaghetti Sureshi. 'You expect best behaviour here in Heaven but you positively encourage dreadful cruelty on earth. For example, you elect politicians who draw you into any number of wretched wars in far-off lands. You lose a generation of innocents, damage the older one and the one to come.'

Bhupi nods thoughtfully.

Jack remains silent.

'I know!' says Bhupi, stepping on to a treadmill for his daily workout. 'Let's have a debate.'

Jack and Spaghetti Sureshi exchange despairing glances.

'Bureaucracy versus democracy,' mutters Jack. 'Centuries could pass.'

'On earth, as it is in Heaven,' Spaghetti Sureshi sighs in agreement.

'Bhupi,' says Jack, 'why not let the clowns have the new extension? They could tease one another to their heart's content without bothering the residents of Heaven. We could call it Purgatory.'

'Ah, sadly, the original had to be closed down when Jean-Paul Sartre demanded too many radical, expensive, minimalist and existential changes,' Bhupi manages to puff out.

'But it could be some might like to join The Fold!' says Bhupi, suddenly enthused by the idea of recruiting clowns keen to be angels. Later, he'll ask Jack to take over the recycling of old souls who are to be reborn in another entity. It'll be the moment Jack and Jezza part company.

112 HOH AND THE MCC

It is the opening of the first Multi-Church Convention and the presiding president, His Overall Holiness, Randall Candelskin, is dressed in flowing robes that change colour and style to match the religion 'speaking' at that moment.

Candelskin suggests that all churches of the MCC join together and build large shopping malls with multi/ no-faith areas for all to use in quiet prayer, Yoga or meditation, as trialled successfully the previous year in the new Dekaydence mall.

Candelskin argues passionately that such a project could provide the various religious and non-religious bodies with a healthy income, make council tax and TV licences irrelevant, and provide somewhere to park the car, if not on earth then in the MCC-owned and -managed clouds (*costs variable and dependent; see small print.*).

Questions and responses come thick and fast, from all quarters – Catholics, Jews, Muslims, Hindus, Christians, Buddhists, Quakers, and Druids, etcetera – so that Candelskin's clothing begins to look like the Blackpool Tower illuminations, flashing on-off-on and on-on-off like some kind of visual Morse code.

'What size income are we talking about, given it's to be shared between us?'

'How much goes into the Dekaydence coffers?'

'We want a place to look after our pets.'

'We want a place to park the kids.'

'We demand at least two dozen ladies loos on each and every floor.'

'And each cubicle must have the facility to accommodate comfortably a woman, at least two small children, several loaded shopping bags, a handbag and a large dripping-wet umbrella.'

'We want to abolish the law that says you, HOH, are the only person permitted to say "Bless you!" when someone sneezes. It's ludicrous, it's...'

'The Office of HOH now issues ticketed books priced from £5 to £5,000,' says Candelskin flintily. 'Each "Bless you!" ticket (at £5) is stamped with my signature and can be used by a person in need, once and once only. Technology enables surveillance of the ticket to be monitored at all times and an electric shock can be administered should someone attempt to use the ticket more than once.

'So, best avoid allergy sufferers or else you could be in for a hefty outlay and a sharp electric shock. But not to worry, a goodly percentage of ticket sales will go to each and every one of you within the MCC.'

The audience tuts and groans. Until someone works out the huge projected income.

The conference grinds on until a police officer comes on stage and speaks softly to Candelskin, who pales significantly under his light tan, grasps the lectern to steady himself, mumbles an apology to the gathering and promises to return to the conference the next day. It's a promise he isn't able to fulfil. He also misses most of the post-Coronation celebrations, as well as a chance encounter with his boss, God.

113 CORONATION CELEBRATIONS

Indigo travels to the Colosseum in a white Dekaydence Orbobubble bearing a gold coronet on the roof. The flying machine creates a welcome light breeze on a swelteringly hot day as it travels along the river Thames from Kew to Tower Bridge.

Ron, once a Dekaydence Guide, now a COP (Chief Orbobubble Pilot), gently steers the vehicle from riverbank to riverbank so that cheering crowds on both sides can see the young queen at close quarters. Finally, to the delight of all, the Orbie flies under Tower Bridge then soars into the sky, showering those below with trailers of gold, green, white and tangerine glittering stars.

'Oh, my!' Indigo exclaims in a shocked tone, as they near the Colosseum. 'It's gone. The Colosseum has disappeared.'

Will yawns and looks the other way.

Indigo presses her nose against the glass.

'Oh, my,' she repeats. 'Look, Will, d'you see?'

Will is beyond disinterest but to oblige his young cousin he glances at the view.

'Oh, my, indeed,' he says, intrigued.

The Colosseum has become an enormous white flower,

a gigantic daisy. It's encased in trillions of long thin plithanium petals – rising from the ground to way beyond the height of the structure – trembling ever so slightly in the light breeze. As the Orbie flies closer and lower they see the arena floor has become a disc of florets, thousands of them, glowing a golden tangerine.

The crowd roars its delight when the Orbie lands and Indigo and Will disembark and wave to the crowds.

'Have a nice Dekaydence Day, Your Majesty!' shouts Ron, saluting the Queen, bowing and blushing simultaneously.

Indigo smiles at Ron, who decides this has to be the best day of his life.

The Orbie departs the Colosseum, leaving clouds of cherub'oids and dov'oids to fly overhead, trailing streamers of dazzling lights in white, green, tangerine and gold.

Indigo waves to the crowd watching her on the enormous wafer-thin fibrene monitors. At her side, Will gives a brief uncomfortable wave and an even briefer smile. He's lost the hang of all the protocol whereas Indigo, he sees, performs the public profile role comfortably and naturally. And appears to enjoy it.

Indigo and Will head for a circle of several hundred men, women and youngsters from across the land, standing to attention in their celebratory best as they face the crowd.

A band plays as the two young royals present

everyone in the circle with a 'Good Citizen' badge and a scrolled certificate for their work in the community. Unfortunately, the sponsor, Dekaydence, has put the company name and logo indiscreetly and prominently on the badge and certificate, much to Will's disgust and Indigo's indignation.

Two announcers – an attractive young woman and a greying older man, as TV oft demands – interview the award-winners about their achievements and explain the programme of events to the global audience.

Indigo and Will enter the Dekaydence Royal Box, which is accommodating some two hundred people – VIPs, world leaders and celebrities, and the celebrity photographer, Lars Sparks.

Di'Abalo gives Indigo and Will a curt nod and turns to talk with the President of the Federation, who is busy smiling and ingratiating himself with the crowd. Will knows the official secret – that the President has been kidnapped in enemy territory – and now, squinting at the stand-in, he spots the 'Made by Dekaydence™' label on the back of his neck.

'Shame you missed the Dipsticks and Stanley Halls.' The President smirks at the recently arrived Ruby Q. 'They were outstanding. Like almost everything Dekaydence does.'

'That's odd. I've only just arrived but I was told the Dipsticks aren't due on stage for at least another twenty minutes or more,' Ruby Q replies, but the Federation

President has already turned to speak to more high-profile guests.

'The President doesn't look quite right,' she whispers to Will, who's standing close by. 'He looks as if he has been freshly washed and ironed.'

'He has. He's a copy. A non-iron copy, at that,' Will whispers back. An 'oid of an 'oid. Ask Grout when you see him.'

Will turns and catches Di'Abalo's eyes. There's something odd about them, he thinks. It's not only that they are unusually bloodshot. There's a fierce anger in them, like a fire waiting to erupt.

Despite the heat, Will shivers.

114 DI'ABALO'S SPEECH

Timpani, bass drum and tam-tam play the opening few bars 'very deliberate', as the composer, Aaron Copland, wrote on his score of his *Fanfare for the Common Man*. The crowd's excitement turns swiftly to something steadier, quieter, an inner intensity of anticipation.

At the conclusion of the music Di'Abalo rises from his chair. The crowd follows suit.

Di'Abalo raises a golden goblet of Dekaydence champagne to Indigo. Those in the box, who now include Ruby Q, who has just arrived, follow suit. While in the crowd many raise bottles of Dekaydence beer or Blooza Jooza or, at the least, remove and raise their Dekaydence logo'd sunhats.

'To our Queen!' declares Di'Abalo. 'Long to reign over us. God save our Queen!'

'To our Queen! To Queen Indigo!' comes the shout, which erupts into applause, cheers, foot-stomping, whistles and singing that rise up and out of the arena, reaching the ears of those miles away in the crumbling, decadent town of Lord di'Abalo's early years – Croy Polloi.

Indigo stands to acknowledge the acclaim. She smiles and waves as she struggles to hide her sorrow. The reason why she is here. The loss of what has been taken from her and the burden of what she has chosen to take on.

Di'Abalo hands his goblet to Phlegm and gestures the crowd to resume their seats.

'Ladies and gentlemen, of all ages,' proclaims Di'Abalo, 'may I welcome you to your new arena, your personal pleasure palace. A project undertaken by Dekaydence, blessed and supported by Her Majesty's late grandfather, His Royal Highness, King Edmund.'

Indigo smiles, but anger and the word 'liar' flash through her head. Her grandfather was kicked out of his own palace by Di'Abalo and forced to live in an old crumbling wooden shack by this monster to make way for his montrosity.

Di'Abalo continues.

'We hope His Majesty even now is watching down on us from an arena in heaven.'

Too true we're watching over you, you cruel, diabolical murderer, says the deceased King Edmund, now resident in heaven.

Indigo's smile freezes on her face as more cheers and polite applause are offered by a sympathetic audience. How can D'Abalo lie like this? she wonders.

'But His Majesty has given us a Queen,' Di'Abalo continues. 'A new and young Queen for a new and young age. Not only is she beautiful on the outside but I have seen the beauty of her soul.'

Indigo grimaces on the inside. No, make that her beautiful inside, she tells herself.

'Yes,' says Di'Abalo. 'Our Queen cares passionately for her country and for its people. And while, at her age, she could be out partying every night, she chooses to visit our citizens and to study. To learn more so that she can do more. Yes, this is a young woman who knows her own mind, and how to improve it, and will not be browbeaten – as I have learnt to my cost.'

The crowd roars with laughter.

'This young lady is a queen for our times. As the world warms, as more hearts freeze with cruelty, unkindness, poverty, debt and unemployment, there stands our clever and compassionate Queen, our guardian angel. Someone who chooses to live as simply as possible despite her noble status. She has seen the future and the dangers it holds and among her good deeds and projects she has created an enthusiasm countrywide for growing organic food. She talks about it on radio, TV and direct to the people. Yes, she can truly lay claim to eating her own words.'

The crowd, VIPs, celebrities, even the world leaders, laugh, cheer and applaud.

D'Abalo holds up his hand for silence.

'And now, before the celebrations begin, let us dedicate this arena to old King Edmund, with his passion for puddings and cake, and to his young granddaughter, Queen Indigo, with her passion for justice and organic food for all!'

At Di'Abalo's nod, Indigo presses a button by her side. She watches the large screen. The camera is focused on the brick wall separating the auditorium from the arena floor. She becomes aware of chiselled script being inscribed on the wall by an unseen hand. The message reads:

In memory of Edmund, our beloved King of Puddings and Custard
and
In praise of Indigo, our Queen of All Things Green, Good, Bright and Beautiful

Oh, but how Indigo longs to discuss with Will and Grout this awful, clammy sugary rubbish that Di'Abalo uses to 'sell' her like a product in a Dekaydence catalogue.

I suppose that's all I am to him, she considers, a product. And one day, no doubt, I'll no longer be fresh or in fashion. And, as my grandfather before me, I shall be discarded like a sweetie wrapper.

MacCavity drums his caber on the floor and announces, 'The arrival of spring.'

115 SPRING

The sky over the arena is ink black. The crowd is quiet, almost apprehensive. A bird sings out, followed by another and another...until a rich carpet, a dense chorus of birdsong fills the air with aural boundary warnings. Dawn begins to drift across the sky like watercolours on canvas as the piercing cry of a cockerel soars high into the air.

MacCavity bangs his caber on the wooden floor beneath him.

'Good morning to a Dekaydence dawn!' he cries.

'Good morning!' the crowd responds.

'Enter a Dekaydence spring!' cries MacCavity, as a pink and tangerine sky lights up a sky canopy.

The crowd rumbles out gasps and applause. The arena has become an English country landscape of green hills and trees, snowdrops, wild primroses, cowslips, crocuses, tulips, the bulbous buttercup, red campion and daffodils, as well as bright yellow bushes of forsythia, peach blossom on quince, and blackthorn, like a white mist within the bare hedgerow.

Mothers nurse babies and watch over children playing hide and seek, football or rounders. Teenagers cycle and race in the hills. Young and old sit on benches, talking or reading.

An acclaimed young actor recites Shakespeare's speech 'Seven Stages of Man', Jacques's speech, beginning 'All the world's a stage...' Young musicians play the music of Elgar, Vaughan Williams and Delius, while other young actors, dotted about the landscape, read nursery rhymes and limericks, and pertinent poems about youth and childhood. And popular characters from Dekaydence books and movies fly into the air, scattering Dekaydence sweeties to youngsters in the audience.

MacCavity drums his caber on the floor and announces, 'The arrival of summer.'

116 SUMMER

'Sumer is Icumen in,
Lhude sing, cuccu...'

...sings a boy's pure treble voice that is powering its way up into the summer sky. A golden sky in which gilt-edged, raven-sized pound and dollar signs drift about but remain alert and swift enough to avoid capture by many a greedy, grasping hand in the crowd.

The spring countryside has been replaced by a cityscape packed with attention-seeking skyscrapers, dense traffic and car horns, impatience and tempers. Young men and women struggle to get somewhere before anyone else. They hustle to work. They bustle to a party. They want to make money. They're hungry for fun. They want big lives. Bigger than the lives of their parents.

A new source of heat and energy arrives on stage — the rock band 2B, four casually dressed young lads on a stage emerging from the depths. A smaller stage rises from within the first, bringing the SS, the Studs & Sluts — two young men, two young women — all dressed in gold extravaganza designed by Petty Masters.

The eight youngsters punch the air, saluting their fans. The audience cheers.

'I'm awright, Jack!' shouts 2B's lead singer, Milky Shake, who then breathes huskily into the microphone, 'Are you awright, Jacqueline?'

Youngsters shout back their delight.

Suddenly, those in the upper rows are distracted by unusual activity above their heads. Sets of giant smiling red lips are cruising among the dollar and pound signs, their great strawberry jam tongues shooting out to entwine dollar and pound signs, devouring them speedily and greedily, as the signs squeak and kick, struggle and scream.

'I'm awright, Jack!' Milky Shake, 2B's lead singer, shouts.

'I'm awright…!' a large section of the crowd shouts back.

'Jack! Jack! Jack!' another section responds.

'Are you awright, Jack?' Milky Shake enquires teasingly.

'Yes! Yes! Yes!' the crowd shrieks.

'Milky! Milky! Milky!' shouts one half of the audience.

'Shake! Shake! Shake!' shouts the other half.

Milky Shake downs a full glass of milkshake, burps, apologises and begins the popular song, 'I'm awright, Jack!'

> My manner and clothing say 'I'm awright, Jack!'
> Got a pad in a cul-de-sac, a personalised Cadillac
> A knack of being…just laid-back
> Yeah, I'm in the fast lane, the fastest track.

I'm a big noise in the City
And I'm sitting OK, pretty.
I eat with the stars.
Drink at private bars.
OK, so there's times I get a tad unable
But remember, I'll be under the *very best* of tables...
et al...

The crowd is happily singing and gyrating in their seats or in the aisles.

Is it only Will who sees a different spectacle?

At the arena's edge a handful of youngsters is hanging about, looking shiftily this way and that. A couple of well-built Black Tartan guards appear, cuff and collar them and herd them away. Will studies the youngsters and sees in their expressions frustration, envy and anger.

These are probably among the growing number of our young, he considers, who have no job, no money, no home, no education, no help and no hope. What chance do they have in life? They remind him of the two lads who set upon him one night, not that long ago, to rob him of his adservarum. They came close to killing him, to get the expensive tablet-watch he was wearing. It didn't happen that way because Sid, his bodyguard, got to them first. It was the two young assailants who ended up dead, quickly disposed of and erased by the state. As though they'd never existed.

MacCavity drums his caber on the floor and announces, 'The arrival of autumn.'

117 AUTUMN

The sky is gold, red, orange and yellow, above myriad trees in their dark, bare skeletal garb.

A huge smoke cloud engulfing the arena's stage disperses to reveal a rising stage on which stands a burnt-out shed, a burnt-out car, a load of twiggy, lifeless shrubs and a lean, mean-looking motorbike.

The audience gasps. Could it be...? They are astounded, confused, shocked and then excited by happy memories reincarnated.

'Ladies and gentlemen, boys and girls,' MacCavity booms forth, commanding, and getting, attention as his caber beats the ground. 'Please put your hands together to welcome a band that we have sorely missed but has returned to us in perfect tribute form — courtesy of Dekaydence. So, please give a warm welcome to the new...Dipstick Five!'

The crowd's applause and cheers rise high into the air. It's difficult to gauge for sure but perhaps the loudest cheers and applause come from Ruby Q.

The fans chant out the names of favourite Dipstick hits and the original Dipsticks — Butt, Lizard, Nevis, the never-present Lincoln, and Mulch the reluctant triangle player — beg their replacements to come out from wherever they are hiding.

The crowd's enthusiasm grows in size and volume. And then...

There they are! Leaping out from the wrecked car – as they did in days of old! Four young men in rubberised wooden suits, trellis braces and plaited ivy ties, gumboots and straw hats. Two pick up guitars, one goes straight to a drum kit. One – sullenly, for it is Mulch – picks up a triangle.

The crowd applauds and shouts out enthusiastically. Ruby Q gyrates on her seat.

'Dipsticks!' Dipsticks! Dipsticks!' she shouts, along with all the others.

But something is missing, or rather someone. The audience looks desperately this way and that for where the missing fifth is likely to be.

Ruby Q spots him. Yes! There he is! Lying prostrate on the bruiser bike. He gets up slowly, drowsily.

Thousands of girls and women squeak, squeal and squeam with delight.

'It *is* him, isn't it? The real, original him,' they whisper for reassurance, one to another.

For a moment, the young man – clad only in his blue-and-white-striped pyjamas, a combat green dressing gown, black boots and a black baseball cap skewed sideways – surveys the crowd with a querulous pout. Then he winks and gives a broad grin, a dimple furrowing deep into one cheek. He teasingly reveals one naked shoulder and puckers up for a kiss.

'It *is* him! *Mmm*!' the ecstatic crowd murmurs, kissing back *en mmm-asse*.

'Stanley Halls! Stanley Halls! Stanley Halls!' they call out, weeping with happiness that the main man is still alive, weeping with deep-seated grief at the loss of the four original Dipsticks.

'Yes!' shouts MacCavity. 'Girls and boys, ladies and gentlemen, let's put our hands, feet and kilts together to give a special welcome to a visitor all the way from the U S of A...the one and only original still standing...Mr Stanley Halls!'

The crowd roars in ecstasy. Stanley Halls in person! The jaw-dropping gorgeous, crowd-pleasing, delightfully dimpled lead singer. The only Dipstick to come out alive from the burning building that had been Dekaydence HQ. (Excepting the fact that, by chance, Stanley Halls, aka Kane Martin, happened to be out already, taking MacNoodle's beloved haggoid, Cromarty, for a walk back to the Martins' house to meet his mum. Only later had the metal mutt been returned to his tartan master.)

The Dipsticks sing all their classics (as do all their fans, including Ruby Q) – the 'Shed Anthem'; 'Bring Dekaydence'; 'Mall Content' and many more, until the golden autumn sky rusts to bronze, then metal grey...

MacCavity drums his caber on the floor and announces, 'The arrival of winter.'

118 WINTER

Stanley and the other Dipsticks finish a third encore and depart the stage, waving and blowing kisses to the crowd, who return the compliment. The stage is now festooned with single red roses, posies, chocolates and cards with words of undying love, and contact details.

A chill wind blows across a wild, rough countryside. The audience shivers. A glittering grey twilight sky hovers overhead, with clouds dense with snow. Flakes fall and settle in abundance. Now it is winter in the arena. People rummage hastily in their carrier bags to find the chunky Schneek-designed fleeces provided by the sponsor, Dekaydence.

The trees are become shrivelled skeletons, their dark branches newly dressed in white feathery frills. Thick smoke emerges from peaty fires burning in cottage fireplaces, along with the rich scent of cooking meat. The audience shivers and salivates as the snowstorm continues. Cottagers encased in fur and woollens venture outside to clear a pathway or wade through snow drifts to collect a Dekyadence food parcel that drops from a small Orbie flown now by a new breed of miniature 'oid.

The cottagers swig sweet cocoa or warming whisky

from their flasks and watch their exhaled breath turn into white mist while trees blossom with icicles.

Suddenly there are different sounds – tinkling bells, foghorns, cymbals and choirs of children's pure voices singing Christmas carols.

A flash of light streaks across the arena. It's so fast it's difficult to see what it is... And then they see it clearly – a long, sleek glass-topped white sleigh, propelled through the air and around the arena by a team of eight black reindeer'oids, their harnesses and reins fashioned from Welsh leather and gold.

Ruby Q follows the sleigh driver with her eyes. He is an old man past his prime, dressed in red tartan and wearing a false white beard. He coughs from time to time, a deep-seated cough that Ruby Q recognises comes from the chest of Phlegm, who almost everyone assumed was dead.

Ruby Q peers at the man sitting in the back seat, smiling and throwing overboard hundreds of tiny black tartan Xmas stockings containing Dekaydence vouchers. Under his thick black cloak, lined in scarlet tartan, he is dressed in a black silk suit and an open-necked white silk shirt. He is wearing red tartan sunglasses, which he removes and stares steadily into Ruby Q's eyes.

She sees the Caribbean-coloured eyes and her heart sinks. This man is the antithesis of Santa Claus. This man is her father, her biological father, Lorenzo di'Abalo.

The audience shivers. The earth shudders. There's a

tension in the air.

MacCavity drums his caber on the ground and announces that it's 'Time for the Grand Finale'.

119 THE JACKPOT PRIZE

The large and noisy crowd returns, sated with Dekaydence food and drink filled with sugar, salt and chemicals that'll sooner rather than later induce death. Yet the knowing and unknowing alike return to their seats laden with large bags full of snacks from the new Dekaydence '2-2 Delicious!' range.

Gradually, the lights are lowered, the crowd quietens. Music begins. Mean and spare. Strings reverberate two notes. There's an electric charge in the air and something akin to menace as a great bell tolls mournfully every 10 minutes.

Those in the shuffling queue of bidders are getting edgy. They're none too pleased that every time they move they're liable to get a sharp electric shock from an invisible barrier on either side. They feel corralled like sheep. Angry sheep, if there ever was such a thing, that someone else has the audacity to try to control them.

The crowd senses the sheep's tension but shrugs it off in a devil-may-care attitude. After all, these bidders are people with twelve-figure wealth and upwards, way beyond the eight-figure sums they are prepared to pay out to win more wealth, perhaps to build on a useful connection with Lord Di'Abalo and his worldwide businesses.

The bidders have nine minutes to study data on the monitors and crack the code that will enable Di'Abalo to access the secrets in the brain of the young man they call the Phoenix, which he will share with the highest bidder.

The crowd hushes itself and hears a sound over the speakers like the sigh of someone breathing their last.

The ground in the arena shudders and emits a rumbling hiccup before it cracks open. The crowd gasps. A large circular block of black granite emerges from the ground on which stand one hundred Black Tartan guards, their eyes shielded by their red tartan glasses. They stand to attention and, by order of their commander-in-chief, MacCavity, Head of Dekaydence Security, 50 guards turn to face inwards.

MacCavity, in his best red tartan, carries his caber while, by his side, is his beloved, giant spider'oid pulling remorselessly on her lead.

'Lucretia!' MacCavity hisses to his pet. 'Desist! What has got into yous, woman?'

Lucretia has nothing to say on this or any other matter. Though she does harbour a grudge at growing black hairy arms for the use of others. More precisely, the wretched, smelly things on two legs – the things called humans.

Soon all is revealed: the black granite block is a catafalque on which lies the body of a young man. He is surrounded by fibrene monitors pulsating with data. And, thus, the star billing of the Dekaydence post-Coronation celebration is presented – tall, skinny, semi-naked, and in a deep coma.

Yes, the mind of this scrawny, comatose young man is billed as the Jackpot Prize.

Once, he was an eco-warrior fighting globally to save the lives of animal and man. Fable and mystery surround him. Where did he come from? What are his roots? Some say that the greedy, war-mongering politician who is the Federation's President is the father of this young humanitarian whose aim is to make the world a better, fairer and kinder place. He became a hero of, and for, the young. He is a hero still to many worldwide. He is the hero best known as the Phoenix.

120 FEAR AND FURY

'Is that who I think it is?' Indigo, wide-eyed, asks Will.

'I believe so, yes, Your Majesty,' says HOH Candelskin, realising Will cannot bring himself to speak. 'It is the Phoenix.'

This Phoenix will not rise, Will tells himself, fury and fear in his eyes where tears are forming. He has known the Phoenix since their first day at school; admired his fellow Noteian for taking such an active part in humanitarian operations. To see him now, the centre of a tawdry auction, and close to death...

Will excuses himself. He throws up in the nearest cloakroom, as his mind hammers on, trying to find a way to save the Phoenix.

'You OK, sir?' says Sid, putting his head round the cloakroom door.

Will nods as he hangs over the basin, wiping his face.

'We can't find a way out,' says Sid. 'Everywhere is covered by armed Black Tartans. They've even armed the Eye-Spys.'

'They must be expecting trouble. Or want to create it for their own ends,' says Will. He punches his fist into the palm of his hand. 'We must get him out of here, Sid. We simply must.'

'Could be someone is already on the case,' says Sid, who's intent on his ad'um. 'Here, take a look at security camera 13.'

Hope settles briefly on Will's face, to be replaced by despair.

'What on earth does he think he's doing?' he says, scanning the screen and seeing the familiar face of another childhood friend and fellow Noteian who's in the long slow-moving queue to reach the mind of the Phoenix.

121 BRAIN FEVER

Those queuing to see into the mind of the Phoenix are restless. They're not used to waiting, they pay others to do that for them. They just want to get on and out with the prize, each convinced that it's theirs.

So it begins. One by the one, the first dozen bidders key in an identity number stamped on their ticket receipt and focus their eyes on the iris check.

'Hang on, there's only three steps to get up there,' says the man at the front of the queue, squinting ahead suspiciously. 'What's going on?'

'You don't need steps,' a Black Tartan guard says. 'You travel on a rising corridor that takes you direct to the catafalque.'

'But I've got a gammy leg,' the man protests, indignant. 'I didn't know about any corridor lark. And I haven't brought my long-distance glasses. Why didn't someone tell me?'

'It's all in the instruction sheet you received, sir.'

'I don't read instruction sheets,' the man snaps. 'The secretary does that. Or the wife.'

'At the end of the day, sir, it's all down to you. So, are you coming or going? Remember there are no refunds.'

'All right, all right. But if I fall over, my lawyers will sue you for—'

'Good for you, sir.' The Black Tartan guard nods. 'But remember, Dekaydence lawyers stand at the left hand of Lord di'Abalo himself. They don't "do" losing. Dekaydence bankers are on his right side. But you'd know that as the data tells me you're on the board of the new Strawberry Jam Bank. Bet that cost a few jammy dough-noughts.'

'Actually, I do gold mostly,' the man says contemptuously, his face as twisted as a parsnip. 'But I got a tip-off and bought into every Dekaydence strawberry field in China. You should try it some time.'

The guard says nothing but sighs as he watches the man mount the steps and proceed into the corridor. Inside, there are ever-changing scenes of luxury – from palaces to castles to stately homes, from shipping cruises to private yachts, from personal islands and jungles, to private jets and fleets of luxury limousines.

All mine for the taking, the man reflects smugly. *Not that I need it, though it's always handy to have in hand a spare fortune or three. My business is global with the best IT department money can buy. They've made me a device that'll scan the Phoenix's monitors so the boffins can read the data through my eyes and immediately give me the code and answers, and tell me which button to press.*

He steps forward, speed-scans the monitors and waits. He drums his fingers on his hand. Nothing. Only silence.

'Hello?' he demands, in a low urgent voice. Silence answers with silence.

The 11 others on the stage are studying monitors, making notes and speaking into their gadgets. They, too, field only silence. Everyone is anxious. Very anxious. All of them, or their bosses, have sunk large sums of money into this project, and on hedge funds as well as strawberrry fields.

'One minute to go,' a Dekaydence voice'oid announces.

Whatever it costs, I shall have the body of the Phoenix, the man promises himself through frustration, anger and gritted teeth. *IT will have more time to use their know-how to get the information, and maybe they'll uncover inside info on Dekaydence that could prove useful.*

'Time's up!' the voice'oid says firmly.

The man and a few others let forth a torrent of angry words. They resort to bribes. The Official Dekaydence HandyMan accepts cash bribes only to ensure media silence on illegal offers that would otherwise see them all sent to prison.

In the queue, the waiting bidders see breaking news on their ad'ums that Dekaydence has just taken over the Federation's entire legal system. It appears the Head of Dekaydence and many more chief executives, politicians and the armed forces march together for a New DisOrder.

There is another 'trough' interval before the Grand Finale. Indigo remains in the Royal Dekaydence Box, reading the souvenir programme. She knows Will is worrying about something that he won't mention in Di'Abalo's presence. She wishes Grout was around to answer her questions and concerns about what's going on and what will be the fate of the Phoenix.

122 ARRIVAL OF THE ALFS

'What now? What comes next?' Indigo enquires.

'A reality break,' says Will gloomily, as he re-enters the box. 'That's right, isn't it, Lord di'Abalo?'

'Yes,' says Di'Abalo.

'This isn't your scene, Indigo,' Will begins. 'Quite the reverse, it's—'

'I agree,' says Candelskin. 'It's not at all Your Majesty's cup of tea.'

Ruby Q says nothing.

'Gentleman, I appreciate your concern,' Indigo responds, 'but I assure you I do know my own mind and I don't want mollycoddling. I am—'

The trumpets announce trough time is at an end and the next stage of the celebrations will begin. The crowd hastens to its places.

A cheer goes up and echoes round the stadium as the faces of four high-profile politicians appear on the monitors, their crimes detailed briefly under their faces and read out by an acclaimed film and Shakespearean actor who has also dabbled in thrillers and Dekaydence film and TV adverts. Ruby Q considers him to have the ultimate dark-chocolate voice.

'Are you ready to press your buttons?' shouts the Actor.

'Yes!' the crowd responds keenly.

'Remember, the green light is for...?' The Actor trails a teasing question.

'Gasbag!'

'Yes!' the Actor underlines heavily. 'Which means...?'

Reasons and demands come thick and fast.

'Lock up the Fleeing Four!'

'Put them back in Parliament, get them talkin'!'

'Yeah! Talkin' day and night!'

'They gotta produce hot air to give us, the people, electricity!'

'Or else!'

'That's right!' shouts the Actor. 'And a red light is for...?'

'E-rase and de-lete. E-rase and de-lete!' the crowd cries out staccato-style.

'You've got it! So...shall we begin?' asks the Actor.

'Yes!' The crowd roars.

'So,' says the Actor, 'first up is the Minister for Culture. Guilty of shutting down every library in the land. Guilty of leaving Parliament for two months without permission in order to act as the front end of a donkey in pantomime. Guilty of coercing the Foreign Secretary to play the back end! Hit your preferred button—green or red...*now*!'

'And your answer is...85 per cent say green! That means elongated talking shifts – for all, *or else*!'

'Gas-*bag*! Gas-bag! *Gas-Bag!*' Sections of the crowd spit out one syllable or the other, back and forth, and then unite in one word. *Gasbag!*

The two politicians are marched away in manacles to a black tartan van, scared and shamefaced but much relieved they got the green light rather than the red.

'Next up, ladies and gentlemen,' says the Actor, 'the Minister of Works and Pensions, working with the Chief Executive of ALF Bs — the new Alien Life Form Bureaux that are forcing the elderly, disabled and needy back into work, or deprivation, or death. They are given a choice and now, ladies and gentlemen, it's time for you to make yours.'

There are boos and hisses among a few cheers.

'Yes,' the Actor continues. 'ALFs ensure disabled, unemployed, disadvantaged, homeless people, young and old, lose all benefits. They are to be left to fend for themselves, in effect left to die alone in unheated homes or on the streets.'

'Press your buttons, ladies and gentlemen, red or green?' says the Actor. There's a drum roll in a pause before the Actor continues. 'And the result is — 50 per cent green and 50 per cent red! A split vote! Now, we can't have that, ladies and gentlemen, can we? We must have a decision!'

'Life for the Minister! And death to the ALF and safety man!' shout a number of people in the crowd.

'No, No!' others cry. 'Life for the ALF man and death to the Minister!'

Candelskin is sweating profusely. His hands are shaking. He heads for the cloakroom, where he dabs his face and neck with cold water. Given his earlier misdemeanours, he realises he could have ended up in the arena, a gladiator, a piece of dead meat on the way to be 'oided. A shiver runs down his spine. With these new popular political, gladiatorial, death games in position, he must be on his guard.

Indigo looks stunned. This is the Dekaydence future, she realises. But is it the future that society really wants? She wonders, should she abdicate to allow more politically experienced people to work things out? She thinks of her grandfather and her forebears. No, she cannot resign her post. She has made her vows. She must be strong – If only for others.

'So, this event is a one-off? For me...?' Indigo asks Di'Abalo hesitantly.

'No, ma'am. It's for all citizens.' Di'Abalo laughs. 'It's a hugely popular game that we've franchised and is now played throughout the Federation and beyond. It's called "Demockrazy".'

Indigo nods, bewildered.

'You must understand, Your Majesty,' Di'Abalo continues, 'it's an efficient way of eradicating worthless and dangerous elements in society. With an added judging panel of popular celebrities and judges it serves two purposes – it's a great opportunity to entertain and essential to control the masses.'

Indigo nods politely but says nothing. Inside, her thoughts are in turmoil. It appears Dekaydence is creating a new world order, a new bullying, brutally cruel way of running, or rather controlling, a country and, as Di'Abalo himself hints, eventually, the entire planet.

What place education to teach young, tender and open minds how to learn, how to live, how to care? she wonders. What place equality? What place justice? What place freedom of speech? What place kindness, compassion and love?

She tries to imagine what her grandfather, the King, might have done in her situation. Or her father, the Crown Prince. She scolds herself. She must not look back. She must concentrate on the present, with an eye to the future. She must develop her own strengths and beliefs.

She glances at Will, who gives her a smile that's organic and natural, not his usual manufactured-for-a-crowd smile. She sighs with relief; she has his support. And somewhere, not far away, there is Grout, she thinks. Just the thought of him makes her feel she has the strength to carry on.

123 'OIDER AND 'OIDER

Di'Abalo is distracted by the sight of an elderly man sweeping the arena floor while the Studs & Sluts perform in a brief interlude before the next entertainment, the Battle of the Glad'oids.

He orders a Black Tartan guard to eject the old man, who is leaning on his motorised broom and spending much time engaging youngsters in long conversations. The last thing Di'Abalo wants is elderly people mixing with the young. They have too much in common, including antipathy towards those of an age in between.

The Studs & Sluts leave the stage to cries for an encore that time and management determine can't be done.

The crowd whoop and holler, and stomp their feet in excitement, as they hear a new wave of glad'oids pounding up the stone stairs from their underground cells and dressing rooms. The metal gates open on to the arena and the glad'oids pour forth and run to their appointed places.

'Let battle commence!' proclaims MacCavity, beating the ground with his caber.

The crowd gives a thunderous roar. Battle commences. Metal against metal. Muscle against tactics, or lack of. The crowd bays for blood as a range of animal'oids darts out of the open gates. The starved animal'oids are ravenous for flesh and blood, as well as machinery, empty drink cans and discarded crisp packets.

Plaudits and abuse are hurled in every direction, from the crowd and the battlefield. Felled bodies of flesh and blood are whisked away, to be re-formed in moments with metal, fibrene and hi-tech methodology. Friends, relatives and strangers become 'oids. No one appears overly concerned until...

Multivarious cries burst forth from the audience. A civilian has wandered into the arena. Smiling and chatting and stopping to congratulate the warriors who are as much bemused as incensed. A madman? No. Or rather, yes! But who is he?

A close-up of a man's face appears on the monitors, a deep and bloody line across his face, like a settlement crack in a building. The man turns. It's the President of the Federation! Or is it? The camera scans the VIP box revealing that Presidents from all over the world have a very similar look. Not surprising, given that many have a not-too-discreet label on the back of their neck declaring — 'Made by Dekaydence'.

'Are they all the same?' Ruby Q whispers aghast to Spiky Hair. 'Are they all 'oids.'

'Not all. Not yet.' Spiky Hair shakes her head. 'But rumour is they'll soon share one brain.'

'So they'll all march to the tune of Dekaydence's New DisOrder!' murmurs Ruby Q.

Ruby Q stares at the Presidents and then scanning the arena sees a man employing his biggest, cheesiest grin, as he hands out cards asking for donations to his favourite charity - himself. Yes, that's him all right! The President of the Federation.

Surrounded by fights, big and small, he's constantly butted and battered by warriors and soon he's looking anxiously for help. But no one responds.

Meanwhile, on the opposite site of the arean, Ruby Q spots a rare happy grouping of Black and Red Tartan guards who are relishing the company of an elderly cleaner who looks vagueuly familiar.

There's a nervous hum in the crowd. The've spotted the President of the Federation shuffling about in ever-decreasing circles. (Don't fret, Spiky Hair advises Ruby Q, that's part of a politician's job.) Suddenly, the President cries out. He's hyperventilating. And muttering in many tongues of other lands. Arabic, Mandarin, Hindi, Russian, *et al* converge into an incomprehensible potage. Then he crashes to the ground. His body is quickly removed by a red Orbie truck.

Di'Abalo sends an urgent message to Grout to get the spare Presidential 'oid to the arena. And put another on charge mode. Pronto.

The elderly man breaks off his conversation to sweep the area clean. The battles rage on. The wounded and dying are taken away speedily in a red Orbie and replaced swiftly by 'oids, animal, vegetable and occasionally mineral. Bets are placed. Fights break out in the crowd. Food and drink flow freely. The elderly man continues to sweep and chat as he moves round the perimeter fence. Meanwhile, the sun bakes on.

'Gosh, that was quick!' Ruby Q remarks suspiciously to Spiky Hair, as the President of the Federation returns to the arena.

Dressed now as a gladiator he appears restored to good health. He waves cheerily to the crowd, who note his slick-backed fibrene coiffure and stare at him (and his knobbly knees) in shock and disbelief. Rumours rumble about the crowd. Is he man or 'oid? No one can be sure.

The President, who has made a career out of extricating himself from crises, sports the familiar cheesy grin and love-me look of a pleading puppy.

Suddenly, he is collared by a big bruiser of a man. He is dragged into a bitter and intense feud between three glad'oids arguing and fighting over a bottle of beer that's lying on the ground.

'I say,' says the President, donning his most ingratiating smile, 'why don't we share the drink and talk things through?'

One of the glad'oids goes to punch him. But, as ever, the President is slippery quick on his feet. He jumps out of the way, inadvertently (possibly) bumping into a tall, skinny, vacant-looking young man who he grabs by the arm. Praising the young man's strength and vigour, he pushes him into a fight between the three arguing glad'oids, who appear not to notice and simply carry on fighting with added intensity.

The President decides to weevil his way towards the exit. But in his haste his step falters. He's trodden on something, but what? He looks down. Two bright red eyes glare into his. The liquorice-thick tail is humming and what looks like thick black oil is dripping slowly from the creature's jaw.

Oh, my God, it's a haggoid! he thinks to himself. *What do I do now?*

He looks around for a Red Tartan guard, the usual haggoid handler, but the only one he can see is on the other side of the arena, deep in conversation with the elderly man holding a broom.

The President waves urgently to the Red Tartan, indicating the haggoid. There's a penetrating screech so agonised that the nearest fighting glad'oids stop briefly to see who's been wounded. When they see it's the President they return relieved to their fight.

'Ross! Get away from that 'oid!' shouts MacNoodle from the barrier. 'You don't know where it's been or what you might catch off it!'

But the message doesn't get through.

The Pres'oid is staring at his foot. The haggoid is devouring it. Everywhere there's blood and stuff, the mere sight of which makes him want to vomit and/or faint. He's swaying from side to side but – with a concerted effort –

he draws his sword from its sheath and brings it down on the haggoid's head.

There's a horrible tin-can sound and a gargulated screech from the haggoid. The Pres'oid sinks to the ground with an almighty clatter. At his feet, or foot, the haggoid lies, its head detached from its body. Its tail hangs loose, as do its ears. The red eyes are freeze-focused on the eyes of the President with a mixture of hatred and sorrow.

'*No!*' MacNoodle cries out, scrambling over the perimeter fence and running faster than he's run in his entire life.

The elderly man espies a tiny red Orbie dustbin on its way to vacuum up the pieces.

'Could you hold this for a moment, dear lady?' says the elderly man, abandoning his broom to the woman in blue standing next to him, without giving her a second glance. 'I won't be a moment.'

Flying metal, fibrene and flesh fists rain down on MacNoodle's body as he runs across the arena. He falls under a scrum of bodies, manages to crawl out, pick himself up and run to where he's seen Ross. But when he gets there, there's nothing. No sign of the haggoid. He looks this way and that, and falls to his knees, pushing the Pres'oid to one side. He's surrounded by blood, bone, metal and gore but nothing haggoidy.

A ray of sunshine settles like a butterfly on something close at hand, near the President's foot. MacNoodle crawls towards it, curious. It's a metal bolt. He scans the ground and sees a random selection of nuts and bolts. He scoops them into a clean handkerchief and carefully places the hankie in his jacket pocket.

MacNoodle gets up, oblivious to almost everything around him, his thoughts focused on Ross. He fails to see the big bruiser of a glad'oid moving slowly towards him from behind. He fails to see the sword rise above his head. He is felled by an almighty blow to his head and his knees crumple under him. Blood is coming from somewhere. There are tears in his eyes. He can focus only on Ross and Cromarty, his two wee boys, his two beloved metal mutts. Who will look after them? he frets, clutching his hankie tight as he slips into unconsciousness.

124 MIXED BOX

The sun shines bright and hot on the arena and on the audience, who eat and drink as though they've never before eaten. Certainly, nothing like the new '2-2 Delicious Dekaydence delights', which is probably correct, given the list of unpronounceable poisonous chemicals the delights contain, up to and beyond the hilt.

Meanwhile, the metal-suited glad'oids are drenched in sweat. Most are not only exhausted but now, increasingly, fearful of being killed and/or re-'oided.

The queue for the Phoenix is diminishing. Only fifty or so remain in the queue to win the Jackpot Prize. As yet, no one has got anywhere near discovering the entry code to access the young man's mind and, therefore, his secrets.

In the Dekaydence Royal Box a party is in full swing. Lord di'Abalo warmly greets his guests, people of power and influence from around the world, most of whom have bought into Strawberry Jam and, equally, Dekaydence's plans for a new world disorder. Di'Abalo says little, encouraging others to chat. More is learnt this way, he knows.

Indigo has few words to say to the guests, who treat her politely but who, she realises, consider her to be an anachronism, as well as a female and not much more than a child, albeit quite a bright one.

Will leans against the edge of the balcony, watching the crowd while contemplating North's enthusiasm for the good things going on around the world. People helping others less fortunate than themselves. People giving their money, their time, their love to others.

He thinks of Piccolo. And is acutely aware of the emptiness in his own life.

He realises the astute among the gathering are drawn to him because they think he is clever, has the ear of the Queen and, most important, Lord di'Abalo. That's why they 'cultivate' him, he considers, though he has no desire to be cultivated or cultivate them.

Of them all, it is HOH Candelskin who spends his time pressing the flesh, listening as well as wheeling and dealing. Dressed in a white free-flowing gown with a rainbow silk sash, he cultivates many he deems to be important while all are mesmerised by the fact that as each individual approaches the HOH, his garb flashes and changes to the religion of the person whose hand he is about to shake.

125 A RELATIVE PROBLEM

A lithe woman, supple and lightly tanned, enters the balcony box. She's dressed in a cornflower-blue silk dress that matches her eyes, while her warm smile draws guests to her. It's as if they know that there is something special about this stranger in their midst.

The woman listens to all and sundry then walks to where Indigo stands alone. The young Queen is looking out over the arena. The fighting continues; the Orbie trucks speed in and out, collecting the remains of the fallen; while the Phoenix lies barely breathing on the catafalque.

'It could be worse, I suppose,' sighs the woman, shaking her head.

'Could it?' Indigo replies sharply. 'Could it really?'

'Let me put it this way,' says the woman. 'It may get worse before it gets better.'

'What does that mean?' sighs Indigo. 'And how can you be so sure?'

Indigo's anger dissolves. Something in the woman's smile disarms her.

She returns a quick smile.

'Should I know who you are?' she enquires.

The woman bursts out laughing. Heads turn; her laughter is contagious and catches hold of the smiles of others, and lifts their spirits.

'I'm an organic gardener,' says the woman casually. 'As I know you are. You've done great things, if I might say so. You and Lady Catgut.'

'Gosh, how come you know so much about me and I know nothing about you? Are you a friend of Lord di'Abalo?'

'No,' the woman says definitely, a wisp of a worry furrowing across her face.

'Then who—?'

'Hello,' Di'Abalo says silkily to the woman. 'We've not been introduced. I am—'

'I know who you are,' says the woman, giving Di'Abalo a curt nod before moving on.

Di'Abalo turns to Phlegm.

'Who is that young woman?' Di'Abalo demands.

Phlegm looks down to examine his feet.

'I can't be sure, my lord, exactly—' Phlegm begins.

'I hear in your voice that you know exactly who she is,' Di'Abalo retorts.

'As I said, I can't be sure,' says Phlegm, knowing that there'll be no easy way out of this.

'Phlegm,' Di'Abalo says softly, his eyes glinting evil, 'give me your answer, or else you will never see home again.'

Phlegm's eyes widen in horror; he looks as if he might disintegrate on the spot.

'So, Phlegm, who is she?' says Di'Abalo.

'Er...' says Phlegm.

'I'm waiting,' Di'Abalo snaps.

Indigo scents an acrid smell in the air. She looks aghast as black smoke emerges from Di'Abalo's fingertips, which glow ember-red. Memories of her grandfather's final moments jolt her mind.

'No!' she shouts. 'Not again!'

Without a second thought she throws the contents of her champagne glass over Di'Abalo's hands.

Witnesses to the event gasp as one and edge away from the protagonists. A few are quick to leave the box; others to accept Dekaydence champagne refills and simply carry on partying.

Ruby Q snatches a serviette from a pile on a nearby table and hands it to Indigo. Phlegm takes one for Di'Abalo. Ruby Q steps back but stays within hearing distance.

'I'm so sorry, it's just that...' Indigo apologises to Di'Abalo as she sees his hands have no trace of any burn, no smell of smoke, nothing that would corroborate what she'd seen moments before.

'Don't give it a second thought, Your Majesty. These things happen,' Di'Abalo says to her, quiet and calm, though she sees his pupils have become tiny dagger-shaped icicles.

She shudders.

As does Phlegm.

'Well, Phlegm,' says di'Abalo, 'can you recall the name of the attractive woman in the blue dress?'

Phlegm hesitates and then, in a rush and a blush, replies quietly.

'Speak up, man!' Di'Abalo commands.

Phlegm swallows hard. Ruby Q, acutely aware of his discomfort, stands closer to the old man, who is trembling horribly, and links her arm through his.

'My lord,' he says, two tads louder, 'the young woman in question is...is your mother.'

More jaws fall in that moment than at any other time over the next century.

126 MOTHER OF REINVENTION

A sardonic smile settles on Di'Abalo's mouth. He watches the woman in blue studying the crowd and moves towards her. He touches her elbow. She flinches and turns sharply, her sparkling blue eyes, now glacial, regard him with disdain.

'You look exceptionally good for your age, Mother,' he says. 'How many facelifts and tucks does that make now?'

The woman's look turns to permafrost. Indigo notices him shudder.

'Come, now, Mother,' Di'Abalo says softly. 'Where's your sense of humour?'

'Almost exterminated by you,' says the woman coldly. 'Like the worries you've ladled on to your poor father over the years. You've come close to exterminating him, but you know that.'

'Father has been gaga for ever, long before I came on the scene. But you, you are constantly refreshing yourself, in mind as well as body. That is what I adore about you.'

He bows, reaches for her hand, intent on kissing it, but she doesn't move.

'Once again you have gone too far,' she says, 'so this time I intend stopping you, now and for always.'

'I shall enjoy seeing you fail, Mother,' Di'Abalo says laconically, and turns on his heel.

Phlegm gives a slight bow to the woman in blue and follows his master.

Suddenly, unexpectedly, black clouds cover the sky, thunder rumbles on the horizon. Rain pours down, drenching everyone in the arena: spectators dressed in their skimpy summer clothing; glad'oids stuck in the soggy ground, trying to fight in what's become a huge mudpit; the Phoenix on his catafalque and those queueing to see him to win the Jackpot Prize. Several guests in the Royal Box shove at others to get out but the traffic of people appears to have solidified, stagnated. No one can move.

Will tries to persuade Indigo to leave the Royal Box. She refuses.

'I'm one with the people,' she says. 'I'll stay.'

'Me, too,' says Ruby Q.

Will stands protectively close to Indigo. Phlegm moves to stand on her other side, Ruby Q holding his arm.

A shard of lightning streaks across the sky and disappears. Moments pass. Thoughts reassemble elsewhere. There's a crack of thunder. Another shard of lightning jets into the arena, flying singeingly close to many while terrifying all who see it.

Some in the crowd realise, with fear or relief, that the lightning is heading directly for the Royal Box.

Lorenzo Di'Abalo stands alone, his eyes alight with

fervour, absorbed in the drama of the spectacle, as if he is there to welcome the visitor.

The lightning strikes his mother in the chest. She staggers.

Inside his head, Di'Abalo cheers.

His mother's body folds before him. He kneels at her side. The focus of many in the Royal Box is centred now not on escape but on the fate of the beautiful woman they so much admired. Has she drawn the sting that could've hit any one of them?

'See how much stronger than you I am now, Mother Nature,' he taunts her.

Slowly, she raises her head, her face and eyes devoid of expression. He smiles at her, a cruel tyrannical smile.

'Father lost out to me years ago and now it is your turn,' says Di'Abalo triumphantly. 'You shall—'

He is stopped momentarily in his tracks by the furious look in his mother's eyes and then laughs.

'Mother, dearest,' he says patronisingly. 'Not to worry. Soon you'll be out there, in the galaxy's wilderness, where you belong.'

She is on her feet, facing him eye to eye. Her hands are clenched tight as though she is holding on to something with all her will. Slowly, she holds out her hands, palm facing palm. She waits a moment, watching his sneering gaze turn a tad uneasy, and then...

She opens her hands and from every finger shoot forth bolts of lightning that strike at every vital part of

Di'Abalo's body. Now it is Di'Abalo's turn to crumple and yell out in pain, to fall to his knees and then to the ground.

'You can duplicate and destroy almost everything, Di'Abalo, but you are not a creator, and never will be,' says Mother Nature disdainfully. 'You steal love but you are incapable of feeling it, let alone giving it. I should've destroyed you at birth. Or cast *you* out to the wilds of the galaxy or beyond. And would've gladly if I'd known how you would exploit the weakness of humans.'

She kneels at the side of her son. Thunder grumbles underground. There is the sound of an explosion. And several more, repeated. It confuses many. Is it more thunder? Or gunfire? The crowd searches itself; the VIPs in the Royal Box shrug and fret. A young woman cries out, pointing vigorously at the catafalque, now thick with Black Tartan guards.

Will holds up his ad'um to zoom into the scene. Someone in the queue has been shot. Someone is on the ground. Someone is not moving. He zooms in closer.

'Oh, God,' he says, under his breath. 'Please, no.'

'What is it?' asks Indigo, hoping, praying fervently it is not Grout.

Will is speechless. He cannot absorb what he has seen, let alone tell Indigo what has happened – that on the ground lies the body of a Noteian. One of the young doctors. One of his closest friends.

127 BEWARE CHAOS

A red medical Orbie flies into the arena and takes away the young Noteian. No one knows for sure whether he is alive or dead. Will contacts Sid and asks him to get on the case. Sid is uneasy.

'I am supposed to be guarding you,' he says.

'I'm fine,' says Will. 'We've got a powerful woman up here who's just brought Di'Abalo to his knees. I don't think you need worry.'

'That must be some woman,' says Sid admiringly. 'Who is she?'

'Not sure,' Will demurs. 'Possibly some powerful renegade 'oid that's being trialled by Dekaydence. Or perhaps, though highly unlikely, it is his mother. But certainly Di'Abalo, courtesy of this woman, is out for the count.'

Sid laughs.

'OK, boss. I'm on the case. But promise me, you'll keep your head down. Something crazy is happening out here.'

Will grunts his assent. Something crazy is out there for sure. He focuses the ad'um on the scene.

'Now what?' he mutters to himself, as he scans the stage.

A fracas has broken out, near the catafalque. Something unseen and intangible is preventing the few remaining in the queue, as well as the Black Tartans, from getting anywhere near the Phoenix. The Black Tartans are not happy, and are looking for some Red Tartans to take the blame.

Someone is close by the Phoenix, bending over him and talking to him. A young cloaked figure is holding the hand of the Phoenix and nodding, as if answering the Phoenix's questions, though Will knows this cannot be. He switches on the sound of the ad'um and realises the unknown figure is that of the Phoen'oid.

128 THE PHOEN'OID'S GIFT

'*Ruva*,' says the Phoen'oid. 'My brother. It is I, Josef. Your brother, or rather the mechan'oid named Josef that you want destroyed.'

The Phoen'oid gently holds the Phoenix's hand. It lies limp in his own. But in his head he hears an almost imperceptible throb of activity in the Phoenix's brain.

'Listen, *mi ruva*,' says the Phoen'oid. 'I speak in Etruscan, one of the old languages that I know you have stored secretly in your head, so few will understand what passes between us. Time is short. I know I am about to self-destruct. And you are on the verge of death. And who knows, the world itself may be next. There is only one thing we can do, *mi riva*.'

The Phoen'oid senses a sudden surge in the Phoenix's mind, indicating he understands time is short. What is it the Phoen'oid is offering? he wants to know.

'I surrender my being to you,' the Phon'oid responds. 'If you accept, you become an 'oid within a millisecond of downloading me. My powers, some infinitely stronger than yours, become yours. Together our powers will be entwined and interlocked. No one will be able to take them away from you. Think what good you can do, Jesu. You will become the eternal Phoenix, until or unless you decide to pass on your powers and your life to another. What do you say?'

The Phoen'oid holds the Phoenix's hand to his forehead. He feels the mind of the dying young man grind slowly as if it has been ransacked and lost the ability to work.

'Make haste,' the Phoen'oid urges. 'The last grains of sand in the timer of my life are falling.'

For a moment the Phoen'oid feels it is too late. That it is all over for them both. That he and the Phoenix will soon no longer be.

He feels a slight pressure on his hand and senses a word struggling to take shape in the Phoenix's brain. It comes to him in the shape of a sword. And the Phoen'oid knows instantly that this is meant to give him courage and that the answer to the question he has asked is, *Yes, I accept your offer*.

The tide turns. The Phoen'oid begins to feel his being turn to liquid that will flow fast and free into a great river. He feels a pang of regret that soon he will be no more. He feels tears but knows also that they, too, will be absorbed into a greater force. He feels the last drops of his mind and his strength are leaving him and being absorbed by the Phoenix.

He feels exhaustion, as if he's done a hard day's work.

There's an outbreak of tiny pinpricks in his head. The program designed to bring about his end is working its way deep into his system. The program will not transfer but will delete itself when the job is done. The Phoenix will inherit much from the Phoen'oid.

The Phoen'oid sighs. He believes he has done what humans would deem to be a good deed. He has given his life so that another, and perhaps more, may live. For the first time he thinks he understands the meaning of love.

'Farewell, Jesu, my brave beloved brother,' he murmurs, aware that the voice of another is mingling with his. The voice of the real brother of the Phoenix, the real Josef, the President's younger son.

Somewhere within his body the Phoen'oid senses a smile. Does it come from the Phoenix, Josef or even himself...? His eyes close, his hand slips from the hand of the Phoenix. He is sailing away on the warmth of a smile.

The outer surface of the Phoen'oid's body is dissolving fast, his innards too.

'May a caring, compassionate God be with you, always, brave Phoen'oid, who I badly misjudged.' The Phoenix sends a farewell from his mind to the final essence of the Phoen'oid.

The Phoenix feels his strength returning and growing, that he is regaining control of his mind as well as his body, that new powers have come to him through the Phoen'oid.

'*Adieu*, my brother,' says the Phoenix, focusing his energy on the Phoen'oid. 'I send you a gift to add to the seed that was with you from the beginning and which you yourself nurtured into growth, the gift of love.'

129 O, FATHER, WHO ART NOT IN HEAVEN

Di'Abalo is on his feet again, lively and laughing. It's as though the incident with his mother had never happened. He is mingling happily with his guests, who also appear to have forgotten the recent drama. Or put it to one side. But that's the way of temptation, of golden promises accompanied by vintage Dekaydence champagne and canapés. Oh, and lucrative business contracts.

Will, Ruby Q and Phlegm remain close by Indigo. Will suggests to the woman in blue that she also stay close by them. She declines politely. He suggests his bodyguard give her a lift home. She thanks him but, again, declines. She moves on. He senses more trouble is brewing. And wonders why Phlegm is so protective of Indigo. Given that he's Di'Abalo's man.

Di'Abalo excuses himself suddenly and hurries from the Royal Box to the other side of the arena, where the fighting has resumed and intensified.

'What are you doing here?' he demands of an old man sweeping up discarded Dekaydence cartons of this, that and the other from the floor.

'Clearing up some of the mess you've made,' the old man responds tartly.

'What side of the cloud did you get out on?' retorts

Di'Abalo. 'And why are you both here, on my patch? Shouldn't you be home, knitting wings, listening to endless prayers and hymns, playing hoopla with your halos, painting everything white?'

'Are you saying your mother's here, too?' says the old man, trying to conceal his excitement.

'Yes. And if you are both here to take me home, I'm not going,' Di'Abalo says stubbornly. 'Now or ever.'

'I don't want you home. Not with your track record down here...'

'Keeping tabs on me?'

'Yes,' says the old man firmly. 'You've gone too far. I've given you many chances and you've given me nothing in return except a sense of despair.'

'Your fault,' says Di'Abalo. 'You rejected and recycled the Alpha and made me the Beta model. I should have been, could have been the gold.'

'No, you could never be gold.' The old man shakes his head. 'You're not good enough. Never were. You were borderline Beta.'

'So you always told me. I don't recall one word of praise from you. Or from Mother. It was all for Him, the golden boy, the chosen one, the Blessed is He who has always stood at Your right hand.'

'So different from you. I don't recall you've done any good deed, whereas he...' says the old man. 'You prefer to wreak havoc, don't you? It's you who has introduced the earth to disease, death and destruction.'

'Mother helped in those departments. She's less sentimental than you. Anyway, I contribute heavily to your population.'

'Yes, it's thanks to you we're overcrowded. In Heaven and on Earth. Tearing down rainforests, building housing and industrial estates on old woodland...' The old man sighs. 'Oh, and while we're here, why this need to procreate incessantly?'

'You told me to follow the instructions in The Book you gave me before I left,' says Di'Abalo. 'It said, simply, "Go forth and multiply."'

'I didn't expect you to take it literally.'

'If you'd been more involved in my upbringing... Mother, too, but she was always off on some nature course or other.'

The elderly man stares into the sky.

'You've brought terrible confusion and unhappiness to young people worldwide,' says the old man. 'To the likes of Ruby Q and Grout, Will and Piccolo, Tommo, and thousands more.'

'I've also spiced up their brains and encouraged them to be more determined than ever they would've been,' says Di'Abalo. 'But don't forget, the poor souls have inherited genes from you and from Mother.'

'God help them,' mutters the old man, with a sigh.

'That'd be nice,' says Di'Abalo sarcastically. 'You never had the time to help me.'

'You are a born liar,' says the old man. 'I am so glad I

destroyed the Beta blueprint of you.'

'Did I ever tell you I found the blueprint of you?' says Di'Abalo.

'There isn't a blueprint for me,' says the old man. 'Only apple pips.'

'Oh, but there is,' says Di'Abalo, with an enigmatic smile. 'I've got it.'

Di'Abalo carefully opens an old slim-line tin, revealing a small piece of stone engraved in old text.

'With this I could make another you,' says Di'Abalo tauntingly.

'Best give it to me, boy,' says the old man, holding out his hand. 'You'd never manage it.'

Di'Abalo retracts the stone. He smiles at the old man, rubs his fingers together, which causes a spark to ignite in the cracks of the stone.

'Don't!' the old man cries out.

Di'Abalo laughs.

'It matters little, time-warped old man,' says Di'Abalo, 'The instructions are sealed into my memory as well as a back-up memory stick.'

'Then you won't mind if I have it,' says the woman in blue, as the stone and tin conjoin in her hand.

Di'Abalo takes a step towards his mother to snatch back what she has taken, but finds himself blocked by an invisible force.

'For God's sake!' he shouts.

'That's precisely my motive,' says the woman in blue.

'Your rudeness and cruelty is beyond measure, Lorenzo.'

'Cruelty is a trait I've inherited from you, Mother dearest,' says Di'Abalo. 'It's your speciality, isn't it? Creating life, in order for it to be killed. Mostly for no reason. What's the point of that?'

'It was to be a garden,' says the old man sadly. 'A place of peace. A place for reflection. A place for growth, hope and happiness.'

'And a place of order,' says the woman in blue.

'And whose great idea was that?' says Di'Abalo offhandedly.

The elderly man and the woman in blue exchange glances but say nothing.

'Someone gives you the orders, don't they?' says Di'Abalo coolly. 'Ha! I always wondered if there was someone pulling your strings. Didn't think you could do it all on your own. You won't tell me who or what it is. But as you know, I am nothing if not resourceful. I'll find out and remind you, just in case you forget again.'

Di'Abalo turns on his heel, to return to his guests in the Royal Box. To return to Dekaydence business. But once again an unseen force stops him in his tracks. All he can do is turn to face them.

'The time of evil must end, Lorenzo,' says the woman in blue quietly. 'It and you have gone on for too long.'

'So you're going to decrease my powers again? Is that your plan? Reduce me to basic magic once more?' Di'Abalo sneers. 'As you do after almost every war, tsunami, banking crisis, murder, rise in income tax...'

'You have managed to do all of those things without any recourse to magic, Lorenzo. You do it easily through your persuasive charm and your money,' says the woman in blue. 'Assets that could be used better for the force of good. Not evil. So it is time for you to reflect on your ways. It is time for you to leave this world.'

'I've no intention of dying and going to Heaven, if that's what you're after,' says Di'Abalo. 'And who is it that's made that decision? It's obviously someone with greater authority than even you two. My, I'd like to meet them.'

The woman in blue shakes her head.

'As you well know, Lorenzo, we deal with the here and now. And for now I have decided you are to go on a voyage.'

'Am I allowed to know my destination? Somewhere hot, I hope. Like me, Phlegm must have heat.'

'Phlegm will not be accompanying you.'

Di'Abalo is taken aback.

'You cannot do this. Phlegm comes everywhere with me. Since I was a microdot on a blueprint. I can't manage without him. Or he without me.'

'You'll have to manage. So will he. As you say, he is much in need of heat. And you have denied him that comfort for too many years.'

'He likes to serve me. He'll be lost without me. I'm not standing for this. Phlegm comes with me to somewhere warm or I don't go.'

'You don't have a choice, Lorenzo. Not this time.'

'So where is it I'm going? If I can be bothered.'

'I repeat, you have no choice.'

'So, where…?'

'You will be travelling south.'

'Good, it's not the frozen north.'

'No. It's the frozen south.'

'What?' Di'Abalo shudders.

'You are going to Antarctica.'

'What? Then I want six electric blankets. And a large one each for the cats.'

'That won't be necessary.'

'Why?'

'The cats will be coming with me as you'll be living in a lake.'

'You mean *on* a lake.'

'No, I mean *in* a lake.'

'What?'

'You'll be residing in Lake Vostok, which lies under four kilometres of ice. It's the largest of some four hundred known sub-glacial lakes in Antarctica. In the 1980s the Russian station above it recorded the lowest temperature on earth: −89°C (−128°F).'

'*What?*' Di'Abalo is close to combustion.

'You'll be made physically capable of survival. The rest is up to you.'

'How shall I survive? And what do you mean, the rest is up to me?'

'You'll have time to think things over. Think how you can improve yourself should you ever be permitted to return to earth.'

'So, in order to improve myself, you'll be providing books, technology, friends, champagne, women...?'

'No. It's not possible or practicable.'

'How come?'

'Because, within the next 60 seconds, you will take on a new form. You will become the lowest form of life, a microbe.'

'You...! I shall not be reduced to a feckin' microbe! You've gone too far this time in your cruelty. I cannot, and will not, live in that base form. Thousands of years of heat, I can't just switch to cold. That's another nice gene you've given me. You're always cold, inside and out. You cannot do this to me! Not if you want to see me again.'

'I don't want to see you again, Lorenzo. And that's God's honest truth.'

Di'Abalo begins to feel the frozen force of her eyes on him. He attempts to create a barrier to protect himself but her look cuts through it as if it's tissue paper and goes on to aim at his head and his heart.

'You cannot do this, Mother!' he pleads with her, taking a step towards her, a cross-shaped dagger in his hand, which he raises above his head to bring down on hers.

But the dagger is wrested from his hand and clatters to the ground.

The elderly man has acted. Although his interference has saved her from further attack, his partner is enraged.

Di'Abalo attempts to move. But his limbs will not let him. So he stands, rooted to the spot. But the struggle remains active in his head.

130 FLYING TONIGHT

A huge bird flies overhead, uttering a long, mournful cry. Everyone looks up. Some get a glimpse of a powerfully built ebony-coloured creature. Some see that its long graceful athletic form is scarred from battle wounds.

In the box next to the Royal Box, Piccolo wants to cry out but instead whispers in his head.

Bianco!

The bird hovers, then swoops down, landing on the edge of the Royal Box. Some VIPs scream and rush out.

'Don't leave me again for so long, Bianco,' says Piccolo.

He strokes the bird's long, sleek neck, hearing words in his head.

'I intended never to leave you, but events occur,' says the bird. 'And my life has always been one of servitude. But I shall never forsake you. Never doubt that, Piccolo.'

So saying, the bird flies up into the air and off to the other side of the arena, where Di'Abalo stands with the woman in blue and the elderly man.

'Here comes your transport, Lorenzo,' says the woman in blue.

'So, you deny me the chance to say farewell to Phlegm,

to Candelskin, to the cats? To make arrangements for the business?'

'As you have denied so many others,' says the eldelrly man.

'When we get there I'll turn that damn bird, Bianco, into an eiderdown,' Di'Abalo snarls.

The old man laughs disparagingly.

'You won't get the chance, boy. You'll need all your energy to keep your head above water, as it were.'

'You... I cannot, I shall not go!' says Di'Abalo. So loud is his voice that they hear it on the sound system in the auditorium.

'What's going on?' Indigo enquires.

'I don't know,' says Will. 'But the woman in blue is there. With an elderly man.'

'How odd!' says Ruby Q. 'The old man sounds like Mr Treasure! And the woman in blue...she could be Mrs Treasure's granddaughter. Well, Mr T will be pleased to have his granddaughter visiting.'

Suddenly, there is a cry so loud, so full of pain, fear and pent-up fury and frustration that the fighting in the arena stops instantly. The gladiators and glad'oids look around, awaiting directions from MacCavity. But he is equally transfixed by the look on his boss's face – the lack of twinkling light in his eyes and the terrified expression on his face as he stares at the elderly man, the woman and now some huge, odd-looking bird.

MacCavity has never seen this enfeebled side of

Di'Abalo and doesn't know what to think. Let alone do. So he stands and stares, nonplussed. The audience emits a quiet hum of interest and concern. Even the time-limited contestants on the stage with the monitors and the Phoenix pause for a moment, and look at one another questioningly.

The agonised cry doesn't stop. Even as the voice reduces in volume, along with the body, to that of a microbe. Even though it is placed inside a thin tin and carried in Bianco's beak. The sound sends shivers through each and every one in the arena. Except Ruby Q. He is gone, she says to herself. He is gone but perhaps not for good.

131 ADIEU

He has not gone for good, Ruby Q. He's gone for evil.

There you are. And being silly again.

Yes, silly is a good mode for me to be in. But now, to be serious, it's time for me to leave you.

For good?

Certainly not for evil.

Will I never hear from you again? It's a bit scary to contemplate aloneness.

You won't be alone. You have friends. And you've discovered yourself, you recognise your strengths and weaknesses. And I couldn't be happier to know that I've helped in some small way. And you've got me a distinction for my dissertation.

I did?

Yes, I shouldn't tell you but, as I'm leaving...

Where are you going?

To another assignment.

Where do you go for that?

Mmm. Over there.

Over where? Up, down, middle earth?

It's called Head Office.

Head Office? You mean Heaven?

Oh, no. Head Office oversees Heaven. I'm studying with

Head Office for higher management and interpersonal relationship skills. And I've been offered a week's work experience with God – as and when He returns to Heaven.

Where on earth does God go when He's not in Heaven?

You've just answered your own question, Ruby Q, so I can speak freely! God comes down to Earth from time to time. You should know, He was living at your place. And you know His partner, Mother Nature, from the Vatican Gardens.

Hang on, hang on. So, is that them over there? Watching the big bird disappear over the horizon?

Yes, that's them. And in the bird's beak is a tin with the lone microbe that is Di'Abalo.

I can't take this in.

Yes, you can and you have. So, you know something more, I think.'

'That Di'Abalo is their son?'

Yes, or rather one side of Him.

What does that mean?

There's the alternative side, the alternative son. Ah, listen, Ruby Q. Listen.

I hear birdsong. Trees rustling. A waterfall busy waterfalling. And music. Vaughan Williams' 'Lark Ascending'.

Look, Ruby Q, Look at the stage where the Phoenix lies.

I am looking. I am... Oh, my word!

13

Will searches the departure lounge at the airport. He can't see much beyond a lively, giggling small convention of clowns, keen to get on the flight before theirs to the Netherlands.

'He's not here, is he?' Will says accusingly to Bodkin.

'No, the commander got him on an earlier flight.'

'With no guard?' Will is trying to control his fury.

'Don't worry, sir, the commander made sure Boston was put in the seat next to him,' says Bodkin. 'They'll be driven to the hotel. And there'll be a message for us to meet them in the courtroom.'

There is indeed a message but when they arrive in the courtroom. Proceedings are all but over and there is no sign of the President. Will questions Boston, who says he hasn't seen the President since yesterday.

'What?' Will exclaims in fury.

The court frowns at Will as a judge calls him to order.

Will looks daggers at Bodkin, who remains utterly calm.

The judge looks down at her notes. She thanks the barristers, including Gerald and Daphne Wiggins who are before her in court, and issues thanks to their father and to Ruby Q Cooper for assembling the necessary details and documents.

'It is the court's decision,' says the judge, 'that the President of the Federation is guilty as charged of war crimes. As and when he is released from captivity he will be brought to the court and told the length of sentence he must serve. Until that time...'

'So where is he?' Will regards Bodkin with narrowed eyes. 'What have you done with him? You can't easily lose such a man, unfortunately.'

Bodkin ignores Will, who stands up and addresses the judge.

'Madam Chairman,' Will begins, 'I beg the court's forgiveness in not being able to bring the President to trial in person. It is regrettable. We have worked round the clock to have him released from the captivity but—'

'We now have him here, Your Honour,' Bodkin pronounces firmly, as he stands up alongside Will.

The courtroom gasps as one, and focuses on Bodkin.

'What are you talking about? Where is he? And what are you doing?' Will whispers sharply to Bodkin.

Bodkin doesn't answer. He's struggling to open the suitcase on wheels that has a travelling mind of its own.

The zip gets stuck and Bodkin has to reach inside with both hands to drag out...

First, comes an injured yelp. Then emerges a small curly yellow wig that is sitting lopsided on the head of a mannikin about two feet high.

'Hello,' says the mannikin, in a nasal flat-vowelled voice known to almost everyone in the courtroom. He proffers an oleaginous smile. 'Sorry to put you out. But this wig was the only way out and so, some'ow...you find me in... well, in seriously reduced circumstances.'

A tear falls from the President's eye. (Not to worry, there's a considerable number banked in an enlarged tear duct, implanted by Dekaydence before the election, that is topped up usually before personal interviews and TV appearances.) Luckily, tears don't cloud his view of the shocked and sympathetic looks he is getting from the courtroom and the Press bench.

He smiles inwardly and confidently. Thus, will come unto him, he concludes, a worldwide tsunami of sympathy votes that will free him at once from prison and guilt and will exalt him from President of the Federation into the first President of All Peoples of the World in the New DisOrder.

The judge ruminates. So does the President, who thinks he'll get Randall Candelskin back on side to work his marketing magic and perform any necessary political footwork and diplomatic shuffling. Given the disappearance of Di'Abalo, the President decides he'll take over and revive Dekaydence and put in place as chief executive the one person suitable for the job – Bodkin.

The sound of the judge's gavel cuts through the thick murmuring of the courtroom.

'Guilty as charged!' the judge pronounces.

The courtroom erupts with cheers. Journalists scramble over strangers and colleagues to call their editors.

'What?' cries a voice that nobody hears above the general brouhaha as it emanates from the wee President, who has slipped off his chair and is attempting to clamber back on to it.

The gavel strikes again.

'And as time is as short as you are now, Mr President,' the judge continues, 'you will serve seven years—'

'Shame on you!' comes a shout. 'He needs hanging!'

The gavel strikes again.

'You will serve seven years in a hospital attending to the needs of soldiers injured during the wars,' the judge continues determinedly. 'In addition, you will serve another seven years attending, seven days a week, the families of the bereaved.'

There is applause, whistles and cheers.

'After that time,' the judge concludes, 'you will return here before this court, which will review the situation for its final verdict. But from this day forward you are no longer President.'

The mannikin shrieks and faints to the floor.

132 THE PHOENIX RISES

The semi-naked prostrate body of the Phoenix is beginning to pulsate. Ruby Q stares, wide-eyed. The crowd whispers to itself. What is happening?

A low hum passes through the crowd, which wonders what is happening. Wondering if this will be a Dekaydence crowd-pleasing trick.

The Phoenix begins to rise slowly from his catafalque. And now an almighty hush descends on the crowd. Even the remaining competitors queueing for the Jackpot Prize appear to have forgotten the competition and ignore commands from their HQs as they kneel in obeisance to watch the ascent of the Phoenix.

The Phoenix summons the ashy remains of the Phoen'oid, which lie cold on the floor, into his warm, cupped hands. He brings his palms together and whispers words to the Phoen'oid's ashes. He breathes into them a spark that ignites flames that grow into a fire, and suddenly, a great and mighty blaze surrounds the Phoenix, who opens his arms wide, as if he is embracing the audience as well as the fire.

The flames mount. The contestants watch in awe. The gladiators and glad'oids kneel. The audience kneel by their seats, or bow their heads in reverence. Some pray, some weep, for the soul of the Phoenix, whose body soon disappears in the flames.

There are tears. There are cries of horror, there are shouts of murder, aimed at Di'Abalo and others who are known to have held the Phoenix captive.

All this stops when the Phoenix emerges unscathed from the flames. He reaches out his open, giving hands to the crowd whose applause grows into a mighty roar as the Phoenix's revived strength and power transform him into half man, half bird, fashioned from the sun, with a body and wings of gold and bronze. Behind him, for all the world to see, is a shimmering rainbow forming an arc above his head, pronouncing both God's promise that the Earth will not be forsaken and, as well, the birth of the new Phoenix.

The Phoenix rises into the summer night, watched by all in the arena and by trillions around the world. He flies higher and sees the star that the Phoen'oid has become, whispers to him, telling him that he will forever shine in the sky. He flies higher and further until he disappears from view.

He will be back. He will be everywhere. Because he is the Phoenix.

Was that a miracle? Ruby Q asks.

Yes, technically and on every count, it's a miracle.

I hope I see him again.

I hope so, too. But you have him in your heart, Ruby Q. It's a good place to keep good stuff.

Then I'll put you there, too.

I am honoured. Truly. You have taught me much, Ruby Q, but now I must leave you. Remember, you are in my heart and always will be. So, adieu, *dearest Ruby Q.* Adieu.

There are tears in her eyes as well as joy in her heart as she looks up at the rainbow now fading from the sky. It's a natural phenomenon, she knows, but it's something else as well. It is a promise, a gift, a smile. Whatever, and overall, she reminds herself that she is fortunate in her life. Luckier than many.

I am not my father's daughter but I am the daughter of a good man, she tells herself. I am also the daughter of a clever woman led into temptation by the false love of a bad man. I have inherited much that is good, and learnt much – good and bad. I want to learn more in order to help make the world a better place. I shall write and campaign for justice, to expose evil and reveal and praise good deeds. I may fail in my efforts but I shall carry on, in word and deed.

Mirror or no mirror, I know at last who I am.

HERE ENDETH BOOK THREE OF
THE CHRONICLES OF DEKAYDENCE

However...
*For those who want to know what happens to some of
the characters in Dekaydence, read on ...*

SO, WHAT DOES

THE FUTURE

HOLD...?

1 GOD AND MOTHER NATURE

'How long before Di'Abalo shows his face again?' God enquires dispiritedly.

Mother Nature shrugs.

'I don't know,' she says. 'I'm just relishing the peace of life without him.'

God nods reflectively.

'He's bound to find a way out, though, even if he is a microbe encased in ice.'

'Let's hope not,' Mother Nature says.

'He was such a handsome little lad,' God reminisces. 'Extraordinarily bright, and old and wise way beyond his years. Where did we go wrong? I don't think we did anything untoward, did we, dearest?'

'You haven't called me that in a long time,' Mother Nature remarks.

'Have I not? I am sorry. Work and forgetfulness. Forgive me. Ah, I see you're thinking. Something else worrying you? The TV licence fines, perhaps?'

'No, they can sing – in or out of church – for their fines, as far as I'm concerned. No, I've been wondering for some time – has Lorenzo inherited his evil nature from us?'

God gasps.

'Oh, my! What a terrible thought!'

'Yes, it is. But it's likely, isn't it?' says Mother Nature. 'I mean, apart from the stories written about us, what do we know about where we came from, who we are, and why?'

'It's not as if we can ask anyone.'

'Yet we both know intrinsically, since our time began, that there is someone, or something, out there, watching us. That Being might be able to help us,' Mother Nature muses. 'The answers might help Lorenzo. They might also help mankind.'

'How on Planet Earth do we do that?' says God.

'I don't really know.' Mother Nature shrugs. 'But we could start at the beginning. Or rather *a* beginning. We could talk to Adam and Eve.'

'Oh, no, must we?' God groans. 'He'll go on and on about the tree, the apple, the rib, the wretched snake... And we'll be forced to eat apple pie, apple pudding, apple sponge, baked apple with roast apple and apple fritters ...'

'I'll make a treacle tart and custard, and a chocolate raisin cake with amoretto. That usually diverts them,' says Mother Nature, soothingly. 'Now, we'll have to think of some pertinent questions that might help uncover the truth.'

'Truth?' reflects God. 'Does anyone know what that means nowadays?'

'Let's put aside semantics and ethics for today. Let's sit

down with a cup of tea to think out our questions,' says Mother Nature.

'Are you coming home with Me?' God enquires nervously. 'To live with me?'

'If we're going to research and work together, as before, it would make sense if we live together, if that doesn't inconvenience you?'

God brushes feathers and crumbs from his trousers and thinks that he must make more of an effort for her sake.

'That suits me very well, dearest,' He says, deciding that He'll try out one of the outfits Petty Masters designed for him, none of which Mother Nature has seen. He ponders: yes, the white slacks, blue and white striped seersucker jacket, designer stubble, and black tartan sunglasses.

He smiles inwardly to Himself, imagining Dearest's utter delight at his smart new look.

2 MACNOODLE AND MACMINOR

Some might say that it wasn't a good idea to attempt the rescue of his pet haggoid, Ross, from the Dekaydence arena, given that a pitched and bloody battle was raging between determined gladiators and crazed glad'oids.

So when MacNoodle opens his eyes and finds he's surrounded by fluffy grey and white curtains and several oddly dressed people twanging harps and guitars while monitoring machines, his heart sinks, believing he's about to end his days in some kind of hippy hospital perhaps better equipped to take life rather than save it. So it comes somewhat as a relief to him to discover he's dead already and has arrived in Heaven. And joy of joys, Ross is by his side. MacNoodle hands Jack the hankie containing the nuts and bolts to mend Ross, who is then noisily and happily reunited with his twin, Cromarty. There are tears of delight and numerous friendly bite marks exchanged as the haggoids' joy is unbounded and unfettered.

A search party is sent out for empty tins and crisp packets as it becomes obvious that being in the state of heaven doesn't affect the haggoids' appetite one bit. Eventually, Jack visits the clowns and finds numerous discarded takeaway pizza packets and bagloads of empty cans of Blooza Jooza-Just for Yousa. From whence they came no one is quite sure, although Jack did espy a motorbike that could well belong to a Hell's Devil.

MacNoodle is soon back on his feet, and gets the two haggoids to help him clean up Heaven and the clowns' new extension. It is full-time work but the place is getting cleaner and tidier. And wherever they go Ross and Cromarty are thoroughly spoilt by all they encounter, from Archimedes to Emile Zola.

MacNoodle misses his friend MacMinor. But he keeps a regular eye on him, in his new job on Earth. And is comforted by the thought that one day they will meet up again.

MacMinor is asked to stay on in Rome, at the invitation of the (real) Pope, whose grandmother was a Scot, born and raised in North Berwick. His Eminence delights in MacMinor's company and knowledge, as well as his Scottish accent that reminds His Eminence of his grandma, her tales of childhood and sitting round a peat fire when hot porridge was laid in a drawer to be cut daily for a slice before school or work.

'No jam, no milk, no salt, no Sissynach [*sic*] additions. That's what my grandmother would say,' the Pope recalls, proudly, in a fair imitation of a tartan brogue.

Soon after, the Pope invites MacMinor to be his personal security guard. His Eminence is more than happy that his guard continues his art history studies with the Open University. In fact, MacMinor becomes so knowledgeable that he's often asked to give private guided tours to heads of state and commerce, and celebrities. He even gets an offer to appear in a Hollywood movie. But that's another story.

In time MacMinor and MacNoodle are reunited and exchange tears of joy and receive plenty of affectionate gnaws, oily licks and gentle bite-marks from the haggoids.

3 PETTY AND HUNKY, THE FACE AND SCHNEEK

Petty Masters continues to create designer clothes for a worldwide market of wild, whacky and wealthy people who are into extreme, new fashion. However, a subtle, elegant streak has crept into her work, in a collection of businesswear that joins Hunky Doré's equally elegant office range for men. Meanwhile, Schneek, working with Petty, is doing well with a baby range, and, under his own name, is proving highly successful with a rollerblade sportswear range.

Schneek has become a regular feature in the PMT/Doré household. He has grown to adore the three boys, who feel the same about him. But his workload has increased such that he has had to give up being their nanny. And when the three girls arrive on the scene so, too, does another nanny.

Schneek has an apartment not far from the PMT/ Doré house. He visits the house daily and is proud to be godparent to all six children. The girls are developing mottled black, tan and white skin resembling something akin to cheetahs or the black and white stripes of zebras. Schneek worries that this may limit their options in husband material. That said, further along the line there'll come a time when someone in the family will produce a spider'oid. And at some point, in another place, Lucretia will know and be ecstatic. Moreover, the new homo-spider'oid will have an interesting life. In the here and now, and the beyond.

Verona – better known as the Face; mostly unknown as Petty's sister – still has one of Hunky's spider black arms, which bothers her not at all. However, she spends a long time feeling lost. She has no work. She was head of the GeeZers, which collapsed, mostly because of her abrupt way of dealing with people. Now, alas, like most of today's youngsters she is finding it difficult to find work. Petty supports her sister, who has her own room in the family home. The Face is grateful but embarrassed at the kindness shown her by her sister. She so wants back her independence.

One day, after months of research and raising funds from doing odd jobs here, there and everywhere, the Face announces she is going to India, to work as a campaigner for women's rights. So that women, young and old, can walk the streets day and night without fear of being accosted, or worse. She wants to change society. To open the eyes of boys and men who consider women's worth as like a half-eaten discarded lollipop on the pavement, to be dropped, trodden on and kicked away.

'It'll be hard work,' says Petty. 'And potentially dangerous.'

'Possibly,' the Face replies. 'But it's more dangerous to ignore the problem. It won't go away unless something is done. Boys will grow into men, hardwired with a negative attitude towards women that could spread worldwide. Did you know that recent figures show that 90,000 cases of rape in India are still waiting to get to court?'

'Yes, I did know. But how long do you intend staying there?'

'As long as it takes,' the Face replies. 'So, don't forget to let me know when you're a grandmother.'

Petty starts to cry. Hunky Doré puts a comforting arm around his wife.

'Listen, honey-pot, I've been thinking of a trip to India for some time. So you tell me when you want to go, we'll go.'

'What about the children?'

'We'll take them, and the nannies.'

'And Schneek?'

'Of course, and Schneek. That goes without saying, honey-pot.'

'Thank you, you dear, kind man,' says Petty Masters, kissing her husband on the cheek.

He feels himself blush, to the tips of his fingers, both white and ebony.

4 GROUT AND INDIGO

Indigo and Grout are walking on the sand and pebble beach at Lyme Regis. Indigo wanted a weekend break and asked Grout if he would join her. He wants to pay his share but she insists that this is her treat.

'I'll take you to dinner on both nights,' says Grout. 'I won't hear otherwise.'

Indigo groans.

'I suddenly feel grown up. And it's a tad scary.' she says, somewhat dazed.

Grout laughs.

'You're in shock or recovery,' he says soberly. 'Look what you've experienced or done in a very short time. You've lost family, you've been crowned Queen, and you've spoken out about your ideas for the new monarchy...'

'And gained an enemy in Di'Abalo!' Indigo mutters.

'I wouldn't worry. He appears to have vanished off the face of the earth.'

'Do you know what's happening to Dekaydence? Will you be able to stay on and continue your research?'

'I don't know. Wiggins is investigating, thank goodness,' says Grout.

'Is he fully recovered?'

'He's not far off. But he can't get rid of the strong smell

of caramel. He's much concerned that guests at his son's wedding might object or even pass out.'

'I'll have a word with Lady C. I'm sure she'll be able to create some herbal remedy. Though caramel is a scent infinitely better than burning flesh.'

Indigo sees Nayr, her bodyguard, standing with two Red Tartan guards and their slavering haggoids. Further along the beach several Black Tartans guards struggle to control their powerful, slavering liz'oids.

'Grout,' says Indigo slowly.

'Majesty,' says Grout, with a slight bow.

'Stop that!' she says, blushing. 'Do you recall a question I put to you some months back?'

'Whether I wanted one spoon of sugar or three in my tea?'

'No!' she says, with a mock cross frown. 'Be serious – I asked if you'd marry me.'

'Oh, Indigo,' sighs Grout. 'If only I'd said yes that first time you asked.'

'Does that mean you've found someone else?' Indigo is taken aback, wondering if the reason for Grout's refusal is Maria.

'No, there's no one else,' says Grout.

'So what's the problem?'

Grout takes a deep breath.

'A while back I was in the laboratory when Di'Abalo showed up. I didn't tell you because I still can't take in what he said. You'd better sit down...'

She perches on a rock.

'I'm sorry, Indigo, but I can't marry you. Ever,' says Grout.

'Why not?' she demands.

'Because I am the son of Lorenzo di'Abalo. One of many, it would seem.'

'Is that all?' says Indigo, quietly indignant. 'I know it's weird! And creepy! 'Cos he's Ruby Q's father, too. But that doesn't make her or you a bad person, does it?'

'But if you and I had children...?'

'Grout,' says Indigo, 'my father was a drunk and a layabout. My grandfather was abominably sexist. Your parents haven't noticed you left home a year or so ago, and have moved abroad anyway. Lovable as they might or might not be, they're not what you'd consider to be ideal parental role models. But that's not going to interfere with my life. And I don't want my life to upset yours.'

'What do you mean?'

'I don't want to marry you, Grout. It's not that I don't love you. I do. What I want is for you to do your own thing — research. You can do so much for this world, Grout. Save the bees. Perhaps find a cure for Tommo and other teenagers like him who've passed through the White Room. Maybe you can find the cure to return Nigel to man size. So I don't want you wasting your time cutting ribbons, opening lavatories, listening to endless speeches, many of them mine, and all that. Cousin Will can do that.'

'So, what do you want from me?' says Grout, with a wry grin.

'I want us to be partners. I want us to have children together, I want—'

'Hang on. We might end up having children who take after their grandfather – Lorenzo di'Abalo.'

'Grout, look at yourself and Ruby Q Cooper. Neither of you show any resemblance to Di'Abalo. And what about me? Am I like my father or grandfather?'

Grout grins.

'In some good ways, Miss Bossy-Boots, you are like your grandfather, the King.'

'OK, says Indigo. 'There is a chance our children may inherit the worst of everyone in our history but I'd hope the two of us could nurture out the nasty, thoughtless bits.'

Grout shakes his head.

'I can't let you do this, Indigo. It contravenes what the Royal Family has stood for over centuries.'

'Grout, every so often the Royal Family needs an injection of fresh blood from a commoner,' Indigo replies sharply. 'Now is one of those times. It's genetic good health. Either that or we get a supply from a friendly, healthy vampire.'

Grout chuckles, and considers for a moment.

'OK, Indigo,' he says at last. 'For genetic purposes and to stop any possibility of you dabbling with vampires, will you *not* marry me?'

'Yes, Grout,' she replies crisply.

'So...do we live together?'

'If you like.'

Grout adopts a thoughtful Rodin-esque pose.

'I think I could do that,' he says, with a considered nod followed by a grin.

'Excellent!' she says, showering him with a scoop of water from a rock pool. 'And that is your *not* coronation as my official partner!'

He laughs as he shakes his head dry, scans the rough beach and picks up a pebble.

'I don't know your position on rings, not that I have one on me, but I wonder if you'd accept this pebble as a symbol of our union?'

'Most kind,' she says, gazing at it. 'Especially as you've chosen the most beautiful pebble on the beach.'

'I never saw you as a pebble,' says Grout teasingly, 'but now you mention it...'

She goes to throw more water at him when he scoops her up in his arms and carries her back to the car.

Indigo contacts the nice young man at the TV studio to ask if she can make a short broadcast some time soon. He is flattered by her direct call and they confirm a date. And so she announces her partnership and introduces Grout as a hard-working young man who has given her much support over several difficult years. They sit side by side on a sofa in a private, elegant room at the Goring Hotel in London, awash with the delicate scent of white lilies in a large vase by the window, answering questions from a distinguished journalist, known to her friends as Spiky Hair.

Later, formal oaths of the civil commitment to the country are taken by the Queen in front of a plethora of heads of state. There follows a formal banquet at which Will and Wiggins sit on either side of Indigo. The proceedings are broadcast.

A party takes place in the Kent countryside with spectacular views of the sea. It's a private affair attended only by friends – including Will, Piccolo, Ruby Q, Nigel, Tommo, the Catguts, Edwina Gardening-Fork, Young Miss Burgess, Maria and the NoBrMi, a trio of Indigo's beloved cousins.

Piccolo plays a new composition dedicated to the Queen, which triggers a few tears of joy and happiness. And like many a wedding, civil ceremony, party or funeral, the occasion triggers reunions and re-ignites friendships.

5 CLAUD CANAPÉ

'Zis is terrible. 'ow did it happen?' Claud Canapé demands in his heavily accented English. 'In fact, all zis is, *actuellement*, to the detriment of humankind.'

Gods shrugs. He's not the least clue what the *homme* is talking about, accent or no accent.

Luckily, or unluckily, He returned a large part of His brain (including all languages) to the third-floor library for a well-earned rest before meeting up with the garrulous Canapé, who is now expostulating and waving his arms about in true Gallic style (TTT, *édition française*).

On Earth, Canapé had been a designer and architect to the rich and famous. In Heaven, he has taken it upon himself to redesign much more.

'Look at this!' says Canapé, prodding a drawing. 'The Great White Shark and his relatives – rows of teeth. If one on the outer working edge goes it is replaced quickly by another. So, fewer problems; less expensive dental treatment for mankind.'

'I see,' says God, playing for time to keep up.

'And what about ze large birds of prey? They have eyes capable of far more resolution than ours. Imagine, no sat-nav, no corrective surgery, no spectacles. You see your supper two kilometres away on a plate on a table outside the village inn.'

'Good point,' says God, warming slowly to the theme.

'And I do not understand why in that wretched fridge-freezer of a northern hemisphere no one knows much about keeping warm at night. This could save money and resources simultaneously. All it comes down to is having, all over our bodies, a full and glossy coat of hair.'

'I see where you're coming from,' says God, nodding slowly and sagely.

'And if animals can sense the presence of objects in darkness, why can't we? We wouldn't need expensive electronic equipment. Tell me,' Canapé commands, 'why on Earth or in Heaven doesn't your technical department talk with your design department and human resources?'

God shakes his head.

'Possibly because Mother Nature would be talking to herself three times over,' God sighs. 'But perhaps it's better you don't tell her I said that.'

6 THE CATGUTS

The Catguts recognise they are getting older and decide the time has come to downsize. The adopted and extended family of Grout, Piccolo, Nigel, Maria, Ruby Q, the Martin family and Indigo are quite taken aback.

'But you can't move,' cries Maria. 'This is home. You love it. And we love it, too.'

'It's not a decision for us to make,' says Grout firmly. 'It's for Lord and Lady Catgut.'

'Is it the cooking, the cleaning, the Tower of Eden, or what, Lady C?' Indigo asks.

'It's everything, dear,' says Lady Catgut, matter-of-factly. 'We're getting on in years. Creaking bones. Memory and limbs rusting up. We'd love to stay here but, as Catgut says, we've got to be sensible and move to a smaller place we can manage without help.'

'First I've heard of Catgut being sensible,' says Edwina Gardening-Fork, when she's told the news by Ruby Q.

Ruby Q grins. Then an idea occurs to her that she puts to the Fork.

'Excellent idea, dear,' says the Fork. 'See what they think.'

And so it comes to pass that the old boathouse used for years as a storeroom and spare room (where Cage hid when on the run from the police) is renovated. Bathroom and shower upstairs and down. A kitchen on the ground floor; a kitchenette upstairs. Indigo helps Lady C with the décor, which Lady C decides must be modern and comfortable but not clinical (which would upset Catgut). So the two women choose a main furnishing colour of soft dove grey, with splashes of purple and aquamarine for cushions, curtains and tiebacks.

When he sees what has been done Catgut is speechless. He is soothed by an examination of the new power shower in the wet room and a deep wallow in a comfortable armchair with a glass of good red wine, and then...

It's the new study that does it. Catgut never said anything but all knew he was sad to leave the old study that had journeyed with him over decades.

So when he is shown his new study with its recording studio, floor-to-ceiling patio doors overlooking the gardens and the river...Catgut realises he's arrived in heaven (on earth, in this case). He tinkers with almost every gadget in the new room before sitting down to play the piano.

As they come and go from the old house into the new with packaging boxes galore the Catguts' 'family' applaud and cheer him. It's only when he senses the house is quiet and empty that Catgut allows himself tears. How odd, he thinks, he has cried in dreadful, desperate times and now he is crying for joy.

He's startled by the entrance of Lady Catgut carrying a

tray of tea and home-made cakes and wearing a beaming smile.

'Etti, dearest,' Catgut says enthusiastically, blowing his nose. 'I've decided I'm going to be a bright semi-breve rather than an old crotchet.'

'Jolly good,' says Lady Catgut, handing him a mug of tea and a piece of his favourite fruit cake.

Catgut takes a bite of cake and sighs with delight. This isn't just heaven. This is heaven de luxe.

7 THE MARTIN FAMILY

As politicians are obliged now to pant out (for free) a higher rate of hot air in Parliament to feed the National Grid, they feed their pension funds with extra-curricular business, mostly with foreign agents, which enables them to invest in multi-million-pound properties at home and abroad. It makes hard times harder for many, including the Martin family.

Mrs Martin, accused of physical assault by an eight-year old child (as likely as a blizzard of chocolate ice-cubes in the Saharan desert) is sacked from her long-term teaching post in a single-faith school – despite witnesses swearing there was no assault, despite police saying there is no case to answer.

Mrs Martin is in shock, and comes close to a breakdown. She worries about losing an income and frets that such an accusation will make it nigh on impossible to get work elsewhere. So the system – if it can be described thus – and the children within it lose a first-class teacher and a good educational and social foundation.

Expecting her children to leave home at any time Mrs Martin decides she will run a bed-and-breakfast from the house. She will offer home-grown, home-made food. And hopefully, being on a direct rail link to London and the airports, she can expect business to be good. Necessary amendments and furnishings are undertaken.

The economic climate isn't good for almost everyone, young people included. Cage and Waat can't find suitable rented accommodation for themselves and baby Jake. Cage manages the business affairs of Kane, his actor brother who lives in the US, which gives him a small income, some of which pays fees needed for Waat, who's training to qualify as a nurse. In time, she'll become a matron of a local hospital and a powerful campaigner within the NHS for prioritising gold standard patient care.

Taylor makes more money as a model than an actress. She considers a regular nine-to-five office job, but where and how to get one? Her agent calls. There's a role in a film being shot in California with several big American names. She stays in Santa Monica with her brother Kane. She gets another film offer and the two siblings sing together at gigs. Taylor tries to repay Ruby Q, who'd bought Taylor's plane tickets and much else beside. A friendly squabble ensues and the money goes to Ruby Q's charity – helping unemployed youngsters find work, and recruiting volunteers to help the lonely and elderly.

Taylor will stay in contact always with Ruby Q, who will interview her friend for a prestigious magazine – as once they dreamt.

The eldest Taylor offspring, Meryl, is producing wondrous metal sculptures but needs a larger customer base. She gets it, courtesy of another artist, Ruby Q's aunt, Lily. Meryl's star will rise and shine and win her awards and accolades.

Mr Martin gets freelance marketing work from Edwina Gardening-Fork and tip-offs from Spiky Hair. Then he meets someone, by chance, in a Fleet Street pub. They chat, have a few drinks and within an hour are firm friends. Mr Martin is intrigued by the young man's investment projects as well as his liquor-buying generosity. So though he knows little of the specifics, Mr Martin buys heavily into the scheme – on borrowed money.

Cage takes Waat and Baby Jake to visit the Catguts in their new apartment. Cage marvels at the newly refurbished place that had been his refuge not that long ago.

A few visits on, Cage reveals to the Catguts that Waat has asked him to marry her. Cage is beside himself with happiness. He confides that he has always felt himself second best to Jack but now... Catgut asks him where they propose to live.

'Not sure of Mum's B&B opening date but we must move out soon,' says Cage. 'We have a baby on the way.'

'Wonderful!' cries Lady Catgut, clapping her hands together. 'Why not move here? Into the main house? There's plenty of room for half a dozen babies, if you so decide. What do you think, Catty?'

'Marvellous idea, Etti, darling,' says Catgut. 'Our family extends still further. Another wee grandson. If I may be so bold, Waat.'

'You may, sir,' says Waat, 'except it might be a girl.' It isn't but there will be boys and girls among the children they have, as well as those they foster and adopt.

'I don't know how to say thank you,' says Cage. 'I hope you don't think we had it in mind when we came to see you. And, please, we shall pay you rent — otherwise we can't take up your kind offer.'

Waat nods her agreement and smiles as she sees her son attempting to nod.

'We'll discuss it anon,' says Lady Catgut. 'But first have a look round. See what you think. We won't be offended if you choose to go elsewhere.'

'Well, I, for one, shall be most offended if you say no,' says Catgut, affecting haughtiness as his eyes twinkle.

Returning home, Cage, Waat and Baby Jake encounter Mr Martin on the front doorstep, shaking hands with a departing visitor. Cage sees an envelope pass into the hands of the young man, who he recognises but can't be sure from where. The young man with shifty eyes hastily departs the scene.

'Who's that?' Cage asks his father, as Waat takes the baby inside.

'My new business partner,' Mr Martin replies, with a satisfied smile. 'Soon riches will fall from the sky and I'll be able to keep your mother in the luxury she deserves, courtesy of that young man.'

'How come, Dad? Who is he? What does he do?'

Mr Martin taps his nose.

'*Entre nous*, old man, that young man is now in charge of the Dekaydence laboratory. He's been stocktaking. And he's found a pile of documents and test tubes that point to a treasure trove and more beside.'

Cage frowns. He can't recall who the young man is. He soon finds out.

'I never trusted that young man,' Waat informs him later. 'A so-called friend of my half-brother Innit. I was glad when In found God and goodness and drifted away from his so-called friend. Just as well, given what I heard the other day. That young man who worked for Dekaydence now works for Randall Candelskin. That means he's still up to no good. That's what he was always up to when I knew him as Big Bully Bodkin.'

8 RUBY Q

Ruby Q works as a reporter on the *Daily News* – formerly the Dekaydence *Daily Unigraph*, now a newspaper and website run as a workers' co-operative that is financed largely by Jarvis, its Deputy Editor. Spiky Hair is the Editor and Spiky Hair's friend The Suit is a popular columnist and blogger and remains happily a man about town and free lunches.

Ruby Q works undercover with the Phoenix, exposing corruption and cruelty worldwide. She never meets him. No one does. They communicate only under the wire. But she keeps him informed of how Maria is doing, which is pretty well. Maria is studying for qualifications that will enable her to work in Piccolo's schools of MAT – Music As Therapy – in Sussex and Scotland. Piccolo is proud of his work with her, and the 'mending' work she now does with others. Her brother, the Phoenix, is proud, too. From time to time Maria receives a book. There is never a note, or an address, not even a word. She knows that's the way it is and understands why but...

Occasionally, Ruby Q gets depressed at the amount of bad news there is in the world. So, with the support of The Suit, she tries to find at least one happy story every month for the paper. One day, a happy story finds her.

It's a love story written by Elsa, her non-grandmother, who, with her beloved dog, has now passed on. And suddenly there's an unexpected rumbling of interest in Elsa's work. Her radio plays, stage productions and film scripts. As and when and if anything happens, Wiggins has a lawyer friend who specialises in the entertainment industry and will help her out. Ruby Q isn't holding her breath but when it does actually happen...

Visits from Mr and Mrs Treasure have tailed off. Courtesy of their holy natural powers, Ruby Q's memory has erased the time spent with them as God and Mother Nature. She recalls a friendly woman in Rome and a grubby old gardener, or was he a cleaner, in the arena? She does see, albeit irregularly, Edwina Gardening-Fork and her friend, young Miss Burgess – the two who helped her in many various ways and have now caught the travelling bug and don't want to lose it.

She keeps in close touch with, and visits, Will, Piccolo, Grout and Nigel. Indigo she sees less frequently. Understandable, given that being Queen is a full-time, lifetime job, with few tea breaks. Although when the two young women do meet they enjoy planning how they can build a better world, full of Towers of Eden.

After a few years her mother's lawyer, Wiggins, writes to advise her of her inheritance. They can assume, he says, that her mother has died on her voyage into the galaxy, which is where her inheritance lies. Somehow Angelica Nera has gained control of vast mineral wealth on other planets that now cede to her daughter, who realises she must again come to terms with losing her mother.

'No one as yet has the power or the finance to do anything about it,' Ruby Q tells Wiggins distractedly. 'I don't have children and am unlikely to have any. So I'd prefer to leave it all to the world, for projects to help health and education, music and sport, to research and grow sustainable, natural crops and fuels.'

'Admirable idea, Ruby Q,' says Wiggins. 'But best leave it for now as it is. You are young. You and the world may change faster than you think.'

Ruby Q frowns.

'Except I want to be a philanthropist. I want to help others.'

Wiggins smiles.

'How about I come back to you after I work out a compromise. I help you to be the philanthropist. You agree to be helped by me on the basis I want to protect you in case of an uncertain future.'

Ruby Q considers and agrees. She sells the old family home and moves to a small riverside flat in London. Her father, suffering from dementia, lives in a specialist care home in Sussex where he's visited regularly not only by his daughter but by her friends who live close by. He stays with Ruby Q when she's not working and they walk along the Embankment or through Hyde Park. Sometimes they take in a concert or two, when Rallan smiles throughout or weeps silently.

She has all but lost the man who was her father in every way except biologically. As she has lost a mother she never really knew. But then she looks around her and sees Indigo, Will, Grout, Maria, Piccolo, the Phoenix, the Martin family, the Catguts *et al* – all have lost someone close through no fault of their own. While Tommo has lost himself, through the workings of Dekaydence. But all carry on as best they can.

Ruby Q tells herself that she must remind herself of this whenever she feels alone or lonely. Tragedy, loss and death visit everyone, every heart, every home. Even a house move to another location, a friend moving a distance away, can feel like bereavement. We don't forget those whom we have lost. We carry on missing them. Our feelings for them don't change. That is the reason we mourn. That is the power of love.

9 HOH RANDALL CANDELSKIN

Candelskin doesn't appear in public for some considerable time. Rumours abound. Spiky Hair heard that he was having a nervous breakdown. Certainly, no one can reach him by phone or internet, or the front door that remains steadfastly shut.

It's when Ruby Q revisits the British Library – to research Rome, Vatican City and the Di'Abalo family – that she comes across him. She gets a whiff of the pungent exclusive celeb and royalty aftershave, Dekaydence 321. Then she sees him sitting with his head in his hands. Quite still. Possibly asleep.

There's an unoccupied seat next to him on the line of desks. She sits down, takes a notebook from her bag and begins writing.

She is lost in research when the chair next to her scrapes across the floor. She looks up. Candelskin is standing behind his chair, looking at her with a blank expression. His face is pale, his cheeks sunken, his hair tousled. He is dressed, unusually, ultra-casual, in faded chinos and an old denim jacket.

'Coffee, Miss Cooper?' he says hopefully.

'OK,' she replies, seeing relief as well as sadness in his expression.

He buys two coffees and they sit outside in the warm sunshine close to the magnificent bronze statue of Paolozzi.

'That's based on William Blake's study of Isaac Newton, underlining how Newton's equations showed that the world is determined by mathematical laws,' says Candelskin, almost to himself.

Neither speaks for some minutes. Candelskin stares into space, seemingly oblivious to her presence.

She coughs.

'You don't seem yourself, Mr Candelskin.'

He turns to her in a daze.

'My dog died,' he says in a wavering voice. 'I had him for years. My best friend. My baby. I don't know how I'm going to live without him.'

'I am sorry,' says Ruby Q.

Candelskin nods.

'He was always there on the mat, waiting for me. He knew my voice, my footstep, the car engine, the sound of my key in the door, as well as the opening of the fridge door... He was the most extraordinary beast.'

'I bet he knew he was a lucky dog to have such a caring dad. I bet he knew he'd fallen on all four paws.'

Candelskin stares into the middle distance and smiles ruefully.

'We spoke on the phone every day, even when I was away.'

Ruby Q nods.

'When the police brought me home from the conference, I found him there, lying on the mat, dead but still warm.' Candelskin's voice is unsteady.

'Gosh, what a shock! But how did the police know your dog had died?'

Candelskin looks surprised.

'They didn't. How could they?'

'But you said they'd come for you.'

'Yes. That was to tell me my mother had died. A neighbour saw her collapse in the garden while she was picking roses.'

'Oh, I am so sorry. How frightful for you.'

Candelskin sighs.

'Yes,' he agrees. 'It is. Or was. But it's the dog I miss the most. That sounds terrible, doesn't it?'

'I've heard that's not unusual,' says Ruby Q, 'but working with the churches will pull you through.'

'No longer,' says Candelskin, with a small, quick smile. 'I thought you of all people would have heard – I've resigned. Too much red tape. Too many control freaks. And in my world the rule is I must be the only control freak.'

'Gosh, so where do you go now? You've done PR and marketing, politics, the Church – what's left? Farming?'

Candelskin laughs, as he eyes her intently.

'I always thought you the clever one, Miss Cooper. Farming it is! Minerals in the sky, fortunes on earth! All to save our failing, depleted planet.'

'Except it'll be years before someone works out how

it can be mined and transported to earth economically,' says Ruby Q.

'Years?' says Candelskin, with the sly-wise smile she recalls so well. 'Not necessarily.'

She waits for him to explain.

'I am working with foreign developers on an idea that's been initiated here.'

He hesitates, noting Ruby Q's interest, but decides not to tell her, as yet, that he knows she will inherit the rights to many valuable minerals in the galaxy, and probably more in galaxies beyond, due to her mother's astute negotiations when travelling through space on Dekaydence business.

'It's down to one man,' Candelskin continues enthusiastically. 'Our scientific home-grown Dekaydence genius.'

'You mean Grout?' says Ruby Q, taken aback.

'Spot on, again, Miss Cooper! Yes, Grout. By chance he has found a DNA sequence that will help launch this work within a few years.'

'It must be very special DNA.'

'Oh, it is, Miss Cooper, it is very special. In fact, it's beyond unique. It is DNA from an everlasting source.'

'How can that be?' Ruby Q looks puzzled.

Candelskin looks around suspiciously before whispering in her ear.

'I know I can trust you, Miss Cooper, not to tell anyone what I'm about to tell you,' he says. 'We are working with the DNA of the Phoenix.'

10 THE NOTEIANS

The Noteian – shot by a sniper while standing on the catafalque in the arena, trying to save the Phoenix – was Driver. He'd flashed a document at the guards showing Di'Abalo's permission to take the Phoenix immediately and urgently to hospital. He nearly succeeded in his plan but didn't realise the Phoen'oid was in front of him, creating an invisible barrier to prevent anyone getting close to the Phoenix. And that MacCavity quickly learnt from Di'Abalo that Driver's documentation was false.

So it is Driver who is rushed to hospital. Handcuffs speeds across London, alerting other Noteian specialists along the way. Six of them are gowned up by the time he arrives. But it is too late. Driver never regains consciousness. For some time afterwards Handcuffs feels he, too, is unconscious, except when any thought of his closest friend comes into his mind. They had been like brothers. And the pain of loss is excruciating. It is physical pain as well as mental. Handcuffs feels he'll never recover.

But, little by little, he does. It is a struggle but he is a fighter. The bruise of loss will always be there, he knows. But he owes it to his friend and to himself to carry on. But how? He is the same person but he is different. From now on he will lead a different life. He will return to medicine but he must also find something else to do.

Noteian friends support him, as do the families of both Driver and Handcuffs, knowing and savouring the deep friendship of the two young men. Will introduces Handcuffs to North and his associates. Gradually, Handcuffs sees a way into a new and worthy life. As with North, he will meet someone like-minded and his life will begin to bud again and then blossom with friendship and love. And in time he will name his son in memory of his Noteian friend, Driver, by his given name, Noah. He'll never forget his best friend, his brother with whom he shared everything except religion and death.

11 MACCAVITY

As the future of Dekaydence remains uncertain, MacCavity returns home to Scotland. He no longer wants to take orders from anyone. Ideally, he'd be happy walking the beaches of North Berwick with Lucretia at his side. But he accepts it'll be a long time before a giant spider'oid is accepted into the 'walking the dog' community. So he sets up as a mercenary, with six trusted former Black Tartan guards, and visits unsettled areas of the globe, i.e. almost anywhere beyond Bognor Regis.

MacCavity will also work increasingly as a personal bodyguard, as do Sid and Nayr.

But for the time being MacCavity walks the beaches on moonless nights when Lucretia will not be seen.

12 MCCARBON

McCarbon, MacCavity's former deputy, is glad to be out of Dekaydence. The place unsettled him in too many ways. He didn't fit in, and others made him only too aware of the fact. Now he is in charge of an exclusive shopping mall where, overall, people are well mannered and friendly. He enjoys the order in his life and work. He works hard and enjoys a settled family life, with regular walking holidays at home and abroad. His family is much relieved. It is so good to hear him laugh again.

13 HILLI

Hilli, the Face's minder, goes to live for a time in an eco-commune he comes across when travelling with Will, North and East. (South and West having gone off in their own direction). It's not far from the Catguts' and when he visits Lady Catgut for gardening advice he takes his guitar and musical skills to help the troubled youngsters being treated by Piccolo and Maria.

14 COMPRENDO

Comprendo and his sidekicks – who kidnapped the Face before agreeing to work under her guidance – now work in the building trade, through contacts of Petty Masters. They receive funding to help young unemployed people back into work from a charitable foundation set up by Ruby Q and supported by the photographer Lars Sparks. They work with different builders – good 'uns and bad 'uns – who, nevertheless, all go to the pub on a Friday night for beer, skittles and crack (that's conversation with an Irish accent). Eventually, they find good, strong-minded women and produce rumbustious children much like themselves at the same age. They all have rescue dogs they adore and make part of the family. Occasionally, Comprendo does gigs as a children's conjuror and clown. He gets his equipment from a small shop in Bognor Regis and meets a wide variety of clowns.

15 BODKIN

Bodkin wears expensive clothes to expensive restaurants, bars and champagne clubs. Work is going exceedingly well for him. He has fingers in many pies. If only he had more fingers, he thinks, and, for a few minutes, he ponders a Hunky Doré-style operation. At the moment he hasn't the time. He's investing heavily in Candelskin's sky mining mineral projects and, on the quiet, he's taking lessons in elocution, etiquette and ballroom dancing. Bods has become a social climber, and has the polished shoes and skilled political footwork to accomplish much. His connection with his old friend Innit is tenuous and rusting. But should anything go wrong, it'll be Innit to whom Bodkin turns for help.

16 LARS SPARKS

Lars Sparks – the photographer who dresses in black designer slacks, sweater and loafers – is completing a coffee-table book on up-market gardens and grand 'floral' displays. The computer book speed-grows a reader's choice of flowers and plants, which readers pick, scent, examine and pay for before planting their purchases into their garden that very day. (It must be said – mustn't it? – that a handsome chunk of Lars Sparks's earnings that used to help the GeeZers now goes to help Ruby Q's charity for the young unemployed, the lonely and the elderly.)

Lars has also taken on the jobless Dekaydence Irish gardener Killivy, whose enthusiasm for the book project knows no bounds. Lars does the research; Killivy provides information on the flora. The two travel together, staying in local hostelries (at Lars's expense) and share their stories in the evening over supper and a drink. They're both solitary men but they rub along well together. Perhaps because both understand the importance and value of silence, and of listening.

17 INNIT

Innit is walking a very different path that involves social consciousness, prison visiting and not inconsiderable hardship. He visits children in schools, talks about the importance of love and commitment to self and others; the importance of choosing a career that inspires. He visits the elderly and infirm in hospital and at home, taking flowers and friendship, and chocolate biscuits. And he prays – regularly and privately – to and for Jezza, the woman he has come to realise that he loved and loves still. At this stage it seems improbable he will settle down with anyone.

He receives a letter from Wiggins advising him of a legacy left to him by Cataract. Innit is taken aback. Why? How? Guilt sits within him. Wiggins invites him to his office. They talk about the Cataract they knew and then...

Innit admits that he has been a mean, grasping young man. And, he knows, much worse, and feels unable to divulge this except to God. It was losing his girlfriend that made him realise he must save the girl called Maria from a life of degradation. And that took him in the direction of God. Not a specific god. Not a god with a rucksack of rules. No, a being that has shown him the path of doing good that he discovers makes him feel good, too. So Innit puts Cataract's legacy to good use – helping others. It's not long before Wiggins decides to deal with the administration of Ruby Q's charity, Lars and Innit's charities, and the one set up by Handcuffs, in memory of his beloved Noteian friend, Noah, and called Noah's Musical Ark, which helps youngsters adrift in the world.

18 WILL AND PICCOLO

Indigo's decision to have a small, private gathering of friends and family (excepting Grout's family who have moved abroad, leaving no forwarding address) enables a happy happening to take place. So it's nigh impossible for Piccolo to avoid encountering Will. He tries, of course, but fails. It's only later, much later, he explains at length to Will that the reason he's done his best to avoid his friend was to ensure God kept up his end of the bargain Piccolo made with Him: that he, Piccolo, keeping well away from Will, would (somehow) ensure that God would keep Will safe.

'I can't believe someone of your age and life experience believes in all that tosh,' says Will, his normal dour expression replaced with eyes bright with joy that he's sitting next to his long-lost friend.

'You make me sound like a war veteran,' says Piccolo.

'You are, in many ways,' says Will. 'In fact, we all are.'

'What will you do now there's talk of closing down Dekaydence?'

'Wiggins is working with CCM to decide its future. But I'm not going to hang around to see what happens. I want to take Tommo back home to Scotland.'

'What about Grout's work on him?'

'That will continue. Scotland's only next door, you know.'

'And what will you do in Scotland?'

'Ach, human life has arrived there, Pix. Bakers, libraries, shops, BBC Radio 4, the *Today* programme, corn plasters, all that sort of thing. It's all there. So I'll help manage the estate. But now Grout, North and I have read so much more on climate change and the need to think about and address problems now...

'We must research how to improve sustainability as opposed to going along with the idea that climate change is man-made. I want to work with North on community projects and, as much as I can, I want to support Indigo when she's on "official" duty. And I want to take Tommo back to his loch, see if he can sail and fish like he used to.'

Piccolo sighs.

'Sounds idyllic.'

'It is.' Will hesitates. 'Want to join me?'

'Yes,' says Piccolo, with no hesitation. 'It's what I've dreamt of for a long time.'

Luckily, having lost none of his mariner's skills, Tommo is in his element, regularly sailing the loch in his boat, *The Black Dog*, with Will and Piccolo.

'This is the life,' says Piccolo, lying on his back, enjoying the warm summer sun on his face and body. 'I could get used to this.'

He takes a drink and another sandwich from the hamper.

'No more music?' Will enquires, with a grin.

Piccolo looks at him in mock disdain.

'Will, there will always be music. I couldn't live without it.'

'And your music therapy centres?'

'Yeah, they're important to me. Man, if I can help kids and adults, show them they can quit the bottom of the heap where I lived for so long...show them they can get a life...I'll know I've done something with mine.'

'You've done a lot already. Check the list of your compositions.'

'I can't help but make music. Helping people is different. It's about giving, isn't it? Who'd have thought it? A slum kid with nothing but desperate need, I've found a real joy in giving to others.'

When the call comes from the police that his mother is in hospital and close to death, Piccolo hesitates.

'I know you don't want to go,' says Will. 'But think how you might feel if you miss saying goodbye.'

Piccolo shrugs.

'Why should I care about her, man? She killed my father. She abused me for years. She ruined my life, everything.'

'On the other hand, maybe your life wouldn't have turned out like this.'

'So you think I should thank her for all she did for me?'

'No.'

For a moment Will is silent.

'Look, you don't have to say anything, Pix. But maybe being there would help you let go. I don't know. I don't think there's an absolute right or wrong. It's something only you can work out and decide. Whatever you do, I'll support you.'

'If you were me, would you go?'

'I really don't know. I think I'd be the same as you... undecided.'

The ward is plain and dull. The one picture on the wall is dull and unmemorable. There are six beds in the room, all occupied by elderly women. All but one is silent, staring into space. A radio blares out a mess of voices but no one listens. One patient cries out repeatedly and is ignored.

Piccolo shudders. The atmosphere feels as inviting as a room full of cold custard.

A nurse, without lifting her head, waves him off in a direction. He finds his mother in a side room in a grey bed that reminds him of a popular TV prison series. She is connected to various machines that wink out data. Her eyes are staring and unblinking as he sits down beside her on an uncomfortable plastic chair.

He hesitates to take her hand that is resting on the bedcover a few inches from his. He sits forward. She has become an old woman, he realises. Her once thick black mane is faded, thin and matted; a city road map has furrowed routes across her face. She is wearing an oxygen mask, kept roughly in place with a thick piece of tape. The tape's edge curls away from the eye, which is now bleeding. Only later he discovers it was the wrong tape, in the wrong place, that cut open her eye. Later, he will be angry and decide to take action. Later still, he will decide to do nothing and get on with his own life, as his dad would have chivvied him to do.

A jug of water sits on the bedside cabinet. Piccolo fills a cracked plastic beaker and wonders how any one of the elderly women in the ward could ever lift such a heavy jug. He soon sees that the women wait in vain.

He wonders. Who had the worse death? His father or mother? Violent but quick? Or slow and torturous? There's little to choose between the two, he considers, dourly.

'Mum, it's Piccolo,' he whispers.

Nothing happens. She doesn't stir.

'Mum, I've come to say goodbye.'

He draws closer to her, and puts his hand over hers.

'Mum, it's time to say goodbye.'

He feels his hand gripped tight.

'I don't want to die, boy.' Her speech is blurred with sobs, her eyes are brimful of fear.

'It happens to us all,' he whispers in return.

'I's scared, boy,' she replies. 'I done you wrong. Now I's scared to meet my Maker. And your dad.'

What can he say that doesn't sound critical or false?

He grips her hand in return.

Her eyes are open but focusing on nothing.

'I goin' blind,' she cries, her trembling voice so soft he can barely hear her. 'Go do good, boy. Forget me and my bad ways. Go mix with good people.'

Her eyes are staring. Her skin is paling, the energy in her eyes diminishing.

His hand tightens on hers.

'Mum?' He tries gently to urge an answer from her.

'Mum? Mum, can you hear me?'

He's aware of the rising drumbeat of his heart. What does he do? What does he say? Don't let her go yet. Not quite yet. This is an important moment and he feels helpless. Think, idiot, he commands himself. Think. What might he say if the roles were reversed?

'Safe journey, Mum,' he whispers softly to her. 'Safe journey.'

He sits with his mother in silence, holding her hand, thinking over his past. The bruises inflicted, inside and out. The love of and for his father. If he had had a 'normal' childhood... But what is normal? And how many children experience 'normal'?

He is deep in thought when he feels a hand on his shoulder, and starts.

He turns, removing his hand from his mother's, and puts his hand over Will's. He smiles, seeing his present and, hopefully, his future.

BREAKING NEWS

Charlie, a child under five, is murdered by his mother and her partner, after suffering months of physical and mental abuse, beatings, punches and being held under cold water in a bath until he's unconscious. He's also been starved and force-fed salt.

Schoolteachers watched a bonny, bright-eyed little boy turn, within a few months, into a concentration-camp lookalike, a wizened old man, the light gone from his being. They saw Charlie's black eyes, his body a bag of bones. They watched as he scavenged for discarded food in bins and sandpits, devouring the remains of a pear, a half-eaten sandwich covered in sand, grit and ants. They smelt the scent of stale urine on his shabby unwashed clothes.

His mother told the school Charlie had an eating disorder and mustn't be fed, and they believed her. When Charlie broke his arm the couple convinced the police that he'd been playing about on a dining chair. Neighbours heard Charlie crying out several times in the night and thought he was having nightmares.

The fact was Charlie's life had become a living nightmare. When he returned home from school he was locked in a tiny room that had no toys, no pictures on

LIVE FROM AN ILLEGAL INTERNET SERVICE PROVIDER

the wall, no drawing pads, no books, no blankets, just an old thin mattress that he was forced to use as a lavatory. When his mother and her partner discovered Charlie's siblings were opening the door to bring Charlie into their room the doorhandle was removed.

So Charlie dies, four years old, weighing as little as an 18-month-old toddler. He dies from a blow to the head, one of the thirty-odd blows his body had received in recent months. He dies because his mother and partner planned to kill him. He dies because the system designed to protect him fails him, utterly and completely.

19 PICCOLO AND WILL

Piccolo weeps as he reads Charlie's story. It so easily could have been his story. Except he'd got lucky. He'd lived long enough to be physically and mentally strong enough to make good his escape. He'd got lucky some more. He'd met Will who had saved his life. He'd met Rallan, who'd cared for him when they'd both been held hostage by Dekaydence. He'd met Lady Catgut, who'd invited him to live in her home, where he'd learnt he could return, as well as receive, care and love.

Piccolo reads that an official inquiry will be set up to examine how and why Charlie died. Will shakes his head. There have been inquiries over the years that have found faults but not solved the problem. He sets about research with Ruby Q, who talks to her boss, Spiky Hair, who talks to a handful of level-headed contacts in places, high and low.

They wonder the lack of meals in the school where Charlie was a pupil. Wasn't that a simple but effective way of watching over children's health, welfare and safety, ensuring youngsters from poor families got fed at least one square meal a day? If that's a cutback, what is its priority in saving – money or lives?

Why isn't communication – or should that be

community, and/or common sense – happening between schools, social and health workers, and the police? Whatever happened to community where neighbours see, hear and smell things of concern, and report it to those in a position to deal with such a problem? Where are the police in charge of our communities? Do they have an up-to-date list of the 'right' contacts?

Not to worry, having cut costs in this area, a government produces a hefty 'help' document that some years later is reduced by 75 per cent. Heavens above! If a life is endangered, isn't a page of A4 enough for emergency and non-emergency contact details in each 'support' area? Maybe the other side of the page can include a few common-sense procedures?

Piccolo recalls social workers visiting his home. He was locked in the bathroom. He had orders, underlined heavily with threats, to be silent. He chewed on a bar of soap; he was too frightened to call out for help. Mostly, the social workers were young and inexperienced. His mother ran rings round them. (He was in awe of her performance of lies.) The social workers had little or no experience, seemingly little training or support to know how to deal with devious carers.

Piccolo reads how vital information isn't passed on. A child dies. Another Charlie. Murders continue: every year some fifty to seventy children are killed by their parents or carers.

Anger takes hold of him. Charlie's carers must be

punished, he decides. They'll get prison terms but what use is that? What use do their lives have? Apart from using up taxpayers' hard-earned money. It's the new norm: the innocent pay for the guilty. Piccolo gets angrier. He goes for long walks, sometimes with Will, sometimes without. One day, on the spur of the moment, he contacts Sid. They talk about Charlie.

'Man, if I was in charge,' says Piccolo, 'I'd make them suffer the abuse they dished out to the little lad. Then I'd leave them to die, like they left him.'

'You're not alone in that feeling,' says Sid quietly.

'So would you be prepared ...?' Piccolo enquires.

'No,' Sid responds, emphatically. 'No. And if you're asking what I think you're about to ask, best we stop talking right now.'

Piccolo is about to reply when the line goes dead.

'It could have been me,' Piccolo says to Will as they take the long circular walk through the Sussex countryside that takes them from and back to the Catguts' house. 'If I hadn't bumped into you and Rallan, Lady Catgut and Ruby Q, the kindness and compassion you showed me...'

'You were lucky,' says Will. 'You got the chance to make a different path for yourself, a better life. And you took it.'

'Charlie didn't have that chance.'

'No,' says Will. 'He was very unlucky. He met with evil. As did Tommo.'

Piccolo's eyes brim over with tears.

Will puts his hand on Piccolo's shoulder as they walk along the path towards home.

'You weren't to blame, Pix,' he says. 'You couldn't do anything and it appears others, trained specifically to help, couldn't either. All we can do is work to try to prevent there being more Charlies. To remember him by saving the lives of others.'

Piccolo nods.

'I so love you, Will,' Piccolo says softly.

'Ach, am I glad?' says Will, with a smile. 'Because, Music Man, I feel the same about you.'

20 THE SUIT AND PHLEGM

Seeking sunshine and heat, a touch of history and culture, the Suit takes a short break in Rome. The guidebook is a treasure trove in itself. The Suit explores the oldest wine bar in town, where he sits sipping soft drinks, before moving to the Vino e Camino in the Piazza dell'Oro, facing the 16th-century church, San Giovanni dei Fiorentini. He's relishing a delicious meal while admiring the building's brick arches and cross vaults when he's aware of someone standing close to his table and who utters a polite, if hacking, cough.

'Phlegm!' says the Suit, astounded and thrilled to find a familiar face. 'How wonderful to see you. What brings you here?'

'I'm going home.' Phlegm's tears of joy glisten on his cheek. The Suit marvels that he looks so extraordinary well. The deathly pallor that has haunted his face, seemingly for ever, has been replaced by a rosy-cheeked glow.

They talk over old times. Phlegm enjoys his whisky, the Suit his carbonated elderflower water.

It's only later, much later, after the two have shaken hands and gone their separate ways, that the Suit learns that the old butler has disappeared. There has been an incident in the square – a fight, a premature birth, an unpaid bill. No one is quite sure what has happened but police and ambulances are on the scene, questioning the tourists, entertainers, hawkers, cafe owners and innkeepers.

The Suit checks out the square, asks a few questions before slipping away and confirming with himself that he'll call into the local police station in the morning to see if they have any news of Phlegm.

He heads back towards his hotel, along a dark dank narrow alleyway that runs between empty decaying tenements.

He hears a cough, at a distance ahead in the shadows. But he can see nothing. He looks over his shoulder. Nothing and no one. He slackens his pace. There's another cough. The Suit stops at a gentle bend in the brick wall. Cautiously, he peers round it. Under an old street light he sees the figure of a man in a dark suit lighting a cigarette, taking a long drag and then throwing it on to the flagstones beneath his feet.

The Suit is on the verge of laughing and calling out Phlegm's name when he sees the butler light a second cigarette, a third, a fourth, until, ultimately, a dozen burning cigarettes lie on the flagstones, in a circle around him, glowing like bright watchful eyes.

The Suit watches, mesmerised.

Phlegm is rubbing his fingers together. Flames shoot from them and feed the circle of fire such that the flames jump into the air, higher and higher. The Suit is seized by shock and frozen panic. What should he...?

He takes a step forward. He can't see Phlegm but he throws what little water he has left in his bottle on to the flames.

'Phlegm!' he cries out. 'Phlegm, old chap, what are you doing? Step away from the flames. Here, take my hand! Oh! Perhaps it's best if I call for help...'

His hands are shaking as he holds his ad'um and demands help from the emergency services. But the voice at the other end is drowned out by a hysterical shriek of delight from amidst the flames.

The Suit hurries to remove his jacket, using it to try to douse the flames. He thinks he is succeeding as the flames appear to diminish. But the old butler stands firm, singing an old song from the 1940s. The Suit, pouring with sweat, makes a grab for Phlegm but gets only a ripped sample of his sleeve and part of the man's arm. The Suit stifles a scream and swallows his vomit. He is shaking as Phlegm carries on singing.

Suddenly, the Suit feels the ground shudder beneath his feet.

He takes a few steps backwards, on to steadier ground.

'Phlegm,' he cries out.

The flames are shooting up into the air, taller, wider and stronger. Then they plummet to the ground, tearing through the flagstones as if they were puff pastry. The Suit stares dumbstruck at Phlegm, who is punching the air as if in celebration and emitting a huge ecstatic, roisterous laugh as all at once...he disappears into the earth.

'Didn't he say anything before...?' Spiky Hair asks him later.

'No,' says the Suit, shaking his head sadly. 'Well, only a number.'

'Which was...?' says Spiky Hair.

The Suit consults his notebook.

'It was six-three-seven-eight,' he says, and sighs. 'Whatever that means.'

Spiky Hair shrugs.

'I'll check,' says Ruby Q, 'but I think that's the distance in kilometres from the earth's surface to its centre.'

'It doesn't make any sense, does it?' says the Suit.

Ruby Q says nothing. She's thinking. Of the times she's encountered Phlegm and seen him shiver, even in hot sunshine. Of the times he has talked about returning home. Of his strong tie and loyalty to her father, Lorenzo di'Abalo, the most evil man she has ever encountered. It makes her wonder... No, it's too outrageous to think that her father is a devil. Because, if he is, what does that make her? And then she thinks some more. So what? She is her own person. She can discard what she doesn't want to be. She is now of her own making.

21 BHUPI AND SPAGHETTI SURESHI

Bhupi and Sureshi Spaghetti get to welcome some holy enthusiastic clowns into Heaven but are glad and relieved when God and Mother Nature, or rather Mother Nature and God, return to take charge of the place. Bhupi is reincarnated and becomes a much-respected expert in worldwide telecommunications. The reincarnated Sureshi Spaghetti establishes several businesses in the community, with the help of his deeply adored wife and two beloved sons. He becomes a thinker, a meditator, and friend and mentor to many.

22 BOSTON

Boston, the young American soldier who worked with the team apprehending the Federation President, completes his army service. He contemplates a life farming, organically and ethically, or a career in politics. He decides to do both and becomes a man who inspires trust and love. His wife, who bears him three fine sons and a fine daughter, adds to the family by establishing a home for infirm and elderly dogs and horses, and raises funds for research into CDRM, a degenerative bone disease that leads to progressive loss of hind-limb function in German shepherds (and other breeds), a dog Boston grew up with and loved to the end of Salika's dark nose to the tip of her dark waggy tail.

23 SPIKY HAIR

Spiky Hair is in the office six or seven days a week. She's determined that there must be more 'good news' stories as well as thought-provoking pieces in the newspaper and its on-line counterpart. She gets her way but Jarvis is concerned that she looks exhausted. He suggests, gently but firmly, that she has a break. In fact, that she becomes a travel writer for, say, three months, while he, Jarvis, will try valiantly to manage without her. She laughs, and, much to her own surprise, accepts his offer. So, she revels in the Edinburgh Fringe Festival, travels to Victoria Island in Canada, to Melbourne in Australia, and to Shanghai, China.

When she returns, refreshed and reinvigorated, with a folder full of stories about the places she's been, the people she's met, she tells Jarvis that she wants travel to play a bigger part in her life. Jarvis grins.

'Go for it!' he says, a great warm grin on his face.

24 GOO AND MACSOYA

Goo and MacSoya, the two culinary talents in the Dekaydence kitchens, set up a café together. It's a delicious mix of British food, Scots, French and Chinese, and is open every day from 6am to 9pm. It proves popular with local schoolchildren and office workers. In time, the two young chefs give talks and demonstrations in schools that decide to bring back kitchens and healthy eating.

Goo and MacSoya's café expands into a nationwide chain that sells their own cookbooks for young people. Goo talks to his dead father and consults Grout when he's stuck. In fact, unwittingly, Goo encourages Grout to fulfill his dream to open a technical college for students of all ages. It's at the first college that Grout helps a student create a range of kitchen and garden gadgets and implements, such as kettles, sweepers, hedge trimmers and lawnmowers that are 100 per cent silent.

Mrs Martin trials the new equipment and gives cookery lessons to students in the technical college and in the local Towers of Eden. She is happy once more.

25 THE MAN IN THE PINK SHORTS

The young man in the bright pink shorts and T-shirt, and red and orange spotted socks, who took the Arena Coronation Celebration tickets from Cage, bumps into Cage at the side entrance to Charing Cross station.

Cage scarcely recognises the young man, now dressed in a smart business suit, collar and tie.

The young man's grin stretches from ear to ear.

'Good to see you, matey. And thank you again. Here...'

He takes a bulging brown envelope from an inside pocket and hands it to Cage.

'If this is money,' says Cage, 'I can't possibly...'

'Yes, you can, matey,' says the suited young man. 'Else I'll follow you home and thrust it though your letterbox. Or your mouth.'

Cage hesitates.

'You did me a good deed,' says the young man. 'And you led me to another.'

'Did I?' says Cage, frowning over blank memories.

'Oh, yes,' says the young man. 'Someone in the street, a young woman, a complete stranger, came up to me and gave me this.'

Cage stares into the young man's open hand, on which

sits a blue stone. He hears the sound of ocean waves; he breathes in the scent of the salty ocean waves, and he absorbs the wondrous warmth of a sandy beach on a summer's day.

'Here, take it,' says the young man.

Cage shakes his head. 'It's too beautiful to give away to a complete stranger.'

The young man grins.

'You gave those tickets to a complete stranger.'

Cage smiles.

'The young woman who gave it to me,' says the young man, 'she told me I'd know when and who to pass it on to. I've carried it around, with your envelope, for months. And then, when I saw you I knew this was the moment. This stone is meant to be with you.'

He presses the blue stone into Cage's hand. Cage grins.

'There, you see. That young woman, Mary or Maria, told me that a young man, a musician, had given it to her. It'd been given to him by some elderly lady who told him there'd come a time when he'd know to pass it on.'

Cage doesn't know what to say or do, except stare into the stone.

'Mesmerising, ain't it?' says the young man. 'Now, listen, I may be talking out of turn but I know you got a young wife and a young baby to care for and times is hard. Take the money, matey, and care for them and the stone until you feel it's time for it to help someone else on their journey. Now, I must get back to work. See you around!'

Cage is about to thank him but the young man is already halfway down Villiers Street before he turns into John Adam Street and waves at Cage, then disappears from view.

At home, Waat cries soundlessly over the amount of money the young man has given them, which will help them in their new home. Her tears soon dry as she holds the stone. Strangely, she realises almost immediately that the stone will not be with them for long which doesn't stop her smiling.

26 RUBY Q

Ruby Q is in a dream, and knows it.

She tosses and turns in her sleep. It's a hot and sticky night but that's not disturbing her. She is searching for something important with no idea what it is. She is confused. And her hand hurts. She unrolls the fingers of her clenched fist and stares at a metal key digging into her skin. It's the key she was given by the elderly man in the Vatican Gardens. How on earth did it get into her hand? And why?

Ruby Q is in a dream, and knows it.

She is travelling at supersonic speed through time and space, inside a tunnel woven of memories. Her own memories. Everyday life, family meals, bedtime stories read to her by Rallan. Moving home, school and friends. Discovering her Aunt Lily. Finding her long-lost mother. Interesting work assignments. Important campaigns. As well as the countless times she has stood, looking at herself in a mirror, wondering who and what she is.

The memories continue. Taylor up a tree, demanding Ruby Q join her. Elsa staring at her from her study window with her grumbly, bumbly old dog by her side watching from the window ledge. A young couple, hand in hand on a beach, smiling and waving to a little girl. The last time she and her parents were all together. She smiles as she watches her young self building castles in the sand, knowing that she is also creating dreams in the air.

Ruby Q is in a dream, and knows it.

She is in a corridor of many doors that coils round the outside of an ivy-covered skyscraper with, seemingly, no beginning and no end, no top and no bottom. She walks alone. There's no one about. No sound. Nothing. Just space and darkness visited occasionally by shooting stars. She wonders if her mother is out there, somewhere, able to see her.

She stops at one of the identical ivy-covered doors, feels for a handle and discovers a lock. Without hesitation, she takes the key from her pocket and isn't surprised that it fits. And the key turns. The door creaks but scarcely moves. What she doesn't expect is that the ivy entwines itself round her wrist and starts to creep up her arm.

Ruby Q is in a nightmare, and knows it.

She attempts to wrest the ivy from her body. But its grip gets tighter. Now it is slithering upwards to her neck. Soon she won't be able to move or breathe. She leans her whole body weight against the old door. It squeaks, spits and groans but succumbs slowly, slowly to her body's pressure. As she falls over the threshhold the ivy shrivels and falls lifeless from her body to the ground.

A giant bright orange paper whistle unfurls at speed and, softly, punches her on the nose. She is startled, then bemused. There's no sound, not even when she screams.

She repeats her scream, the same silence is repeated back.

A man behind the whistle steps forward. He is dressed as a clown in a white silk playsuit with large black spots and oversized boots. He sports bright red lipstick, layers of white foundation, and a long flowing curly red wig. He beams and winks at Ruby Q as he hands her a headset, indicating she put it on. She hesitates then slowly follows his advice.

'Climbing ivy!' swears the clown, in a rare silent Scouse accent (rarer still in TTT). 'Why are you using the back door rather than the main entrance? I s'pose you've lost the copy of your death certificate, like everyone does nowadays?'

Ruby Q is distracted by the fact that she can now hear and understand this silent talk and also speak it.

'I'm sorry,' she says, 'I've no idea where I am or who you are or what I'm doing here, but I can tell you, for sure, I am alive.'

'Pfff! That's what they all say.'

'Possibly. But in my case, it happens to be true.'

'Ruby Q Cooper!' A familiar voice calls out.

She spins round.

'Jack!' she exclaims (in her own voice that changes to TTT). 'Oh, it's so good to see you. Are you OK? We all miss you, Jack.'

'And I miss you. All of you. Can you tell me how Waat and Baby Jake are?'

Ruby Q is aware that the searing rage and jealousy she felt in the past towards Waat, her rival for Jack's love, is gone.

'They're doing fine, Jack. Your son, Jake, is going to be as clever and good looking as you, and...and Waat is...a brilliant mum!'

Jack smiles.

'You don't have to protect me, Ruby Q. I know Cage and Waat have got married. And that *they* have a baby on the way. I know Cage will care always for Waat and Jake and the new baby. I know that for sure.'

For a moment they are both silent.

'I still don't know where I am and what's happening,' says Ruby Q.

'You're in Heaven, Ruby Q,' says Jack. 'Well, on the outskirts. But you're here ages before your official, listed date of arrival. So I wonder who or what sent you here? And why?'

Ruby Q shrugs.

'As far as I'm aware, I'm inside a dream. And I got in here only because I was given a funny old key by a funny old gardener in the Vatican Gardens that could unlock an old door I was standing at. So this, with fresh paint everywhere, is Heaven? It could just as easily be Bognor Regis...'

Jack laughs.

'You entered heaven by the back door!' says the clown, named Albert Ross, respectfully. 'Man, that's class. In all my time here, I've never known that to happen.'

Jack laughs.

'Albert, you arrived here only ten minutes ago, so that's hardly surprising,' he says. 'But it has happened before, and recently. Our last visitor, Ruby Q, was your mother, Angelica Nera. She had a bit of an accident but our team soon put her together. She went off into deep space and isn't due back here for some time.'

'So, she could be watching me, even now,' Ruby Q muses.

'All things are possible,' says Jack. 'Archangel Gabriel has become an accomplished painter and decorator, and pianist. And up here, pigs do fly.'

'So I could go after her,' Ruby Q ponders.

'No,' says Jack emphatically. 'It's dangerous out there.'

'That's for sure,' says Jezza, standing at Jack's side. 'Gangs of clowns and thugs roam space, Ruby Q, just looking for trouble.'

'Man, we're not all thieves and vagabonds,' Albert Ross interjects sadly. 'Many of us are simple clowns and jokers trying to escape memories of a sad childhood.'

'We know that, Albert Ross,' says Jack. 'But if Ruby Q's mum hadn't dropped the key Jezza and I would still be out there, lost in space for ever, courtesy of the space thugs. As it was, that key saved us, as your key saved you, Ruby Q.'

'It's as though there's a hand on a steering-wheel,' says Ruby Q.

'Possibly. But it could be Bhupi, the newsagent, who is standing in for God. He likes to be at the helm. Or it could be the Clives making sure everything is in working order.'

'Bhupi and the Clives sound like an ancient pop group,' says Ruby Q.

'They could be one, they can do almost everything else,' says Jack.

'Oh, dear, I'm feeling really sleepy.' Ruby Q yawns. 'I think I'm on the way home. I had so much to tell you, Jack, so much to ask...'

'We have to go, too, Ruby Q. Jezza and I are leaving Heaven any moment.'

Ruby Q's eyes widen in surprise.

'Where are you going? Isn't Heaven the final resting place?'

'Yes,' says Jack. 'But we're not going to rest.'

'What are you going to do?'

Jack hesitates. Jezza takes over.

'We're travelling through nature, in land, sea and sky,' she says. 'It's research for Mother Nature. She has taken over Planet Earth, and much else besides, from God. You might find soon that the new earth may have a more feminine, gentler touch.'

'If I could join you, I could write about it,' says Ruby Q, her head nodding towards sleep. Her eyelids too heavy to keep open.

'Tell her, Jack. So when her time comes she will die

happy,' Jezza whispers in TTT.

'It's not policy, Jezza.'

'It's old policy, Jack. Mother Nature has other ideas.'

'Then we ought to wait and see what they are.'

'It'll be too late. Look, Ruby Q's already disappearing like the Cheshire cat. It'd be so good for her to leave us with a smile, Jack. You must tell her, she's your friend. Maybe just give her a hint?'

Jack smiles at Jezza – the Martin dimple appearing in his cheek.

'OK, Mrs Kindness,' he says, and leans closer to Ruby Q.

'Ruby Q, it's me, Jack. We want you to know that we shall meet again. In Heaven. With our family and friends. But first, as one of the seven chosen ones, you will become part of the new rainbow above a new Earth. I shall smile because you will be the red in the rainbow, as bright and as wild as your hair, with an energy and passionate commitment to grow compassion and kindness in the world. And, at last, I shall join you as green and discover that the Q in your name stands for Quaestor, the investigator who, I know, will work to expose evil and encourage good, for ever and always, whomsoever you are and whomsoever you become.'

Ruby Q is in a dream, smiling happily.

27 LORENZO DI'ABALO

A white sheet of snow stretches out in all directions, across a landscape twice the size of Australia. It is the coldest, driest, windiest continent. It is Antarctica. No one originates from these parts; only researchers and technicians visit, and perhaps several thousand investigating animals, birds, plants and microscopic organisms. But always there are sounds of life – the sea cracks and breaks; a seal underwater emits a kettle-pitched squeal that suddenly falls off as if it's reached boiling point; penguins twitter like small birds, older penguins sound like an experienced singers.

Deep below the surface, beneath four kilometres of ice, there is water that hasn't seen the light of day for, maybe, millions of years. And yet, and yet, there are spiders, wood lice, centipedes, some three dozen or more, hitherto unknown, species. Colourless, blind, and unusually energetic, hustle-bustling, this way and that. Surviving on a yellowy scum, hydrogen sulphide from hot springs deep in the earth, that provides the energy that light would normally provide.

But at this moment the visitors are tucked up in bed. Animals cluster together for warmth. The wind groans, moans and heaves its huge, powerful body, this way and that, across the landscape where all else is quiet.

It's difficult to say how much time elapses before a tiny crack appears in the ice. It grows slowly. Another crack appears. And another. Creating sounds like creaking boards on a wooden ship, stretching and reaching out, this way and that.

And out of the cracks come strange little creatures – colourless, blind and soundless – that emerge from holes and run off in every direction and ever-increasing numbers.

From deep within the earth a sound comes like a woman's breath exhaling in the late stages of a pregnancy. The wind's groans increase, and whip round the cracks, noisily exploring a mound or a crevice, this way and that. And then, from the depths, a tiny rumbling noise begins and grows in strength as it ascends.

The sound is joined by another, different and odd. Is it, can it be, a laugh? Whatever it is, there is a sense of jubilation approaching the top of the expanding hole. A sound that becomes triumphant. And then a roar, like that of a mighty lion king, shreds the silent night, as an almighty volcanic explosion of ice mingled with fire and embers burst forth from the ground, shooting high into the air.

From deep within the volcanic fountain a body takes shape and grows in the flames. Its face and body flesh a mass of glowing coals and embers, its long flowing hair made of snakes of fire, its eyes glittering with a deadly, fiery fury.

'*Yes!*' cries the figure, punching a burning arm and clenched fist into the sky. The voice sounds as if it is sitting in a large metal bowl. It rumbles with thunder that then becomes a cackling laugh, crazed and raucous, that bounces round the landscape and flies high into the sky, whirling and spinning, diving down to the ground and soaring into the skies, over and over again, cackling and screeching all the while.

See the smile? The jagged blackened teeth mixed with teeth fashioned as tiny skulls?

See the piercing Caribbean sea-blue-green eyes that somehow glitter more brightly than the fire? And listen to that triumphant scream that cries out...

'I have succeeded! I am immortal evil!

I am Lorenzo di'Abalo!

I am the Devil Incarnate!

28 RUBY Q

Ruby Q awakes in the early hours of the morning. Cold and still as the house. The garden, too.

Shivering, she reaches for her fleece jacket. It was only one dream among many but... She saw his eyes, glinting blue-green in a face comprised of fiery red and orange embers. Somehow she knows the dream is a reality. That Di'Abalo is once more on the move. That he is returning to the world to do his di'abolic worst. Fear grips hold of her stomach and her mind.

She goes to the window. Light is oozing into the sky, alongside the rain. Birdsong fills the air as birds and squirrels chase rivals away from their food sources. Is this greed or evil? Or the fight for survival? Greed and evil, it seems, cannot be eradicated. But is the answer to focus on encouraging good in the world? So what can she do? Carry on as a journalist, highlighting wrongs, trying to make the world a better place? Yes, this will be her life's work.

What must she have about her person? she wonders. Steadfastness, kindness, strength, patience and humour to sow in the world. Not brambles of hatred and greed but seeds of compassion, hope and love.

Bright and beautiful, the rainbow makes an archway

to somewhere or nowhere. But no matter as to how or from where it derives, however short or long its stay, she knows the rainbow will bring her hope, always.

She will build her work on the foundations of others who lost their lives trying to save the planet, including Jack, a number of GeeZer and Real GeeZer friends, and Will's brother Tommo – tragically remodelled by Dekaydence in the White Room – whom she'd met and befriended at an eco-activist meeting long before her encounter with Jack.

She will build her work also in memory of children who never had the chance to know the world, good and bad. Who were never able to enjoy the warmth and fun of friendship, the beauty of a bluebell wood in springtime, the magnificence of the sun over the sea, or the taste of raspberries and chocolate. Or the joy of watching a film, listening to music or to birdsong, or reading a book, thinking, feeling, loving or sharing a smile. She will build her work also for the children who will one day be your children.

29   LORENZO DI'ABALO

Di'Abalo stands in the centre of a raging inferno, savouring the taste of brimstone. He runs his fingers through his hair, which has become a torrent of flames. Oh, the relief of breaking free from the ice and wallowing in a fierce and furious heat that reminds him of home.

He glances up. The black sky is losing out to light.

A feather brushes his face. He shudders. For a sudden, brief moment it feels as if an arrow of ice from the freezing lake pierces his very being, causing him excruciating cramps and nausea.

What is it? Who is it that's interrupting his reverie? Someone who has discovered he is on the loose again? God? Or Mother Nature?

He hears the sighs and groans of the east wind as it ruffles the bleak white landscape.

Cautiously, he opens his eyes, now red, orange and citric yellow. He feels his old powers returning.

He senses the presence of someone or something close by. He is ready to confront and to fight. Be it with his father or mother.

He looks about him. The land is deserted and desolate. He is aware of a great dark shadow in the sky. Its black wings outstretched like a cleric, ready to embrace, or consume, all before it.

'Bianco?' Di'Abalo whispers, lest the name slips out into the wider world.

Black wings are attached to strong, rippling muscles of flesh, black and strong like polished ebony. Ivory teeth gleam in the broad characteristic grin.

'You sound surprised to see me, man,' says Bianco.

For once, Di'Abalo is speechless. Even though he it was who locked the young man into the body of a bird.

'You think I'm going to throw you back into that brrr-ing ice pond?' Bianco's look is mischievous.

'I'd like to see you try,' di'Abalo snarls through clenched teeth.

As he speaks, Di'Abalo sinks to his feet, clutching his head. He is being tortured by a tsunami of good thoughts and kind feelings that multiply over and over again within his brain.

He retches. Out of his mouth comes a torrent of tiny twinkling balls of crystal, diamond, ruby, emerald, sapphire, gold and silver that disappear up into the air and spread their colour across the dark canvas of the sky.

Di'Abalo lies on the ground, exhausted. Panting quietly, he wipes away any light and colour that has smeared his mouth and face.

His eyes narrow, he takes a deep breath and, staring intently at Bianco, opens his mouth and directs at him a mighty force of fire.

Bianco holds out a hand to stop the fire force. He stands resolute. The fire falls to the ground, petering out into blackened soot and ash on the snow.

One of Di'Abalo's eyebrows rises in mild surprise.

'Who or what are you?' he asks. 'That can do such things?'

Bianco smiles.

'I am the writing on the wall,' he says.

'Possibly, but I don't read much.'

'What you must miss,' says Bianco, with a wry smile. 'But I am here to persuade you that good can come out of evil.'

Di'Abalo snorts.

'Not possible, or acceptable.'

'We'll see,' says Bianco.

'Anyway, who are you to dare to attempt a change in me?'

'I am what you could have been,' Bianco continues. 'You were the model chosen to be the first Alpha. You shone above all the Betas. All was progressing well until you revealed the other side of yourself. One that we had never seen before. A selfish, greedy, cruel side. And you crashed, falling below Beta level. When you could have been—.'

'The Gold,' di'Abalo interrupts sharply. 'I know all this. But you, Bianco or Birdman, whatever you were or are, you are always black.'

Bianco laughs.

'I can't be held responsible for what you and artists over centuries have done to me, now, can I? It's a free world, so I'm led to believe, perhaps mistakenly.'

Di'Abalo stares into Bianco's eyes. He is taken aback by something he has never seen before. That Bianco's eyes are blue-green like a Mediterranean sea... Like his own.

'So are you the Gold?' Di'Abalo enquires, curious.

'Yes, I am the Gold,' Bianco replies quietly. 'I am the son of God, or whatever name He chooses to work under.'

'No, no,' says Di'Abalo, firmly. 'I am the son of God. I am The Prodigal Son.'

'Possibly, but ...' Bianco shrugs. 'You were the most beautiful angel in Heaven. Lucifer, leader of the choir, the cub pack, God's library, and more besides. But you wanted more. You were determined to discover how God's gold standard is achieved. You fell to Beta level, carrying on over centuries, most recently using numerous innocent teenagers in the White Room experiment, thinking that they would show you how it happens. The experiment failed. You failed. Because you fell below the required standards. You are the Fallen Angel, you are the Devil, you are Satan. Now I am come to help you reach Gold, to return you to the beautiful Lucifer you were once, through good works and deeds. Or, my brother, I must and shall contain you again or destroy you.'

'You think destroying me will destroy evil?' Di'Abalo says sarcastically. 'If you do, you are a fool of false gold, and not a god. I have fathered more devils and done more evil deeds than you have said prayers. To eliminate me will be hard enough; to eliminate all my heirs and their "talents" impossible. Evil will have the upper hand always.'

Within a moment's breath Di'Abalo becomes a long, wild, swirling, coiling rainbow-hued snake – red, orange, yellow, green, blue, indigo and violet – that entwines and engulfs Bianco, trying to suffocate the life and heaven out of the black bird's body.

Bianco cries out. He feels an excruciating evil pierce his soul before he, too, transforms into a huge ball of bright shining golden light that consumes all the surrounding darkness, and singes the Di'Abaloic rainbow snake to grey, stone, camel, beige, sour cream, brown, and ember black, twisting it with an intense heat into a curling matchstick.

There is no winner. The fight continues, going one way and then the other. Between good and evil. Between Bianco and Di'Abalo. God weeps. So much so that there are floods in the northern provinces and an ocean falls off the planet. Spaghetti Sureshi gets together a group of like-minded clowns who – wearing outrageous flippers, snorkels, swimwear and small umbrellas on their heads – return to earth to lift people's spirits.

AN UNKNOWN SOLDIER

'I heard tell I was killed in the eastern provinces by FF, that's to say friendly fire. How friendly is that? I suppose at the end of the day – or, in my case, the morning – the fatal bullet is despatched and neither the sniper nor you has any idea of the person on the other side. In civilian life, who knows? That sniper and I could be off to play football, having a drink in the pub, talking about our families. If we'd met in no man's land, maybe we'd be talking about what this war is about. I reckon we'd agree it's a criminal waste of life – for both sides, or rather the many sides, most of which appear to want to keep the engine of destruction going at full and bloody power.

'I understand now that war is all about money and power. Naively, I joined up to fight for my country. To defend it. I came to realise that I wouldn't be serving the monarch, the president, the public or my family. I'd be serving hungry businessmen and powerbrokers, vultures who rape and pillage the minerals, the oil, the gas, whatever will make them another fortune, from lands condemned to be battlefields, and from men, women and children condemned to die.

'Not long before the FF encounter I was reading research that said war is never lawful, except in self-defence. In fact, I read that war was outlawed in 1928 when major nations signed the Treaty for the Renunciation of War (the Kellogg-Briand Pact).

'The researcher and campaigner writes that this war makes every UK taxpayer complicit and as liable for breaking that law (by paying taxes to fund, support wars or genocide and other crimes against humanity) as are the military, the government, the judiciary and the monarchy. (Article 25.3 of the International Criminal Court, Nuremburg Principle V11, Section 52 International Criminal Court Act 2001 – well, what else would you call it?).

'The researcher also discovered that it is illegal to wilfully kill another human being. That the UN charter allows only a proportionate armed force in self-defence but only until the Security Council takes control of the situation.

'There's much more. I've listed some of statutes so for now I'll leave you. I want to discover if Heaven is all it's cracked up to be. And you, you've got to get on with your life.

'I'll be flown home with all ritual. But I won't get a hug

from my folks, from my young brother and my big sister. Or from the woman I love, who is the mother of my two young boys, who I'll never see grow up. I won't be there for them. That hurts me most. I've given my life and therefore I've robbed the ones I love of what they needed from me.

'Advice? From me? Well... Don't vote in leaders whose priority is to be re-elected; whose aim is to ride forever the Federation gravy train; who see wars as a way to gain wealth and power, mostly for self. Never minding the de-construction of a country, a family, a community, a way of life. Be aware the uprising, the revolution funded into existence to mask activities far and away more sinister. Drugs, prostitution, human trafficking. No. Strive to build your life, your relationships, your world not through hate and greed but through love and compassion. Man and beast, as well as flowers, blossom better that way.'

30 HQ

'How's it going?' says the girl, as she appears in the room.

'It'll be over soon,' says the boy, focused on the monitor floating in front of him.

'Really?' says the girl, peering over his shoulder at the picture of Planet Earth. 'Such a waste.'

The boy shrugs.

'I know more than I want to about humans and their jumbled concept of good and evil,' he says. 'I'll be glad to get shot of the lot of them. Hopefully, my grades will be so good I'll be moved onwards. And upwards!'

The girl nods distractedly, and glances idly around the room.

'You're unusually quiet,' says the boy. 'That means you've got something to say. And that means you've heard something.'

The girl laughs, a warm, rich and cosy sound.

'Yes. You're right. You are being moved.'

'Yippee! Wow! Fantastic!' The boy jumps to his feet, punches the sky and starts throwing his work into the jaw of an ancient rusty haggoid, which devours everything slowly in gulps and through belches. 'So my grades are that good that I'm promoted, as of now?'

'Kind of,' says the girl, with noticeable ambivalence.

The boy stops in mid-throw of paper and memory sticks. The haggoid's jaws yatter and drip oil in irritation at this break in food supply.

'What do you mean, kind of?' asks the boy suspiciously.

'You leave today. Now, in fact. And your new project is Mars.'

'*What?* Oh, no! What on Planet Earth for?'

'They want you to try again, from the beginning. See if you can do better this time!'

The boy looks as if he might explode with fury.

'But I've been there, done that and I didn't get any T-shirt, or any thanks for my trouble!' he shouts as he bangs both fists on the desk lid.

'I told them it wouldn't work and it didn't. Those alleged intelligent life forms on Mars ruined the planet, came to Earth and did the same thing there. It's likely they've ruined most everything in the solar system simply through their ignorance and greed. I told them all this before I started work on this pesky Earth project. I told them it'd be the same as Mars. It won't work, I said. And it hasn't... So, any other good news?' he concludes sharply.

The girl blushes, her eyes bright with joy.

'I've got a new assignment.'

'Which is...?' The boy stares at her, sulky and goggle-green-eyed.

'It's part of a new directive,' the girl says excitedly.

'God is on gardening leave – well, you know that, you've seen his trousers. So, from now on, Mother Nature is in charge of the solar system. She's hinted that there'll be more women in senior positions, if not in every position. And guess what?'

'You get to be a goddess?' says the boy snidely.

'No, silly,' says the girl, with a smile. 'But we Alpha-plus graduates have contained the deadly virus that was loose on earth and all research material is now under lock and key. And now we're helping to save the bees. We have to persuade the pesticide producers to stop what they're doing so bees can live and thrive naturally. If pesticides win out, Earth is done for. It has no future.'

'Great.' The boy yawns, widely and with exaggerated boredom. 'Anything else of momentous importance?'

'Well...yes!' says the girl. 'Mother Nature has appointed me her right-hand assistant. I am so excited, I can't tell you!'

'Good, because I don't want to know any more,' says the boy, with another loud, over-dramatic yawn.

'We'll be working on a new model of Planet Earth, starting with Creation, as of Monday week,' says the girl. 'The first matter on the agenda is to inject into the system more love. Did you know that Mother Nature has been on an anger-management course to try to control her temper tantrums over tsunamis, volcanic eruptions, earthquakes and other allegedly "natural" disasters?'

'Blagh!' says the boy, as if he was throwing up.

'Whatever therapy Mother Nature tries, I warn you, both she and the system cannot take a "love" overdose.'

'We'll have to wait and see, won't we?' says the girl teasingly, her eyes sparkling as she skips from the room, singing a song that has yet to be written.

31 MOTHER NATURE

Mother Nature sits on a faraway hilltop overlooking the sea, thinking and planning.

As she strokes the blue dress that God gave her many, many years ago, Mother Nature – aka Papatuanu, Maka, Papamama, Nokomis, Eingana, Dewi Sri – decides she will, she must include men in her new Earth, her new Creation. They have an equal role to play. She thinks tenderly of God and, despite their titanic tempers, their happy years together. Yes, of course, the new world needs as many men as women. What was she thinking when she decided on a world ruled by women only?

A short distance away sits a new black clown in Heaven, Albert Ross, who meditates between the occasional request from Mother Nature for soothing music from his ancient oboe.

Nearby, Albert's friends, Louis and Ianoladadamski Sackbutt, ponder health and safety issues in the new Creation. At a further distance, the two Clives with their new friend, Clive, pore over the human and creature design and how to improve it.

As it was in the beginning, an unknown voice whispers in Mother Nature's head.

'Who's that?' asks Mother Nature.

Just a voice in your head, clocking in.

Mother Nature's mind swiftly scans her memory.

'I've met, or rather heard, you before, haven't I?' she enquires.

Yes. I didn't think you'd remember me. It was ages ago.

'Was it at the beginning of time?'

Strictly speaking, it was a few seconds before. You were a bit nervous so I dropped by. I know you're not nervous this time round. So, good wishes with your plans to create a better, more caring, honourable world. Oh, and when you next see Him do please pass on good wishes to God from all of us at HQ.

'HQ? Has He been there, without telling me?' asks Mother Nature, cross and suspicious.

No.

'So, where and what is HQ?' asks Mother Nature. 'Can it answer the vital questions about Creation, His and Hers? We need to know of our beginnings to help the present and the future.'

It's never been done before and I don't know the answers. But I wonder if you'll find what you're looking for somewhere over the rainbow.

'Interesting thought,' says Mother Nature reflectively, while hearing Sackbutt softly play a song on his oboe. 'I think you may be right.'

32 ANGELICA NERA

Angelica Nera is travelling intergalactic with orders from Lord di'Abalo to buy out any mineral of value. She sends him up-to-date information but receives no message in return. She is not much bothered. She enjoys making deals, and now that she understands what kind of young woman her daughter is, and that Wiggins is there to support her, Angelica Nera knows that Ruby Q will put her inheritance to good use.

The thought brings her comfort, as well as strength to continue. She has steered her small craft away from the pirates and thugs that haunt the one billion or more galaxies, hunting for easy prey. She has no memory of her accident in a previous craft that left her the sole survivor. She accepts that the long, dangerous journey means certain death at some uncertain point.

On her first encounter with alien life she is met by a band of tall, handsome warriors, their glistening faces bronzed as though fashioned from flesh, silk and metal itself. It is they who present her with the gift of a tiny implant that converts any language in the galaxies that she hears or speaks to the language she understands best.

'Will you pass this way again?' asks one warrior.

'No. My business here is done,' she says, shaking her head.

He nods, thoughtfully.

'Where do you go from here?'

She shrugs.

'I'll turn right, and go on till Xmas.'

He smiles.

Angelica's craft is coming in to land, descending through thick meringue clouds on to a new planet. The chief here is multilingual and eager to do business. Separated by time and space, they have communicated via TTT and other alien devices and now she is looking forward to a face-to-face meeting with someone who sounds a like-minded soul.

When she lands she finds the place is deserted. The sky is ink dark. There's no one about. There's nothing but a long ramshackle hut and a cold, mournful wind. Are the creatures here away from camp, mining? Whatever, she decides to explore the hut.

She steps carefully over the uneven pebbled landscape, the wind biting at her face. As she nears the building she hears music. Debussy. 'The Girl with the Flaxen Hair'. The Earl Wild version.

The music stirs bitter-sweet memories in her head and heart. Loneliness has lived always within Angelica. She hopes, so hopes, that Ruby Q will escape it and the melancholia it brings. She will pray for her daughter, asking a God she's not entirely sure exists that He keep her daughter safe, away from loneliness and depression.

She knocks on the door. No response. She knocks again. Silence, but the door opens slowly. She takes a cautious step over the threshold and walks into a dark, shadowy sitting room in which a fire crackles and spits in the grate. There's something else. In a corner of the room stands a Christmas tree, covered with ivory and gold bows and baubles and scores of tiny bright sparkling ivory-coloured lights.

She recalls Ruby Q as a small child, the look of awe and wonder in her face as she stared at her first Christmas tree.

She hears slow, unsteady footsteps on a tiled floor. She tenses, checking the proximity of the door for a quick escape, as an elderly man, stooped with age, enters the room with a silver tray on which stand two glasses of champagne. He puts the tray on a small table and exits the room. She wonders why he looks so familiar.

She sits and dreams. There is still so much she wants to achieve in her work. Still so much she wants to give to Ruby Q and...

Steadier footsteps approach and stop. A tall man in evening dress is standing in the doorway. He steps forward to hand her a small black velvet box.

'Merry Xmas, Miss Nera,' the man says. 'I'm so glad you took the right turning to my territory and my home.'

A grin appears on the bronze man's face.

'It's you!' she cries out. 'How did you know I'd be here?'

'I read your mind. Although leaving behind a copy of your itinerary helped.'

'Did I?' she asks. 'But where is everyone else?'

'There is no one else, Angelica Nera. Only the two of us.'

'And the butler.'

'Yes, there's always S'not, the butler, a gift from the father I never met.'

'But why...?'

The man sits down beside her.

'Are you going to open your present?'

'But I've got nothing for you,' she says.

'You have everything for me,' he says.

She feels uncertain, nervous as she unwraps and opens the box.

'Oh!' she exclaims, staring at a magnificent emerald and gold necklace. 'But I can't accept this.'

'Yes, you can. My grandmother never wears it. Her preference is sapphires.'

'But—'

'I'd like you to have it because it'll suit you. Besides,' says the man, 'my grandmother told me one day I'd know instantly who to give it to. She was right. It's you, Angelica Nera. I've fallen in love with you. I knew it the moment I saw you.'

'But you don't know me. Or anything about me. And I know nothing about you.'

'But we do know one another. We have shared laughter as well as mining messages. Now we can exchange more information. The weather forecast is bad. Best you stay here tonight, but remember, a night here lasts seven of your Earth days.'

When she awakes, Angelica sees the freshly kindled fire. She scents several delicious aromas – fresh coffee and chocolate, freshly baked bread, strawberry jam, peaches and nectarines...

She's hungry but something else is gnawing at her. She gets up and crosses to the window. The vast landscape is grey and bleak; the vast grey and bleak sea throws itself mercilessly at the beach and the steep cliffs of the shoreline.

Suddenly, he is standing behind her, his hand on her shoulder.

'Do you know something?' he says.

'Yes,' she replies calmly. 'I am pregnant with your child.'

'With our son,' he amends.

'How did you know?' she says.

'A gift inherited from my grandmother.' He shrugs. 'How did *you* know?'

She shrugs.

'I don't know. Maybe this translating device in my head does internal body language.'

'Maybe.' He laughs. 'And now I think in your condition it's best you stop travelling.'

'I can't. I'm committed. And I have a tough boss to answer to.'

'We can travel together in my craft. I'll sort out your boss another time.'

'Do you know there's one thing you haven't told me?'

The warrior frowns.

'What's that?' he asks.

She smiles.

'Your name.'

He laughs, a rich, cosy enveloping sound.

'Apologies. I am Louis,' says the warrior. 'I am named after the Sun King of France by the father I never met. I'd like to name our boy Lorenzo, after my father and his father, who I also never met. So, with our family name, our boy will be...Lorenzo di'Abalo.'

He catches her as she stumbles.

'What is it?' he asks, concerned at her ashen face.

She shrugs.

'The baby kicked me.'

She hesitates.

'I want to tell you something that might make you change your mind.'

'Is this necessary?' he asks, as she hands back the emerald and gold necklace.

'Yes,' she says. 'I work for Lord di'Abalo in his London office of the Company of Dekaydence. I have known him since I was young and... And I have a grown-up daughter by him. Ruby Q is a good, bright, kindly young woman.

But he is a hard and complex man, often cruel beyond measure.'

'As my grandmother has told me,' says Louis.

'So I am fearful that this child may be cruel, like his grandfather.'

'Then we educate him to behave and think differently,' says Louis. 'It sounds as if his half-sister will be much more than a half-good influence.'

'Here,' he says, placing the necklace round her neck. 'It suits you, Angelica Nera. It's as if it was designed for you.'

She is distracted by thoughts.

'There are times,' he says, taking her hand, 'when a happy ending is the order of the day. Luckily, for us, we are blessed also to have a happy beginning.'

Angelica nods, trying to ignore the boy child in her womb who kicks her again, with strength way beyond his age. She chokes back a sob. Her eyes close, her knees buckle but again he catches her in time and holds her close. She must run away, she decides – to Mars, to Kepler-22b, Gliese-581d or the Jupiter moons – to spare them, Ruby Q, Louis and the baby, Lorenzo. She must save them from hurt, pain and...something, she knows, which could be much, much worse.

And then she sees more clearly the honesty, strength, and kindness in this man's face. If she stays with him, who knows what might happen? She might come to know happiness or...

All things considered, says a voice in her head, *your Ruby Q has turned out rather well. Maybe this is fate. For baby Lorenzo, for Louis and for you, Angelica Nera.*

33 HEAVEN

There are rumours in Heaven that God is tired and wants to retire. It's a shock to all but almost everyone is understanding of His plight. Even Petty Masters, who, much to her own surprise, enters a church for the first time in many years to wish Him well in His new ventures, which involve rescuing ageing motor vehicles and destitute donkeys and other animals worldwide. Petty isn't quite sure why, but she becomes a regular fundraiser for the donkeys and a patron of their charity.

There are rumours of a list of candidates for the post of God. He doesn't know it but Wiggins features in the top three, although he has a good few more years on earth, watching his grandchildren grow. Another candidate is Randall Candelskin, who cannot bear to part with his new dog O'Reilly. The third, deemed a rank outsider, is Mother Nature. Mother Nature is anything but an outsider, argue the OldTimers, while a giggle of new angel clowns point out that a woman's amazing ability to multi-task also comes Mother-Naturally.

34 WILL AND PICCOLO

Piccolo takes a few musical commissions from around the world, donating a large part of his fee to MAT, his music therapy charity. Funds help establish a therapy centre in wooded fields close to the Catguts' Sussex home; and another next to Will's family estate in Scotland. The centres are for those whose lives and minds are disrupted and disturbed. People come from far and wide for treatment given by trained and experienced therapists who will soon include Piccolo and Maria. And there are regular fund-raising shows with performances by residents that raise the spirits of all concerned.

From time to time the centres are visited by Hilli, formerly the Face's bodyguard, who always brings his guitar to help out. He also gives talks on TV and radio on the work done at the centres on national radio and TV while former patients give interviews to say how they have been helped. Ruby Q writes updates for her paper and each year Jarvis runs a Christmas auction in his newspaper for the charity, and others, that brings in support and funds.

Will oversees the running of the estate in Scotland, taking pressure off his ageing mother. He spends time in his father's old study, reading and researching more on climate change. And he spends time on the lake with Tommo. Grout is still working on a cure, as well as thinking of ways to cut carbon emissions. And so it is that Will, who did dour for so long, now has a smile that travels to both sides of his face and shines out of eyes that regard Piccolo with respect, admiration and love.

35 RUBY Q

Ruby Q picks up an old, much-loved copy of a childhood book that strangely, every so often, finds itself in her hands. As she turns the pages of the spiky-humoured, thyme-travelling adventures, something flutters to the floor. She picks up a photograph and sees a familiar face.

She puts the photo on the mantelpiece, next to a picture of her father.

'It seems we're destined to be apart,' she says to her mother, who, in the photo, is wearing the crystal heart necklace that Ruby Q is now wearing. 'Wherever you are, Angelica Nera, I pray that there is love and humour in your life and a kindly being watching over you, watching over us all. And that one day, however dark and bleak the world, we shall meet again.'

Ruby Q carries on with her work, some done in memory of those who lost their lives trying to save the planet - including Jack, a number of GeeZer and Real GeeZer friends, and Will's brother Tommo, tragically remodelled by Dekaydence in the White Room, who she'd befriended at an eco-activist meeting before she met Jack.

Some of her work will be in memory of children who never had the chance to know the world, good and bad. Who were never able to enjoy the warmth and fun of friendship, the beauty of a bluebell wood in springtime, the magnificence of the sun over the sea. Who never tasted fresh food, the taste of raspberries, chocolate, not even fresh water. Neither did they ever experience watching a film, reading a book, loving, or sharing a smile. Ruby Q will work also for your children. Your children who will pick up the pieces of this fractured world and build a better, fairer, and more just world.

36 GROUT

A smile is never far from Grout's face, especially when he and Indigo watch their two sons and two daughters exploring, investigating, and playing happily together.

He tries to put work worries to one side. But he is working hard on Bodkin's notes, on the three stages of exploration of teenage minds in the White Room. Luckily, there are no longer experiments but there are recordings of every experiment undertaken. Alpha, Beta and Gold, Grout repeats to himself, but what exactly does it mean in Dekaydence terms?

He ponders. Alpha is the first stage in a development, Beta the improved second version, and Gold is the final, 'perfect' version and standard. Grout ponders some more. It's when he sees the footage taken by the invisible Eye-Spys in the frozen wastelands of the terrifying fight between Di'Abalo and Bianco that Grout understands better that whatever Di'Abalo may be Bianco is pure Gold.

As he gets older, Grout understands more. That this was, and still is, a never-ending fight between good and evil. Despite, or perhaps because of, the power of Mother Nature. There will be neither peace nor reconciliation. In this unusual instance there is one son comprising two separate people, opposites, albeit with identical determination. And that is it, for ever and ever. Until there is an end. Amen.

37 GROUT

It may never happen again but for now, here they are, Will, Ruby Q, North, The Face, Cage, Grout, Indigo and Piccolo, sitting round a table in the garden of the Catguts' riverside home. The floods have subsided, damaged buildings, farms, roads and rail repaired, the sun is shining and everywhere there are trees are in blossom, pale green and pink, and white, like bridesmaids awaiting the arrival of the bride.

The young adults are discussing, debating and arguing about climate change. What concerned them years before concerns them to this day. Even Piccolo – who had thought it all a strictly middle-class self-indulgent fret that had nothing to do with him, guv – has been won over.

A UN report says there is now overwhelming evidence that the impacts of global warming are likely to be 'severe, pervasive and irreversible'.

'Natural systems, such as water resources and sea levels, have borne the brunt,' Will tells the others, 'but the thought is now that there'll be a growing impact on humans as health, homes, food, and safety are likely to come under threat from rising temperatures.'

'Knowing you two, you'll change your minds again.' The Face snorts, regarding Will and North disparagingly.

'Possibly, 'says North. 'Because science doesn't give finite answers. There's aways another question to ask and examine.'

'All we know for sure is that climate change is a natural, continuing process,' says Will. 'Now we know that human beings are adding to the problem. By how much is anyone's guess. So we need to understand better what's happening, and what we can do to manage climate change and its associated risks.'

'You can do that, Grout, dear,' says Indigo, 'you and your scientific and technical friends from around the world.'

'Yes,' says Grout. 'It should take us only a couple of hours.'

Indigo laughs.

Grout smiles. But deep down he feels a nagging worry.

And you know what that worry is, don't you, dear boy? says a familiar musical voice in his head.

Yes, you do, dear boy! says Di'Abalo, as though he was one of his own cats relishing stolen cream. *Humans will have to be 'oided in order to survive on earth. And then up-'oided to survive the journey to another galaxy, which they'll destroy as they have every other. So there will be super-intelligent 'oids and there will be drone'oids. And you know the ending already, don't you, Grout – that, in time, we shall see the passing of all human beings.*

Grout gives an imperceptible nod but says nothing. If there is a trace of a smile on his lips it's because he knows the super-advanced Noteian software in his brain will keep out even the likes of di'Abalo.

But he accepts there are more important things to address. The bloody wars that have broken out across the globe; the dwindling lack of resources above and below the earth's crust; toxins in the atmosphere; and the worldwide plight of women and young girls married against their will, raped, beaten and murdered. This is not the world that Grout wants for his children, or for anyone's children. He realises he must consider how to bring about change. He will continue to work on scientific projects.

And he'll work to establish peace and justice throughout the world, to show how and why it is essential man and his world cherish kindness and compassion.

37.5(RECURRING) RUBY Q

Ruby Q reads of the high water content inside planets and moons. Of microbes that have travelled millions of miles, taking life to other worlds. Somehow that brings her comfort, a reassurance that there may well be life on other worlds, and that her mother may still be alive. Thus, it comes to pass that Ruby Q understands and experiences a sense of contentment, even happiness, that requires no mirrors of proof but, instead, flourishes deep inside.

GARRET
BOOKS

ACKNOWLEDGEMENTS

The Open University
Walton Hall
Milton Keynes MK7 6AA
a fount of knowledge and understanding

A World Without Bees by Alison Benjamin and Brian McCallum
guardianbooks £9.99
a fascinating honeytrap of a book

Clive Coker
www.cqprojects.co.uk
*a talented designer and engineer who looked beyond my basic
construction for the Towers of Eden and who saw advantages in
Nature that could help mankind*

Heaven forfend that you've not read the first two books.
But if you haven't, here they are ... *Black Light* and *Green Fire*.

BLACK LIGHT

available in paperback £6.99
on the iPad £4.99
Kindle £2.99

GREEN FIRE

available in paperback £6.99
on the iPad £4.99
Kindle £2.99

THE LOST JOURNAL

Have some interactive fun with some of your favourite characters in
The Lost Journal
the prequel to the Dekaydence trilogy

available on the iPad £2.99

Reviews

Fiction

BLACK LIGHT

Like Philip Pullman on speed! – Piers Plowright

A rollicking read that a modern Jonathan Swift would have been proud to produce.
– Patience Wheatcroft

A fast-paced, well-plotted thriller with futuristic details ... A must-read.
– Fran Crumpton, The Book Partnership

wholly innovative ... a modern classic. – John Lloyd, Waterstones

GREEN FIRE

a cross between Alice in Wonderland *and* Dr Who, *liberally sprinkled with* Spooks *and* 1984 – Tom Boyle

Brilliant ... so inventive. – Keith Turner, former Fleet Street journalist

RED ICE

Early warning preview ...

Usually, fiction follows news. Here, it's the reverse. Satirically, politically and sci-fi-ly, this is a revolution of a book. – R. C. Lacey

Non-fiction

FAREWELL, MY LOVELY

absolutely enchanting – Jilly Cooper

perfect bedside reading for animal lovers of every kind – Susan Hill, *The Lady*

contains so much happiness I couldn't put it down until I'd read every page.
– B. J. Kerks, *Fur & Feather*

Poetry

CATCH 36

Charming...with a satirical bite – Scott Pack

History

THE QUEEN'S PRIZE

a magnificent job ... a superb story ... has style and flow to the point of almost having a taste – Guns Review